WHISPERS OF THE DEAD

A Collection of Sister Fidelma Mysteries

WHISPERS OF THE DEAD

A Collection of Sister Fidelma Mysteries

Peter Tremayne

headline

Copyright © 2004 Peter Tremayne

The right of Peter Tremayne to be identified as the Author of
the Work has been asserted by him in accordance with the
Copyright, Designs and Patents Act 1988.

First published in Great Britain in 2004
by HEADLINE BOOK PUBLISHING

10 9 8 7 6 5 4 3 2 1

Cataloguing in Publication Data is available from the British Library

ISBN 0 7553 0229 X

Typeset in Times by Palimpsest Book Production Ltd,
Polmont, Stirlingshire

Printed and bound in Great Britain by Clays Ltd, St Ives plc.

HEADLINE BOOK PUBLISHING
A division of Hodder Headline
338 Euston Road
London NW1 3BH

www.headline.co.uk
www.hodderheadline.com

For the wonderfully supportive members of
The International Sister Fidelma Society
with gratitude

Contents

Introduction

❧

W elcome to the second volume of Sister Fidelma short mystery stories.

The Sister Fidelma mysteries are set during the seventh century AD, mainly in her native Ireland.

Sister Fidelma is not simply a religieuse. She is, indeed, a member of what we now call the Celtic Church, whose conflicts with Rome on matters of theology and social governance are well known. As well as the differences in rituals, the dating of Easter and the wearing of a dissimilar tonsure, celibacy was not widely practised and many religious houses contained individuals of both sexes who raised their children to the continued service of God. However, Fidelma is basically a qualified *dálaigh*, an advocate of the seventh-century law courts of Ireland, and using the ancient Brehon Law system. In those days women were co-equal with men and could aspire to all the professions, and many women were lawyers and judges and even wrote law texts as well as interpreting them. Indeed, we even know the names of many of them.

Those who have followed Sister Fidelma's adventures in the series of novels and in the previous volume of short stories, *Hemlock at Vespers*, will no doubt be acquainted with the historical and social background to these stories. The volumes contain an explanatory 'Historical Note'. Such background details have also been put on the amazing International Sister Fidelma Society website at www.sisterfidelma.com and I feel it is superfluous to add it to this volume.

In these short stories, as with the previous fifteen tales collected in *Hemlock at Vespers*, Fidelma usually appears without her companion the Irish-trained Saxon Brother Eadulf of Seaxmund's Ham, from the land of the South Folk. There is an exception in this volume. 'The Lost Eagle' features Brother Eadulf because it is an event that occurs while Sister Fidelma is visiting Canterbury with him, and falls chronologically between the events in the novels *Smoke in the Wind* and *The Haunted Abbot*. Every other tale is set in Ireland.

In Fidelma's own chronology, 'The Blemish' is the earliest story because it occurs while she is still studying law under the Brehon Morann at his law school. The bulk of these stories have been written at the request of editors who sought particular themes, such as my good friend Peter Haining who wanted to know if Fidelma would be averse to appearing in a drinking story. 'Gold At Night' was the inevitable outcome. Another editor wanted to know if Fidelma ever took a vacation, or what passed as a vacation for a seventh-century religieuse. 'Corpse on a Holy Day' was the response. Now and then references have been made in the stories to Fidelma's interest in cosmology and astrology. Astrology was an art widely practised in those days. An editor asked me to expand on that and thus we have 'The Astrologer Who Predicted His Own Murder'.

With the demand for Fidelma short stories coming from various quarters, the energetic and creative editor of *The Brehon*, the journal of The International Sister Fidelma Society, David R. Wooten, approached me. The Society produces *The Brehon* three times a year for its members. With such support and a membership spanning many countries, I decided that *The Brehon* should have the opportunity of publishing some original Fidelma stories and 'The Blemish' and 'Dark Moon Rising' first appeared in its columns.

When my editors asked me if I would consider putting together a second volume of short stories, they also asked me if I could add a couple of original tales on aspects of Brehon Law which I had not covered in previous stories. For example, how was an Irish chief elected? That is the theme of 'The Heir Apparent'. What was 'fosterage' in ancient Ireland and were there laws to protect children? Hence 'The Fosterer'. And also the complicated subject of inheritance from a person deemed to be insane: 'Cry "Wolf!"' is one aspect.

In the short stories a character has appeared several times whom I have a fondness for: Abbot Laisran of Durrow, Co. Laois (from *dearmach* in Middle Irish or *darú* in Modern Irish, Durrow means 'the oak plain'). The abbey was founded by St Colmcille before his exile from Ireland c. AD 563. Durrow was one of the most important ecclesiastical teaching centres in Ireland and during the mid-seventh century, in Fidelma's day, it is recorded that its students came from no less than eighteen different nations in Europe. Today, Durrow is best remembered for its famous Illustrated Gospel Book, *The Book of Durrow*, dated by some to the mid-seventh century.

Abbot Laisran regards Fidelma as his protégée. It was he who persuaded her, once she had qualified in Brehon Morann's law school to the level of *anruth*, one degree below the highest that the secular and ecclesiastical colleges of ancient Ireland could bestow, to join the abbey of Kildare. As many readers will know, Fidelma is more concerned with law than religion and when she found out that her abbess was not averse to breaking the law, she left Kildare (see the story 'Hemlock at Vespers' in the collection of the same name). As a base, she returned to the court of her brother, Colgú, King of Muman, who ruled at Cashel, in what is now Co. Tipperary.

In stories such as 'A Canticle for Wulfstan' and 'The Horse That Died for Shame' (collected in *Hemlock at Vespers*) Abbot Laisran's good humour acts as a balance to Fidelma's sterner thoughts of duty and the search for truth. I have received not a few letters from readers asking why I did not bring the good Abbot Laisran into more of Fidelma's adventures. Those readers will, I hope, be pleased to know that Abbot Laisran appears in the title story, 'Whispers of the Dead', 'Who Stole the Fish' and in 'Gold At Night'.

Here, then, are another fifteen mysteries that try Fidelma's abilities to the limit. As in some of the earlier mysteries, Fidelma, and you, will discover – as in 'The Fosterer' – that law is not always synonymous with justice.

Peter Tremayne

Whispers of the Dead

∾

Abbot Laisran sat back in his chair, at the side of the crackling log fire, and gazed thoughtfully at his cup of mulled wine.

'You have achieved a formidable reputation, Fidelma,' he observed, raising his cherub-like features to his young protégée who sat on the other side of the fireplace, sipping her wine. 'Some Brehons talk of you as they would the great female judges such as Brig or Dari. That is commendable in one so young.'

Fidelma smiled thinly. She was not one given to vanity for she knew her own weaknesses.

'I would not aspire to write legal texts as they did, nor, indeed, would I pretend to be more than a simple investigator of facts. I am a *dálaigh*, an advocate. I prefer to leave the judgement of others to the Brehons.'

Abbot Laisran inclined his head slightly as if in acceptance of her statement.

'But that is the very thing on which your reputation has its foundation. You have had some outstanding successes with your investigations, observing things that are missed by others. Several times I have seen your ability first-hand. Does it ever worry you that you hold so much responsibility?'

'It worries me only that I observe all the facts and come to the right decision. However, I did not spend eight years under instruction with the Brehon Morann of Tara to no avail. I have come to accept the responsibility that goes with my office.'

'Ah,' sighed the abbot, '"Unto whomsoever much is given, of him shall much be required." That is from—'

'The Gospel of Luke,' Fidelma interrupted with a mischievous smile.

1

Abbot Laisran answered her smile.

'Does nothing escape your attention, Fidelma? Surely there must be cases when you are baffled? For instance, there must be many a murder over which it is impossible to attribute guilt.'

'Perhaps I have been lucky,' admitted Fidelma. 'However, I do not believe that there is such a thing as a perfect crime.'

'Come now, that must be an overstatement?'

'Even when we examine a body with no evidence of who he, or she, was in life, or how and when he, or she, died, let alone by whose hand, a good observer will learn something. The dead always whisper to us. It is our task to listen to the whispers of the dead.'

The abbot knew it was not in Fidelma's nature to boast of her prowess; however, his round features assumed a sceptical expression.

'I would like to make a wager with you,' he suddenly announced.

Fidelma frowned. She knew that Abbot Laisran was a man who was quick to place wagers. Many was the time she had attended the great Aonach Lífé, the fair at the Curragh, for the horse racing and watched Abbot Laisran losing as well as winning as he hazarded money on the contests.

'What manner of wager had you in mind, Laisran?' she asked cautiously.

'You have said that the dead whisper to us and we must have ears to listen. That in every circumstance the body of a person will eventually yield up the information necessary to identify him, and who, if anyone, is culpable for the death. Have I understood you correctly?'

Fidelma inclined her head in agreement.

'That has been my experience until now,' she conceded.

'Well then,' continued Abbot Laisran, 'will you take a wager with me on a demonstration of that claim?'

'In what circumstances?'

'Simple enough. By coincidence, this morning a young peasant woman was found dead not far from this abbey. There was no means of identification on her and inquiries in the adjacent village have failed to identify her. No one appears to be missing. She must have been a poor itinerant. One of our brothers, out of charity, brought the body to the abbey. Tomorrow, as is custom, we shall bury her in an unmarked grave.' Abbot Laisran paused and glanced slyly at her. 'If the dead truly whisper to you, Fidelma, perhaps you will be able to interpret those whispers and identify her?'

Fidelma considered for a moment.

'You say that she was a young woman? What was the cause of her death?'

'That is the mystery. There are no visible signs of how she died. She was well nourished, according to our apothecary.'

'No indication of violence?' asked Fidelma, slightly bemused.

'None. The matter is a total mystery. Hence I would place a wager with you, which is that if you can find some evidence, some cause of death, of something that will lead to the identification of the poor unfortunate, then I will accept that your claim is valid. So, what of the wager?'

Fidelma hesitated. She disliked challenges to her abilities but, on the other hand, some narcissistic voice called from within her.

'What is the specific wager?' she asked.

'A *screpall* for the offertory box of the abbey.' Abbot Laisran smiled. 'I will give a *screpall* for the poor if you can discover more about the unhappy woman than we have been able to. If you cannot, then you will pay a *screpall* to the offertory box.'

A *screpall* was a silver coin valued to the fee charged by a *dálaigh* for a single consultation.

Fidelma hesitated a moment and then, urged on by her pride, said: 'It is agreed.'

She rose and set down her mulled wine, startling the abbot.

'Where are you going?' he demanded.

'Why, to view the body. There is only an hour or two of daylight left, and many important signs can vanish in artificial light.'

Reluctantly, Abbot Laisran set down his wine and also rose.

'Very well,' he sighed. 'Come, I will show you the way to the apothecary.'

A tall, thin religieux with a beak of a nose glanced up as Abbot Laisran entered the chamber where he was pounding leaves with a pestle. His eyes widened a little when he saw Sister Fidelma enter behind the abbot. Fidelma was well known to most of the religious of the Abbey of Durrow.

'Brother Donngal, I have asked Sister Fidelma to examine our unknown corpse.'

3

The abbey's apothecary immediately set aside his work and gazed at her with interest.

'Do you think that you know the poor woman, Sister?'

Fidelma smiled quickly.

'I am here as a *dálaigh*, Brother,' she replied.

A slight frown crossed Brother Donngal's features.

'There is no sign of a violent death, Sister. Why would an advocate have an interest in this case?'

Catching the irritable hardening of her expression, Abbot Laisran intervened quickly: 'It is because I asked Sister Fidelma to give me her opinion on this matter.'

Brother Donngal turned to a door.

'The body lies in our mortuary. I was shortly to prepare it for burial. Our carpenter has only just delivered the coffin.'

The body lay under a linen sheet on a table in the centre of the chamber that served as the abbey's mortuary where bodies were prepared for burial.

Sister Fidelma moved towards it and was about to take a corner of the sheet in her hand when the apothecary coughed apologetically.

'I have removed her clothing for examination but have not dressed her for the coffin yet, Sister.'

Fidelma's eyes twinkled at the man's embarrassment, but she made no reply.

The corpse was that of a young woman, perhaps no more than twenty years old. Fidelma had not entirely hardened herself to premature death.

'She is not long dead,' was Fidelma's first remark.

Brother Donngal nodded.

'No more than a day and a night, I reckon. She was found this morning and I believe she died during the night.'

'By whom was she found?'

'Brother Torcan,' intervened Abbot Laisran, who was standing just inside the door observing them.

'Where was she found?'

'No more than a few hundred paces from the abbey walls.'

'I meant, in what place, what were the conditions of her surroundings?'

4

'Oh, I see. She was found in a wood, in a small clearing almost covered with leaves.'

Fidelma raised an eyebrow.

'What was this Brother Torcan doing there?'

'Gathering edible fungi. He works in the kitchens.'

'And the clothes worn by the girl . . . where are they?' Fidelma asked.

The man gestured to a side table on which clothing was piled.

'She wore just the simple garb of a village girl. There is nothing to identify her there.'

'I will examine them in a moment and likewise will wish to speak to this Brother Torcan.'

She turned her gaze back to the body, bending forward to examine it with careful precision.

It was some time before she straightened from her task.

'Now, I shall examine the clothing.'

Brother Donngal moved to a table and watched while Fidelma picked up the items. They consisted of a pair of sandals called *cuaran*, a single sole of untanned hide, stitched together with thongs cut from the same hide. They were almost worn through. The dress was a simple one of wool and linen, roughly woven and threadbare. It appeared to have been secured at the waist by a strip of linen. There was also a short cape with a hood, as affected by many country women. Again, it was obviously worn and fringed with rabbit fur.

Fidelma raised her head and glanced at the apothecary.

'Is this all that she was wearing?'

Brother Donngal nodded in affirmation.

'Was there no underclothing?'

The apothecary looked embarrassed.

'None,' he confirmed.

'She did not have a *ciorbholg*?'

The *ciorbholg* was, literally, a comb-bag, but it contained all the articles of toilet, as well as combs, which women carried about with them no matter their rank or status. It served women in the manner of a purse and it was often tied at the waist by a belt.

Brother Donngal shook his head negatively once more.

'This is why we came to the conclusion that she was simply a poor itinerant,' explained the abbot.

'So there was no toilet bag?' mused Fidelma. 'And she had no brooches or other jewellery?'

Brother Donngal allowed a smile to play around his lips.

'Of course not.'

'Why of course not?' demanded Fidelma sharply.

'Because it is clear from this clothing, Sister, that the girl was a very poor country girl. Such a girl would not be able to afford such finery.'

'Even a poor country girl will seek out some ornaments, no matter how poor she is,' replied Fidelma.

Abbot Laisran came forward with a sad smile.

'Nothing was found. So you see, Fidelma, this poor young woman cannot whisper to you from her place of death. A poor country girl and with nothing to identify her. Her whispers are silent ones. You should not have been so willing to accept my challenge.'

Fidelma swung round on him to reveal the smile on her face. Her eyes twinkled with a dangerous fire.

'On the contrary, Laisran. There is much that this poor girl whispers; much she tells us, even in this pitiable state.'

Brother Donngal exchanged a puzzled glance with the abbot.

'I don't understand you, Sister,' he said. 'What can you see? What have I missed?'

'Practically everything,' Fidelma assured him calmly.

Abbot Laisran stifled a chuckle as he saw the mortified expression on the apothecary's face. But he turned to her with a reproving glance.

'Come now, Fidelma,' he chided, 'don't be too sharp because you have been confronted with an unsolvable riddle. Not even you can conjure facts out of nothing.'

Abbot Laisran stirred uncomfortably as he saw the tiny green fire in her eyes intensify. However, when she addressed him, her tone was comparatively mild.

'You know better of me, Laisran. I am not given to vain boasting.'

Brother Donngal moved forward and stared at the body of the girl as if trying to see what it was that Fidelma had observed.

'What have I missed?' he demanded again.

Fidelma turned to the apothecary.

'First, you say that this girl is a poor country girl. What makes you arrive at such a conclusion?'

Brother Donngal regarded her with an almost pitying look.

'That was easy. Look at her clothing – at her sandals. They are not the apparel of someone of high rank and status. The clothes show her humble origins.'

Fidelma sighed softly.

'My mentor, the Brehon Morann, once said that the veil can disguise much; it is folly to accept the outside show for the inner quality of a person.'

'I don't understand.'

'This girl is not of humble rank, that much is obvious.'

Abbot Laisran moved forward and peered at the body in curiosity.

'Come, Fidelma, now you are guessing.'

Fidelma shook her head.

'I do not guess, Laisran. I have told you,' she added impatiently, 'listen to the whispers of the dead. If this is supposed to be a peasant girl, then regard the skin of her body – white and lacking colour by wind and sun. Look at her hands, soft and cared for as are her nails. There is no dirt beneath them. Her hands are not calloused by work. Look at her feet. Again, soft and well cared for. See the soles of the feet? This girl had not been trudging fields in those poor shoes that she was clad in, nor has she walked any great distance.'

The abbot and the apothecary followed her instructions and examined the limbs she indicated.

'Now, look at her hair.'

The girl's hair, a soft spun gold colour, was braided behind her head in a single long plait that reached almost to her waist.

'Nothing unusual in that,' observed Laisran. Many women in the five kingdoms of Éireann considered very long hair as a mark of beauty and braided it in similar style.

'But it is exceptionally well tended. The braiding is the traditional *cuilfhionn* and surely you must know that it is affected only by women of rank. What this poor corpse whispers to me is that she is a woman of rank.'

'Then why was she dressed as a peasant?' demanded the apothecary after a moment's silence.

Fidelma pursed her lips.

'We must continue to listen. Perhaps she will tell us. As she tells us other things.'

'Such as?'

'She is married.'

Abbot Laisran snorted with cynicism.

'How could you possibly know that?'

Fidelma simply pointed to the left hand of the corpse.

'There are marks around the third finger. They are faint, I grant you, but tiny marks nevertheless which show the recent removal of a ring that has been worn there. There is also some discoloration on her left arm. What do you make of that, Brother Donngal?'

The apothecary shrugged.

'Do you mean the marks of blue dye? It is of little importance.'

'Why?'

'Because it is a common thing among the villages. Women dye clothes and materials. The blue is merely a dye caused by the extract of a cruciferous plant *glaisin*. Most people use it. It is not unusual in any way.'

'It is not. But women of rank would hardly be involved in dyeing their own materials and this dye stain seems fairly recent.'

'Is that important?' asked the abbot.

'Perhaps. It depends on how we view the most important of all the facts this poor corpse whispers to us.'

'Which is?' demanded Brother Donngal.

'That this girl was murdered.'

Abbot Laisran's eyebrows shot up.

'Come, come, now. Our apothecary has found no evidence of foul play; no wounds, no bruising, no abrasions. The face is relaxed as if she simply passed on in her sleep. Anyone can see that.'

Fidelma moved forward and lifted the girl's head, bringing the single braid of hair forward in order to expose the nape of the neck. She had done this earlier during her examination as Brother Donngal and Abbot Laisran watched with faint curiosity.

'Come here and look, both of you. What, Brother Donngal, was your explanation of this?'

Brother Donngal looked slightly embarrassed as he peered forward.

'I did not examine her neck under the braid,' he admitted.

'Well, now that you are examining it, what do you see?'

'There is a small discoloured patch like a tiny bruise,' replied the apothecary after a moment or two. 'It is not more than a fingernail in width. There is a little blood spot in the centre. It's rather like an insect bite that has drawn blood or as if someone has pricked the skin with a needle.'

'Do you see it also, Laisran?' demanded Fidelma.

The abbot leaned forward and then nodded.

Fidelma gently lowered the girl's head back on to the table.

'I believe that this was a wound caused by an incision. You are right, Brother Donngal, in saying it is like a needle point. The incision was created by something long and thin, like a needle. It was inserted into the nape of the neck and pushed up hard so that it penetrated into the head. It was swift. Deadly. Evil. The girl probably died before she knew that she was being attacked.'

Abbot Laisran was staring at Fidelma in bewilderment.

'Let me get this straight, Fidelma. Are you saying that the corpse found near this abbey this morning is a woman of rank who has been murdered? Is that right?'

'And, after her death, her clothes were taken from her and she was hurriedly dressed in poor peasant garb to disguise her origin. The murderer thought to remove all means of identification from her.'

'Even if this is true,' interrupted Brother Donngal, 'how might we discover who she was and who perpetrated this crime?'

'The fact that she was not long dead when Brother Torcan found her makes our task more simple. She was killed in this vicinity. A woman of rank would surely be visiting a place of substance. She had not been walking any distance. Observe the soles of her feet. I would presume that she either rode or came in a carriage to her final destination.'

'But what destination?' demanded Brother Donngal.

'If she came to Durrow, she would have come to the abbey,' Laisran pointed out. 'She did not.'

'True enough. We are left with two types of place she might have gone. The house of a noble, a chieftain, or, perhaps, a *bruighean*, an inn. I believe that we will find the place where she met her death within five or six kilometres of this abbey.'

'What makes you say that?'

'A deduction. The corpse newly dead and the murderer wanting to dispose of it as quickly as possible. Whoever killed her reclothed her body and transported it to the spot where it was found. They could not have travelled far.'

Abbot Laisran rubbed his chin.

'Whoever it was, they took a risk in disposing of it in the woods so near this abbey.'

'Perhaps not. If memory serves me right, those woods are the thickest stretch of forest in this area even though they are close to the abbey. Are they that frequented?'

Abbot Laisran shrugged.

'It is true that Brother Torcan does not often venture so far into the woods in search of fungi,' he admitted. 'He came on the corpse purely by chance.'

'So the proximity of the abbey was not necessarily a caution to our murderer. Well, are there such places as I described within the distance I have estimated?'

'An inn or a chieftain's house? North of here is Ballacolla, where there is an inn. South of here is Ballyconra where the lord of Conra lives.'

'Who is he? Describe him.'

'A young man, newly come to office there. I know little about him although he came here to pay his respects to me when he took office. When I came to Durrow as abbot the young man's father was lord of Ballyconra but his son was away serving in the army of the High King. He is a bachelor newly returned from the wars against the Uí Néill.'

'Then we shall have to learn more,' observed Fidelma drily. She glanced through the window at the cloudy sky.

'There is still an hour before sunset,' she reflected. 'Have Brother Torcan meet me at the gates so that he may conduct me to the spot where he found the body.'

'What use would that be?' demanded the abbot. 'There was nothing in the clearing apart from the body.'

Fidelma did not answer.

With a sigh, the abbot went off to find the religieux.

Half an hour later Brother Torcan was showing her the small clearing. Behind her, Abbot Laisran fretted with impatience. Fidelma was looking at a pathway which led into it. It was just wide enough to take a small cart. She noticed some indentations of hooves and ruts, undoubtedly caused by the passage of wheels.

'Where does that track lead?' she asked, for they had entered the clearing by a different single path.

It was the abbot who answered.

'Eventually it would link to the main road south. South to Ballyconra,' he added significantly.

The sky was darkening now and Fidelma sighed.

'In the morning I shall want to see this young lord of Conra. But it is pointless continuing on tonight. We'd best go back to the abbey.'

The next morning, accompanied by the abbot, Fidelma rode south. Ballyconra itself was a large settlement. There were small farmsteads and a collection of dwellings for workers. In one nearby field, a root crop was being harvested and workers were loading the crop on to small carts pulled by single asses. The track twisted through the village and passed a stream where women were laying out clothes to dry on the banks while others stirred fabrics into a metal cauldron hanging over a fire. The pungent smell of dyes told Fidelma what process was taking place.

Some paused in their work and called a greeting to the abbot, seeking a blessing, as they rode by. They ascended the track through another field towards a large building. It was an isolated structure which was built upon what must once have been a hill fort. A young man came cantering towards them from its direction, sitting easily astride a sleek black mare.

'This is young Conri, lord of Conra,' muttered Laisran as they halted and awaited the man's approach.

Fidelma saw that the young man was handsome and dark-featured. It was clear from his dress and his bearing that he was a man of rank and action. A scar across his forehead indicated he had followed a military profession. It seemed to add to his personality rather than detract from it.

'Good morning, Abbot.' He greeted Laisran pleasantly before turning to Fidelma. 'Good morning, Sister. What brings you to Ballyconra?'

Fidelma interrupted as Laisran was opening his mouth to explain.

'I am a *dálaigh*. You would appear to be expecting visitors, lord of Conra. I observed you watching our approach from the hill beyond the fortress before you rode swiftly down to meet us.'

The young man's eyes widened a little and then he smiled sadly.

'You have a sharp eye, *dálaigh*. As a matter of fact, I have been expecting the arrival of my wife during these last few days. I saw only the shape of a woman on horseback and thought for a moment . . .'

11

'Your wife?' asked Fidelma quickly, glancing at Laisran.

'She is Segnat, daughter of the lord of Tir Bui,' he said without disguising his pride.

'You say you have been expecting her?'

'Any day now. I thought you might have been her. We were married only three months ago in Tir Bui, but I had to return here immediately on matters pertaining to my people. Segnat was to come on after me but she has been delayed in starting out on her journey. I only had word a week ago that she was about to join me.'

Fidelma looked at him thoughtfully.

'What has delayed her for so long?'

'Her father fell ill when we married and has only died recently. She was his only close kin and she stayed to nurse him.'

'Can you describe her?'

The young man nodded, frowning.

'Why do you ask?'

'Indulge me for a moment, lord of Conra.'

'Of twenty years, golden hair and blue eyes. What is the meaning of these questions?'

Fidelma did not reply directly.

'The road from Tir Bui would bring a traveller from the north through Ballacolla and around the abbey, wouldn't it?'

Conri looked surprised.

'It would,' he agreed irritably. 'I say again, why these questions?'

'I am a *dálaigh*,' repeated Fidelma gravely. 'It is my nature to ask questions. But the body of a young woman has been found in the woods near the abbey and we are trying to identify her.'

Conri blinked rapidly.

'Are you saying that this might be Segnat?'

Fidelma's expression was sympathetic.

'We are merely making inquiries of the surrounding habitations to see if anything is known of a missing young woman.'

Conri raised his jaw defiantly.

'Well, Segnat is not missing. I expect her arrival any time.'

'But perhaps you would come to the abbey this afternoon and look at the body? This is merely a precaution to eliminate the possibility of its being Segnat.'

The young man compressed his lips stubbornly.

'It could not possibly be Segnat.'

'Regrettably, all things are possible. It is merely that some are more unlikely than others. We would appreciate your help. A negative identification is as helpful as a positive one.'

Abbot Laisran finally broke in.

'The abbey would be grateful for your co-operation, lord of Conra.'

The young man hesitated and then shrugged.

'This afternoon, you say? I shall be there.'

He turned his horse sharply and cantered off.

Laisran exchanged a glance with Fidelma.

'Was this useful?' he asked.

'I think so,' she replied. 'We can now turn our attention to the inn which you tell me is north of the abbey at Ballacolla.'

Laisran's face lightened.

'Ah, I see what you are about.'

Fidelma smiled at him.

'You do?'

'It is as you said, a negative is as important as a positive. You have produced a negative with young Conri, so now we will seek the identity of the murdered one in the only possible place.'

Fidelma continued to smile as they turned northwards back towards the abbey and beyond to Ballacolla.

The inn stood at a crossroads, a sprawling dark building. They were turning into the yard when a muscular woman of middle age driving a small mule cart halted, almost blocking the entrance. The woman remained seated on her cart, glowering in displeasure at them.

'Religious!' She almost spat the word.

Fidelma regarded her with raised eyebrows.

'You sound as if you are not pleased to see us,' she observed in amusement.

'It is the free hospitality provided by religious houses that takes away the business from poor people such as myself,' grunted the woman.

'Well, we might be here to purchase some refreshment,' placated Fidelma.

'If you can pay for it, you will find my husband inside. Let him know your wants.'

Fidelma made no effort to move out of her way.

'I presume that you are the innkeeper?'

13

'And if I am?'

'I would like to ask you a few questions. Did a young woman pass this way two nights ago? A young woman who would have arrived along the northern road from Tir Bui.'

The big woman's eyes narrowed suspiciously.

'What is that to you?'

'I am a *dálaigh* and my questions must be answered,' replied Fidelma firmly. 'What is your name, innkeeper?'

The woman blinked. She seemed ready to argue, but then she compressed her lips for a moment. To refuse to answer a *dálaigh's* questions laid one open to fines for obstructing justice. A keeper of a public hostel had specific obligations before the law.

'My name is Corbnait,' she conceded reluctantly.

'And the answer to my first question?'

Corbnait lifted her heavy shoulders and let them fall expressively.

'There was a woman who came here three nights ago. She merely wanted a meal and fodder for her horse. She was from Tir Bui.'

'Did she tell you her name?'

'Not as I recall.'

'Was she young, fair of skin with spun gold hair in a single braid?'

The innkeeper nodded slowly.

'That was her.' Suddenly an angry expression crossed the big woman's face. 'Is she complaining about my inn or of the service that she received here? Is she?'

Fidelma shook her head.

'She is beyond complaining, Corbnait. She is dead.'

The woman blinked again and then said sullenly: 'She did not die of any food that was served on my premises. I keep a good house here.'

'I did not specify the manner of her death.' Fidelma paused. 'I see you drive a small cart.'

Corbnait looked surprised at the sudden switch of subject.

'So do many people. I have to collect my supplies from the outlying farms. What is wrong with that?'

'Do you also dye clothes at your inn?'

'Dye clothes? What games are you playing with me, Sister?' Corbnait glanced from Abbot Laisran back to Fidelma as if she

14

considered that she was dealing with dangerous lunatics. 'Everyone dyes their own clothes unless they be a lord or lady.'

'Please show me your hands and arms,' Fidelma pressed.

The woman glanced again from one to another of them but seeing their impassive faces she decided not to argue. She sighed and held out her burly forearms. There was no sign of any dye stains on them.

'Satisfied?' she snapped.

'You keep your hands well cared for,' observed Fidelma.

The woman sniffed.

'What do I have a husband for if not to do the dirty work?'

'But I presume you served the girl with her meal?'

'That I did.'

'Did she talk much?'

'A little. She told me she was on the way to join her husband. He lives some way to the south of the abbey.'

'She didn't stay here for the night?'

'She was anxious to reach her husband. Young love!' The woman snorted in disgust. 'It's a sickness you grow out of. The handsome prince you thought you married turns out to be a lazy good-for-nothing! Take my husband—'

'You had the impression that she was in love with her husband?' cut in Fidelma.

'Oh yes.'

'She mentioned no problems, no concerns?'

'None at all.'

Fidelma paused, thinking hard.

'Was she alone during the time she was at the inn? No one else spoke to her? Were there any other guests?'

'There was only my husband and myself. My husband tended to her horse. She was particular about its welfare. The girl was obviously the daughter of a chieftain for she had a valuable black mare and her clothes were of fine quality.'

'What time did she leave here?'

'Immediately after her meal, just two hours to sunset. She said she could reach her destination before nightfall. What happened to her? Was she attacked by a highway robber?'

'That we have yet to discover,' replied Fidelma. She did not mention that a highway robber could be discounted simply by the means of the poor girl's death. The manner of her death was, in fact, her most important clue. 'I want to have a word with your husband now.'

Corbnait frowned.

'Why do you want to speak to Echen? He can tell you nothing.'

Fidelma's brows drew together sternly.

'I will be the judge of that.'

Corbnait opened her mouth, saw a look of steadfast determination on Fidelma's face, and then shrugged. She suddenly raised her voice in a shrill cry.

'Echen!'

It startled the patient ass and Fidelma's and Abbot Laisran's horses. They shied and were skittish for a few moments before they were brought under control.

A thin, ferret-faced man came scuttling out of the barn.

'You called, my dear?' he asked mildly. Then he saw Abbot Laisran, whom he obviously recognised, and bobbed servilely before him, rubbing his hands together. 'You are welcome, noble Laisran,' before turning to Fidelma and adding, 'You are welcome, also, Sister. You bless our house by your presence . . .'

'Peace, man!' snapped his burly wife. 'The *dálaigh* wants to ask you some questions.'

The little man's eyes widened.

'*Dálaigh?*'

'I am Fidelma of Cashel.' Fidelma's gaze fell on his twisted hands. 'I see that you have blue dye on your hands, Echen.'

The man looked at his hands in bewilderment.

'I have just been mixing some dyes, Sister. I am trying to perfect a certain shade of blue from *glaisin* and *dubh-poill* . . . there is a sediment of intense blackness which is found in the bottom of pools in bogs which I mix with the *glaisin* to produce a dark blue . . .'

'Quiet! The Sister does not want to listen to your prattling!' admonished Corbnait.

'On the contrary,' snapped Fidelma, irritated by the bullying woman, 'I would like to know if Echen was at his dye work when the young woman was here the other night.'

Echen frowned.

'The young woman who stayed only for a meal and to fodder her horse,' explained his wife. 'The black mare.'

The man's face cleared.

'I only started this work today. I remember the girl. She was anxious to press on to her destination.'

'Did you speak to her?'

'Only to exchange words about her instructions for her horse, and then she went into the inn for a meal. She was there an hour or so, isn't that correct, dearest? Then she rode on.'

'She rode away alone,' added Corbnait, 'just as I have told you.'

Echen opened his mouth, caught his wife's eye, and then snapped it shut again.

Fidelma did not miss the action.

'Did you want to add something, Echen?' she prompted.

Echen hesitated.

'Come, if you have something to add, you must speak up!' Fidelma said sharply.

'It's just . . . well, the girl did not ride away entirely alone.'

His wife turned with a scowl.

'There was no one else at the inn that night. What do you mean, man?'

'I helped her on to her horse and she left the inn but as she rode towards the south I saw someone driving a small donkey cart join her on the brow of the hill.'

'Someone joined her? Male or female?' demanded Fidelma. 'Did you see?'

'Male.'

Abbot Laisran spoke for the first time.

'That must be our murderer then,' he said with a sigh. 'A highway robber, after all. Now we shall never know who the culprit was.'

'Highway robbers do not drive donkey carts,' Fidelma pointed out.

'It was no highway robber,' confirmed Echen.

They swung round on the little man in surprise.

'Then tell them who it was, you stupid man!' yelled Corbnait at her unfortunate spouse.

'It was young Finn,' explained Echen, hurt by the rebuke he had received. 'He herds sheep on Slieve Nuada, just a mile from here.'

'Ah, a strange one that!' Corbnait said, as if all was explained to her satisfaction. 'Both his parents died three years ago. He's been a recluse ever since. Unnatural, I call it.'

Fidelma looked from Corbnait to Echen and then said, 'I want one of you to ride to the abbey and look at the corpse so we can be absolutely sure that this was the girl who visited here. It is important that we are sure of her identity.'

'Echen can do it. I am busy,' grumbled Corbnait.

'Then I want directions to where this shepherd Finn dwells.'

'Slieve Nuada is that large hill you can see from here,' Abbot Laisran intervened. 'I know the place, and I know the boy.'

It was not long before they arrived at the shepherd's dwelling next to a traditional *lias cairach* or sheep's hut. The sheep milled about over the hill indifferent to the arrival of strangers. Fidelma noticed that their white fleeces were marked with the blue dyed circle that identified the flock and prevented them from mixing into neighbouring flocks during common grazing.

Finn was weathered and bronzed – a handsome youth with a shock of red hair. He was kneeling on the grass astride a sheep whose stomach seemed vastly extended, almost as if it were pregnant but unnaturally so. As they rode up they saw the youth jab a long, thin, needle-like *biorracha* into the sheep's belly. There was a curious hiss of air and the swelling seemed to go down without harm to the sheep which, when released, staggered away, bleating in irritation.

The youth looked up and recognised Abbot Laisran. He put the *biorracha* aside and came forward with a smile of welcome.

'Abbot Laisran. I have not seen you since my father's funeral.'

They dismounted and tethered their horses.

'You seem to have a problem on your hands,' Abbot Laisran said, indicating the now transformed sheep.

'Some of them get to eating plants that they should not. It causes gas and makes the belly swell like a bag filled with air. You prick them with the needle and the gas escapes. It is simple and does not hurt the creature. Have you come to buy sheep for the abbey?'

'I am afraid we are here on sad business,' Laisran said. 'This is Sister Fidelma. She is a *dálaigh*.'

The youth frowned.

'I do not understand.'

'Two days ago you met a girl on the road from the inn at Ballacolla.'

Finn nodded immediately.

'That is true.'

'What made you accost her?'

'Accost? I do not understand.'

'You were driving in a donkey cart?'

'I was.'

'She was on horseback?'

'She was. A black mare.'

'So what made you speak to her?'

'It was Segnat from Tir Bui. I used to go to her father's fortress with my father, peace on his soul. I knew her.'

Fidelma concealed her surprise.

'You knew her?'

'Her father was chieftain of Tir Bui.'

'What was your father's business in Tir Bui? It is a long journey from here.'

'My father used to raise the old horned variety of sheep which is now a dying breed. He was a *treudaighe* and proud of it. He kept a fine stock.'

The *treudaighe* was a shepherd of rank.

'I see. So you knew Segnat?'

'I was surprised to see her on the road. She told me she was on her way to join her husband, Conri, the new lord of Ballyconra.'

Finn's voice betrayed a curious emotion which Fidelma picked up on.

'You do not like Conn?'

'I do not have the right to like or dislike such as he,' admitted Finn. 'I was merely surprised to hear that Segnat had married him when he is living with a woman already.'

'That is a choice for the individual,' Fidelma reproved. 'The New Faith has not entirely driven the old forms of polygyny from our people. A man can have more than one wife just as a woman can have more than one husband.'

Abbot Laisran shook his head in annoyance.

'The Church opposes polygyny.'

'True,' agreed Fidelma. 'But the judge who wrote the law tract of the Bretha Croilge said there is justification for the practice even in the ancient books of the Faith for it is argued that even the chosen people of God lived in a plurality of unions so that it is no easier to condemn it than to praise it.'

19

She paused for a moment.

'That you disapproved of this meant you must have liked Segnat. Did you?'

'Why these questions?' countered the shepherd.

'Segnat has been murdered.'

Finn stared at her for some time, then his face hardened.

'Conri did it! Segnat's husband. He only wanted her for the dowry she could bring into the marriage. Segnat could also bring more than that.'

'How so?'

'She was a *banchomarba*, a female heir, for her father died without male issue and she became chieftainess of Tir Bui. She was rich. She told me so. Another reason Conri sought the union was because he had squandered much of his wealth on raising war bands to follow the High King in his wars against the northern Uí Néill. That is common gossip.'

'Gossip is not necessarily fact,' admonished Fidelma.

'But it usually has a basis of fact.'

'You do not appear shocked at the news of Segnat's death,' observed Laisran slyly.

'I have seen too many deaths recently, Abbot Laisran. Too many.'

'I don't think we need detain you any longer, Finn,' Fidelma said after a moment. Laisran glanced at her in astonishment.

'Mark my words, you'll find that Conri is the killer,' called Finn as Fidelma moved away.

Abbot Laisran appeared to want to say something, but he meekly followed Fidelma to her horse and together they rode away from the shepherd's house. Almost as soon as they were out of earshot, Abbot Laisran leaned forward in excitement.

'There! We have found the killer. It was Finn. It all adds up.'

Sister Fidelma turned and smiled at him.

'Does it?'

'The motive, the opportunity, the means, and the supporting evidence, it is all there. Finn must have killed her.'

'You sound as if you have been reading law books, Laisran,' she parried.

'I have followed your successes.'

'Then, tell me, how did you work this out?'

'The *biorracha*, a long sharp needle of the type which you say must have caused the girl's mortal wound.'

'Go on.'

'He uses blue dye to identify his sheep. Hence the stain on the corpse.'

'Go on.'

'He also knew Segnat and was apparently jealous of her marriage to Conri. Jealousy is often the motive for murder.'

'Anything else?'

'He met the girl on the road on the very night of her death. And he drives a small donkey cart to transport the body.'

'He did not meet her at night,' corrected Fidelma pedantically. 'It was two hours before sunset.'

Abbot Laisran made a cutting motion with his hand.

'It is as I say. Motive, opportunity, and means. Finn is the murderer.'

'You are wrong, Laisran. You have not listened to the whispers of the dead. But Finn does know the murderer.'

Abbot Laisran's eyes widened.

'I fail to understand . . .'

'I told you that you must listen to the dead. Finn was right. It was Conri, lord of Ballyconra, who murdered his wife. I think the motive will be found to be even as Finn said . . . financial gain from his dead wife's estate. He probably knew that Segnat's father was dying when he married her. When we get back to the abbey, I will send for the local *bó-aire*, the magistrate, to take some warriors to search Conri's farmstead. With luck he will not have destroyed her clothing and personal belongings. I think we will also find that the very black mare he was riding was the same the poor girl rode on her fatal journey. Hopefully, Echen will be able to identify it.'

Abbot Laisran stared at her blankly, bewildered by her calmness.

'How can you possibly know that? It must be guesswork. Finn could have just as easily killed her as Conri.'

Fidelma shook her head.

'Consider the death wound. A needle inserted at the base of the neck under her braid.'

'So?'

'Certainly, a long sharp needle, like a *biorracha*, could, and probably

21

did, cause that wound. However, how could a perfect stranger, or even an acquaintance such as Finn, inflict such a wound? How could someone persuade the girl to relax unsuspecting while they lifted her braid and then, suddenly, insert that needle? Who but a lover? Someone she trusted. Someone whose intimate touch would arouse no suspicion. We are left with Segnat's lover – her husband.'

Abbot Laisran heaved a sigh.

Fidelma added, 'She arrived at Ballyconra expecting to find a loving husband, but found her murderer who had already planned her death to claim her inheritance.

'After he killed her, Conri stripped her of her clothes and jewels, dressed her in peasants' clothes and placed her in a cart that had been used by his workers to transport dyed clothing. Then he took her to the woods where he hoped the body would lie unseen until it rotted or, even if it was discovered, might never be identified.

'He forgot that the dead can still tell us many things,' Fidelma concluded sadly. 'They whisper to us and we must listen.'

Corpse on a Holy Day

T he day was hot in spite of the breeze blowing off the sea from the south. The procession of pilgrims had left the sandy beach and were beginning to climb the steep green hill toward the distant oratory. They had stood in reverent silence before the ancient granite stone of St Declan, a stone that, it was said, had floated to that spot across the sea bearing on it vestments and a tiny silver bell. It had floated ashore on this isolated part of the Irish coast and was found by a warrior prince named Declan who knew it was God's way of ordaining him to preach the New Faith. So he began his mission among his own people, the Déices of the kingdom of Muman.

There the stone had stood since the moment it had landed bearing its miraculous gifts. The young brother who was conducting the pilgrims around the sites sacred to Declan had informed his charges that if they were able to crawl under the stone then they would be cured of rheumatism but only if they were already free from sin. None of the band of pilgrims had ventured to seek proof of the stone's miraculous property.

Now they followed him slowly up the steep hill above the beach, straggling in a long line, passing the grey abbey walls, and moving towards the small chapel perched on the hilltop. This was the final site of the pilgrimage. It was the chapel that St Declan had built two centuries before and in which his relics now reposed.

Sister Fidelma wondered, and not for the first time, why she had bothered to join this pilgrimage on such a stifling summer's day. Her thought was immediately followed by a twinge of guilt, as it had been before. She felt an inner voice reprimanding her and pointing out that it was her duty as a religieuse to revere the life and works of those great men and women who had brought the Faith to the shores of Ireland.

Her peripatetic journey, fulfilling her main duty as a *dálaigh*, or advocate, of the law courts of the five kingdoms of Ireland, had brought her to the sub-kingdom of the Décis on the south coast of Muman. When she had realised that she was staying a few days at the great abbey of Ardmore, which St Declan had founded, coinciding with the Holy Day set aside for his veneration, she had attached herself to the band of pilgrims being conducted around the principal sites associated with his life and work. Fidelma was always keen to acquire knowledge. She pressed her lips in a cynical grimace as she realised that she had answered her own question as to why she was part of this pilgrim group.

Brother Ross, the young man in charge, had been prattling on about the life of Declan as he preceded them up the hill. He was an intense young man, scarcely more than the 'age of choice', hardly out of his teenage. Even the steep climb did not seem to make him breathless or cause him to pause in his enthusiastic monologue.

'He was one of the four great saints who preached in the five kingdoms of Éireann before the coming of the Blessed Patrick. They were Ailbe, the patron saint of our kingdom of Muman, Ciarán also of Muman, Ibar of Laigin, and Declan of the Déices of Muman. So we may boast that this kingdom of Muman was the first to convert to the New Faith . . .'

Brother Ross was naively passionate as he began to enumerate the miracles of the saint, how he raised people who died of the Yellow Plague. The pilgrims listened in a respectful and awed silence. Fidelma had assessed the dozen or so men and women who were trudging up the hill and came to the conclusion that she appeared to have nothing in common with them except a membership of the religious.

They were now approaching the brow of the bare hill where the small oratory of grey granite stood. It was perched on the top of the round hump, surrounded by a low stone wall. From a distance, it had appeared a small speck of a building. As they drew nearer Fidelma could make out its rectangular dry-stone walls. It was scarcely thirteen feet by nine feet in dimensions and its steep sloping roof was in proportion.

'This is where the earthly remains of the blessed saint repose,' announced Brother Ross, halting and allowing the pilgrims to gather

24

around him by the gate in the low wall. 'After the end of his arduous mission through the countryside he returned to his beloved settlement of Ardmore. He knew he was not long for this world and so he gathered the people and the clergy around him and counselled them to follow in his footsteps in charity. Then, having received the divine sacrament from Bishop Mac Liag, he departed this life in a most holy and happy fashion, escorted by a chorus of angels to the kingdom of heaven. Vigils were held and solemn masses celebrated, signs and wonders were seen, a conclave of saints gathered from all corners of the land.'

Brother Ross spread one hand towards the oratory, his voice warming to his theme.

'His earthly remains were escorted to this, his first little church, to be laid to rest within it. I will lead you inside. Only three may accompany me at a time for, as you can see, it is very small. In the oratory lies a recess in the ground in which is a stone-built coffin. This is the resting place designated by Declan himself at the bidding of an angel. His relics are there and great signs and miracles are worked through the intervention of the Blessed Declan.'

He stood with bowed head for a moment while the pilgrims mumbled their respectful 'Amens'.

'Wait here for a moment until I enter the oratory and ensure we are not disturbing any worshipper. This day is holy to the saint and many people come to pray here.'

They paused by the wall as Brother Ross instructed while he turned inside the enclosure and crossed to the lintel door and disappeared inside.

A moment or two later, the young man burst out of the oratory, his face flushed, his mouth working yet uttering no sound. Sister Fidelma and the others stood staring at him in total surprise. The sudden change from the quiet respect to such agitation was bewildering. For several moments, the young man could not utter a word and then they came out in a spluttering staccato.

'Uncorrupted! A miracle! A miracle!'

His eyes were wide and rolled as if he had trouble in focusing.

Fidelma stepped forward in front of him. 'Calm yourself, Brother!' she demanded, her voice rising in sharp command to quell his excitement. 'What ails you?'

Brother Ross seemed finally to focus on her with his wide staring eyes.

'The body of the saint . . . it is uncorrupted!'

'What do you mean?' Fidelma demanded in irritation. 'You are not making sense.'

The young man swallowed and breathed deeply for a moment as if to gather his composure.

'The sarcophagus! The stone has been swung aside . . . the body of the blessed Declan lies there . . . the flesh is uncorrupted . . . truly . . . a miracle . . . a miracle! Go and spread the news . . .'

Fidelma did not waste time on trying to make further sense of the young man's incoherent claims.

She strode quickly by him, shaking aside his restraining hand, and went into the oratory, crouching a little to pass under the lintel. There was only one small window to give natural light and she paused, blinked, and waited a moment for her eyes to adjust. Two tall candles on an altar at the end of the small chapel were unlit but, surprisingly, a small stub of candle stood splattering on the tomb slab.

This stone slab had been pushed at an angle from the recess in the ground revealing the contents of the shallow grave. She strode forward and peered down. Brother Ross had been right in so far that a body lay there. But it was not the body of someone who had been interred two centuries before. She bent down to examine it. Two things she noticed: the blood was still glistening and wet, and when she touched the forehead, the flesh was still warm.

When she emerged, she found Brother Ross still lyrical with excitement. The pilgrims were gathered excitedly around him.

'Brethren, this day you have witnessed one of the great miracles of Declan. The saint's body has not corrupted and decayed. Go down to the abbey and tell them and I will stay here and watch until you return with the abbot . . .'

He hesitated as the eyes of the pilgrims turned expectantly as one to where Fidelma exited from the oratory with a grim face.

'You saw it, didn't you, Sister?' demanded Brother Ross. 'I told no lie. The body is uncorrupted. A miracle!'

'No one is to enter the chapel,' Fidelma replied coldly.

Brother Ross drew his brows together in anger.

'I am in charge of the pilgrims. Who are you to give orders, Sister?'

'I am a *dálaigh*. My name is Fidelma of Cashel.'

The young man blinked at her brusque tone. Then he recovered almost immediately.

'Lawyer or not, these pilgrims should be sent to tell the abbot. I will wait here . . . This is truly a miracle!'

Fidelma turned to him cynically.

'You who know so much about the Blessed Declan may provide the answers to these questions. Was Declan stabbed through the heart before being laid to rest?'

Brother Ross did not understand.

'Was the Blessed Declan, in reality, a young woman?' went on Fidelma, ruthlessly.

Brother Ross was outraged and said so.

Fidelma smiled thinly.

'Then I suggest you examine your uncorrupted body a little further. The body in the grave is that of a young woman who has recently been stabbed in the heart. It has been placed in the grave on top of old bones which presumably is the skeleton of Declan.'

Brother Ross stared at her for a moment in horror and then hurried back into the oratory.

Fidelma instructed the pilgrims to wait outside and then hurried after the young man, pausing just inside the door.

Brother Ross, kneeling by the tomb, turned and glanced up towards her. His face, even in the semi-gloom, was white.

'It is Sister Aróc, a member of the community of Ardmore.'

Fidelma nodded grimly.

'Then I think we should despatch the pilgrims back to Ardmore and ask them to inform the abbot of what has been found here.'

The band of pilgrims were spending the night in the hostel at Ardmore anyway.

'Shouldn't we go . . . ?'

Fidelma shook her head.

'I will stay and you may stay to assist me.'

Brother Ross looked bewildered.

'Assist you?'

'As a *dálaigh*, I am taking charge of the investigation into how Sister Aróc met her death,' she replied.

When the pilgrims had been despatched down the hill towards

the monastery, Fidelma returned into the chapel and knelt by the tomb. Sister Aróc was no more than twenty years old. She was not particularly attractive; in fact, rather plain-featured. A country girl with large-boned hands whose skin was rough and calloused. They lay in a curious clawlike attitude at her sides, as if the fingers should be grasping something. Her hair was mouse-coloured, an indiscernible grey-brown.

As Fidelma had previously noticed, there was one wound on the body. There was no need to ask what had caused it. A thin knife blade with its rough-worked handle still protruded from it. Her habit was ripped just under the left breast where the knife had entered and doubtless immediately penetrated her heart. The blood had soaked her clothing. It was not dried and that indicated death had not occurred long before. In fact, she thought the time could probably be measured in minutes rather than hours.

A thought had occurred to Fidelma and she examined the floor of the chapel, tracing her way carefully back to the door and outside. She was looking for blood specks but something else caught her eye – droplets of wax near the sarcophagus. The fact alone was not surprising. She would imagine that many people over the years had entered with candles and bent to examine the stone that had covered the relics of the saint. What was surprising was the fact that the tallow grease lay in profusion over the edge of the sepulchre on which the flat covering stone would have swung shut.

Fidelma, frowning, seized the end of the flat stone and exerted her strength. It swung. It was not easy to push it but, nevertheless, it could be moved with a rasping sound back into place across the tomb. Thoughtfully, she returned it to the position in which she had found it.

She let her gaze wander back to the body to examine the knife again. It was a poor country person's knife; a general implement used for a variety of purposes.

She made no effort to extract it.

She turned her attention to the accoutrements worn by the girl. A rough, wooden crucifix hung around her neck on a leather thong. It was crudely carved but Fidelma had seen many like it among the poorer religious. Her eyes wandered down to the worn leather *marsupium* that hung at the girl's waist.

She opened it. There was a comb inside. Every Irish girl carried a comb. This one was made of bone of the same poor quality as her other ornaments. Long hair being admired in Ireland, it was essential that all men and women carried a *cíor* or comb. She also found, rather to her surprise, there were half a dozen coins in the *marsupium*. They were not of great value but valuable enough to suggest that robbery was no motive in this killing even if the thought had occurred to Fidelma. It had not.

The more Fidelma looked at the corpse, at the position of it, the more she realised that there was something bizarre about this killing; more peculiar than even the usual aberrant fact of violent death. She could not quite put her finger on it. It was true that the corpse's facial muscles seemed slightly distorted in death as if there was a smile on its features. But that was not what bothered her.

By the time she left the oratory, three senior religious were entering the low gate to the oratory grounds. Fidelma immediately recognised the pale, worried features of Rian, the Abbot of Ardmore. With him there was a tall woman, whose face was set and grim, and a moon-faced man, whose expression looked permanently bewildered, whom she also recognised as the steward of the abbey. What was his name? Brother Echen.

'Is it true, Fidelma?' asked the abbot. He was a distant cousin and greeted her familiarly.

'True enough, Rian,' she replied.

'I knew it would happen sooner or later,' snapped the tall sister with him.

Fidelma turned inquiring eyes on her.

'This is Sister Corb,' Abbot Rian explained nervously. 'She is the mistress of the novices in our community. Sister Aróc was a novitiate under her charge.'

'Perhaps you would be good enough to explain the meaning of that remark,' invited Fidelma.

Sister Corb had a long, thin, angular face. Her features seemed permanently set in a look of disapproving derision.

'Little explanation needed. The girl was touched.'

'Touched?'

'Crazy.'

'Perhaps you might explain how that manifested itself and why it would lead to her death?'

The abbot interrupted anxiously.

'I think it might be better explained, Fidelma, by saying that the girl, Sister Aróc, isolated herself from most of us in the community. Her behaviour was . . . eccentric.'

The abbot had paused to try to find the correct word.

Fidelma suppressed a sigh.

'I am still not sure how this manifested itself. Are you saying that the girl was a half-wit? Was her behaviour uncontrollable? Exactly what marked her out as so different that death was an inevitable outcome?'

'Sister Aróc was a fanatic about religious beliefs.' It was the moon-faced steward of the abbey, Brother Echen, who spoke up for the first time. 'She claimed that she heard voices. She said that they were' – he screwed up his eyes and genuflected – 'she said they were voices of the saints.'

Sister Corb sniffed in disapproval.

'She used it as an excuse not to obey the Rule of the community. She claimed she was in direct communication with the soul of the Blessed Declan. I would have had her flogged for blasphemy but Abbot Rian is a most humane man.'

Fidelma could not help the censure that came into her voice.

'If, as you say, the girl was touched, not of the same mental faculty as others, what good would a flogging have done?' she asked drily. 'I still do not see how this behaviour would have led to her death . . . her death *sooner or later* was the phrase I think you used, Sister Corb?'

Sister Corb looked disconcerted.

'What I meant to say was that Sister Aróc was otherworldly. Naive, if you like. She did not know how . . . how lecherous men can be.'

The abbot seemed to have a coughing fit and Brother Echen seemed to have taken an intense interest in his feet.

Fidelma stared hard at the woman. Her eyebrow rose in automatic question.

'I mean . . . I mean that Aróc was not versed in the ways of the world. She let herself enjoy the company of men without realising what men expect from a young girl.'

The abbot had regained his composure.

30

'Sadly, Sister Aróc was not possessed of good sense but I think that Sister Corb might be overstating the attraction that Aróc could stir in the minds of any male members of our community.'

Sister Corb's lips twisted cynically.

'The Father Abbot sees only the good in people. It does not matter the extent of the attractive qualities, a young girl is a young girl!'

Fidelma raised her hands in a gesture indicating hopelessness and let them fall.

'I am trying to understand what is implied here and how this is providing a clue to how and why Sister Aróc came by her death in such bizarre circumstances.'

Sister Corb's eyes narrowed slightly and she stared across the chapel ground to where Brother Ross was leaning against the low dividing wall, still looking pale and shaken.

'Have you asked him?'

'Brother Ross? Why?'

Sister Corb's lips compressed.

'In fairness, I should not say another word.'

'You have either said too much or too little,' Fidelma replied dourly.

'Where was he when the killing took place?'

'That I can answer,' Fidelma replied. 'Brother Ross was conducting the band of pilgrims around the sites associated with the Blessed Declan. I was part of that band.'

Sister Corb was not convinced.

'How can you be so sure?' she demanded.

'Brother Ross had been with us during the last two hours.'

'So why could he not have killed the girl before he met you?' pressed Sister Corb, refusing to be budged from her suspicion.

'Because' – Fidelma smiled – 'she was killed not long before we arrived at the chapel and found her. In fact, I would say she was killed only minutes before.'

Sister Corb's mouth snapped shut. She seemed irritated at Fidelma's logic.

'Why would you accuse Brother Ross anyway?' asked Fidelma with interest.

'I have had my say,' muttered the mistress of novices, her lips forming into a thin line of defiance.

31

'I will tell you when you have answered my questions to my satisfaction,' replied Fidelma softly. The fact that there was no belligerence
in her voice made it that much more imposing. Sister Corb was well
aware of the powers of an advocate of the law courts.

'It is well known that Brother Ross desired the girl,' she replied
defensively.

'Desired?'

'Lusted for her.'

Brother Echen snorted with derision.

'That is, with all respect, only Sister Corb's interpretation. Her
jaundiced view of the intention of men in any situation leads her to
make leaps of imagination.'

Fidelma swung round to him.

'You do not share Sister Corb's view?'

'Ask Brother Ross himself,' the steward replied casually. 'He liked
the girl's company. They were often together and he did not ridicule
her, as some did. But he had no lecherous intentions.'

'How do you know this?'

'As steward of the community, it is my job to know things, especially
to keep a watch for anything which might lead to a disturbance among
the brethren.'

'What, in this matter, might have led to a disturbance?'

Brother Echen glanced at Sister Corb meaningfully.

Fidelma turned and smiled at the abbot.

'Father Abbot, if you and Sister Corb will wait with Brother
Ross . . . ?'

She waited until they had moved out of earshot before turning back
to Brother Echen.

'Well?' she prompted.

'Sister Corb was creating trouble for Brother Ross. She was jealous.'

'Jealous?'

Brother Echen shrugged eloquently.

'You know . . .'

'I don't know. Tell me.'

'Corb was jealous of Ross because she wanted Aróc for herself.
Sister Corb is . . . well, that is why she has a peculiar attitude to men
and ascribes lust as their only motive.'

'Did Aróc respond to Corb's advances, if that is what she made?'

'No. Aróc was otherworldly, as we have said. She did not care for any physical contact. She was one of the aesthetes sworn to a life of celibacy. She rejected Corb even as she would have rejected Ross had he thrust his attentions on her.'

'What makes you sure that he did not?'

'He told me that he did not. He enjoyed her company and speaking to her of the saints and of the Faith. He respected her too much.'

'How well did you know Sister Aróc?'

Brother Echen shrugged.

'Not well at all. She had been six months with the community. She was still technically under the instruction of the mistress of the novitiates – Sister Corb. Truth to say that I spoke only once to her and that was when her case had come up before the council.'

'Her case?'

'Corb had been asked to report on her novitiates by the abbot when we sat in council to discuss the affairs of the community. That was when Corb talked of Sister Aróc's eccentric behaviour. It was decided that I should question her about the voices she claimed to hear.'

'And what did you decide?'

Brother Echen shrugged.

'She was not mad in any dangerous sense, if that is what you mean. However, her mind was not sound. I have met one or two religious who claim to have spoken with Christ and his Holy Saints and known many who have claimed as much and more who have become saints themselves.'

'Just one point more, where were you during the last hour?'

Brother Echen grinned broadly.

'With ten witnesses who will account for my presence, Sister. I was giving a class in calligraphy to our scribes for I am considered to have a good, firm hand.'

'Ask Sister Corb to come to me,' Fidelma dismissed him.

Sister Corb came but was still belligerent.

'Why haven't you spoken to Ross?' she demanded without preamble. 'There is some way he must have killed her . . .'

'Sister Corb!' Fidelma's sharp tone quelled her. 'We will speak of matters of which you are competent to give evidence. Firstly, where were you during this last hour?'

33

Sister Corb blinked.

'I was in the abbey.'

'And you can prove this fact?'

The mistress of the novices frowned for a moment.

'Most of the time I was instructing the novitiates this morning.'

Fidelma picked up her hesitation.

'During this last hour?'

'Are you accusing me . . . ?'

'I am asking where you were and whether you can prove it.'

'After instructing the novitiates I spent some time in the abbey gardens. I do not know whether anyone saw me there or not. I was just returning when I heard the pilgrims coming to tell the abbot what had happened here and so I joined him and Brother Echen.'

'Very well. How long did it take you to climb the hill to this chapel?'

Sister Corb looked surprised.

'How long . . . ?'

'Approximately.'

'Ten minutes, I suppose. Why . . . ?'

'That is most helpful,' Fidelma replied, cutting the woman short. She left Sister Corb, ignoring the look of anger on her angular features, and walked across to Brother Ross.

'Death is not a pleasant thing to look on, is it, Brother?' she opened.

The young man raised his light blue eyes and stared at her for a moment.

'It was gloomy in the oratory. I did not see too well. I thought I saw . . .'

Fidelma smiled reassuringly.

'You made it plain what you thought you saw.'

'I feel stupid.'

'I understand that you knew Sister Aróc quite well?'

The youth flushed.

'Well enough. We . . . we were friends. I could say that . . . that I was her only friend in the abbey.'

'Her behaviour was described as a little eccentric. She heard voices. Didn't that bother you?'

'She was not mad,' Brother Ross replied defensively. 'If she believed it then I saw no cause to question her belief.'

'But the others thought that she was insane.'

'They did not know her well enough.'

'What do you think she was doing up here in the oratory?'

'She often came to the oratory to be near to the Blessed Declan. It was his voice that she claimed that she heard.'

'Did she tell you what this voice told her?'

Brother Ross gave the question consideration.

'Aróc believed that she was being chosen by the saint as his handmaiden.'

'How did she interpret that?'

Brother Ross grimaced.

'I don't think that even she knew what she was talking about. She thought she was being told to obey the will of someone two centuries dead.'

'And what was that will?'

'Celibacy and service,' replied Brother Ross. 'At least, that is what she said.'

'You say that she liked to come to the oratory to be close to St Declan. Did you help her remove the lid of the sarcophagus and then grease it with tallow candle wax to allow her to swing it to and fro at will?'

Brother Ross raised a startled face to meet her cool gaze.

Fidelma went on rapidly.

'Do not ask me how I know. That is obvious. I presume that you did help her for there was no one else to do so.'

'It was not an act of sacrilege. She just wanted to look on the bones of the Blessed Declan and touch them so that she could be in direct contact with him.'

'Did you know that Sister Aróc would be here this morning?'

Brother Ross quickly shook his head.

'I had told her that the pilgrims would be coming to see the oratory this morning – it being the Holy Day.'

'It sounds as though she was strong-willed. Maybe she did not care. After all, today would be a day of special significance for her. As the feast of St Declan, the day on which he departed life, it would be obvious that she would come here.'

'Truly, I did not know.'

'What I find curious is, knowing her so well as you did, even knowing

35

her habit of opening the tomb and gazing on the relics of the saint, why you came rushing out crying the saint's body was uncorrupted. Had you not known what the relics were like, had you not known what Aróc looked like, it might have been explicable . . .'

'I told you, it was dark in the oratory and I truly thought . . .'

'Truly?' Fidelma smiled cynically. 'Not for one moment did you consider any other option than to rush forth and proclaim that Declan's dusty relics had been suddenly translated to incorrupt flesh?'

Brother Ross wore a stubborn look.

'I have told you all I know in this matter.' He folded his arms defiantly.

Fidelma's lips thinned and she gazed an inordinately long time on him; examining, particularly, the front of his robe.

'Do you have any suspicion of who killed Sister Aróc?' she finally asked him.

'I know only that she died a violent death here when there was no need for such an end to her life,' he replied belligerently.

Fidelma turned away towards the agitated figure of Rian, the Abbot of Ardmore.

'I am grieved, Fidelma. I am the head of my community, the shepherd of my flock. If there was violence brewing I should have felt it.'

'You are only a man and not one of the prophets, Rian,' Fidelma admonished. 'There is no need for you to take any blame for this on to your shoulders.'

'How can I help resolve this matter?'

'By answering a few questions. Did you know Sister Aróc?'

'I am abbot,' he responded gravely.

'I meant, know her on a personal level and not merely as one of your flock.'

The abbot shook his head.

'She was brought to me six months ago by Sister Corb, who wished to induct her into the school of the novices. She was of the age of choice. She struck me as a religious girl although not overly bright. Apart from my one interview with her, I have only seen her at a distance.'

He paused and then glancing swiftly across the chapel ground towards Sister Corb he continued.

'Sister Corb came to me a few days ago to lodge an official complaint. It was only then that I heard of her curious behaviour;

what was it that Sister Corb described it as – "otherworldly"? Echen
was sent to speak to her but he reported that she was eccentric but not
dangerous.'

'Do you know whether Sister Corb might have other motives for
complaining about Aróc?'

The abbot flushed slightly and then grimaced.

'I know what you mean. I had not thought that applied in this
case. But Sister Corb does have several liaisons which I would not
approve of. But, as abbot, sometimes it is diplomatic to feign a lack
of knowledge.'

'Several?' Fidelma's brows arched. 'Could it be that some of
her – her liaisons, as you call them, might have been jealous of
Sister Corb?'

The abbot looked startled.

'Do you mean . . . ?'

'Questions again,' snapped Fidelma. 'Every question I ask, I seem
to get answered by a question!' She repented at once as the Father
Abbot seemed to wince at her outburst. 'I apologise. It is just that it
is so difficult to extract information.'

'No, it is I who should apologise, Fidelma. There are several
members of the community who would be angered by Corb's attention
to Sister Aróc, if that is what you are asking. But I do not think that
they would be worth considering in this case.'

'Why not?'

'If my meagre knowledge of law is anything to go by, as well as
being a suspect by motive, you must also be suspect by opportunity.'

'Your knowledge is correct,' affirmed Fidelma.

'Well, you indicated to Brother Echen and to Sister Corb that this
murder took place shortly before your group of pilgrims arrived at the
hilltop. Look around you.'

The Father Abbot spread his arms.

Fidelma knew what he meant without looking. The hill, as they
wound their way up the only track, was just a round grassy hump
without trees, without bushes, and only the small oratory on top.
Anyone leaving the oratory shortly before the arrival of the band of
pilgrims would have no place to hide.

She smiled quickly.

'No, Father Abbot, I suppose it was not a sound thought to imagine

37

someone sneaking up from the abbey and killing Sister Aróc and then sneaking away moments before a party of pilgrims arrived at the oratory.'

'Then what are you saying? Who killed Sister Aróc?'

Sister Fidelma turned to the others and waved them to come forward.

'My investigation seems to have drawn to its close,' she said, addressing the abbot.

He looked bewildered.

'Then I must ask you again, who killed Sister Aróc?'

Fidelma glanced towards Brother Ross.

Sister Corb was smiling in grim satisfaction.

'I knew it,' she muttered. 'I . . .'

Fidelma raised her hand for silence.

'I made no accusation, Sister Corb. And you should know the penalty for false accusation.'

The mistress of the novitiates was suddenly silent, staring at her in bewilderment.

'But if Brother Ross is not the murderer . . .' began Brother Echen helplessly, 'who killed her?'

Fidelma glanced again to the young religieux.

'Brother Ross will tell you,' she said quietly.

'But you said . . .' began the abbot.

Fidelma shook her head impatiently.

'I said nothing. I implied he did not murder Aróc but I did not say that he did not know who killed her.'

Brother Ross was regarding her with frightened eyes.

'You would not believe the truth,' he said quietly.

'I know the truth,' Fidelma replied.

'How? How could you know . . .'

'It was not that hard to work out, given the time factor and the situation of the oratory where no one could hide.'

'You'd better explain it to us, Sister Fidelma,' the abbot said.

'Our group of pilgrims came to the oratory and, as I have pointed out, Aróc's death occurred, judging by the condition of the corpse, moments before,' Fidelma explained. 'Ross went into the oratory first. Moments later he came out. He might well have had time to stab Aróc and then return to us to pretend that he had discovered the body. But the evidence is against that. Such a stab wound would have caused blood to spurt on his robes.

'It was obvious that Aróc was killed while lying in the open tomb. She was not killed elsewhere and dragged to the open tomb. There were no blood splatters leading to the tomb which would have been made. If Brother Ross had killed her, then his robes would have been drenched in spurting blood from the wound. Instead, he has some spots of blood on his right hand and his sleeve. They were made when he bent to touch the corpse.'

She pointed to his robes so that they could verify her statement.

The abbot was worried.

'You have presented us with a conundrum. Tell us the answer. The killer was hiding in or behind the oratory, is that it?'

Fidelma sighed shortly.

'I would have thought it obvious.'

Brother Ross gave a little groan.

'I confess! I confess! I killed her. I did it.'

Fidelma looked pityingly at him.

'No you did not.'

Sister Corb was indignant.

'That will not do, Sister. The man has confessed. You cannot deny his confession.'

Fidelma glanced at her.

'Brother Ross is even now trying to save his friend's soul. He believes that the Penitentials would prohibit Sister Aróc's being accorded the last rites, a forgiveness of sins and burial in sanctified ground in a state of spiritual peace. It is time to tell the truth, Brother Ross.'

'The truth?' pressed Brother Echen. 'What is the truth?'

'She killed herself.'

Brother Ross groaned piteously.

'When you have eliminated every other explanation as being impossible, that which remains must be the truth,' Fidelma said drily. 'Am I right, Brother Ross?'

The young man's shoulders had slumped in resignation.

'She . . . she was not of this world. She heard voices. She thought she was being instructed by spirits, from the otherworld. By the Blessed Declan. She had visions. She made me open the tomb so that she could touch the holy relics. I greased the stone so that she could swing it open

39

by herself when she wanted. She often spoke of joining the holy saint. I did not think she meant to kill herself.'

'What happened?' demanded the abbot.

'I brought the pilgrims to the oratory and went inside before them in case there was a worshipper at prayer. I had no wish to disturb anyone. I saw her body lying in the open grave with both hands gripping the knife in her breast. I realised with horror what she had done. There was no time nor place to hide the body from the pilgrims. If I had attempted to swing the tomb shut those outside would have heard me. I forced her hands from their grip on the knife and put them at her sides. I tried to remove the knife but it was buried to the hilt, that was when the spots of blood stained my sleeve and hand. I think I panicked, believing the pilgrims would come in at any moment. The only thing I could think of was to pretend the saint's body was uncorrupted and hope it would distract the pilgrims to run down to the abbey to report the news, giving me time to dispose of the body. I did not count on . . .'

He glanced towards Fidelma and shrugged.

'The crime of suicide forbids her being laid in hallowed ground,' pointed out Sister Corb. 'The suicide is classed as a *fingalach*, a kin-slayer; a person no better than a murderer.'

'That is why I tried to protect her so that her soul could journey on to the otherworld in peace,' sobbed the youth. 'I loved her that much.'

'There is no need to worry,' Fidelma assured him gently. 'Sister Aróc can be buried in consecrated ground.'

Here the abbot began to protest. Fidelma cut him short.

'Sister Aróc, for legal purposes, was classed a *mer*, one of unsound mind. The law states that the rights of the mentally disturbed should take precedence over other rights. A lenient view is taken of all offences committed by them.'

'But Brother Ross lied,' pointed out Sister Corb, angry and determined that someone should be punished.

Fidelma countered her anger softly.

'The law also looks kindly on those whose concern it is to protect those unable to protect themselves. Brother Ross may now rest assured that Sister Aróc's soul can now depart in peace.'

The abbot glanced around hesitantly before heaving a low sigh of acceptance.

'Amen!' he muttered softly. 'Amen!'

The Astrologer Who Predicted
His Own Murder

'I can appreciate why the Bishop has sent you to defend Abbot Rígán, Sister. However, I think that you will find this is an open and shut case. The abbot is demonstrably guilty of the murder of Brother Eolang.'

Brehon Gormán was a tall, dark man, swarthy of complexion. He sat back regarding Sister Fidelma, seated across the table opposite him, with a look of cynical amusement. He had an arrogance of manner which irritated her. They were using the chamber of Brother Cass, the steward of the abbey of Fota, who stood nervously to one side.

'As I understood the circumstances, there were no eyewitnesses. How, then, can the abbot be demonstrably guilty?' she asked coldly with an emphasis on the words he had used.

The sharp-faced Brehon smiled even more broadly. The smile made Fidelma feel a coldness at the nape of her neck. It had all the warmth of a shark about to snap at its prey.

'Our law takes cognisance of the words of a man uttered before his death,' remarked the Brehon in the manner of a teacher explaining something to a backward child.

'I do not follow.'

'The victim named the abbot as his murderer before his death.'

Sister Fidelma was stunned into silence by his calm announcement.

It had been only that morning when the Bishop of Cashel had called her into his chambers and asked her if she, being a *dálaigh*, an advocate of the courts, would undertake the defence of Abbot Rígán, whose abbey of Fota stood on an island in a nearby lake. The abbot had been accused of killing one of his own brethren. Brehon Gormán was

41

to hear the case and it was known that Gormán was no lover of the religious. The Bishop of Cashel was concerned for the abbot, who, by all accounts, a man with a reputation for kindliness and largesse, was a man whose good works had distinguished him among the brethren. However, the abbot was also known to be a man of strict obedience to the Rule of Rome which brought him into conflict with many of his fellow religious.

The community of the Abbey of Fota was a small exclusive brotherhood of leather workers and a few scholars. They were a self-sufficient community. As protocol required, Fidelma had introduced herself to the worried-looking steward, Brother Cass, who had then introduced her to Brehon Gormán who had ensconced himself in the steward's chamber. She had asked to be informed of all the facts of the case.

The facts seemed simple, according to the Brehon. Brother Eolang, a member of the community, had been found by the lake under a wooden landing pier. He had evidently been drowned but there was bruising and cuts to his head. The community's apothecary, Brother Cruinn, had expressed suspicion about the death. Brother Eolang had not been an elderly man. He was in the prime of his life and the bruising seemed to indicate that he had been struck on the forehead and pushed into the lake where he had drowned.

Brehon Gormán had been sent for. After some initial inquiries he had placed Abbot Rígán in custody pending a full trial.

For a moment or two Fidelma sat gazing at Brehon Gormán in astonishment.

'My understanding of what I have been told is that Brother Eolang was dead when he was discovered in the lake. Is this not so? But you say he was able to name the abbot as his killer. How was this miracle accomplished?'

'He was certainly dead when his body was found,' agreed the Brehon.

'Then explain this riddle which you have set me.'

'It is quite simple. Brother Eolang told several of his brethren a week ago that he would be murdered on a particular day and that the abbot would be responsible.'

Fidelma found herself in the unusual position of being unable to comment for a moment or so. Then she shook her head in bewilderment, trying to control the growing sarcasm in her tone.

'This is the evidence? He predicted he would be murdered by the abbot?'

Brehon Gormán smiled again, even more coldly.

'Brother Eolang also foretold the exact manner of his death,' he added.

'I think you need to explain more precisely, Brehon Gormán,' Fidelma said. 'Was Brother Eolang a prophet?'

'It would appear so for we have the accusation and prediction written in Brother Eolang's own hand.'

Sister Fidelma sat back and folded her hands in her lap.

'I am listening attentively to your explanation,' she said quietly. 'Please tell me the facts so that I do not make any assumptions.'

'There was no love lost between Abbot Rígán and Brother Eolang,' replied the Brehon. 'There are witnesses to several arguments between them. They arose because the abbot did not agree with some of Brother Eolang's beliefs and activities . . .'

Fidelma frowned, still feeling lost.

'Activities? What activities?'

'Brother Eolang was the assistant to the apothecary of the abbey and an adept at making speculations from the patterns of the stars.'

'Medicine and astrology are often twins in the practice of the physician's art,' conceded Fidelma. 'Its use is widespread throughout the five kingdoms of Éireann. Why was the abbot so condemning of the practice?'

Fidelma herself had studied the art of star charts and their interpretation under Brother Conchobar of Cashel who had once told her that she would have made an excellent interpreter of the portents. However, Fidelma placed no great reliance on astrologers, for it was a science which seemed to rely solely on the interpretive ability of the individual. However, she did accept that much might be learnt from the wisest among them. The study of the heavens, *nemgnacht*, was an ancient art among the people of Éireann and most who could afford to do so had a chart cast for the moment of their children's birth which was called *nemindithib*, a horoscope.

The more ancient forms of astrology used by the Druids before the coming of Christianity had fallen out of use because the New Faith had also brought in new forms which were practised among the Greeks and Romans and originated in Babylon.

'The abbot did not approve of astrology, Sister,' interrupted the steward of the community, Brother Cass, who had been standing quietly by during the initial exchange. 'The abbot disliked Brother Eolang on account of his practice of astrology. The abbot had read a passage in one of the Scriptures which denounced astrology and so he took his teaching from it. He tried to forbid its practice within our community.'

Fidelma smiled softly.

'Forbidding anything is a sure way of encouraging it. I thought we were more tolerant in such matters? The art of the *réaltóir*, the astrologer, has been one that has its origins from the very time our ancestors first raised their eyes to the night sky. It is part of our way of life and even those who have accepted the New Faith have not rejected the fact that God put the stars in the sky for the obedience of fools and the guidance of the wise.'

There was a silence then Brother Cass spoke again.

'Yet there was an animosity between Eolang and the abbot over this matter.'

'Over a week ago,' commenced the Brehon, 'according to certain members of the community, and as they will testify, Brother Eolang became so worried about the animosity that he cast a chart, what is called a horary chart, to see if he was in any danger from the abbot. He did this because the abbot's language had grown quite violent in the denunciation of Brother Eolang's beliefs.'

Fidelma did not make any comment but waited for the Brehon to continue.

'Eolang told certain of his comrades among the brethren that within a week from the time he had cast that chart, he would be dead. The chart, he said, showed that he was powerless against the abbot and would suffer death at his hands either by drowning or poisoning.'

Brehon Gormán sat back with a smile of triumph.

Fidelma regarded him with some scepticism.

'You appear to believe this.'

'I have seen the chart. I am an amateur in such things but my knowledge is such that the accuracy of the prediction becomes obvious. I shall accept it into evidence along with the testimony of those of the brethren to whom Brother Eolang discussed the meaning of it before his death.'

Fidelma considered the matter silently for a moment. Then she turned to Brother Cass.

'Do you have someone available who could take a message to Cashel for me?'

Brother Cass glanced at the Brehon, who frowned.

'What do you propose, Sister Fidelma?'

'Why, since this chart is apparently central to the abbot's supposed guilt, I would send to Cashel for an expert witness to verify its interpretation.'

'What expert witness?'

'Doubtless, as someone who has dabbled in the art, you have heard of Brother Conchobar, the astrologer of Cashel? He was taught by the famous Mo Chuaróc mac Neth Sémon, the greatest astrologer that Cashel ever produced.'

The Brehon's frown deepened.

'I have heard of Conchobar, of course. But do we need worry him when everything is so clear?'

'Oh, for the sake of justice,' smiled Fidelma, without humour, 'we need to ensure that the abbot has the best defence and that implies someone who is an expert in the evidence against him. You have admitted to having only an amateur's knowledge. I also have but a passing knowledge so it is best to consult a real expert.'

The Brehon examined her features carefully. A suspicion crossed his mind as to whether she was being facetious. Then he glanced to Brother Cass and inclined his head in approval.

'You may send for Brother Conchobar.'

Sister Fidelma smiled briefly in acknowledgement.

'And if we are to take this star chart seriously as evidence,' she went on as Brother Cass departed on his mission, 'then I shall want to have proof that it was drawn up by Eolang at the time it is claimed. I shall want to examine those brethren with whom he discussed it and its conclusions. And, having some slight knowledge of the art, I shall want to see it for myself.'

Brehon Gormán raised an eyebrow.

'It sounds as if you do not trust my judgement?' There was a dangerous quality to his voice.

'You are the Brehon,' Fidelma replied softly. 'When you sit in your court and pronounce your judgement, having heard all the evidence

45

and the plea from myself, as a *dálaigh* defending my client, then your judgement demands and receives respect. Until that time, I shall presume that you have not made any judgement for if you had that would have been contrary to law.'

Her features seemed inscrutable but he noticed her green eyes glimmering with an angry fire as they returned his stare.

The Brehon's cheeks crimsoned.

'I . . . of course, I have made no judgement. All that I have done is point out to you that I have accepted this chart as essential evidence. Also that the people to whom Brother Eolang spoke about its conclusions are satisfactory witnesses. The chart and witnesses will be presented to the court.'

'Do you have the chart here?'

'I have it and written on it is testimony as to when it was written and its interpretation in the very hand of Brother Eolang and witnessed.'

'Show me,' demanded Fidelma.

Brehon Gormán drew a vellum from a case and spread it on the table between them.

'Note the date and time and Eolang's signature in the corner. You will also note that a Brother Iarlug has signed his name as witness and dated it on the same day.'

'This Brother Iarlug is available to testify?'

'Of course, as are Brothers Brugach, Senach and Dubán to whom Eolang spoke of his prediction. They all will testify when this chart was drawn up and when he spoke to them.'

Fidelma pursed her lips sceptically.

'With five of the brethren, including the victim, forewarned of the day when the abbot would commit this alleged murder, it seems a curiosity that Brother Eolang was not given protection against the event.'

Brehon Gormán shook his head, his face serious.

'You cannot alter fate. Fate has no reprieve.'

'That is a concept brought to us by Rome,' Fidelma rebuked. 'Our own wise men say that whatever limits us, we call fate. Fate is not something which is inevitable whether we act or not. It is only inevitable if we do not act.'

Brehon Gormán glowered at her for a moment but she was oblivious of his stare.

'Now, let us examine this chart. You may explain it to me as you confess to be something of an amateur in its deciphering.'

It took a moment or two before Brehon Gormán became involved in the task and, in spite of his antagonism to Fidelma, his voice took on an enthusiastic tone.

'The chart is easy to follow. See here.' He thrust out a finger to the symbols on the vellum.

Sister Fidelma bent over it, silently thanking the time she had spent with old Conchobar learning something of the mysteries of the art.

'It seems that Eolang was so worried that he asked a question "Am I in mortal danger from Abbot Rígán?" This is called a horary question and the chart is timed for the birth of the question. It is like looking at a natal chart but, in this case, it is the birth of the question.'

Fidelma suppressed a sigh of impatience. She knew well what a horary question was. But she held her tongue.

'It seems from the chart that Eolang was ruled by Mercury ruling the Virgo ascendant with the moon as co-ruler. His enemy, the abbot, is represented by the ruler of the seventh house, signified by Jupiter in the seventh house in Pisces.'

'Very well. That I can follow. Continue.'

'Brother Eolang's first impression was that Mercury was very weak in Pisces, being in detriment and fall and also retrograde. Also Mercury was close to the cusp of the eighth house of death. Jupiter on the other hand was powerful. It was in its rulership and angular and disposed Mercury. Jupiter, importantly, also ruled the eighth house of death.'

Sister Fidelma followed the Brehon's pointing finger as he indicated the positions on the chart.

'Now, see here: the moon applied to the sun, ruler of the twelfth house of self-undoing, and was combust. We astrologers . . .' he smiled deprecatingly, 'have long regarded this as the worst condition for any planet. The sun and moon were in the eighth house and the moon in Aries is peregrine or totally without power.'

Fidelma now found herself struggling to understand the various angles which were depicted on the chart. Her knowledge was insufficient to discern the nuances.

'In Brother Eolang's interpretation, what did all of this mean?' she asked.

'All these indications told Brother Eolang that he was powerless against Abbot Rígán. It told him that he would suffer death at the abbot's hands either by drowning or poisoning. Drowning was more likely with Pisces being a water sign. And, see, Jupiter in Pisces indicates a large, powerful man, religious and well respected in the community. Who else did that identify but the abbot?'

'And from your knowledge, you find this interpretation acceptable?' Fidelma asked curiously. Certainly, from her own limited knowledge of how astrologers worked, she could see no flaw in his presentation.

'I accept it completely,' affirmed Brehon Gormán.

'Very well. Let us now send for these witnesses to see what they have to say. Firstly, Brother Iarlug who signed the chart as a witnesses to its provenance.'

Brother Iarlug was thin and mournful and had no hesitation in verifying that he had witnessed Eolang drawing up his chart. Eolang had also explained what the chart portended. That within the week Eolang would be dead and at the hands of the abbot.

'Why, then, was nothing done to protect Eolang if he believed this knowledge,' demanded Fidelma, not for the first time.

'Eolang was a fatalist. He thought there was no escape,' Brother Iarlug assured her while Brehon Gormán smiled in satisfaction behind him.

One after the other, Brothers Brugach, Senach and Dubán all told how Brother Eolang had showed them his chart over a week before. He had predicted the very day on which he would be found in the lake. Each of them confirmed that they believed in inescapable fate.

Fidelma was exasperated.

'Everyone here seems a slave to predestination. Has no one free will?' she sneered.

'Fate is . . .' began Brehon Gormán.

'Fate is the fool's excuse for failure,' she snapped at him. 'Am I to believe that you believed this event would happen and simply sat down and waited for it?'

'It is the fate of the leaf to float and the stone to sink,' intoned Brother Dubán. 'We cannot change our destiny. Even the New Faith tells us that. In this place we have all studied the writings of the great Augustine of Hippo – *De civitate Dei*, The City of God. Does he not argue that we cannot escape our fate? Our fate was predestined even before we were born. Even before God made the world, the Omnipotent One had decreed the fate of the meanest among us.'

'On the contrary. Did not our own great theologian Pelagius argue in *De Libero Arbitrio* – On Free Will – that meek acceptance of fate is destructive to man's advancement? We are given information to make choices upon, not to sit back and do nothing. Doing nothing, as Augustine suggests we do, imperils the entire moral law of mankind. We have to take the initial and fundamental steps for our salvation. If we are not responsible for our actions, good or bad, then there is nothing to restrain ourselves from indulging in sin.'

'But that's a Druidic teaching . . .' protested the Brehon.

'And Pelagius was accused of trying to revive the Druidic philosophy,' interrupted Brother Dubán in annoyance. 'That was why he was declared a heretic by Rome and excommunicated by Pope Innocent I.'

'But that judgement was not accepted by the churches here, nor in Britain nor Gaul nor even by many of the Roman bishops,' answered Fidelma sharply. 'Even Pope Zosimus, who succeeded Innocent, rescinded that degree and declared Pelagius innocent of heresy. Only the African bishops, the friends of Augustine, refused to accept the Pope's ruling and persuaded the Roman Emperor Honorius to issue an imperial decree denouncing him. It was for political reasons, not those of faith, that Pope Zosimus had to reconsider and change his ruling which lifted the excommunication.'

Brehon Gormán was studying Fidelma with an expression of suspicion and annoyance.

'You seem well informed on this?'

'As lawyers, is it not our duty to imbibe as much information as we can?' she demanded. 'Our knowledge must surely be as wide as we can make it, otherwise how can we profess to set ourselves up as judges of other people's actions?'

Brehon Gormán seemed confused for a moment.

Fidelma continued in a confident tone: 'Now, I shall want to see the person who found Brother Eolang's body, the apothecary who examined it and, of course, the abbot.'

'The body was found by Brother Petrán,' the Brehon responded sourly. 'The apothecary is Brother Cruinn and you will find the abbot confined to his chamber. I do not think there is need for me to accompany you for I am conversant with their evidence. It is of little importance.'

Sister Fidelma raised an eyebrow but said nothing. She glanced at the surly Brother Dubán.

'Then perhaps Brother Dubán will show me where I may find them?'

Brother Dubán reluctantly led the way to the herb garden of the community. There was a single brother working in it.

'Petrán tends the garden and you will see our apothecary's shop in the far corner. There you will find Brother Cruinn.'

Brother Dubán turned and walked swiftly off without another word.

The rotund, red-faced religieux who was tending some bushes in the garden turned as she approached. He frowned for a moment and then gave a friendly smile.

'Sister Fidelma?'

'Do you know me?' she asked, puzzled by the greeting.

'Indeed. But you would not know me. I was in the court when you defended Brother Fergal from a charge of murder. Have you now come to defend our abbot?'

'Only if I believe him to be innocent,' agreed Fidelma.

'Innocent enough.' The man was now serious. 'I am Brother Petrán and I found the body of poor Eolang.'

'But you do not believe that the abbot is guilty?'

'I do not believe that a man should be condemned on the evidence of a claim based on obscure maps of the stars.'

'Tell me what happened?'

'I was going to go to market to buy new plants for the herb garden. This involved crossing the lake,' he added unnecessarily. 'I went to the pier where our boat was tied up. It was then that I saw the body of Brother Eolang in the water under the pier.'

'Under the pier?' Fidelma asked quickly with emphasis.

'The pier is made of thin wooden planking. Some of it is loose and missing. You have to look down to make sure you step surely. That was how I was able to see him. I was keeping my eyes on where I was placing my feet. I saw the body between a gap in the planking. Mind you, I do not suppose I would have looked down so closely at that spot had it not been for the man calling to me and pointing down.'

Fidelma tried not to show her surprise.

'What man?' she asked slowly.

Brother Petrán did not seem perturbed.

'There was a man on horseback on the far bank. As I came on to the pier he started to shout and wave to me. I wondered what was up. It was too far distant to hear any words distinctly. He kept gesturing with his arm towards the water and that was when I looked down and saw the body.'

'Are you saying that this man might be a witness to what happened?' she asked quietly.

Brother Petrán shrugged.

'He certainly spotted the body and drew my attention to it.'

'Did you tell the Brehon this?'

'He thought it was irrelevant because of the evidence that showed the abbot's involvement.'

'Can you describe the man on horseback? Did you know him?'

'He was a stranger. But he rode a fine horse and was dressed as a warrior. He carried the standard of the King of Cashel.'

'Then he must have been a messenger of the king, passing on his way to Cashel,' Fidelma cried in relief. 'We can find him.' Fidelma paused a moment and then continued: 'What then? What happened after your attention was drawn to the body?'

'I raised a cry for help and, being a good swimmer, I jumped into the water and brought the body ashore. By that time Brother Cruinn, our apothecary, had arrived to help me.'

'And the man on the far bank?'

'When he saw that I had brought the body out of the water, he raised his hand and rode off. There was little else he could do for there was no boat on his side of the water.'

'You say that you could swim?' Fidelma went on. 'Do you know if Brother Eolang was a swimmer?'

Brother Petrán shook his head immediately.

'He came from a small fishing community, islanders, who believe that it is wiser not to know how to swim for it is best to be drowned outright, falling into heavy, merciless seas, than prolonging the agony and torture of the body and soul by vain struggle.'

Fidelma suppressed a shiver at the idea.

'I have heard the philosophy although I do not agree with it. Was there no one else who came except the apothecary?'

'No one.'

'Do you know how long Brother Eolang had been in the water?'

'I do not. But the apothecary, Brother Cruinn, said . . .'

Fidelma held up her hand to silence him.

'Perhaps we should leave Brother Cruinn to recount what he said,' she advised. 'You can only give evidence as to your own views.'

Brother Petrán's glance wandered past her shoulder and focused.

'Then there is no better opportunity to hear his words for here is Brother Cruinn.'

Fidelma turned and saw an elderly man coming through the garden. He was strongly built, the arms of his robe rolled up around the elbows showing strong, muscular forearms. His hair was grey and eyes deep blue. He seemed puzzled at seeing the female religious in the herb garden.

Brother Petrán introduced her and the apothecary's face relaxed.

'I was the one who noticed that this was no mere drowning, Sister,' he said with complacency. 'Poor Eolang. He assisted me as apothecary, you know.'

'Perhaps you will accompany me to the wooden pier and explain, on the way, the circumstances which aroused your suspicions?'

They left the herb garden and passed through a small door in a high stone wall which led immediately on to the bank of the island. Fidelma saw that the lake was very wide at this point. The pier, standing on wooden piles, was certainly old. Some of the planking was rotten and did not seem secure.

'This is in need of repair,' Fidelma commented.

'Indeed. It is only used for landing materials for our garden. The primary landing stage is at the main gate as you will have doubtless observed when you arrived.'

'Was there a specific reason why Brother Eolang was here?'

The apothecary rubbed his chin.

'He had gone out in the boat that morning to deliver something to the mainland and so, I presume, he was returning it so that Brother Petrán could use it to go to the market. Brother Petrán found his *marsupium*, his purse, still in the boat.'

'His purse was found in the boat?'

'He had probably forgotten it when he climbed on to the pier.'

'I understand that Brother Petrán retrieved the body of Brother

52

Eolang from the water and then you answered his cries for assistance. Is that so?'

'I heard Brother Petrán from the herb garden and came straight away,' confirmed Brother Cruinn. 'I saw immediately that poor Eolang was dead.'

'How long had he been dead? Could you tell?'

'I am proficient in my work, Sister.' The apothecary was proud of his professional capabilities which made him sound a trifle haughty in manner. 'He had not been dead long. The blood was still flowing from the wound on his forehead and that was when I realised that murder had been committed.'

'Because of the wound? What was it like?'

'It was on the forehead, between the eyes. It was clear that someone had picked up a cudgel of some sort and smitten the brother who fell into the water and drowned.'

'And had you heard the story of how Brother Eolang had predicted that he would be murdered on that day?'

Brother Cruinn shook his head firmly.

'It was only afterwards that I learned this story from Brother Senach.'

'But you worked with him. He was your assistant apothecary. Is it not strange that he did not mention this prediction?'

'He knew my views. I knew of Eolang's reputation as an astrologer. Personally, I did not think much of it. I am a practical man but there are many in my profession who use it as an aid to their medical arts. However, it seems that this time, Eolang was right.'

'This time?' queried Fidelma.

Brother Cruinn smiled deprecatingly.

'I have known many of Eolang's predictions to fail. That is probably why he did not raise the matter of the prediction with me.'

Fidelma nodded thoughtfully.

She made her way back to the chamber of Brother Cass, the steward of the community, and found him in conversation again with Brehon Gormán.

'Have you sent for the messenger of the King of Cashel to hear his evidence?' she asked the Brehon without preamble.

Brehon Gormán looked bewildered.

'The man on horseback who drew Brother Petrán's attention to the body,' she explained impatiently.

'Oh, that man? How did you find out he was a king's messenger?' He paused at her expression and then added defensively: 'I did not think his evidence would be relevant. After all, we have evidence enough about the incident.'

Fidelma scowled in annoyance.

'Don't you realise that he might have witnessed the entire incident?' She turned to Brother Cass. 'You must send another messenger to Cashel immediately to find this man. He is one of the king's messengers so his identity should be easy to discover. He must be brought here as an important witness.' She turned on her heel but at the door she paused and glanced back at the scowling Brehon and then looked at the unhappy steward. 'I shall expect my orders to be carried out, Brother Cass. I shall now speak with the abbot.'

Abbot Rígán was, at first meeting, a likeable man; friendly, concerned and bewildered at the situation in which he found himself. Only after talking to him for a time, did Fidelma find that he was, indeed, rigid in his beliefs and a passionate supporter of the Roman Rule of the Faith.

'Did you kill Brother Eolang?' Fidelma demanded in opening the conversation after she had introduced herself.

'As God is my witness, I did not,' replied the abbot solemnly.

'Have you heard the nature of the evidence against you?'

'It is ridiculous! Surely no reasonable person would countenance such evidence as worth considering.'

'Brehon Gormán does. There is much to be explained in that evidence. Over a week ago Brother Eolang foretold that on such a day he would be killed by either drowning or poisoning. No one can deny that he did die in such circumstances.'

The abbot was silent.

'Brother Eolang said that if that circumstance happened, you would be responsible for his death.'

'But that is rubbish.'

'The Brehon says that if one part of the prediction is true, why not the other?'

'I refuse to answer the prattling of superstition.'

'I am told, Father Abbot, that you and Brother Eolang were not friends. That you criticised him because he practised astrology. Superstition, as you have just called it.'

Abbot Rígán nodded emphatically.

'Doesn't Deuteronomy say – "Nor must you raise your eyes to the heavens and look up to the sun, the moon, and the stars, all the host of heaven, and be led on to bow down to them and worship them . . ."?'

Fidelma inclined her head.

'I know the passage. Our astrologers would say that they do not worship the stars, but are guided by their patterns for that very passage of Deuteronomy continues where you left off – ". . . the Lord your God created these for the various peoples under heaven." If He created them, why should we be afraid to follow their guidance?'

The abbot sniffed disparagingly.

'You have a quick tongue, Sister. But it is clear that God forbade star worship. Jeremiah says, "Do not be awed by signs in the heavens" . . .'

'Our astrologers would point out that Jeremiah is actually admitting that there are, indeed, signs in the heavens and he merely admonishes us not to be awed by them with the implication we should understand them and learn by them.'

'Not at all!' snapped the abbot. 'Isaiah says –

Let your astrologers, your star-gazers
who foretell your future month by month,
persist, and save you!
But look, they are gone like chaff;
fire burns them up . . .'

'Isaiah was addressing the Babylonians during the exile of the Israelites in Babylon. Naturally, he would belittle their leaders. The point is, Abbot, whether you like it or not, astrology accuses you and astrology must, therefore, defend you.'

'I will not be defended by that which my Faith denies.'

'Then you cannot be defended at all,' said Fidelma, rising. 'If a man comes with a stick to beat you, would you say that I will not defend myself for that man has no right to use that stick as a weapon?'

She was at the door when the abbot coughed nervously. She turned back expectantly.

'In what way would you defend me?' he muttered.

55

'Where were you when Eolang was drowned?' she asked.

'That morning I was engaged in the accounts of the community. Our brethren make leather goods and sell them and thus we are able to sustain our little community.'

'Was anyone with you?'

Abbot Rígán shrugged.

'I was alone all morning until Brother Cass came to report the finding of Brother Eolang to me. I detected a strange atmosphere in the community for I was unaware of this nonsense about a prediction. I was therefore surprised when Brother Cass informed me that he had already sent for a Brehon based on information he had received. I was more surprised when the Brehon arrived and I found myself accused of killing Eolang.'

'The prediction is damning,' pointed out Fidelma.

'Could it be that Brother Eolang killed himself to spite me?'

'In my experience, suicides do not hit themselves over the head and drown nor is spite considered a sufficient motive for killing oneself.'

'It sounds as if you believe this prediction and therefore my guilt.'

'My task, Father Abbot, is to investigate the facts and if the facts show you to be guilty, then my oath as a *dálaigh* forbids me to hide your guilt from the court. My task would only be to explain any special circumstances which caused your guilt. A *dálaigh* cannot intentionally protect the guilty before the courts. But, I emphasise, judgement must be based on facts.'

When the abbot tried to speak again she raised her hand to silence him.

'At the moment, I have no judgement one way or the other. I have a suspicion of what happened but I cannot prove my suspicion before the Brehon. I am not, therefore, in full possession of the facts.'

Twenty-four hours had to pass before Brother Cass announced that his messengers were returning from Cashel.

Sister Fidelma went to the main gate to watch the boat crossing the lake towards the pier. Her sharp eyes immediately spotted the bent figure of the elderly Brother Conchobar in the stern of the boat. Her anxious eyes found a second figure, a young warrior, seated next to him.

'Brother Conchobar, I am glad that you have come,' she greeted as they stepped ashore.

The old man smiled, a slow, sad smile.

'I heard of your curious case from the messenger you sent. This is Ferchar, by the way.'

The young warrior bowed to Fidelma. He did not forget that Fidelma was sister to the King of Cashel.

'Lady, I heard that the man drowned. I am sorrowful that I was not able to do anything more than I did. Alas, it was too far for me to swim across the lake to his rescue.'

Fidelma glanced anxiously from Ferchar to Conchobar as a thought struck her.

'Have you discussed this matter with one another on your journey here?'

Brother Conchobar shook his head. It was Ferchar who answered.

'Lady, we know that the method of giving evidence says that no witness may confer with another about the event. We have kept our silence on this matter.'

One of the brethren, whom Brother Cass had sent to bring them to the abbey, came forward.

'I can swear to this before the Brehon if need be, Sister. These men have not spoken of the matter since we found them and brought them hither.'

'Excellent,' Fidelma was relieved. 'Come with me.'

Fidelma led them to Brother Cass's chamber where Brehon Gormán was waiting impatiently.

'The judgement on this matter has been delayed a full twenty-four hours. I hope this has not been a waste of time.'

'Justice, as you must know, Brehon Gormán, is never a waste of time. I have asked Brother Conchobar to wait outside while we now hear from an eyewitness.'

She motioned to Ferchar.

Brehon Gormán examined the young warrior.

'State your name and position.'

'I am Ferchar of the bodyguard of King Colgú and act as his messenger.'

'What is your evidence in the matter of the murder of Brother Eolang?'

57

Ferchar looked puzzled and Fidelma intervened.

'He means the death of Brother Eolang, the brother found by the pier.'

Brehon Gormán scowled in annoyance at her correction.

'That is what I meant,' he said tightly.

'I was riding along the shore on my way to Cashel,' began Ferchar. 'Across, on the island, I saw a religieux mooring his boat at the end of one of the side piers of the abbey.'

'I do not think we need bring forward evidence that this was Brother Eolang bringing the boat to the herb garden pier where he was found,' intervened Fidelma.

Brehon Gormán motioned Ferchar to continue with an impatient gesture.

'The religieux had moored the boat and was walking along the pier when it seemed that he stopped abruptly and turned back to the boat. This meant that he was facing towards me. Then, curiously, he started back as if something had stopped him. I heard a crack. He staggered back and fell off the edge of the pier. I started shouting to attract attention. I shouted for some minutes and then I saw another religieux exit from a gate. He heard my voice but I doubt if he heard my words. I gestured to where the religieux had fallen in. He must have seen him for he waved acknowledgement and jumped in and started to haul the body to the shore. Seeing that another religieux had arrived, and that there was nothing else I could do, I continued on my journey, not realising in that short time, the first religieux had met his death.'

'Are you sure there was no one else around at the time the religieux fell into the water? The religieux was by himself on the pier?'

'No one else was there,' affirmed Ferchar.

'But you heard a crack?' intervened Brehon Gormán.

'I did. Like a branch breaking.'

'Perhaps someone had cast a spear at him to make him fall back or . . . yes, a sling shot perhaps?' suggested the Brehon.

'He was facing towards me on the shore. The distance was too far to cast a sling shot nor any other weapon. No, there was no one around when the man fell into the lake.'

'Are you claiming that this was the act of some supernatural force?' demanded the Brehon turning to Fidelma. 'What of the prediction? You cannot explain away the accuracy of the prediction.'

Fidelma smiled at Ferchar.

'Wait outside and ask Brother Conchobar to enter.'

A moment later the old man did so and Fidelma asked the Brehon to spread the astrological chart before him.

'Conchobar, will you examine this chart and give me your advice?' she invited.

The old man nodded and took the chart from her hands. He spent some time poring over it and then he looked up.

'It is a good chart. A professional one.'

Brehon Gormán smiled approvingly.

'You agree, then, learned Conchobar, with the conclusions of Eolang?'

'Most things are correct . . .' agreed the old man.

Fidelma could see the Brehon's smile broaden but Brother Conchobar was continuing.

'. . . except one important point. Brother Eolang appears to have predicted that within a week following his drawing and judging his horary question he would die. It would happen on the day that Mercury and Jupiter perfected conjunction.'

'Exactly. The first day of the month of Aibreán. And that was the very day that he was killed, exactly as he predicted,' the Brehon confirmed. 'You cannot deny that.'

The old man tapped on the chart with his finger, shaking his head.

'The error, however, is that he failed to note that Mercury turned direct a few hours later and never perfected the conjunction. Brehon, as you have some knowledge of the art, you should know that we call this phenomenon refrenation. Alas, I have seen this carelessness, this overlooking of such an important fact, among many astrologers. To give Brother Eolang his due, perhaps he was too confused and worried to sit and spend time calculating the planetary movements accurately.'

'But he was accurate. He did indeed die on the predicted day. How do you explain it?' protested Brehon Gormán.

'But he was not murdered,' insisted Brother Conchobar. 'The chart does not show it.'

'Then how can it be explained?' demanded the Brehon in bewilderment. 'How did he die?'

Fidelma intervened with a smile.

'If you come with me, I will show you what happened.'

At the end of the old pier, Fidelma paused.

'Brother Eolang brought the boat to the end of the pier. He climbed on to the pier and started to head to the abbey. He forgot something in the boat. His *marsupium* to be exact. This was found by Brother Petrán later. So, halfway along the pier, he turned back for it. This much did our friend, Ferchar, observe from the far shore.'

There was a murmur of agreement from Ferchar.

'Now, look at the condition of the planks on the pier. Some are rotten, some are not nailed down. He stepped sharply towards the boat and . . .'

Fidelma turned, examined the planking critically for a moment, stepped sharply on one. The far end rose with a cracking noise and she had to step swiftly aside to avoid being hit by it as it flew up into the air. She turned back triumphantly to the onlookers.

'Brother Eolang was hit by the end of the plank between the eyes, causing the wounds found by the apothecary. It also knocked him unconscious and he fell back into the water. Drowning does not have to be a long process. By the time he was hauled out of the water he was dead.'

'Then the prediction . . . ?' began the bewildered Brehon.

'Was false. It was an accident. It was nobody's fault.'

Some time later as Ferchar, Conchobar and Fidelma were being rowed back to the mainland, the old astrologer turned to Fidelma with a lopsided smile.

'I can't help thinking that had Brother Eolang been a better astrologer, he would have made a correct prediction. It was all there, danger of death from water and he was accurate as to the day such danger would occur.'

Fidelma nodded thoughtfully.

'The fault was that Brother Eolang, like our friend, Brehon Gormán, believed that the patterns of the stars absolved man from using his free will; that man no longer had choice and that everything was predestined. That is not how the ancients taught the art of *nemgnacht*.'

Brother Conchobar nodded approvingly.

'So you do remember what I taught you?'

'You taught that there are signs that serve as warnings and give us information from which the wise can make decisions. They are options, possibilities from which we may select choices. The new learning from the east seems more fatalistic. Even the Christian teachings of Augustine of Hippo would have it that everything is predestined. That is why I am more happy with the teachings of Pelagius.'

'Even though Augustine's supporters have sneered at Pelagius as being "full of Irish porridge"?'

'Better Irish porridge than blind prejudice.'

Brother Conchobar chuckled.

'Have a care, Fidelma, lest you be accused of a pagan heresy!'

The Blemish

❧

'Fidelma!'

The young monk nearly collided with a tall girl as she came round the corner of the building with such speed and force that he barely had time to flatten himself against the wall to avoid her.

'Can't stop,' she flung breathlessly at him as she hurried on with her hair and robes flying with the speed of her progress.

'Brehon Morann is looking for you,' the religieux shouted after her retreating form.

'I know,' her voice called back. 'I'm on my way.'

'You're late for your examination,' the young monk added before realising that she could no longer hear him. He stood for a moment, looking disapprovingly after her as she disappeared towards a grey stone building that was the centre of the college, then he shrugged and continued on his way.

Fidelma did not need to be reminded that she was late for her examination with Brehon Morann of Tara. The examination was one of several she was taking which, she hoped, would result in her achieving the degree of *dos* and thus ending her fourth year of study at the college of which Morann was Principal. The degree of *dos*, so called because the student was regarded as a young tree ready to develop – for such was the literal meaning of the word – marked the start of her graduation from the school of law studies. It was the lowest rung of the graduate ladder. With such a degree one could go forth and practise as a minor magistrate or legal adviser. Fidelma had a higher ambition than that. But if she did not present herself within the appointed hour she would not be graduating at all.

The Brehon Morann sat at his desk, alone in his study, as Fidelma obeyed his gruff instruction to enter after she had timidly tapped upon his door. He was an elderly man with a kindly face but whose features could mould into a look of stern disapproval within a moment. He wore such an expression now.

'Well, Fidelma,' he said softly, as she came breathlessly to stand before him, 'is it not said that judges begin to count the faults of those who keep them waiting?'

Fidelma coloured in annoyance.

'*Fer-leginn*,' she addressed him by his official title of 'Principal', 'it is not my fault that I . . .'

She saw him begin to scowl and her mouth snapped shut.

'They are truly good who are faultless,' sighed Brehon Morann. His face was still sombre but his twinkling bright eyes regarded her for a moment. She swore that he was laughing at her. 'What were you saying, Fidelma?'

She shook her head.

'I am sorry for my lateness.' She tried to sound contrite. It was no use explaining that for some inexplicable reason the key had been turned in the lock of her door from the outside and it had taken her some time to attract attention and extricate herself from her room. She harboured ill thoughts against the student who had played such a silly and petty trick on her. That they did it this morning of all mornings, when she was due for her examination, increased her thoughts of vengeance on the perpetrator. Morann had doubtless heard many excuses from students over the years and, even though her excuse was, in fact, a reason, any attempted explanation would not enhance her image in the eyes of her venerable examiner.

'Then I accept your contrition,' replied the Brehon solemnly, sitting back and placing his fingertips against one another, hand to hand, so that the tips of the thumbs touched just under his chin. 'Sit down.'

Fidelma sat down, feeling hard done by.

'Tell me what you know of The Blemish?'

Brehon Morann asked the question without preamble and for a second Fidelma had to compose her thoughts.

'The Blemish? You mean, what is a blemish in legal terms?' she countered, playing for time.

Again, the frown of annoyance crossed Brehon Morann's brow.

'You are in a college for the study of law,' he pointed out drily, leaving her to make her own deduction.

Fidelma began to speak, hoping as she did so that the information would come to her mind.

'The law text Uraicecht Becc opens with the sentence that our system of law is founded on truth, right and nature. Judges must give a surety of five ounces of silver that the judgement they give is truthful to the best of the knowledge provided to them. They forfeit that sum if an appeal against their judgement is upheld. If it is found that they have made an erroneous judgement when the facts presented to them are clear then they are fined one *cumal*.'

'Are you saying that honest error is not allowed in law?' snapped Morann.

'It is allowed for isn't there a saying which is "to every judge an error"? But a judge must pay for his error if that error is obvious, and if the error arises from bias then it is said that a blemish will raise itself on his face. A serious false judgement will result in the judge's being deprived of his office and his honour.'

Brehon Morann nodded slowly. He ignored the expression of triumph that crossed Fidelma's face as she finally arrived at the answer to his initial question on 'The Blemish'.

'And this blemish – how would you describe its physical manifestation?' He smiled softly.

Fidelma hesitated for a moment and then decided that she would put forward her own concept.

'When the ancients talked about a blemish's being raised, I do not think that they meant it to be taken literally.'

Brehon Morann's brows drew together sternly.

'Ah, so you are an interpreter of the meaning of the ancient texts?'

Fidelma's chin came up at his tone of mockery.

'I make no such pretension although, surely, it is the task of the Brehon to elucidate the texts? I believe that what is meant by this reference to a blemish is that the loss of a judge's honour and the fact that he becomes known in public as someone who has delivered a false judgement puts a blemish on his character in the minds of the people; the blemish is in the mind not physically on the skin.'

'Indeed?' Brehon Morann's voice was dry and non-committal.

He leaned forward and picked up a small silver hand bell. As its tinkling tones died away the door opened and a short, wiry man with an abundance of white curly hair entered. He closed the door behind him and made his way to a chair at the side of Morann's table facing Fidelma. His face bore no expression at all. His features were bland.

'This is the *druimcli* Firbis of Ardagh. He will set a case before you and you will tell me if and why a blemish should have been raised on the judge involved in the case.'

Fidelma stirred nervously in her chair. A *druimcli* was a person who had mastered the entire course of learning and was not merely a Brehon but could be appointed to the most important legal positions. She turned slightly to face him.

Firbis's tone was high-pitched and querulous and he had a habit of sniffing every so often as if in disapproval.

'Pay attention and do not make any notes. I do not approve of the writing of notes as a means to aid the memory. In the old days, before the coming of the New Faith, the writing of our wealth of knowledge was not allowed. The old religion forbade us to commit our teachings to writing and it is a good rule for pupils who rely on the written word and neglect to train their memories. When pupils have the help of notes, they are less diligent in learning by heart and so their memories rust. Is that not so, young woman?'

The abruptness of the question startled Fidelma for a moment.

'It is an argument that I have heard, *Druimcli*,' she acknowledged solemnly.

The corners of Firbis's mouth turned down.

'But you do not agree?' He spoke sharply, his eyes perceptive.

'Our ancestors failed to record many essential matters before the coming of the New Faith and the result is that much has been lost to posterity. Philosophy, religion, history, poetry . . . these things went unrecorded. Because of this refusal to set forth all knowledge in writing, have we not lost much that would be most valuable to our civilisation?'

Firbis stared at her in disapproval and sniffed.

'I suppose that you are one of the young generation who applauds the work of those scribes in the foundations of the New Faith who spend their time setting forth such matters in the new Latin alphabet?'

Fidelma inclined her head.

'Of course. How will future generations know the poetry, the law, the ancient stories and the course of our history unless it is set forth? I would only make this criticism, that such scribes feel constrained to dress many of the ancient stories of the old gods and goddesses in the images of the New Faith.' Fidelma suddenly felt herself warming to the theme. 'Why, I have even seen one text in which the scribe tells how the hero Cú Chulainn is conjured out of Hell by the Blessed Patrick to help him convert the High King Laoghaire to the New Faith and when Laoghaire becomes a Christian Cú Chulainn is released from Hell to go to Heaven.'

Brehon Morann leaned forward. 'You disapprove?'

Fidelma nodded. 'We are told, in the New Faith, that God is good, loving and forgiving. Cú Chulainn was a great champion whose life was devoted to aiding the weak against the strong. He would surely not have been consigned to Hell by such a God and . . .'

Firbis cleared his throat noisily.

'You seem to have radical ideas, young woman. But in reply to your question, future generations should learn by adhering to the old ways, learning by heart, passing on the knowledge one voice to another voice down the ages. Our tradition is that knowledge must be passed on and preserved in oral tradition so that outsiders do not steal it from us.'

'It cannot be. The old ways are gone. We must progress. But, hopefully, not by distorting the images of our past.'

Brehon Morann interrupted impatiently. 'You say, we must progress. Agreed. Progress in the matter we are dealing with today,' he said heavily. 'The day grows short and there are other students to be tested before sundown.'

Inwardly, Fidelma groaned. She had obviously alienated *Druimcli* Firbis by her attitude and annoyed Brehon Morann by her lateness and her inability to keep her views to herself.

Firbis sniffed rapidly. 'Very well. Pay attention. I will not repeat myself and, whatever happens outside these walls, I will tolerate no writing of notes.'

He stared sharply in challenge at her but she did not demur.

After a moment's silence, he began. 'This case involved a Brehon. We will not name him. A case came before him in which he found a woman not guilty of theft. Let us call the woman Sochla.'

He paused as if he expected a challenge to his opening statement.

'The circumstances were as follows: Sochla worked in the hall of the King of Tethbae. Do you know where that is?'

Fidelma nodded automatically. 'It is a petty kingdom bordering on the west of Midhe, not far from here,' she answered. Fidelma prided herself on her geographical knowledge.

'Indeed,' muttered Firbis, as if disappointed that his question had received a correct answer. 'It was a small kingdom founded two hundred years ago by Maine, a son of the High King, Niall of the Nine Hostages.'

Fidelma also knew this information but did not say anything further.

'As I was saying,' began Firbis querulously, as if she had interrupted him, 'Sochla worked in the hall of Catharnaigh, the king. In a casket, in the hall, the kings of Tethbae kept an oak and bronze casket. In this casket was the preserved skull of Maine, founder of the kingdom, who died in battle. Maine of the Bright Deeds was how the poets described him. His skull was preserved in the ancient tradition as the rallying symbol of his people in Tethbae. It was valued beyond price by them.'

'There are many similar icons in other kingdoms,' observed Fidelma quietly.

'We are not speaking of other kingdoms,' snapped Firbis. 'I speak of Tethbae! The skull of Maine was beyond price and kept in pride of place in the hall of Catharnaigh.'

He stared at Fidelma, challenging her to speak. When she did not, he continued less querulously.

'Catharnaigh and his retinue had left the hall to go to the Field of Contentions to attend a game of hurley. No one was left in the hall except for Sochla whose task was to prepare the feasting hall for the king's return. When Catharnaigh returned, he found the casket, containing the skull, was missing. Only Sochla had been in the hall during Catharnaigh's absence and she was summoned. She denied any knowledge. Yet Catharnaigh was suspicious. Sochla's quarters were searched and the casket was found under the woman's bed. A learned Brehon was summoned and the case was heard. Sochla was found guilty of the theft.'

Firbis paused and sat back.

'This was the case. Did the Brehon render a true or a false judgement?'

Fidelma sat quietly for a moment. Then she raised a slender shoulder and let it fall.

'It is impossible to make an answer based on the facts that you have cited.' She glanced quickly at Brehon Morann. 'I presume that I am allowed to ask questions of the *druimcli* before expressing any opinion?'

Firbis interrupted before the Brehon could answer.

'I thought the facts were plain enough, young woman. The casket was found under the bed of Sochla. Have you overlooked that fact?'

'I have not,' replied Fidelma.

'Bearing that fact in mind, do you tell me that you do not think it is a simple, open and shut case? Surely you do not wish to waste time here? The answer is simply a negative or positive one. Was a true or false judgement rendered when Sochla was pronounced guilty of the crime?'

Fidelma turned to Brehon Morann.

'I think it is right that I should ask questions,' she said stubbornly, determined not to be cowed by the *druimcli*. 'No one would be able to express support for a judgement without knowing all the facts.'

The Brehon smiled gravely. 'You may ask, but do not waste time.'

Fidelma turned back to Firbis. 'What was the motive according to the Brehon who pronounced the woman guilty?'

Firbis blinked and glanced at Brehon Morann with a raised eyebrow. Then he turned back to Fidelma and shrugged indifferently.

'With a priceless relic, I would have thought that the matter of motive was obvious.'

'Really? I would have thought that the motive became more obscure.'

Firbis's eyes narrowed. Before he could respond, Fidelma asked another question: 'Was this Sochla an intelligent woman? Was she half-witted or did she have any other defects that would cause her a lack of common sense?'

'She was intelligent,' replied Firbis tightly.

'Then she would have known that it is impossible to make financial gain from a priceless article such as the skull of Maine of Tethbae. Who would want to buy such a relic apart from those to whom it is priceless?'

'She could have taken it to demand a ransom from Catharnaigh, the King of Tethbae, for its safe return,' pointed out Brehon Morann quietly.

'That would be equally preposterous,' replied Fidelma. 'Once she had revealed that she had the casket and skull, she would be in a vulnerable position and, even if she succeeded in the negotiation, thereafter she would condemn herself to a life of exile from Tethbae and from the reach of its king. No, there is no motive in theft for profit . . . if, as you say, the woman was intelligent.'

Firbis shifted uncomfortably in his seat.

'Are you saying that, on this reasoning alone, you believe that the judge made a false judgement?'

Fidelma shook her head at once.

'Not on that reasoning alone.' She smiled softly. 'In all cases, as you know, there must be motive, means and opportunity. All three things must come together in one pattern. You tell me that the opportunity was there . . . that she was in the hall alone when everyone had gone to watch a game of hurley. Presumably we can be assured that the casket and skull were observed to be in their place before people departed for the game and then were gone when they returned? To remove a casket containing a skull does not require any great means.'

'So you admit that the judge was correct on means and opportunity?' pressed Firbis.

Fidelma pursed her lips thoughtfully. 'I have heard no evidence that this Sochla possessed the only means and opportunity. Is there such evidence? Is it not possible that someone could have happened by and removed the casket while Sochla was elsewhere in the hall of Catharnaigh? Is it not possible that some other person could have planted the casket under Sochla's bed?'

Firbis laughed, amused by the suggestion. 'For what motive?'

'There might be several motives but one would need to ask a great many questions to find and validate them.'

'It seems to me, Fidelma, that you are attempting to make the woman in this case, Sochla, innocent,' observed the Brehon Morann.

Fidelma shook her head quickly. 'Not at all. I am attempting to find out the facts before rushing to judgement. I certainly would have asked more questions on means and opportunity. Tell me more about this Sochla. Is she young or old, what is her disposition, is she married, does she have lovers and, if so, who are they?'

'She is of young age,' Firbis replied. 'She is barely over the "age of choice". Her father was of the *daer-nemed* class, that is a manual worker. In this case he worked as an assistant to the king's blacksmith, while the girl worked as a manual worker, a cleaner, in the king's hall.'

'And why was one so young and of such a class left alone in the king's hall while all others went to a ball game? Did the king fear no enemies, no envious hands, that he would leave his house and wealth unguarded?'

Firbis exchanged another glance with Morann.

'Presumably this line of questioning was pursued with Catharnaigh?' pressed Fidelma when there was no response to her question.

Firbis sniffed. 'What are you implying?'

'*Druimcli*, surely you should know that I could not *imply* anything. It is merely my duty to ask questions and through the answers to discover the truth.'

The *druimcli* looked uncomfortable. 'The king had no cause to fear his enemies nor to fear envious hands in his property.'

'Yet, is it not unheard of that such a noble would vacate his hall and possessions in this manner?'

'The facts are as I have told them. It is not my task to comment or speculate on why a person should do this or that.'

Fidelma leaned forward quickly. 'But isn't that the very task of a Brehon – to examine motivation behind each fact and ascertain what lay behind the fact and whether the person had criminal intent or not?'

Druimcli Firbis sat up more stiffly. 'I declare, you now exceed the parameters of your position, young woman. You are here to answer my question, which you have not yet done.'

'I have not done so because the question cannot be answered in the manner in which it is given,' she replied stubbornly. 'You said that Sochla was young. Was she married?'

'She was not.'

'Did she have a lover?'

Firbis hesitated and inclined his head.

'And where was he on this day?'

'Apparently he was with Sochla.'

Fidelma pursued her lips in astonishment at this new revelation. 'And Sochla? What does she say?'

'That after the king and his entourage left, she began to work and then her lover came by. That they spent some time together . . .'

'Was she out of sight of the casket?' interrupted Fidelma.

Firbis blinked and paused a moment before responding.

'The casket is kept in a place of honour in the main feasting hall, on a stand behind the king's seat. She claimed that they were out of sight of it for nearly an hour.'

'So anyone might have entered the hall and taken it.' Fidelma pouted. 'It seems a very weak case against the girl, indeed. Who was this lover? Will he confirm what she says?'

Firbis smiled thinly.

'I hardly think so.'

'Why so?'

'He fled after the girl was accused.'

'Fled?'

'He was from the lands of Calraige.'

Fidelma was frowning now. 'But that is in the land of . . .'

Firbis interrupted her with a thin smile. 'Exactly so, in the lands of the Uí Ailello, the deadly foes of the kings of Tethbae.'

'Are you trying to say that she and the lover collaborated in this theft?' mused Fidelma. 'If so, then you are proposing a motive which you should have made clear when I questioned you earlier about it.' There was irritation in her voice.

Firbis blinked at the belligerent tone.

Brehon Morann's brows drew together,

'May I remind you that you are addressing a *druimcli*?' he said icily.

'And I remind you,' added Firbis sourly, 'that it is not my task to feed you all the answers to this conundrum.'

Fidelma turned to Brehon Morann.

'I do not mean to sound disrespectful but this is an example of what I meant when I said that the case could not be judged on the facts initially given by the *druimcli*. The introduction of this nameless lover into the story is an integral part of the evidence . . .'

'The Brehon in this case did not think so,' interrupted Firbis, 'other than to reflect that it simply supported the guilt of the girl. It was clear to him that they colluded in this theft and that both meant to flee to the sanctuary of the lands of the Uí Ailello where the chief of the clan would have lavished a reward on them for bringing the skull.'

Fidelma shook her head. 'It is a weak story.'

Firbis looked taken aback and the Brehon Morann leaned forward in his seat. He was smiling gently.

'You seem to take issue with all the facts, Fidelma.'

'Consider these facts,' replied Fidelma with a shrug. 'A servant girl is left alone in the king's hall. She has a lover who is a member of a clan that comprises the most deadly foes of the King of Tethbae and his people. Left alone in the hall, the girl is working when her lover comes by. For an hour they claim to make love. Then they take the skull in its casket and hide it under the girl's bed in the servants' quarters. The lover then departs. The people return, find the skull and casket missing. It is then found under the girl's bed and the lover has fled back to his people.' She paused. 'It is an improbable story. I'd say it is almost nonsense.'

Druimcli Firbis's lips thinned. 'Are you saying that the Brehon in this case could not differentiate what was nonsense and what was fact?'

'It seems so,' Fidelma responded with seriousness.

Druimcli Firbis was now smiling cynically.

'So, are you saying, finally, that it is a matter of a false judgement?'

'False enough, if the Brehon involved judged this matter merely on this evidence alone.'

'Very well, Fidelma,' Firbis said, sitting back slightly. 'We will continue with the facts. The *dálaigh*, the advocate of the king, argued that the intention of Sochla and her lover was to flee with the casket immediately. But they dallied and in their dalliance did not realise that time had passed. They heard the people returning and all they could do was hide the casket under the bed and the lover left, waiting in the vicinity to see what happened. When he realised that Sochla was caught, he then fled leaving her to face punishment alone.'

'And what did the girl's *dálaigh*, her advocate, say in rebuttal?'

'She did not have an advocate.'

'Who pled for the girl?'

'The Brehon did so.'

Fidelma gazed at Firbis's bland expression with amazement.

'A Brehon must be unbiased,' she said slowly.

'Just so,' agreed Firbis, 'and is therefore allowed to enter a case to plead for the accused . . .'

'But only if the accused or witness is incapable of representing or speaking for themselves. You have already told me that Sochla was intelligent, in no way retarded. Why wasn't she allowed to speak for herself or instruct a *dálaigh*?'

Brehon Morann stirred. 'Is it your claim that the Brehon acted improperly?'

'It would seem that the rights of the accused were infringed,' replied Fidelma, choosing her words carefully.

Firbis snorted derisively. 'Infringed? No Brehon of Ardagh would . . .' He hesitated and then asked: 'What of the rights of the king?'

'The law is stronger than a king. It is an old saying,' replied Fidelma calmly. 'The Brehon, from what you have told me, so far seems biased in the extreme.'

Firbis's mouth tightened a little.

'You are talking of a respected Brehon who holds more qualifications in legal affairs than you will ever attain.'

Fidelma's irritations boiled over.

'As well as being a *druimcli* I presume that you are also a prophet or have the gift of clairvoyance?' Her voice was ice cold.

Firbis's brows came together.

'Do you mean to insult me?' His tone was equally studied.

'Insult? Not at all. I merely seek information. You have said that I will never attain the qualifications that this unnamed Brehon holds or held. To make such a statement one needs firstly to know exactly what qualifications the unnamed Brehon held and also to know the future as to what qualifications I am likely to attain to. Being interested in my future, I wondered how this could be. With due respect, I merely asked you the basis of your prognostication – whether you were a prophet or held the gift of clairvoyance? What insult is there in that?'

There was a sound from Brehon Morann.

Behind a hand that covered the lower part of his mouth he appeared to be stifling a laugh.

The *druimcli* seemed to make a conscious effort to control his features.

'Fidelma,' Brehon Morann, having controlled his amusement, spoke

73

softly. 'Fidelma, I think on reflection you will find that the *druimcli* was speaking figuratively.'

'I think he was also speaking without due regard to the law,' replied Fidelma, unappeased by the explanation.

This time Firbis kept his lips pressed tight.

'Explain yourself,' Morann said quietly. It was a dangerous tone.

'Simply, that the law holds everyone to account. Because someone is a Brehon does not exclude them from criticism any more than it allows a *druimcli* to insult a student who has not yet attained to the degree of *dos*.'

There was coldness in the room.

Suddenly, *Druimcli* Firbis seemed to relax and actually smile. It was a thin, wan smile but a smile nevertheless.

'You are right, young woman. It was wrong of me to make such a personal outburst. A Brehon is not above examination and where error has occurred he is not beyond correction and fine. Nor should I have implied that you do not have the right to express your opinion of any error because you have not yet graduated.'

Fidelma bowed her head slightly.

'Indeed, isn't the reason that we are discussing this matter to see whether the unnamed Brehon in question gave a false judgement or a true judgement?' she asked.

Brehon Morann smiled softly.

'That is precisely what we are here for. Have you reached any conclusion?'

'My conclusion, so far, is the verdict is still unsafe. What witnesses were called by the king's *dálaigh*?'

'The king's high steward, for one,' replied Firbis.

'What was his name and the effect of his testimony?'

'His name?' Firbis hesitated then said, 'Feranaim. He deposed that Sochla had been employed as a menial worker in the king's hall. That he had seen her at work when the household left to attend the game and most importantly he had seen the casket in its usual place.'

'He was the last to leave the hall?'

'That is so,' replied Firbis hastily. 'How did you know?'

Fidelma did not reply directly. She continued: 'And was he the person who spotted the casket missing on the return from the game?'

The *druimcli* shook his head. 'No, in fact it was the king himself

74

who spotted that the casket was not in its usual place. The steward was sent for and . . .'

'The steward was sent for?' Fidelma asked quickly. 'Where was he when everyone returned from the game?'

'In his quarters. The steward has a house near the king's hall.'

'But surely, the steward would know that his presence would be needed in the hall with the return of the king and his retinue?'

'He probably did not know they had returned,' Firbis assured her.

She smiled quickly. 'He did not know they had returned? Why not, if he had returned with them?'

Firbis regarded her with a bland expression and did not respond.

'The evidence was that the household went to the game leaving only Sochla in the king's hall,' Fidelma pointed out.

'That is so. She was left in the king's hall.'

'But the steward, the man called Feranaim, obviously did not go to the game and was in the vicinity of the royal complex?'

Neither Firbis nor Morann answered.

She stood thinking a moment. 'Did the Brehon pick up on this point?'

Druimcli Firbis shrugged. 'Was there any need to?'

'I would say there was great need.'

'Why?'

'Because it is evidence that challenges the whole case. Not only does it show that Sochla was not the only person in the vicinity of the casket, nor, as we have found, was her lover the only other person there, but now we have the high steward in the vicinity of the hall. What if Sochla was right? What if her lover and she had been otherwise engaged, and the high steward had slipped into the hall and removed the casket, later hiding it under Sochla's bed for reasons we do not know of?'

'There are a many "what ifs" here, Fidelma. With an "if" you might place all Tara in a bottle.'

'Questions and probabilities are what this case is all about.' Fidelma was not dissuaded. 'Were any questions put to this high steward called Feranaim about his background?'

'None directly,' confirmed Firbis.

'What does that mean?'

'That no direct question was put to the steward,' snapped back Firbis.

Fidelma thought for a moment. 'And was Sochla questioned on her relationship with Feranaim?'

'Her relationship?'

'Was she friendly with the steward?'

Firbis shook his head.

Something prompted Fidelma to press him.

'Did she volunteer any statement at all about Feranaim?'

'The Brehon deemed her statement about Feranaim inadmissible.'

'But what was that statement?'

'She claimed that Feranaim had attempted to seduce her and that she had rejected him. She claimed, because of this, that he held a hatred for her.'

Fidelma's intake of breath was sharp.

'It now seems that the motive and opportunity are not all one-sided matters,' she said coldly. 'Others might have motive and opportunity as well. On what ground did the Brehon rule this information inadmissible?'

The *druimcli* shifted his position.

'The Brehon cited the law text the Berrad Airechta. I suppose you are acquainted with it?'

'It contains the text of the categories of evidence that are inadmissible,' replied Fidelma with confidence. 'If my memory serves me correctly, there are nine major exclusions and four special exclusions. As I recall, evidence may be excluded if it comes from someone known to have been bribed, someone who has a relationship with the person they give evidence against, and someone known to hate the person . . .'

Firbis held up his hand.

'You give us little doubt that you know the law in this respect, Fidelma. The Brehon excluded the evidence on the grounds that Sochla knew and hated Feranaim and thus the evidence was invalid . . .'

'That was a wrong decision.'

'Why?' snapped Firbis.

'Because it would not apply to Sochla, being the accused. Her evidence in rebutting the accusations against her is not inadmissible. In this respect, I believe the Brehon was unjust. He should have included this evidence.'

Fidelma used the legal term *gúach* whose connotation meant that the injustice arose not from error but bias.

76

Firbis sat quietly examining her for a moment or two.

'Then you have decided that there was a false judgement here?

Fidelma did not reply for the moment then she said quietly: 'An injustice in dismissing evidence does not necessarily imply that the overall judgement of the case was wrong or false within the definition by which a blemish might arise on the character of the Brehon. Were I to press forward, would there be any more revelations to come forth?' The question was suddenly sharp and directed to the *druimcli*.

Brehon Morann coughed, suddenly restive. 'There are several other students to be examined this day, Fidelma. I believe you have taken up enough of our time.' The Brehon's face was stern again, his brows drawn together in disapproval.

'Then you wish a judgement from me?' Fidelma said quietly, her head bowed. 'Yet I do not feel that I have been given sufficient time nor all the facts in this case.'

Brehon Morann gave a soft sigh, a quiet hiss of breath that seemed to indicate his displeasure.

'Fidelma, today was the appointed day for your final examination in this series. The result of this day will determine whether you achieve the degree of *dos*, the minimum graduate degree. Those that pass this degree can continue their studies and should they pass six to eight more years of study here then the accolade of *ollamh* might await them at which they could sit with the High King himself and speak a judgement even before he speaks. But the person who has the quickest hand, let them have the white hound and the deer in the hunt. So let me remind you of certain facts.'

Brehon Morann paused, his eyes piercing upon her.

'Certain facts?' murmured Fidelma, trying to concentrate.

'Knowing these things, you came late to your examination. Did you not attempt to make an excuse for doing so?'

Fidelma hesitated for a fraction of a second and then said: 'There was no excuse.'

'You came here and instead of responding to a direct question, you began to question a *druimcli*, someone who has achieved the seventh and highest grade of wisdom, and your questions have been . . . severe and condemning in tone. Let us put it this way, Fidelma: you have not set out to win our approval and yet the decision whether you obtain the degree of *dos* lies in our hands.'

Fidelma flushed. 'I did not think that obtaining a degree lay with attempts to win approval from anyone. I thought it depended on an assessment of my knowledge of law,' she said quietly.

'Of law and your ability to apply it. Do you feel that you have displayed the knowledge that is relevant to judge the question that has been put before you?' Morann replied, his tone not changing.

'A very wise judge once told me that one should not give judgement on hearing the first person's story but to wait until one has heard the other side.'

Brehon Morann, in spite of his gravity, looked amused. 'Are you now trying to win my approbation by quoting me?'

'Not at all. What is true is true no matter whose mouth gives it utterance.'

'So you are saying that you cannot make a judgement?' intervened the *druimcli*.

Fidelma turned to him and shook her head. 'I cannot make a judgement on the particular case that I have heard but I can make a decision on the judgement given by the Brehon in that case.'

Druimcli Firbis sat back with a half smile and made a gesture of invitation with one hand.

'You have a choice – the choice between *firbrith* or true judgement or *cilbrith* or false judgement.'

Firbis put the choice in the correct legal terms.

'I say that the judgement given by the Brehon in this case was *cilbrith* – a false judgement. I also believe, *Druimcli*, that the blemish rests on you; that you were the Brehon in this case.'

Firbis's eyes narrowed a fraction. 'Why do you say this?'

'Because you seem to have an extraordinary knowledge of why the judge did certain things in this case. I also take into account the manner in which you selected the evidence, always in the judge's favour, to present to me. You frequently showed how protective you were of the Brehon. That is, as I say, because I believe that you were the Brehon.'

Druimcli Firbis smiled. 'Belief is not evidence.'

'No. But you are a *druimcli* at Ardagh, which is the principal town of Tethbae where you said this case took place. In your haste to defend the Brehon in this case you also mentioned that he came from Ardagh. There is one conclusion to all these things. You spoke with the authority of the Brehon involved in the case and therefore you were the Brehon.'

Firbis's expression was, curiously, one of approval.

Brehon Morann was smiling with equal accord. 'Well, Fidelma . . .'

'There is one thing more,' Fidelma interrupted.

Morann hesitated and raised an eyebrow in query. 'Something more?'

Fidelma nodded. 'This entire case was a fiction. It never happened. The reason why Firbis spoke with the authority of the Brehon in the case was because he invented the whole story and developed it as we went along as a means of testing me. No one of Firbis's attainment would have acted in the way this Brehon would have done and yet, it was clear, the Brehon involved was none other than Firbis. What was I to make of that? Feranaim, indeed! The very word means "man without a name"! This was a test. Therefore, I concluded that Firbis invented the story to test the student.'

Brehon Morann was smiling. 'You are the first student that has ever seen beyond the nature of the test to that fact,' he said.

'The first student that has even spotted the identity of the Brehon,' agreed Firbis. 'Most students try to make a guess answer at the moment I ask the initial question.'

'But some others demand more knowledge?' queried Fidelma.

'Others do, but when we,' Firbis motioned to Morann, 'argue and try to dissuade them from pressing their questions, they usually give up long before you did so. You kept on tenaciously. You have a good inquiring mind.'

'The purpose of this test is not only to show an inquiring mind and not spring to snap judgements,' Brehon Morann explained, 'but to show to us that you have the tenacity in the face of opposition to carry on against odds, against authority, in your efforts to seek out the truth. Truth might be great and always prevail, but sometimes it needs someone who is tenacious in the face of apparently insurmountable barriers to prise it out of its hiding places. You have done well, Fidelma.'

Fidelma stood up, looking from Firbis to Morann.

'Does that mean that I have passed this test?' she inquired blandly.

Brehon Morann almost grinned. 'The results will be announced in the morning assembly. You shall hear the result then – that is if you are not late again.'

Fidelma nodded, her gesture encompassing both Morann and Firbis.

At the door, she paused and turned back to them with a thoughtful expression.

'Will you also tell me tomorrow whether I passed today's other test?' she asked brightly.

Brehon Morann regarded her warily. 'Other test?'

'I presume that locking me in my room on the morning of this test so that I might be late and therefore distracted was also to test my tenacity and whether I would function under stress?'

The expression on Brehon Morann's face told her that she was correct in her assumption. With a mischievous, almost urchin-like smile, she closed the door quietly behind her.

Dark Moon Rising

'I have come to you in order to seek compensation for the loss of my goods.'

The man with the moon-like face stood before Fidelma in the court of the Brehons of Dair Inis with such an air of woe that he looked almost comical. Distress did not sit easily on his almost cherubic, virtuous features. His blue eyes stared as if in wondering innocence and his lower lip protruded slightly like a child expecting an admonition from an adult.

'Abaoth's claim is without foundation,' interrupted the second man who stood at his side.

Sister Fidelma did not like this thin, wiry individual. His voice grated in her ears with its high-pitched almost whining note. He was richly, almost ostentatiously, dressed and wore too much jewellery. Rich clothes ill became his physical appearance. She suddenly smiled to herself as she realised that his name suited his cunning looks. Olcán – the very name meant a wolf. He had the appearance of a scavenger.

Fidelma had been staying in the abbey established by Molena on Dair Inis, the island of oaks, standing in the waters of Abhainn Mór, the great river, not far from the trading settlement known as Eochaill, the yew wood, which guarded the estuary of the river. It was a busy port and Fidelma had often passed through it. She had only been in the abbey one night when Abbot Accobrán had succumbed to a fever, which caused him to retire to his bed. He had requested that Fidelma, being duly qualified in law, take his place as Brehon and deliver the judgements during the court proceedings which were due the next day.

Now Fidelma sat, trying to suppress her prejudice, as she viewed the two merchants from Eochaill making claim and counter-claim before the court.

'I seek compensation for the loss of my goods,' repeated Abaoth stubbornly.

'And I reject it,' replied Olcán with vehemence.

'The *scriptor* has already informed me of the nature of your claims,' replied Fidelma sharply. 'However, I am lacking in details. Let us begin with you, Abaoth. You are a merchant in Eochaill?'

The round-faced man jerked his head in assertion.

'That I am, learned *ollamh*,' he replied in an obsequious manner.

'I am not an *ollamh*,' retorted Fidelma. She was sure that the man knew that fact. 'I am a *dálaigh* but still qualified to hear your case. Proceed with the details.'

'Most learned *dálaigh*, I trade with the lands of the Britons, Saxons and Franks. I have a small fleet of trading vessels that take leather goods and the skins of otters and squirrels especially to the lands of the Franks and they return laden with corn and wine. My ships offload their cargoes at Eochaill where I hire the barges of Olcán to transport them along the Abhainn Mór to Lios Mór.'

'So you sell your goods to the abbey there?'

Fidelma was acquainted with the abbey founded thirty years before by Carthach and which was now a prominent centre attracting religious from all five kingdoms of Éireann.

'Some portion of the goods are sold to the abbey,' nodded the merchant, 'but most of the wine is purchased by the prince of the Eóghanacht Glendamnach.'

'Very well. Proceed.'

'Learned *dálaigh*, on the last two occasions, Olcán claims that he has lost my cargoes. He refuses to pay me for that loss. I am not so rich that I can sustain the loss of two cargoes. The goods were lost while being transported by his barges. He is responsible for compensating me.'

Fidelma turned to the wiry, thin-faced man with a frown.

'In what manner have the cargoes been lost?' she demanded.

Olcán made a gesture as if dismissing the matter.

'On two nights my vessels have set off upriver for Lios Mór and disappeared,' he replied. 'My loss has been greater than Abaoth's loss.'

Fidelma raised her head in surprise to study the man's face. He was serious.

'Disappeared?' she echoed. 'In what way did they disappear?'

'Having taken Abaoth's cargoes on to my barges – these are the river-going vessels crewed by three men, the type known as *ethur* . . .'

'I am acquainted with such vessels,' Fidelma intervened in a weary tone.

'Of course,' the man acknowledged. 'The cargo was loaded into the barges. They set off up the river to Lios Mór and did not arrive. This has happened twice. The barges have disappeared. If anyone should be compensated it is I.'

Abaoth broke in with almost a whimper in his voice.

'It is not so. The prince of Glendamnach is refusing to trade further with me because I do not deliver the goods he contracts for. I am not a rich man, learned *dálaigh*. Two cargoes lost in as many months. It is clear that thieves are at work and I must seek restitution.'

'What of the crews on these barges? What do they say?'

Again the thin-faced merchant shrugged eloquently.

'They have disappeared as well.'

This time Fidelma could not conceal her surprise.

'Six of your men have disappeared. Why was this not reported before?'

The merchant shuffled his feet in response to her sharp tone.

'I do so now in my counter-claim for compensation for my lost barges and . . .'

'These men might be dead,' she broke in. 'I presume that you are looking after their dependants?'

Olcán grimaced irritably.

'I am a merchant not a charity . . .'

'The law is specific,' snapped Fidelma. 'You should know that you are responsible for all those who work for you, especially their medical expenses if injured in your employ. It is clearly stated in the Leabhar Acaill. I can only think that you are more concerned with your lost barges than the disappearance of your boatmen.'

Olcán regarded her with a sour expression.

'Without my barges and trade I cannot pay my boatmen.'

'When did these cargoes disappear?' she asked Abaoth.

'The last cargo disappeared two weeks ago. The first was almost exactly four weeks before that.'

'And why haven't you reported this before now?'

'I have. I reported it to the master of the port. I was told to bring the matter before the Brehon at the next session of the court here on Dair Inis.'

Fidelma was irritated.

'It is a long time that has passed. The matter should have been investigated before this. Before any decision on whether you merit compensation in this matter, or whether Olcán's counter-claim is valid, it must be investigated. I will consult Bretha im Gata, the law of thefts. You will give the details to the *scriptor* of this court and return here when summoned to do so to hear my decision.'

Abaoth inclined his head, turning as if eager to be away from the court. Olcán, however, glowered at her, obviously dissatisfied, hesitated a moment but left the court after his fellow merchant. At a gesture from Fidelma, the *scriptor* followed them out.

That afternoon, Fidelma found herself wandering along the quay in Eochaill, looking at the ocean-going boats loading and unloading. Her mind was turning over the problem of the disappearance of the barges. A figure was standing blocking her path. It was familiar. She halted and focused and a mischievous grin spread on her features.

The man was elderly. A short, stocky man with greying close-cropped hair. His skin was tanned by sea and wind almost to the colour of nut. His stance and appearance marked him out as a grizzled veteran of seafaring.

'Ross? Is it you?'

She knew him of old as the captain of a coastal barque sailing the waters around her brother's kingdom.

'Lady,' grinned the old seaman, touching his forehead in salutation. Ross never forgot that Fidelma was sister to Colgú, King of Muman.

'What are you doing here?' she asked and then chuckled as she realised it was a foolish question to ask of a sailor in a coastal port. She gestured towards a nearby *bruiden*, a tavern, which stood nearby. 'Let us slake our thirst and talk of old times, Ross, and . . .' she suddenly had a thought, 'and perhaps you can help me with a problem that I have.'

'Of course, lady,' agreed Ross at once. 'I am always prepared to help if you are in need.'

Seated at a table in the hostel, with a jug of honey-sweetened mead between them, Fidelma asked Ross if he knew of the merchants Abaoth and Olcán.

Ross grimaced immediately at the name of Olcán.

'Olcán? He is a greedy man. I've shipped cargoes for him along the coast and he always tries to cheat on his payments. I no longer take his cargoes. Indeed, he has lost trade recently because people do not trust him. He is reduced to a fleet of river barges whereas he had two sea-going ships some years ago. What have you to do with him?'

Fidelma explained, adding: 'What of Abaoth?'

'I know nothing bad about him. He had a fleet of three ships trading mainly with the Frankish ports. I know he has had bad luck recently for one of his ships foundered and was destroyed in a storm. I think he trades hides in return for wine. But as for Olcán – compensation for stolen cargo? I wouldn't lift a finger to get him compensation. In fact, I might pay the thieves to take his cargoes in order to compensate for the times he cheated others.'

Fidelma smiled grimly.

'At the moment I am more concerned with the boatmen who have disappeared.'

Ross sighed and nodded.

'I know Olcán never treated his men well but I see what you mean. I have heard that several good river men had disappeared of late. I did not know that they worked for Olcán although, come to think of it, I do not recall seeing as many of Olcán's barges on the river in recent days.'

Fidelma was intrigued. 'Are you saying that you know Olcán's barges by sight?'

Ross grinned. 'Even barges bear names, lady. And Olcán's barges have the head of a wolf burned into the bow to brand the owner's identity on them. Where did these barges disappear?'

She told him what she knew.

'Between Eochaill and Lios Mór?' he said reflectively. 'That's over thirty miles of river, maybe more. That's a long stretch of river to examine.'

Fidelma was thoughtful.

'There has been something troubling me about it, something Olcán said which struck a thought in my mind and then it passed and now I cannot remember it,' she confessed. Then she clicked her fingers

85

abruptly. 'I know, it was the fact that these boats disappeared at night. That they undertook their journey by night.'

Ross shook his head with a smile.

'Nothing unusual in that. Night is often the safest time to travel and the speediest time for boats like the *ethur* or cargo-carrying boats, as we call them. Often during the day, on rivers such as these, you get many people out in small boats who really don't know the ways of the river. Many skippers of *ethur* try to avoid them because of the accidents that they cause. The answer is that they choose night to travel and so they can move speedily along.'

'I see.' Fidelma was disappointed. However, Ross was rubbing his chin thoughtfully.

'Did you say that Olcán said the last boat to disappear was two weeks ago and the other was four weeks before that?'

'He did. Is that significant to you?'

Ross pursed his lips.

'Not really. Only that it must have coincided with the new moon on both occasions. Usually skippers avoid that period when travelling at night.'

'I don't understand. I thought you said they liked travelling at night?'

'But during the three days of the new moon they usually avoid travel for it is the dark time. The day of the new moon, the day before and the day afterwards.'

'I still do not understand.'

'Even boatmen need moonlight to see by and while they like to travel at night, they do not like total darkness. You must know that we call that the period of the Dark Moon for on those three days the moon is so weak it shows little light.'

'Of course. It is said that the moon holds sway over the night and that things happen at the period of the Dark Moon that never happen in the full moon. Hidden acts take place at the Dark Moon.'

Ross nodded quickly. 'She is the sailor's strength, the Queen of the Night. But she is a hard taskmistress. That is why we have so many names for her in our language and none dare pronounce her real name. Once a sailor steps on shipboard he must never refer to the moon by other than a euphemism such as "the Queen of the Night", "the brightness" or . . .'

86

Fidelma had been looking thoughtful and interrupted him.

'Ross, can you find someone to take me upriver? I'd like to examine its course between here and Lios Mór.'

Ross grinned. 'If it's a trip upriver that you are wanting, lady, then I am your man. I was born on this river. I have a curragh moored a short distance away.'

'But there is only a few hours of daylight left today. The sort of trip I had in mind needs daylight. If your offer still holds at dawn tomorrow, then I accept.'

Ross nodded agreeably. 'Dawn tomorrow it is, lady. I'll bring the curragh to the quay at Dair Inis.'

'Good.' She rose. 'Then I shall take this opportunity to visit some of the wives of the boatmen who disappeared and see in what condition Olcán has left them. The *scriptor* has made me a list of their names and their families live mostly around Eochaill.'

The first three boatmen who had disappeared had been Erc, Donnucán and Laochra. The second crew were Finchán, Laidcenn and Dathal.

On inquiring for the families of the first two names on the list prepared by the *scriptor* Fidelma was informed by neighbours that they had departed from Eochaill. As soon as the news of their husbands' disappearance had been reported, the womenfolk and their children had left the area, presumably to go to stay with other members of their families.

The third family Fidelma found was still living in Eochaill. A woman with heavy jowls and a baby in her arms stood on the threshold of a poor house, and glowered in suspicion at Fidelma.

'My man was a steersman on Olcán's barges,' she acknowledged. 'Six weeks ago now he was contracted to take a cargo up to Lios Mór and has not returned.'

Fidelma was aware of several children playing around the house.

'You have a large family?'

The woman nodded.

'Times must be hard with the loss of your man. Does Olcán help support the family?'

The woman laughed unpleasantly. 'The wolf? That sly one? He would not give a *pingín* that he did not have to.'

Fidelma sighed. Obviously, the woman did not know her rights.

'Do your family help with the feeding of your children?'

Again the woman laughed. 'It is the generosity of Abaoth that feeds my children, Sister. A blessing on his name.'

Fidelma raised her eyebrows in surprise.

'Abaoth?' While it was technically Abaoth's cargo, the legal responsibility was on the employer, Olcán, to compensate the families of the men who were injured in his employ. Disappearance could well be interpreted by the Brehons as a form of injury.

'He is a generous man,' repeated the woman. 'It was his cargo that my man was transporting.'

'Does he help all the families of the boatmen who have disappeared?'

'So I am told. I know he helps me and will do so until the time my man returns.'

'And you have no idea what has happened to your man and his fellow boatmen?'

'None. Now I have things to attend to, Sister.' The woman turned abruptly to her house and closed the door behind her.

Thoughtfully, Fidelma went to find another of the families. According to the *scriptor*, one of the boatmen had recently married a young wife named Serc. The house was a small but better-kept one near the quay. As she came to the door Fidelma heard voices raised, a man's and a woman's. She could not hear what was said but some altercation was taking place. Fidelma knocked loudly and the voices fell silent. She knocked again. There came the sounds of whispering. Then Fidelma heard the noise of a door opening softly on the far side of the house. Something prompted her to move swiftly to the corner of the building where there was a narrow passage leading to the back of it. She had a brief glimpse of a semi-clad male figure, some of his clothes in hand, moving hurriedly away. A second's glimpse and then he had disappeared.

Behind her the front door had opened.

Fidelma turned back to find herself being confronted by a young, attractive but sulky-looking girl with a shawl around her. It was clear that she was naked underneath. Her hair was tousled and her lips were pursed in a surly expression. There was something promiscuous about her even in this state. Her stare was disapproving as she looked at Fidelma.

'Is your name Serc? I am told your husband disappeared two weeks ago while working as a boatman for Olcán the merchant.'

'What's it to do with you?' demanded the girl, still sulky.

'I am a *dálaigh* of the Brehon Court and my inquiry is official.'

Serc was still defiant. 'If you are who you say then you must know the answer to the question.'

Fidelma controlled her irritation.

'Since your husband disappeared, I presume that you are being cared for by the employer of your husband?'

The girl raised her chin a little.

'Abaoth has ensured that I do not want.'

'Abaoth? Not Olcán.'

'Olcán is a lecherous old bastard!' the girl replied without rancour. 'He came here and said he would take care of me if . . .' Her mouth clamped shut.

Fidelma was not surprised.

'You do not know what happened to your husband?'

'Of course not. Why should I?'

'I am trying to find out what happened to him and to the others.'

'Let me know when you do. I'd be interested. Now I am cold, standing here. Have you finished?'

It was clear that even though her husband had vanished with his fellow boatmen, Serc would lack for nothing now or in the future so long as she retained her looks.

There were two other families on her list. One of them, like the first two Fidelma had inquired after, had left Eochaill and, presumably, moved off to live with relatives, since their husbands had gone missing. The other was a large, broad-faced woman who had several children. She seemed anxious when confronted with Fidelma. She and her children seemed to lack for nothing and Fidelma confirmed that this was due to Abaoth rather than the miserly Olcán. Once again, Fidelma was not able to pick up any useful information either about the missing boatmen or their last trip for Olcán.

It was dawn the next day when Fidelma joined Ross in his curragh and they began to move upriver from Eochaill. The Abhainn Mór was well named. It was a 'great river' whose black waters were deep and dark. Once out of the estuary waters and entering the river proper around the place called the Point of the Sacred Tree since pagan times – a hill on which a small fortress stood to protect the river passage – progress was more interesting. They went through the wooded banks of the still broad river, the trees rising on hills along either side as it kept a moderately straight course north.

Apart from small streams that fed the river Fidelma saw nothing that excited her suspicions. Isolated farmsteads could be seen now and again but there were no major settlements once they were beyond Dair Inis.

Ross eased on his oars for a moment.

'Have you seen anything of interest yet, lady?' he asked.

She shook her head negatively.

'Everything seems as it should be.'

'What did you expect to see?'

She shrugged. 'I don't know. Something out of the ordinary per-haps.'

Ross sighed. 'We should break for a meal soon. The sun is already at the zenith.'

She nodded absently.

'The Abhainn Mór is a long river, lady.' Ross had a quiet sense of humour. 'I trust that you don't want to explore its whole length? It rises on the slopes of a mountain in the country of the Muscraige Luachra and that is a long, long journey from here.'

'Don't worry, Ross. Whatever happened to the barges happened before Lios Mór and I think it happened to them before dawn. Whoever or whatever was responsible for their disappearance would not want any witnesses and with daylight would come such witnesses.'

'Well, the next settlement is Conn's Plot, Ceapach Choinn. It is there that the river makes a forty-five-degree turn towards Lios Mór. I doubt whether they could reach that settlement before dawn. Whatever happened to them must have happened long before the river turns.'

Fidelma was grateful for Ross's knowledge.

They pulled into the bank to take a midday snack of bread and goat's cheese and the flask of mead. It was a warm, pleasant day, and Fidelma felt herself sinking into a lazy drowsing state beneath the tall oaks soaring up from the bank above her with the sound of songbirds in her ears.

'We should be on our way, lady,' Ross reminded her after a while.

She started nervously from her reverie.

'I was thinking,' she said defensively. Then smiled. 'No, I think I was dreaming. But you are right. We must press on. There must be somewhere that these barges were taken and hidden before the bend in the river.'

Ross rubbed his chin thoughtfully.

'The only place I can think of is where the River Bríd joins this river.'

Fidelma frowned. 'The River Bríd? Of course, I had forgotten that.'

'It joins the Abhainn Mór less than a kilometre from here.'

Fidelma leaned forward excitedly. 'We will turn off into the River Bríd and see where it takes us.'

The Bríd was a powerful river, although not so wide as the Abhainn Mór, and it was difficult to negotiate against the surge where it flooded into the greater river, joining its slow progress to the sea. There were tiny whirlpools and currents that sent Ross's curragh this way and that in a helter-skelter fashion. Finally, they broke through to calmer water and began to move slowly through a green plain with distant hills on either side. It was a fertile valley in which Fidelma had never been before.

'Do you know this area, Ross?'

'This is the territory of Cumscrad, prince of the Fir Maige Féine.'

Fidelma suddenly shuddered. 'They are a non-Eóghanacht people whose prince claims that he descended from Mogh Ruith, a sinister Druid who was a disciple of Simon Magus, the magician who opposed the Blessed Peter, the disciple of Christ.'

Ross grimaced but without concern.

'If it is a villain that you are seeking, you may seek no further than Cumscrad,' he said. 'There is a local chieftain here who acts in his name, Conna.'

'I have not heard of him.'

'He has a small fortress on a rock above the river but it is some way further on. We have to come to the main settlement first.'

'That's called Tealach an Iarainn, the hill of iron, isn't it? I have heard of that because it is famous for its wealth.'

'That's the place, lady. The people extract iron ore and smelt it and trade it. In fact, Olcán trades for iron cargoes here.'

'Does he now?' Fidelma asked reflectively.

They had come nearly three kilometres along the winding river when Ross, glancing over his shoulder, indicated the settlement on the south bank of the river. There were several barges and small boats moored along the riverbank where wooden quays showed that trade was carried on here.

'We'll stop here and make some inquiries,' Fidelma instructed and Ross pulled in, looking for a mooring.

On firm land, Fidelma took a moment or two to recover her balance having been for some hours seated in the curragh. She looked about along the line of vessels. Tealach an Iarainn was certainly a busy little settlement. There were a lot of people about. By their appearance it seemed that they were mainly merchants or boatmen. There were a large number of blacksmith forges along the quays as well.

'What now, lady?' asked Ross. 'Where do we make our inquiries?'

'Let's take a stroll along the quay first.'

She was surprised at how busy the settlement was. In the hills behind she realised that people were mining and extracting iron ore. She could see wagons bringing it down to the forges where she presumed the iron was extracted and then sent in the barges to be sold at various destinations. It suddenly came to her memory that the plains beyond this settlement were called Magh Méine, the Plain of Minerals.

'Lady!'

Ross's urgent whisper made her turn her head.

They had been walking by a series of barges that were being filled with cargoes of iron ore. It was the end one by which Ross had paused. There was no one on board and he had halted and was staring at the bow.

'What is it?' she asked.

'Take a look at the bow, lady.'

Fidelma looked.

The wooden planking of the vessel seemed to have been recently tarred and for a moment she could not see what he was trying to indicate. Then she saw the slight indentations on the wood. Only by looking at them in a certain way, the way the sunlight glinted and formed shadows, could she make out the deep lines that had been seared into the wood.

She turned excitedly to Ross.

'I see the head of a wolf.'

Ross nodded grimly. 'This was one of Olcán's barges. They did their best to remove the outward signs and paint over the brand mark with tar . . . but not quite.'

A sailor was passing nearby.

'Excuse me,' called Fidelma.

The sailor halted and took in her religieuse robes.

'You want me, Sister?'

'Can you tell me whose barge that is?'

'That one? The end one there? Surely I can.'

Fidelma smiled to hide her impatience. 'And to whom does it belong?'

'That is the barge of the merchant Ségán.'

'Ségán, eh? And where might I find this man?'

'Across in that tavern there, I'll warrant. He's just loaded a cargo and is probably having a last drink before going downriver.'

She thanked the man and turned for the tavern with Ross in her wake.

Inside, the room was packed mainly with boatmen. Several heads turned as she entered. The landlord, or such she presumed him to be, came across to her immediately.

'God be with you, Sister. We do not often have ladies of your cloth in this poor place. We mainly serve the river boatmen. There is a tavern not far away that I can recommend that is better suited . . .'

'I am told that I might find a merchant named Ségán here,' she cut him short.

The landlord blinked and then he pointed to a corner where a fat-looking individual was seated before a plate on which the remains of what had obviously been a small joint reposed. He was sipping at a great pottery mug of a liquid which he was obviously savouring.

With a curt nod to the landlord, Fidelma moved across and took a vacant seat opposite the merchant.

'Your name is Ségán, I believe?'

The fleshy-faced man paused, the mug halfway to his lips, and stared at her.

'Why would a religieuse know my name?' he said, a little surprised.

'I am a *dálaigh* and I am here on official business.'

The man set down the mug with a bang, closed his eyes and groaned.

'I knew it. I knew it.' He shuddered.

Fidelma stared at him speculatively.

'Perhaps you will share your knowledge with me then?' she asked, a little sarcastically.

'It's my wife, isn't it? She is seeking a divorce and . . .'

Fidelma gave an impatient gesture of her hand.

'It's not about your wife. It's about your boat.'

At once a look of suspicion crossed the man's features.

'My boat? You mean the barge? What of it?'

'When did you acquire it?'

Ségán was still frowning.

'I bought it legally. Two weeks ago.'

'From whom?'

'What is this? What are you implying?'

'From whom?' she insisted.

'A man at Conna's fortress.'

'Does he have a name?'

'No more questions until you tell me what this is about.'

Two burly boatmen had risen and made their way over to where Ségán was sitting.

'Something wrong, master?'

'Tell them nothing is wrong unless they are also to be charged as parties to theft,' Fidelma said calmly without taking her eyes from the merchant.

The fleshy-faced man's eyes widened. 'Theft?'

'Your barge and its cargo and crew disappeared two weeks ago. It was then in the ownership of a merchant in Eochaill named Olcán.'

The merchant was shaking his head rapidly. He glanced at the boatmen and waved them away.

'How can you know this?'

'Did you examine the markings on the barge when you bought it?'

Ségán shook his head. 'I know that it had been repainted. There is new tar. What markings?'

'The image of a wolf's head is branded into the woodwork at the prow. That is Olcán's mark. Now where did you get this barge?'

'As I said, I bought it. I bought it from a boatman.'

94

Fidelma frowned. 'And what was his name?'

'Name?' He shook his head. 'There were some boatmen up at Conna's fortress upriver and they were trying to sell the barge. I offered them a good price.'

'You bought the barge from someone whose name you do not even know?'

'I know Conna,' replied the fat merchant. 'He knew the boatmen. That was good enough for me.'

Fidelma sighed.

'Then we must have a word with Conna,' she said to Ross. Turning back she viewed the merchant with disfavour. 'I would advise you not to travel far. The boat you now claim to own was stolen and doubtless its owner will seek restitution.'

The merchant paled a little.

'I bought it in good faith . . .' he began to protest.

'From someone whose name you didn't know,' interrupted Fidelma sharply. 'You therefore share some of the culpability.'

She stood up and left the tavern followed by Ross.

'Would it not be wise to keep an eye on the merchant?' the old sailor ventured.

'I do not think he will be hard to find in the future. I am sure that he was telling the truth although I suspect that he probably realised something was wrong with the transaction.'

'Where now?'

'As I said, to Conna's fortress. How far is that from here?'

'About four or five kilometres.'

Conna's fortress was perched on a rocky outcrop beside the river. There were several barges and boats moored beneath its walls and signs of boatmen unloading cargoes. As they climbed out of the curragh, with Ross securing it, several armed warriors approached. They were not friendly. Fidelma saw it from their faces and so she assumed her haughtiest manner.

'Take me to Conna at once.'

The leading warrior halted and blinked in surprise, unused to being addressed in such a fashion by someone in religieuse robes.

Fidelma followed up the advantage.

'Don't stand there gawking, man. It is Fidelma, sister of Colgú your king, who demands this.'

Nervously the man glanced at his companions and then, without a word, turned and led the way. Ross, following a step behind Fidelma, was trying to hide his nervousness. Fidelma's royal rank apart, Ross knew that Conna owned allegiance to the prince of Maige Féine who was an hereditary enemy of the Eóghanacht kings of Muman.

Their guide had instructed one of his men to run on and announce Fidelma's coming to Conna.

The chieftain met them at the door of his hall, a thinly built man with beady dark eyes, like those of a snake. He gave the impression of someone close to starvation, so gaunt and elongated of limb was he.

'The fame of Fidelma of Cashel precedes her,' he greeted, almost sibilantly. 'How may I serve you?'

Fidelma was not impressed with the man.

'You may best serve me by telling me the truth. I have spoken to the merchant Ségán.'

Did a nervous look appear in the man's dark features?

'You recommended Ségán to a boatman who sold him a stolen barge.'

The features of Conna became immobile.

'I am not responsible for that.'

'If you recommended a thief to persuade another to receive stolen property, then there is your responsibility – chieftain or not.'

'This boatman was trading here at the time. I did not vouch for his character. I simply told Ségán of the fact. Ségán was saying that he wanted to expand the number of barges he had. I introduced them, that is all.'

'Tell me about this boatman.'

'What can I tell you?'

'His name, where he came from, where he is now.'

'His name was Dathal. He came from a downriver port.'

'You say that you had never seen him before?'

'I didn't say exactly that. I know that he traded along the rivers.'

'You have bought cargoes from him?'

'He was only a boatman. The man he worked for owned the cargoes. The man who imports the cargoes from the land of the Britons or the Franks.'

'With whom did you transact your business, then?'

Conna was hesitant but no match for Fidelma in her most assertive manner.

'I always gave the money to Dathal,' he admitted. 'I presumed that he was selling the barge on behalf of his master.'

'Do you know where this Dathal went?'

'Back to Eochaill, I presume.'

Fidelma let out a sighing breath.

'This is not the first time that boatmen have bought you a cargo and then sold their barge before leaving, is it?'

The expression on Conna's face confirmed the suspicion that was in her mind.

'Dathal sold the barge two weeks ago, is that right?' pressed Fidelma. 'Who sold a barge four weeks before that?'

'I bought a cargo then. The boatman's name was Erc and he was from Eochaill. Erc and his men sold their barge to a trader from the Ford of the Cairn not far upriver. That was six weeks ago.'

Fidelma suddenly smiled brightly. The smile seemed to disconcert Conna.

'Then I have no need to bother you further. You may be required to attend the Brehon Court at Dair Inis. It depends. You will be informed in due course. In the meantime, I shall trouble you no more.'

She turned swiftly and with Ross trotting in bemusement at her heels she returned down from the fort to where they had moored the curragh.

'Where now, lady?' demanded Ross, scrambling in after her. 'Upriver to the Ford of the Cairn?'

Fidelma shook her head with a smile of satisfaction.

'No, back to Eochaill. I think the mystery is cleared up.'

Two days later the merchants Abaoth and Olcán stood before her.

'Ah yes. Abaoth, you claim compensation for the loss of your cargoes due to the disappearance and theft of Olcán's barges. Two losses in as many months. One six weeks ago and one two weeks ago. Is that right?'

'It is, learned *dálaigh*,' agreed Abaoth nervously.

Fidelma turned to the glowering Olcán.

'And you counter this claim, Olcán?'

'Of course,' snapped the man. 'The loss of my barges and crews and the loss of the money for the transportation of cargoes for which I have not been paid is the compensation that I seek.'

Fidelma nodded absently and sat back.

'I have made some investigation into this matter,' she said slowly. She turned to Olcán. 'You may rest easy in that your barges and crews have not disappeared.'

The merchant returned her gaze in astonishment.

'What do you mean?' he demanded.

'Both boats were, indeed, the subjects of theft. Their cargoes were sold, sold to Conna of the Maige Féine. The barges were then disposed of by selling them to local merchants – after they had been repainted, of course.'

Abaoth was shaking his head.

'Who was responsible?' he asked wonderingly. 'What has Conna to say of this?'

Fidelma was suddenly grim.

'The crew of each barge willingly diverted from their course and took the barges upriver along the Bríd to Conna's Fort. There they sold the cargoes and then the barges and disappeared.'

'The crews were the thieves?' Abaoth sounded aghast.

'They were acting under orders,' replied Fidelma. 'They acted under the orders of the man they were working for.'

Abaoth turned to Olcán, whose face was reddening in rage.

'How dare you . . . ?' he began.

Fidelma shook her head.

'The plot was yours, Abaoth.'

The fleshy merchant was stunned.

'Are you accusing me of stealing my own cargoes?' he demanded, suddenly pale.

'It was a good way of getting double the money for the same cargo. Money you wanted in order to compensate for the loss of one of your ships. You sold your cargo to Lios Mór. Then you did a deal selling your cargo to Conna who, of course, supplies the prince of Maige Féine. Now, if you could persuade the crews of Olcán to work with you and disappear with their barges after they had delivered the cargoes to Conna then you would have the added bonus. You could also come here and seek compensation from Olcán for the loss of your cargoes. If successful that would cover compensation to Lios Mór and obtain more money for you. It was a complicated and ingenious plot, Abaoth.'

'You cannot prove it.'

'I can so. Olcán's men were willing to do your bidding because Olcán was not a generous master anyway. There is a lesson for you to learn there, Olcán.'

Olcán scowled angrily but said nothing. Fidelma continued to address Abaoth.

'You paid the crews some initial money but, as their major share of the deal, you allowed them to sell the barges and pocket that money. Now it would look peculiar if the boatmen and all their families disappeared at the same time from Eochaill. When I checked these families I did find that half of them had already left the port. Those that remained behind told me that you, Abaoth, were looking after them. I wondered why. It was not your responsibility. I found it difficult to believe that a man with financial problems would be such a great philanthropist. There was another thing. When I visited Serc I surprised her with her husband Dathal who, I believe, was your main contact with the crews and acted as your intermediary with Conna.'

Abaoth was standing white-faced and silent.

'Do I have to waste my time in presenting the proof of these matters, Abaoth? I shall not be so generous in allotting fines and compensation if I have to spend unnecessary time in doing so.'

Abaoth's shoulders had slumped in resignation.

Fidelma turned to Olcán who was a picture of anger as he regarded the merchant.

'Olcán,' she said sharply, 'you would do well to ponder on what motivated your men to be persuaded to betray you. There is a saying that a closed hand only gets a shut fist. It is bad fortune that always attends a mean person.'

Like a Dog Returning . . .

'It's very beautiful,' Sister Fidelma said softly.

'Beautiful?' Abbot Ogán's voice was an expression of disbelief. 'Beautiful? It is beyond compare. Worth a High King's honour price and even more.'

Fidelma frowned slightly and turned towards the enthusiastic speaker, a question forming on her lips. Then she realised that the middle-aged abbot was not looking at the small marble statuette of the young girl in the robes of a religieuse, which had caught her eye as she had entered the chapel of the abbey. Instead, he was looking beyond the statuette, which stood at the entrance to a small alcove. In the recess, on a small altar, stood an ornate reliquary box worked in precious metals and gemstones.

Fidelma regarded the reliquary critically for a moment.

'It is, indeed, a valuable object,' she admitted. But the reliquary box was not unusual in her experience. She had seen many such boxes in her travels, all equally valuable.

'Valuable? It is breathtaking, and inside it is the original *Confessio* penned in the hand of Patrick himself.' Abbot Ogán was clearly annoyed at her lack of homage before the reliquary.

Fidelma was unimpressed and not bothered at all by his look of disfavour.

'Who is the young girl whose statuette guards the entrance to the alcove?' she demanded, turning the conversation to what she considered to be the object of greater interest. Somehow the artist had brought the young religieuse to life, endowing her with a vibrancy that burst through the lines of the cold stone. It seemed that she would leap from the pedestal and greet the worshippers in the tiny abbey church with outstretched hands.

The abbot reluctantly turned from his contemplation of his community's most famous treasure – the reliquary of St Patrick. His face darkened slightly.

'That is a likeness of Sister Una,' he said shortly.

Fidelma put her head to one side to examine it from every angle. She could not get over the extraordinary vitality of the piece. It was almost as if the artist had been in love with his model and only thus able to draw forth some inner feeling into the cold marble.

'Who was the sculptor?' she asked.

The abbot sniffed, clearly not approving of the interest she was showing.

'One of our brethren, Duarcán.'

'And why is her statuette in this chapel? I thought only the holy saints could achieve such honour?'

The corner of Abbot Ogán's mouth turned down. He hesitated and then, observing the determination on Fidelma's face, asked, 'Have you not heard the story of Sister Una?'

Fidelma grimaced irritably. It was surely obvious that she would not be asking the question had she heard the story. The abbot continued: 'She was killed on this very spot some twenty years ago.'

'What happened?' Fidelma's eyes had widened with greater interest.

'Sister Una entered the chapel when someone was attempting to steal the holy reliquary. The thief struck her down and fled but without the reliquary.'

'Was the thief caught?'

'He was overtaken.'

'How did the Brehons judge him?'

'Sister Una was very beloved by our local community.' The abbot's features were set in deep lines, and there appeared a defensive note in his voice. 'Before the culprit could be secured and taken before a Brehon for judgement, the people hanged him from a tree. This small marble statuette was erected in the chapel in Una's honour to guard the reliquary for all eternity.'

'Who was the thief and murderer?'

The abbot again hesitated. He clearly was unhappy at her interest.

'A man who worked in the abbey gardens. Not one of our community.'

'A sad tale.'

'Sad enough,' the abbot agreed shortly.

'Did you know Sister Una?'

'I was a young novitiate in the abbey at the time, but I hardly knew her.' The abbot turned, clearing his throat as if in dismissal of the memories. 'And now . . . I believe that you are staying with us until the morning?'

'I will be continuing my journey back to Cashel in the morning,' Fidelma confirmed.

'Stay here then and I will send Brother Liag, our hostel keeper, to you. He will show you to the dormitory of the religieuses. We eat after Vespers. You will forgive me leaving you here. There are matters I must now attend to.'

Fidelma watched as he hurried along the aisle and vanished beyond the doors of the chapel. As they banged shut behind him, her eyes were drawn back once again to the extraordinary statuette. It held a curious fascination for her. The artist had, indeed, given the poor Sister Una life and, for a while, she was lost in examining the lines of the fine workmanship.

There was a sound behind her: a shuffle of sandals and an exaggerated cough.

She turned. A religieux had entered and stood a little distance off with his arms folded inside his robe. He was balding and wore a doleful expression.

'Sister Fidelma? I am the hostel keeper, Brother Liag.'

Fidelma inclined her head towards him. Yet her gaze was still reluctant to leave the intriguing statuette. The newcomer had observed her interest.

'I knew her.'

Brother Liag spoke softly and yet there was a curious emotion in his voice that caught her attention immediately.

'Yes?' she encouraged after a pause.

'She was so full of life and love for everyone. The community worshipped her.'

'As did you?' Fidelma interpreted the controlled emotion of his voice.

'As did I,' Brother Liag confirmed sadly.

'It is an unhappy story. I have heard it from your abbot.'

Did a curious expression flit across his features? She was not sure in the gloomy light.

'Did you also know the man who killed her?' she pressed when it seemed that he was saying no more.

'I did.'

'I gather he worked in the gardens of the abbey?'

'Tanaí?'

'Was that his name?'

'That was the man who was lynched by the community for the crime,' Brother Liag affirmed.

Fidelma exhaled softly as she gazed at the marble face of the young girl.

'What a miserable waste,' she observed, almost to herself.

'Grievous.'

'What sort of man was this Tanaí? How did he think that he, a gardener, could steal that precious reliquary and sell it – for presumably he did it for mercenary gain?'

'That was the theory.'

Fidelma glanced quickly at him.

'You do not agree?'

Brother Liag returned her gaze and his expression had not changed. It was still mournful.

'I think that we share the same thought, Sister. The only way such an object could be sold for gain is by its destruction. Where and to whom could such a priceless treasure be sold? Jewels pried from the box might be sold individually. The value of the box itself and the greater value of that which is contained in it would be entirely lost. There would be no market for anything so invaluable. Who would purchase such a treasure?'

'Yet if Tanaí was merely a labourer in the garden here, he might not have considered that aspect of the theft. He might simply have seen a precious jewelled box and been overcome by greed.'

The hostel keeper smiled for the first time, more a motion of his facial muscles than indicative of any feeling.

'It is true that Tanaí worked here as a gardener. He was an intelligent man. He had been an apothecary and herbalist. One day he mixed a wrong prescription and one of his patients died. He answered before the Brehons for manslaughter and was fined. The Brehons said it was an accident, and there was no guilt of intent involved – only the guilt of error. But Tanaí was conscientious and, although he could have continued to practise as a herbalist, he withdrew here to the abbey and did penance by returning to study the plants and herbs, living a life of penury and self-sacrifice.'

Fidelma glanced at Liag cynically.

'Until he coveted the reliquary, for what you are telling me is that he was intelligent enough to know its real value. Maybe he thought he would find someone who would endanger their immortal soul for possession of it?'

Brother Liag sighed deeply.

'That is what everyone has thought these last twenty years.'

'You sound as though you still do not agree?' she commented quickly.

Brother Liag was hesitant, and then he sighed reflectively. 'The point that I was making is that he was intelligent enough to know that he could never sell the reliquary, if that was his motive. There are some questions to which I have never found satisfactory answers. Tanaí had removed himself to the monastery with his wife and young daughter because he felt he must do penance for a mistake. That strikes me as the action of a man of moral principle. He worked in the abbey gardens in a position of trust for five years. Never had there been a whisper of anyone's distrusting him. He could have been appointed apothecary of the abbey for the old abbot – he died many years ago now – who had several times urged him to take the position, saying that he had paid for his mistake more than enough.

'Why did he have such a sudden mental aberration? For over five years he was in a position in which he could have stolen the reliquary or, indeed, any one of the several treasures of the abbey. Why did he attempt the theft at that point? And to kill Una! He was never a violent man, in spite of the mistake that led to the manslaughter charge. The killing of poor Sister Una was so out of character.'

'What actually connected him with the attempted theft in the first place?' Fidelma asked. 'The abbot said that he fled without the reliquary.'

Brother Liag inclined his head.

'The reliquary was untouched. Sister Una had disturbed the thief before he could touch it, and she was killed while trying to raise the alarm.'

'Where was Tanaí caught?'

'Trying to enter the abbot's rooms.' Brother Liag shot her a keen glance. 'The community caught up with him at the entrance and dragged him to the nearest tree. God forgive all of us. But Sister Una was so beloved by all of the community that common sense was displaced by rage.'

'The abbot's rooms? That is a strange place for a man to run to when he has apparently just committed murder,' murmured Fidelma.

'A question that was raised afterwards. Abbot Ogán, who was one of the community, a young brother at the time, pointed out that Tanaí must have known that he would be caught and was trying to throw himself on the old abbot's mercy and seek sanctuary.'

'I suppose that it is plausible,' Fidelma conceded. 'What happened to Tanaí's family?'

'His wife died of shock soon after, and his young daughter was raised by the sisters of the abbey out of charity.'

Fidelma was perplexed.

'There is something here that I do not understand. If Tanaí was found at the abbot's rooms, if the only witness was killed and the reliquary had not been touched, and there was no eyewitness, what was there to link Tanaí with the crime? Indeed, how do you know that theft was even the motive for the murder?'

Brother Liag shrugged.

'What else could have been the motive for killing poor Sister Una? Anyway, everyone was crying that it was Tanaí who did the deed and that he had been seen running from the chapel. I presumed that this was without question since everyone was shouting it.'

'How much time had passed between the time the crime was committed and when Tanaí was found?'

Brother Liag shifted his weight as he thought over the matter, trying to stretch his memory back two decades.

'I can't really recall. I know it was some amount of time.'

'An hour?'

'No, well under an hour.'

'A few minutes?'

'More than that. Perhaps fifteen minutes.'

'So who identified Tanaí as the culprit?'

Brother Liag gestured helplessly.

'But everyone was shouting that . . . I saw Brother Ogán, the abbot as he now is. In fact, it was Ogán who was foremost in the hue and cry; but there was Brother Librén, the *rechtaire* . . . the steward of the abbey. Everyone was shouting and looking for Tanaí . . . I have no idea who identified him first.'

'I see,' Fidelma replied with a sigh. 'Why do you now have doubts of Tanaí's guilt?'

Brother Liag appeared slightly uncomfortable.

'I know that this community has his death on its conscience because he was unjustly killed by the anger of the mob and not by legal process. That is enough to lay the burden of guilt on us. There is always doubt if a man has not had a proper chance to defend himself.'

Fidelma thought for a moment.

'Well, on the facts as you relate them, you have a right to be suspicious of the guilt of Tanaí. Had I been judging him at the time, I would have acquitted him on grounds that there was insufficient evidence. Unless other witnesses could have been produced. However, there is little one can do after twenty years.'

Brother Liag gave a troubled sigh.

'I know. But it is frightening to consider that if Tanaí was not guilty, then all this time the real murderer of Sister Una has dwelt within these walls nursing this dark secret.'

'We all live cheek by jowl with people who nurse dark secrets,' Fidelma pointed out. 'Now, perhaps you'll show me to my room?'

After the evening Angelus bell and a frugal meal in the refectory of the abbey, Fidelma found herself almost automatically making her way to the chapel to once again examine the marble statuette of Sister Una. She disliked unsolved mysteries; they kept nagging at her mind until she had made some resolution of the problem. The face of Sister Una, alive in the marble, seemed to be pleading, as if demanding a resolution to this now ancient murder.

Fidelma was standing before the statuette when, for the second time, a voice interrupted her meditation.

'He didn't do it, you know.'

The voice was a soft feminine one. Fidelma quickly glanced around and saw a religieuse standing nearby. She was, so far as Fidelma could place her, somewhere in her thirties. The face could have been attractive, but even in the softening candlelight it seemed bitter and careworn.

'To whom do you refer?' Fidelma asked.

'To Tanaí, my father. My name is Muiríol.'

Fidelma turned to her and examined the woman carefully.

'So you are the daughter of the gardener who was hanged for the killing of Sister Una.' It was a statement rather than a question.

'Unjustly so, for, as I say, he did not do it.'

'How can you be so sure?'

'Because I was here at the time and he was my father.'

'Daughters are not the best witnesses to their father's deeds. I would need more than a statement of belief. You were surely young at that time?'

'I was twelve years old. Do you think that day is not impressed on my mind? I was with him in the abbey gardens, for I used to often play there. I remember seeing Sister Una passing to the chapel. She greeted us and asked my father a question about his work. Then she passed on into the chapel.'

Muiríol paused and swallowed slightly. Her dark eyes never left Fidelma's face. There was a haunted look in them as if again seeing the scene – a vivid scene that appeared to torment her.

'Go on,' Fidelma encouraged softly.

'A few minutes after she passed into the chapel, there came a scream. My father told me to remain where I was and ran to the chapel. He disappeared inside. Others of the community had heard the scream, and some came into the garden to inquire what it portended. There came shouting from the chapel, a man's voice was raised.'

'Was it your father's voice?'

'I did not think so at the time. But time often confuses some details.'

'Your memory appears clear enough.'

'It is the truth, I tell you,' she replied defensively.

'What happened then?'

'I saw my father emerge from the chapel. A voice was crying – "Tanaí has murdered Una!" – or words to that effect. I saw my father running. Later I realised that he was running to the abbot's rooms in fear for his life. But there was an outcry, and the people were angry. I did not know what had happened. I was taken to our rooms by one of the religieuses and remained there until my mother, prostrate with grief, was carried inside. She had seen my father being . . .' Her voice caught and she paused a second before continuing. 'She had seen my father being lynched outside the abbot's rooms. She never recovered and died soon afterwards.'

There was a silence between them for a while.

'From what you tell me, your father could not have killed Una,' Fidelma finally observed. 'Did you never tell your story?'

Muiríol nodded.

'I told it to the old abbot, but I was not believed.'

'But did you tell it to the Brehon who investigated the matter?'

'The matter was kept secret within the abbey for years until the old abbot died. The abbot felt guilty that the lynching had taken place with members of the community involved, and he wished to conceal it. So it was not reported to the Brehons. That was why the religious here were kind to me and raised me as one of the community. After the old abbot had died, no one bothered about the story of Una and my father.'

'Knowing this, why did you remain in the abbey?'

The girl shrugged.

'One day, so I hoped, I would find the guilty one. Someone in this abbey killed Sister Una and was also responsible for my father's death.'

'So you wished your father's name to be cleared?'

Muiríol grimaced.

'That was my original purpose. Twenty years have passed. Is anyone still interested?'

'Justice is always interested in justice.'

'Isn't there a saying that there is little difference between justice and injustice?'

'If I believed that I would not be an advocate of the courts,' Fidelma returned.

Fidelma was irritated. She could not sleep. Her mind was filled with the thoughts of young Sister Una's death. She turned and twisted for an age, but sleep would not come to her. She sat up and judged it was long past midnight.

Finally, she rose from her bed, put on her robe, and decided to go down to the abbey gardens to walk in the cool of the summer night. The only way to the garden that she knew of led through the chapel.

She heard the sound almost immediately as she opened the door into the chapel – a low groaning sound followed by a thwack as if of leather on a soft substance. The groan rose in a new note of pain.

Then she heard a voice: '*Mea culpa, mea culpa, mea maxima culpa!*'

Her eyes narrowed at the familiarity of the masculine voice. She peered into the gloom to seek out the penitent.

A figure was kneeling before the marble statuette of Sister Una, head almost to the ground. The back was bare where the robe was stripped down to the waist. In one hand was a broad leather belt that, every so often, the figure would strike his back with, drawing blood, as she saw by the candlelight. Then the groan would issue a second or so after the impact of the leather on the flesh. The words of contrition were mumbled in Latin.

Fidelma strode forward.

'Explain this, Abbot Ogán!' she demanded coldly.

The abbot froze for a moment and then slowly straightened himself up, still kneeling on the chapel floor.

'This is a private penitence,' he replied harshly, trying to summon anger to disguise his shock at being thus discovered. 'You have no right to be here.'

Fidelma was unperturbed at his animosity.

'On the contrary. As a *dálaigh* of the Brehon Court, no doors are barred to me, Abbot Ogán, especially when it is deemed that a crime has been committed.'

The abbot rose from his knees, pulling his robe around his shoulders. Fidelma had noticed that his back was scarred. It was of no concern to her that the abbot practised flagellation: many mystics of the Church did, although she found such practices distasteful in the extreme. The scars, obvious even in the candlelight, indicated that the abbot had practised the self-abuse for many years.

Ogán was defensive before her hard scrutiny.

'What crime?' he blustered.

With a slight forward motion of her head, Fidelma indicated the statuette of Sister Una.

109

'You seem to be expressing some guilt for her death. Were you guilty of it?'

The last sentence was suddenly sharp.

Abbot Ogán blinked rapidly at the tone.

'I was responsible, for had I been in the chapel at that time she would not have been alone to confront Tanaí.'

Fidelma's brows came together.

'I do not follow.'

'It was my task on the day she was killed to clean the chapel. I had delayed my task out of simple sloth and indolence.'

'I see. So you were not here when you should have been. If you feel guilt then that is within you. So when did you become involved in leading the hue and cry after Tanaí?'

A frown passed the abbot's face.

'Who said I did?' he asked cautiously.

'Are you saying that you did not?'

'I . . . I came on the crowd as he escaped across the garden. Everyone was shouting. They caught and hanged Tanaí from the tree outside the old abbot's quarters. That was when I first knew about her death and realised my guilt, for if I had been here . . .'

'An "if" will empty the oceans,' Fidelma snapped. 'So you did not witness the event? You did not identify Tanaí as the murderer and would-be thief?'

Abbot Ogán shook his head.

'Everyone was proclaiming that Tanaí was the guilty one.'

'But someone must have done so first. Who first identified Tanaí as the culprit?'

The abbot again shook his head in bewilderment.

'Perhaps a few of those who were there that day and who have remained in the abbey might recall more than I do.'

'Who might they be?'

'Brother Liag, Brother Librén, Brother Duarcán and Brother Donngal. Everyone else who was here at the time has either died or moved on.'

'You have neglected to mention Tanaí's daughter, Sister Muiríol,' observed Fidelma.

The abbot shrugged.

'*And* Sister Muiríol. But she was only twelve years old at the time.

No one took any notice of her, for like any loyal daughter, she swore her father was innocent.'

Fidelma paused for a moment and looked once again at the vibrant features on the statuette. An idea suddenly occurred to her.

'Tell me, Ogán, were any of the community in love with Una?'

The abbot looked bewildered and then pursed his lips sourly.

'I suppose that we all were,' he said shortly.

'I think you know what I mean.'

Celibacy was not forbidden among the religious of the Church in Ireland. Most houses, like this abbey, were mixed communities in which the religious, male and female, lived and brought up their children in the service of the new religion.

Fidelma noted that Ogán's chin jutted out a little more.

'I believe that some of the brethren were emotionally and physically enamoured of her. She was a very attractive woman, as you may have noticed, because this statuette is an excellent likeness.'

'Were you, yourself, in love with her?'

The abbot scowled.

'I was not alone in my feelings.'

'That was not my question.'

'I admit it. There was a time when I thought we could have been together under God's holy ordinances. Why are you asking such questions? It has nothing to do with her murder.'

'Does it not?'

Abbot Ogán's eyes narrowed at her tone.

'What are you accusing me of?'

'You will know when I am accusing you. At the moment I am simply asking questions.'

'Una was killed protecting the holy reliquary when Tanaí attempted to steal it. There is nothing else to consider.'

'How can you be so sure? There were no witnesses. The reliquary was not even stolen.'

'I do not understand,' frowned the abbot.

'You mentioned that you were not alone in your love for Una,' she went on, ignoring his implied question. 'Is there anyone else in the abbey today who fell into that category?'

The abbot thought for a moment.

'Liag, of course. And Duarcán.'

'Did Una show particular affection for any one person?'

Ogán scowled for a moment, and then he shrugged in dismissive fashion.

'It was rumoured that she and Liag would be married. I thought they were going to leave the abbey and set up a school together.'

'And you mentioned Brother Duarcán. Is that the same Duarcán who sculpted this statuette? You mentioned that name when I asked you earlier who the artist was.'

The abbot nodded reluctantly.

'It is the same man,' he confirmed. 'I think he was very jealous of Liag. After he sculpted the statuette, he refused to undertake any more work of a similar nature. A waste of a great talent.'

'It is late,' Fidelma sighed. 'Before I leave the abbey tomorrow morning, I would like to speak to Brother Duarcán. Where will I find him?'

'He will be in the abbey kitchens. He now works cleaning and cooking for the community.'

The next morning, Fidelma found Duarcán, a tall dark man, washing kitchen utensils. He glanced up as she approached him and paused in his task. He smiled nervously.

'You are Fidelma of Cashel. I have heard of you.'

Fidelma inclined her head in acknowledgement.

'Then you will have also heard, perhaps, that I am an advocate of the Brehon Court?'

'I have.'

'I understand that you were in love with Sister Una.'

The man flushed. He laid down the pot he was cleaning and turned to her, clasping his hands loosely before him.

'I'll not deny it,' he said quietly.

'I am given to understand that she did not return your sentiments?'

Duarcán's mouth tightened at the corners.

'That is not so. We were going to be married.'

Fidelma raised an eyebrow.

'What of the story that she was going to marry Liag and set up a school with him?'

'Brother Liag is a liar to tell you that. It is not so. That was *our* plan; mine and Una's.'

Fidelma examined his expression carefully. His eyes met hers with a frankness that she found hard to doubt.

'I am told that you were a good sculptor once and that you executed the exquisite statuette of Una in the chapel. Is that so?'

'It is.'

'Why are you now wasting your talent?'

'Wasting? My talent died after I had given Una life in marble. I have nothing else to give. I exist, waiting for the time when I can rejoin Una in spirit.'

The dramatic words were rendered without drama, offhanded, as someone makes a mere statement of fact about the condition of the weather.

'Do you recall where you were when Una was killed?' pressed Fidelma.

'Do you think that I would forget the events of that day?' There was a controlled passion in his voice. 'Yes, I recall. I was in my studio that overlooked the gardens. I was the abbey's stonemason and sculptor. Una had been with me that morning, and we were planning to see the old abbot – he is now dead – to tell him of our decision to marry and leave the abbey. When Una left me, I saw her walk towards the chapel.'

'So you saw her cross the abbey gardens?'

Duarcán nodded.

'And you saw her go to the door of the chapel?'

'No. Not as far as that. The door was obscured by the shrubs and trees of the garden.'

'What did you see then?'

'Tanaí and his daughter were in the garden. Tanaí was doing some work. I saw Una pass by, pausing momentarily to speak to them. Then she went on. A few moments later, I was looking out, and I saw Tanaí rise and move off rapidly after Una. There was something suspicious about the way he moved. Rapidly, I mean, purposefully.'

'Did you hear anything?'

'Hear anything?' He frowned and shook his head. 'I was intent on cutting some stone at the time. I do not even know what made me glance out of the window. It was the sight, shortly afterwards, of people running through the garden that caught my attention rather than the noise. It caused me to go to the door, and that was when

I was told that Una had been killed, that Tanaí had tried to steal the reliquary and had killed her.'

'Who told you that?'

'Brother Liag.'

Fidelma looked thoughtfully at him for a while.

'Did it ever occur to you that if Tanaí was going to steal the reliquary, he would hardly have waited for Una to pass by on her way to the chapel and then attempt to steal it while she was actually there?'

Duarcán stared at her as if he had difficulty following her logic.

'But, Brother Liag said . . .'

Fidelma raised an eyebrow.

'Yes? What did he say?'

'Well, it became common knowledge that is what happened.'

'Was it at your instigation that the statuette was placed in the chapel?'

Duarcán frowned.

'Not exactly. In those long, lonely days and nights that followed, I felt compelled to recreate her likeness in marble from fear that it would be lost in the mists of receding memories. One day, Brother Ogán, as he then was, came to my studio and saw the finished statuette. It was he who persuaded the old abbot that it should be placed in the chapel where it has stood ever since. After that, I did no more work as a stonemason or sculptor. I now merely work in the kitchens.'

Sister Fidelma drew a deep sigh.

'I think I am beginning to understand now,' she said.

Duarcán looked at her suspiciously.

'Understand? What?'

'The cause of Una's death and the person responsible. Where can I find Brother Liag?'

Duarcán's face filled with surprise.

'I saw him pass on his way to the chapel a moment or so ago . . . Are you saying . . . ?'

But Fidelma was gone, hurrying towards the chapel. Inside, she saw Brother Liag talking with the abbot.

'Sister Fidelma.' Brother Liag seemed surprised to see her. 'I thought that you had already started your journey back to Cashel.'

'There was some unfinished business. Just one question. Cast your mind back twenty years to the events surrounding Una and Tanaí's death. There was tumult in the abbey gardens, shouting and so forth. You passed by the door of Duarcán's studio, and he came out to see what was amiss. You told him what had happened. That Una had been killed; that Tanaí had committed the deed, and you also told him the reason – that Tanaí had attempted to steal the reliquary and was prevented by Una.'

Brother Liag frowned, trying to recall, and then he slowly and reluctantly nodded.

'I seem to recollect that I did so.'

'This was before Tanaí had been caught. It was a short time after the community had heard Una's last scream, and Tanaí was even then being chased across the gardens. How did you know, so soon, all these details?'

Brother Liag stared at her, his face going suddenly pale.

Abbot Ogán exhaled loudly.

'Liag, did you . . . ?'

He left the question unfinished, for Liag was returning the abbot's look in horror as a further recollection came to him.

Fidelma's lips compressed for a moment in satisfaction as she turned to the abbot.

'You told Liag your version in the garden. You were heard to cry that Tanaí was the murderer. Your and Liag's versions differ so much that one of you is lying.

'The truth, Ogán, was that you were in love with Una, not Liag. When you found that Una was going away with Duarcán, that love turned to hatred. Sometimes what is thought of as love is merely the desire to possess, and thus it and hate become two sides of the same coin. Was it here, in this chapel, that Una told you of her love and her decision to leave the abbey? Did you then strike her down in your jealous rage? Her scream of terror as you struck was heard by Tanaí, who came rushing into the chapel . . . too late. He was not running to the abbot for sanctuary, but to tell the abbot what he had seen. You raised the alarm, denouncing Tanaí as the murderer, and the first person you told was Liag. The death of both Una and Tanaí are your responsibility, Ogán.'

The abbot stood, head bowed.

When he spoke it was in a dull, expressionless tone.

'Do you not think that I haven't wished for this moment over the years? I loved Una. Truly loved her. I was overcome with a mad rage that I instantly regretted. Once Duarcán's statuette had been placed here, I returned each night to seek her forgiveness . . .'

'Your contrition could have been more readily believed had you made this confession twenty years ago. I would place yourself in the hands of Brother Liag; prepare to answer for your crimes.'

Brother Liag was regarding the abbot in disgust.

'Some of us knew that you were secretly flagellating yourself before her statuette. Little did we realise you were merely as a dog, as the Book of Proverbs says; a dog returning to its own vomit. There is no pity for you.'

The Banshee

'For three days the Banshee had been heard wailing outside his door at night. It was no surprise when his body was discovered. His time had come.'

Sister Fidelma gazed at Brother Abán with surprise.

The elderly monk was sitting slightly forward on his chair, shivering a little although the day was not cold. His thin mouth trembled slightly; a fleck of spittle from one corner caught on the greying stubble of his unshaven chin. His pale eyes stood out in his bony, almost skeletal head over which the skin was stretched taut and parchment-like.

'He was fated to die,' repeated the old man, almost petulantly. 'You cannot deny the summons of the death wail.'

Fidelma realised that the old man was troubled and he spoke with deadly seriousness.

'Who heard this wailing?' she asked, trying to hide her natural scepticism.

The old man shivered.

'Glass, the miller, whose house is not far away. And Bláth has confirmed that she was disturbed by the sounds.'

Fidelma pursed her lips and expelled a little air through them in an almost soundless whistle.

'I will speak with them later. Tell me what you know about this matter, Brother Abán? Just those facts that are known to you.'

The elderly religieux sighed as if suppressing irritation.

'I thought that you knew them. Surely my message was clear?'

'I was told that a man had been found dead in suspicious circumstances. The messenger requested that the Chief Brehon of Cashel send a *dálaigh*, an officer of the court, to come and ascertain those

117

circumstances. That is all I know so far, except that this man was named Ernán, that he was a farmer, and that he was found dead on the doorstep of his house with a jagged wound in his throat.'

Fidelma spoke without irritation but in a precise manner.

'This is a peaceful spot.' Brother Abán was suddenly defensive. 'We are just a small farming community here by the banks of the Siúr river. Even nature bestows her blessings on us and that is why we call this place "the Field of Honey". Nothing like this has ever happened before.'

'It would help if I knew exactly what has happened,' murmured Fidelma. 'So, tell me what you know.'

'I am the only religious in this community,' went on Brother Abán, as if ignoring her request. 'I have been here forty years, tending to the spiritual needs of this little community. Never before . . .'

He fell silent a moment and Fidelma was forced to control her impatience and wait until the old man was ready to begin.

'The facts?' he suddenly asked, his bright eyes upon her. 'These are the facts. Yesterday morning I was at my morning prayers when Bláth came to my threshold, crying in a loud voice that Ernán had been found just outside the door of his house with his throat torn out. I went to his house and found this to be true. I then sent to Cashel for a *dálaigh*.'

'What was so suspicious about the circumstances that you needed to do so?'

Brother Abán nervously rubbed the stubble on his chin.

'Bláth told me . . .'

Fidelma held up a hand.

'First, tell me exactly who Ernán was?'

'Ernán was a young farmer who farmed the lower fields along the riverbank. A handsome young man, married and without an enemy in the world. I knew his parents before they died. Good Christians leading blameless lives.'

'And Bláth? Was she his wife?'

Brother Abán shook his head.

'Ernán's wife was Blinne. Bláth is her sister. She lived with them. She helps about the farm. A good girl. She comes to sing the psalms in the chapel each week.'

'And where was Blinne at this time?'

'Distraught. Beside herself with grief. She loved her husband very much.'

'I see. And Bláth told you . . . what?'

'Bláth said that she had been awoken on the last three nights hearing a terrible wailing outside the farmhouse.'

'Did she investigate the cause of this sound?'

The old monk laughed sarcastically.

'This is a rural community. We live close to nature here. You do not go to investigate the wailing of a Banshee.'

'Surely the New Faith has taught us not to be fearful of Otherworld creatures? As a Christian, do you really accept that there is a woman of the hills, a wraith, who comes to the threshold of a person about to die and then wails and laments in the middle of the night?' demanded Fidelma.

'As a Christian, I must. Do not the Holy Scriptures talk of the spirits and ghosts who serve both God and Satan? Who knows which the woman of the hills serves? In the old days, it was said that the Banshee was a goddess who cared for a specific noble family and when their time came to be reborn in the Otherworld, the spirit would cry to announce their impending death in this world.'

'I know the folklore,' Fidelma said quietly.

'It is not to be dismissed,' Brother Abán assured her earnestly. 'When I was a small boy I heard a story from a neighbour. It seems that the time had come for his father, an old man, to pass on. A plaintive wailing was heard within the vicinity of their dwelling. The son went out the next morning and found a strange comb, which he picked up and took into the house. The following night the wailing returned but this time the doors and windows rattled as if someone was trying to get in.

'Realising it was the Banshee the man placed the comb in a pair of tongs and held the comb out of the window. Unseen hands seized the comb and the tongs were twisted and bent out of recognition. Had he handed the comb out through the window, then his arm would have been wrenched off. That is the power of the Banshee.'

Fidelma dropped her gaze and tried to contain her smile. Obviously, Brother Abán was steeped in the old ways and superstitions.

'Let us return to the case of Ernán,' she suggested gently. 'Are you saying that his sister-in-law, Bláth, heard this wailing and did so on three consecutive nights?'

'The third night was when Ernán was found dead.'

'And Blinne had heard this wailing as well?'

'I only spoke to Glass the miller who confirmed that he had heard it also.'

'So you have not spoken to Blinne, Ernán's wife?'

'She has not been well enough to speak to me, as you can imagine.'

'Very well. Who discovered the body?'

'Bláth was up in the morning to milk the goats and found Ernán outside the house. He had been dead some hours. Bláth believes that . . .'

Fidelma held up her hand.

'I will see what she believes when I speak to her. At this point, she came to you?'

'That is right. I went to see the body while she went inside to comfort Blinne.'

'Where is the body now?'

'In the chapel. We shall bury it tonight.'

'I would like to examine this wound of which you speak.'

Brother Abán stirred uncomfortably.

'Is that necessary? After all, you are . . .'

'I am a *dálaigh* and used to such sights as the corpses of people who have died in violent ways.'

The old monk shrugged.

'It is not often that you would see the corpse of one who has been taken by the Banshee,' he muttered.

'Has there been much wolf activity in these parts recently?'

The question was innocent enough but Brother Abán realised what she was implying and he pulled a sour face.

'You will not be able to pass off this death as a wolf attack, Sister,' he said. 'I know the marks made by a wolf when it is driven to attack a human. A wolf rarely attacks a full-grown man, a strong and muscular man. And the wailing was certainly not that of a wolf. You will have to think again if you want to dismiss this death with a rational reason.'

'I want to find the truth, that is all,' Fidelma replied evenly. 'Now let us inspect the corpse.'

The old monk had been right that Ernán had been young and handsome in life. He was obviously well muscled and strong. The only disfigurement on his body was the jagged wound beneath his chin, which severed his windpipe and arteries. Fidelma bent forward and saw immediately that no teeth marks could have made the wound. It had been made by something sharp although it had been drawn across the throat, tearing the flesh rather than cutting cleanly.

She straightened up after her inspection.

'Well?' demanded the old man.

'Ernán was certainly attacked but not by some Otherworld entity,' she said softly.

She led the way out of the small chapel and stood in the sunshine looking down through the collection of buildings to where the broad expanse of river was pushing sedately along, glistening and flickering in the bright light. There were several dwellings clustered around including a blacksmith's forge and grain stores. The main part of the community dwelt in outlying farmsteads. There were very few people about. Most people would probably be in the fields at this time. However, the blacksmith stood deep in conversation with someone who stood with a thick-legged workhorse.

Fidelma saw the only other people in sight were a couple at the far end of the square who had just emerged round the corner of a storehouse. One was an attractive woman with auburn hair, young and pretty, and slim. Her companion was a young man, long-faced, intense.

Fidelma's keen eyes deduced that neither was happy. The young man was stretching out a hand to the woman's arm with an almost imploring gesture. The woman seemed irritable and knocked the hand away, turning swiftly and striding towards the chapel. The young man gazed after her for a moment then seemed to catch Fidelma's gaze. He suddenly walked rapidly away, disappearing behind the far building.

'Interesting,' muttered Fidelma. 'Who are they? The woman seems to be coming here.'

Brother Abán, standing at her shoulder, whispered: 'This is Blinne, the widow of Ernán.'

'And who was the young man with whom she seemed annoyed?'

'That was Tadhg. He is a . . . he is a bard.'

Fidelma's lower lip thrust out a moment in amusement at the disapproval in the old man's voice.

'That is appropriate.'

The name Tadhg meant a poet.

Brother Abán was already moving to greet the woman called Blinne.

'How are you, my child?'

'Only as can be expected,' Blinne replied shortly. Fidelma noticed that her face seemed an expressionless mask. Her lips were thinned in the set of her jaw. She had a tight control of her emotions. Her hazel eyes caught those of Sister Fidelma and her chin came up defiantly. 'I have come to see the body of Ernán one last time. And Bláth says that she will sing the *caoine*, the keening, at the interment.'

'Of course, my child, of course,' muttered the old monk. Then he remembered his manners. 'This is Sister Fidelma from Cashel. She is . . .'

'I know who she is,' replied the young woman coldly. 'She is sister to our king as well as being a *dálaigh*.'

'She has come to inquire into the death of your husband.'

Was there a slight blush on Blinne's cheek?

'So I have heard. The news is all round the community.'

'I am sorry for your troubles, Blinne,' Fidelma greeted her softly. 'When you have finished,' she nodded slightly to the chapel, 'I would like to ask you a few questions.'

'I understand.'

'I shall be at Brother Abán's dwelling.'

It was not long before Blinne came to Brother Abán's threshold.

Fidelma bade her be seated and turned to the old monk.

'I think that you said that you had something to attend to in the chapel?' she suggested pointedly.

'No, I . . .' Brother Abán caught her gaze and then nodded swiftly. 'Of course. I shall be there if you need me.'

After he had left, Fidelma took her seat opposite the attractive young woman.

'This must be distasteful to you, but your husband has died in suspicious circumstances. The law dictates that I must ask you certain questions.'

Blinne raised her chin defiantly.

'People are saying that he was taken by a Banshee.'

Fidelma regarded her thoughtfully.

'You sound as if you give that story no credence?'

122

'I have heard no wailing messengers of death. Ernán was killed but not by a ghostly visitation.'

'Yet, as I understand it, the wailing on three separate nights thrice awakened your own sister, who dwells with you. This wailing was heard by one of your neighbours.'

'As I said, I did not hear it nor was I awakened. If wailing there was, it was that of a wolf. He was killed by a wolf, that is obvious.'

Fidelma regarded her thoughtfully then she said: 'If it was obvious, then there would be no need for this inquiry. Tell me about Ernán. He was a farmer, handsome, and I am told he was well liked. Is that true?'

'True enough.'

'I am told that he had no enemies?'

Blinne shook her head but responded too quickly, so Fidelma thought.

'Are you sure about that?' pressed Fidelma.

'If you are trying to tell me that you suspect that he was murdered then I . . .'

'I am not trying, Blinne,' interrupted Fidelma firmly. 'I tell you facts. A wolf did not create the wound that caused his death. Now, are you saying that he had no enemies that you know of? Think carefully, think hard, before you reply.'

Blinne's face had become a tight mask.

'He had no enemies,' she said firmly.

Instinctively, Fidelma knew that she was lying.

'Did you love your husband?' she asked abruptly.

A red flush spread swiftly over her features.

'I loved him very much!' came the emphatic response.

'You had no problems between you? Nothing Ernán said that might have led you to think that he nurtured some problem and tried to hide it from you?'

Blinne was frowning suspiciously.

'It is the truth that I tell you when I say that there were no problems between us and that I loved him very much. Are you accusing me of . . . of murdering my own husband?'

Her voice rose sharply, vehemently.

Fidelma smiled disarmingly.

'Calm yourself. I am required to ask certain questions and must do so. It is facts I am after, not accusations.'

123

Blinne's mouth formed a thin line and she still stared belligerently at Fidelma.

'So,' Fidelma continued after a moment or two of silence, 'you are telling me that he had no problems, no enemies, that your relationship was good.'

'I have said as much.'

'Tell me what happened on the night that he died.'

Blinne shrugged.

'We went to bed as usual. When I awoke it was dawn and I heard Bláth screaming outside the house. I think that was what actually awoke me. I rushed out and found Bláth crouching on the threshold with Ernán's body. I cannot remember much after that. Bláth went for Brother Abán who is also the apothecary in the community. I know he came but could do nothing. It is all a blur.'

'Very well. Let me take you back to the time you went to bed. You say – "we went to bed"? Both of you at the same time?'

'Of course.'

'So, as far as you know, you both went to bed and fell asleep together?'

'I have said so.'

'You were not disturbed by Ernán getting up either in the night or at dawn?'

'I must have been very tired for I remember that I had been feeling sleepy after the evening meal and was almost asleep by the time I reached the bed. I think we have been working hard on the farm in recent days as I have been feeling increasingly tired.'

'You heard no disturbances during the night or during the previous nights?'

'None.'

Fidelma paused thoughtfully.

'How was your sleep last night?'

Blinne was scornful.

'How do you think? My husband had been killed yesterday. Do you think I slept at all last night?'

'I can understand that,' agreed Fidelma. 'Perhaps you should have had Brother Abán mix you a sleeping draught.'

Blinne sniffed.

'If there was need for that, I would not have needed to bother him.

My sister and I were raised knowing how to mix our own herbal remedies.'

'Of course. How do you feel now – physically, I mean?'

'As can be expected. I am not feeling well. I feel nauseous and have a headache.'

Fidelma smiled softly and rose. 'Then I have taxed you too long.'

Blinne followed her example.

'Where would I find your sister, Bláth?'

'I think she went to see Glass the miller.'

'Good, for I have need to see him as well.'

Blinne stood frowning at the door. 'You have been told that Glass is claiming that he heard this wailing in the night?'

'I have been told.'

Blinne extended her front teeth over her lower lip for a moment, pressing down hard.

'I did not hear any noises in the night. But . . .'

Fidelma waited. Then she prompted: 'But . . . ?'

'Could it have been true? Bláth said . . . people believe . . . I . . . I don't know what to believe. Many people believe in the Banshee.'

Fidelma reached out a hand and laid it on the young woman's arm.

'If the wailing woman of the hills exists, it is said her task is to be the harbinger of death, lamenting the passing of a soul from this world to the Otherworld. The belief is that the Banshee merely warns but is never the instrument of death. Whether you believe that, is your own affair. Personally, I believe that the Banshee – indeed, all the ghostly visitations that I have encountered – is merely visible manifestation of our own fears, fears whose images we cannot contain within the boundaries of our dreams.'

'And yet . . .'

'I tell you this, Blinne,' Fidelma interrupted in a cold voice, 'that your husband was killed neither by a Banshee, nor by an animal agency . . . A human hand killed him. Before this day is out, the culprit will stand before me.'

Brother Abán directed her along the path towards Glass's mill. The path ran alongside a small stream, which twisted itself down to feed the broad river, the Siúr. As she followed the path through a copse of birch trees she heard a strong masculine voice. It was raised in a recitation.

125

'No pleasure
that deed I did, tormenting her
tormenting her I treasure . . .'

Fidelma came upon a young man, sitting on a rock by the stream. He heard the snap of a twig beneath her feet and swung round, his face flushing crimson as if he had been caught in a guilty deed.

'Greetings, Tadhg,' Fidelma said, recognising him.

He frowned, the crimson on his cheeks deepening. 'You know me?'

Fidelma did not answer for that much was obvious.

'I am Sister . . .'

'Fidelma,' broke in the young man. 'News of your arrival has spread. We are a small community.'

'Of course. How well did you know Ernán?' she went on without further preamble.

The young man grimaced.

'I knew him,' he said defensively.

'That's not what I asked. I said, how well? I already presume that everyone in this community knew each other.'

Tadhg shrugged indifferently.

'We grew up together until I went to the bardic school, which has now been displaced by the monastery founded by Finnan the Leper.'

'The place called Finnan's Height? I knew of the old school there. When did you return here?'

'About a year ago.'

'And presumably you renewed your friendship with Ernán then?'

'I did not say that I was his friend, only that we grew up together, as most people here of my age did.'

'Does that mean that you did not like him?' Fidelma asked quickly.

'One does not have to like everyone one knows or grows up with.'

'There is truth in that. Why didn't you like him?'

The young man grimaced.

'He was arrogant and thought himself superior to . . . to . . .'

'A poet?' supplied Fidelma.

Tadhg looked quickly at her and then lowered his gaze as if in agreement.

'He was a farmer and thought strength and looks were everything.

He called me a weak parasite fit for nothing, not even to clean his pigsty. Most people knew how arrogant he was.'

'Yet I am told that Ernán was well liked and had no enemies in the world.'

'Then you were told wrong.'

'I was told by Blinne.'

'Blinne?' The young man's head jerked up and again came an uncontrollable rush of blood to his cheeks.

Fidelma made an intuitive leap forward.

'You like Blinne very much, don't you?'

There was a slightly sullen expression which now moulded the young poet's features.

'Did she tell you that? Well, we grew up together, too.'

'Nothing more than an old friendship?'

'What are you saying?'

'Saying? I am asking a question. If you disliked Ernán so much, you must surely not have approved of Blinne's being married to him.'

'You would soon find that out from anyone in the community,' admitted Tadhg sullenly. 'I do not deny it. Poor Blinne. She did not have the courage to leave him. He dominated her.'

'Are you saying that she did not love him?'

'How could she? He was a brute.'

'If she disliked the marriage, there are nine reasons in law why she could have divorced him and more why she could have separated from him.'

'I tell you that she did not have the courage. He was a powerful, controlling man and it is poetic justice that he was taken by the Banshee, whether you call it Banshee or wolf. That he was a beast and the stronger beast of the night attacked him and tore out his throat was poetic justice.'

The young man finished his speech with defiance.

'Poetic?' Fidelma gazed thoughtfully at him. 'Where were you the night before last? Where were you when Ernán was killed?'

'In my house. Asleep.'

'Where is your house?'

'Up on that hillside.' He raised an arm to gesture in the direction.

'Was anyone with you?'

127

The young man looked outraged.

'Of course not!'

'A pity,' Fidelma said softly.

'What do you mean?' Tadhg blinked, disconcerted.

'Just that I would like to eliminate you from the vicinity of Ernán's farmstead. He was murdered, his throat cut, and you have just given me a very good reason why you might be suspected of it.'

Now Tadhg's face was suddenly drained of blood.

'I was told that he had his throat ripped out,' he said quietly. 'I presumed that it was by a wolf, although many superstitious people are talking about the Banshee.'

'Who told you that this was how he died?'

'It is common talk. You say that he was murdered? How can you be so sure?'

Fidelma did not bother to answer.

'Well, I did not do it. I was in my bed, asleep.'

'If that is the truth then you have presented me with another suspect,' she said reflectively. 'Blinne.'

Tadhg swallowed rapidly.

'She would never . . . that is not possible. She had not enough courage to divorce Ernán. She was too gentle to strike him down.'

'Human beings react in peculiar ways. If not Blinne nor you, then who also had cause to hate Ernán – a man who was supposed to have no enemies?'

Tadgh raised his hands in a helpless, negative gesture.

'I will want to see you again later, Tadhg.'

Fidelma turned and resumed her progress along the path, her brow furrowed in thought.

Bláth had already left Glass's mill when Fidelma reached there.

The miller was a genial, round-faced man of middle age with twinkling grey-blue eyes, which might well have been the reason for his name which indicated such a colouring. He was a stocky man, clad with a leather apron and open shirt, his muscles bulging as he heaved a sack of flour on to a cart.

'A bad thing, Sister, a bad thing,' he said, when Fidelma introduced herself.

'You were a close neighbour of Ernán, I believe.'

The miller turned and pointed. From where they stood the ground

128

began to descend slightly towards the broad river across some fields to where an elm grove stood.

'That is Ernán's farmhouse, the building among those trees. We are scarcely ten minutes' walk away from each other.'

'And were you a friend of his?'

'I saw young Ernán grow to manhood. I was a friend of his father and mother. They were killed when Crundmáel of Laighin came raiding along the Siúr in his battle boats in search of booty. Only Ernán survived out of his entire family and so took over the farm and continued to make it prosperous. Blinne, his wife, is my niece.' He grinned briefly. 'So is Bláth, of course.'

'And Ernán was well liked?'

'Not an enemy in the world,' Glass replied immediately.

'He and Blinne were happy?'

'Never happier.'

'And Bláth lived with them?'

'She could have come here to live but Blinne and Bláth were always close. There is only a year between them and they are almost like twins. Blinne wanted her sister to be with her and Ernán did not mind for she helped with the farm work. But why do you ask me these questions?'

Fidelma did not answer.

'Tell me about the Banshee,' she said.

Glass smiled briefly.

'I heard the sound only too well.'

'When did you first hear it?'

'I would not want to hear that sound more than once.'

Fidelma frowned.

'You heard it once?'

'Yesterday morning about dawn.'

'Not before, not before the morning Ernán was found dead?'

'No. Only that one morning. That was enough. It wailed like a soul in torment.'

'What did you do?'

'Do? Nothing at all.'

'You weren't curious?'

'Such curiosity about the Banshee can endanger your immortal soul,' replied Glass solemnly.

'When did you realise that Ernán was dead?'

'When Brother Abán came to tell me and asked me if I had heard anything in the night.'

'And you were able to tell him that you had?'

'Of course.

'But only yesterday morning?'

Glass nodded.

'As a matter of interest, if Ernán was the only survivor of his family, I presume that his farm passes to Blinne?'

'Blinne is his heir in all things,' agreed Glass. His eyes suddenly flickered beyond her shoulder in the direction of what had been Ernán's farmstead. Fidelma turned and saw a figure that she initially thought was Blinne making her way up the hill. Then she realised it was a young woman who looked fairly similar.

'Bláth?'

Glass nodded.

'Then I shall go down to meet her as I need to ask her some questions.'

Halfway down the path were some large stones which made a natural seat. Fidelma reached them at the same time as Bláth and greeted her.

'I was coming back to my uncle's mill for Blinne told me that you had gone there in search of me. You are the *dálaigh* from Cashel, aren't you?'

'I am. There are a few questions that I must ask. You see, Bláth, I am not satisfied about the circumstances of your brother-in-law's death.'

Bláth, who was a younger version of the attractive Blinne, pouted.

'There is no satisfaction to be had in any death but a death that is encompassed by supernatural elements is beyond comprehension.'

'Are you sure we speak of supernatural elements?'

Bláth looked surprised. 'What else?'

'That is what I wish to determine. I am told that you heard the wailing of the Banshee for three nights?'

'That is so.'

'You awoke each night and investigated?'

'Investigated?' The girl laughed sharply. 'I know the old customs and turned over and buried my head under the pillow to escape the wailing sound.'

130

'It was loud?'

'It was fearful.'

'Yet it did not wake your sister or her husband?'

'It was supernatural. Perhaps only certain people could hear it? Glass, my uncle, heard it.'

'But only once.'

'Once is enough.'

'Very well. Were your sister and Ernán happy?'

Fidelma saw the shadow that passed across Bláth's face.

'Why, yes.' There was hesitation enough and Fidelma sniffed in annoyance.

'I think that you are not being accurate,' she responded. 'They were unhappy, weren't they?'

Bláth pressed her lips together and seemed about to deny it. Then she nodded.

'Blinne was trying to make the best of things. She was always like that. I would have divorced Ernán but she was not like that.'

'Everyone says that she and Ernán were much in love and happy.'

'It was the image that they presented to the village,' shrugged the girl. 'But what has this to do with the death of Ernán? The Banshee took him.'

Fidelma smiled thinly.

'Do you really believe that?'

'I heard . . .'

'Are you trying to protect Blinne?' Fidelma snapped sharply.

Bláth blinked rapidly and flushed.

'Tell me about Tadhg,' Fidelma prompted, again sharply so that the girl would not have time to collect her thoughts.

'You know . . . ?' Bláth began and then snapped her mouth shut.

'Did this unhappiness begin when Tadhg returned to the village?'

Bláth hung her head.

'I believe that they were meeting regularly in the woods,' she said quietly.

'I think that you believe a little more than that,' Fidelma said drily. 'You think that Tadhg and Blinne plotted to kill Ernán.'

'No!' Bláth's face was crimson. 'There was no reason. If things became so unbearable, Blinne could have sought a divorce.'

131

'True enough, but the farmstead was an attractive proposition. If Blinne divorced Ernán, she would lose it.'

Bláth sniffed. 'You know the laws of inheritance as well as I do. Land cannot pass to a female heir if there are male heirs.'

'But in Ernán's case, he had no male heirs. The land, the farmstead, would go to the *banchomarba*, the female heir.'

Bláth suddenly gave a deep sigh of resignation.

'I suspected something like this might happen,' she confessed dolefully.

'And you invented the story of the Banshee to throw people off the scent?' queried Fidelma.

Bláth nodded rapidly. 'I love my sister.'

'Why not claim an attack by a wolf? That would be more feasible.'

'Anyone would realise the wound in Ernán's throat was not the bite of a wolf. Questions would be asked of Blinne and . . .'

'Questions are now being asked.'

'But only by you. Brother Abán was satisfied and people here would not question the old ways.'

'The old ways.' Fidelma echoed the words thoughtfully.

The girl looked nervously at Fidelma.

'I suppose that you intend to have Blinne and Tadhg arrested?'

'Tonight is the funeral of Ernán. We will see after that.'

'There is some doubt about your suspicion of them?'

Fidelma smiled sadly.

'We will see,' she said. 'I would like a word alone with your sister.'

Bláth nodded towards the farmstead.

'I forgot something at my uncle's mill. You'll find Blinne at the farmhouse.'

The girl left Fidelma and continued up the path to the mill while Fidelma went on to the farmhouse. As she approached she heard Blinne's voice raised in agitation.

'It's not true, I tell you. Why do you bother me so?'

Fidelma halted at the corner of a building. In the farmyard she saw Tadhg confronting the girl. Blinne was standing looking distracted.

'The *dálaigh* already suspects,' Tadhg was saying.

'There is nothing to suspect.'

'It is obvious that Ernán was murdered, killed by a human hand.

Obvious that Bláth was covering up with some story about a Banshee. It did not fool me nor will it fool this woman. I know you hated Ernán. I know it is me that you really love. But surely there was no need to kill him? We could have eloped and you could have divorced him.'

Blinne was shaking her head in bewilderment.

'I don't know what you are saying. How can you say this . . .'

'I know. Do not try to fool with me. I know how you felt. The important thing is to flee from this place before the *dálaigh* can find the evidence. I can forgive you because I have loved you since you were a child. Come, let us take the horses and go now. We can let Bláth know where we have gone later. She can send us some money afterwards. I am sure the *dálaigh* suspects and will be here soon enough.'

With a thin smile Fidelma stepped from behind the building.

'Sooner than you think, Tadhg,' she said quietly.

The young man wheeled round, his hand going to the knife at his belt.

'Don't make it worse for yourself than it already is,' snapped Fidelma.

Tadhg hesitated a fraction and let his hand drop, his shoulders slumping in resignation.

Blinne was gazing at them in bewilderment.

'I don't understand this.'

Fidelma glanced at her sadly and then at Tadhg.

'Perhaps we can illuminate the situation?'

Blinne's eyes suddenly widened.

'Tadhg claimed that he has always loved me. When he came back from Finnan's Height he would waylay and annoy me like a sick dog, mooning after me. I told him that I didn't love him. Is it . . . it cannot be . . . did he . . . did he kill . . . ?'

Tadhg glanced at her, his face in anguish.

'You cannot reject me so, Blinne. Don't try to lay the blame for Ernán's death on me. I know you pretended that you did not love me in public but I had your messages. I know the truth. I told you to elope with me.'

His voice rose like a wailing child.

Blinne turned to Fidelma.

'I have no idea what he is saying. Make him stop. I cannot stand it.'

Fidelma was looking at Tadhg.

'You say that you had messages from Blinne? Written messages?'

He shook his head.

'Verbal but from an unimpeachable source. They were genuine right enough and now she denies me and tries to blame me for what has happened . . .'

Fidelma held up her hand to silence him.

'I think I know who gave you those messages,' she said quietly.

After the burial of Ernán, Fidelma sat on the opposite side of the fire to Brother Abán in the tiny stone house next to the chapel. They were sipping mulled wine.

'A sad story,' sighed Brother Abán. 'When you have seen someone born and grow up, it is sad to see them take a human life for no better reason than greed and envy.'

'Yet greed and envy are two of the great motivations for murder, Brother.'

'What made you suspect Bláth?'

'Had she said that she heard this Banshee wail once, it might have been more credible because she had a witness in her uncle who heard the wail. All those with whom I spoke, who claimed to have heard it, said they heard it once, like Glass, on the morning of Ernán's killing. The so-called Banshee only wailed once. It was an afterthought of Bláth but when she had killed her brother-in-law.'

'You mean that she was the one wailing?'

'I was sure of it when I heard that she had a good voice and, moreover, knew the *caoine*, the keening, the lament for the dead. I have heard the *caoine* and know it was a small step from producing that terrible sound to producing a wail associated with a Banshee.'

'But then she claimed she had done so to lay a false trail away from her sister. Why did you not believe that?'

'I had already been alerted that all was not well for when I asked Blinne about her sleep, I found that she had not even awoken when Ernán had risen in the morning. She slept oblivious of the world and woke in a befuddled state. She was nauseous and had a headache. Blinne admitted that both she and Bláth knew all about herbal remedies and could mix a potion to ensure sleep. Bláth had given her sister a strong sleeping draught so that she would not wake up. Only on the third night did an opportunity present itself for her to kill Ernán.

'Her intention all along was to lay the blame at her sister's door but she had to be very careful about it. She had been planning this for some time. She knew that Tadhg was besotted by Blinne. She began to tell Tadhg an invented story about how Blinne and Ernán did not get on. She told Tadhg that Blinne was really in love with him but could not admit it in public. She hoped that Tadhg would tell someone and thus sow the seeds about Blinne's possible motive for murder.'

Brother Abán shook his head sadly.

'You are describing a devious mind.'

'To set out to paint another as guilty for one's own acts requires a clever but warped mind. Bláth was certainly that.'

'But what I do not understand is why – why did she do this?'

'The oldest motives in the world – as we have said. Greed and envy.'

'How so?'

'She knew that Ernán had no male heirs and so on his death his land, under the law of the *banchomarba*, would go to Blinne. And Bláth stood as Blinne's *banchomarba*. Once Blinne was convicted of her husband's death then she would lose that right and so the farm and land would come to Bláth, making her a rich woman.'

Fidelma put down her empty glass and rose.

'The moon is up. I shall use its light to return to Cashel.'

'You will not stay until dawn? Night is fraught with dangers.'

'Only of our own making. Night is when things come alive and is the mother of counsels. My mentor, Brehon Morann, says that the dead of night is when wisdom ascends with the stars to the zenith of thought and all things are seen. Night is the quiet time for contemplation.'

They stood on the threshold of Brother Abán's house.

Fidelma's horse had been brought to the door. Just as Fidelma was about to mount a strange, eerie wailing sound echoed out of the valley. It rose, shrill and clear against the night sky, rose and ended abruptly, rose again and this time died away. It was like the *caoine*, the keening sounds that accompanied the dead.

Brother Abán crossed himself quickly.

'The Banshee!' he whispered.

Fidelma smiled.

'To each their own interpretation. I hear only the lonely cry of a wolf searching for a mate. Yet I will concede that for each act there is a consequence. Bláth conjured the Banshee to mark her crime and perhaps the Banshee is having the last word.'

She mounted her horse, raised her hand in salute and turned along the moonlit road towards Cashel.

The Heir Apparent

'There's bound to be trouble. Mark my words!'

Brehon Declan was gloomy with pessimism as he and Sister Fidelma walked slowly across the main courtyard of the rath of Cúan, chieftain of the Uí Liatháin, towards the great feasting hall. Already many others were moving through the darkening twilight in the same direction.

'I don't understand,' replied Fidelma. She had been on her way to the abbey at Ard Mór on the coast. Her route lay through the territory of the Uí Liatháin, one of the larger and more influential clans of the kingdom of Muman, and she had decided to visit her old colleague, Declan. He had been a fellow student at the law school of the Brehon Morann. On her arrival at the rath, or fortress, of the Uí Liatháin, she found a state of great agitation and excitement. The heir apparent of the chief had been injured and died in a stag hunt and, having mourned for the prescribed time, the clan was about to elect a new *tánaiste*, who would be successor to the chief. 'I don't understand,' repeated Fidelma. 'Is it that the chief's nominee for the office, Talamnach, is so unpopular that he will be opposed?'

Declan, a dark, saturnine man, eased his lean features into a thin smile and shook his head.

'You must know that the choosing of a *tánaiste*, an heir apparent, to the chieftain, can be a problematic business. At least three generations of the ruling family must meet in conclave and cast their votes for who should be the successor. There are always going to be factions and what suits one group will not suit another, even though they are part of the same family.'

Fidelma sniffed in disapproval.

'Even Cicero centuries ago wrote of the *bellum domesticum* – the strife of families. It is nothing new.'

'That is certainly true,' admitted Declan, 'but the strife within Cúan's family is particularly vicious now that he has named his nephew Talamnach as his nominee for successor.'

'Why so?'

'Firstly, Cúan's own son, Augaire, is unhappy to say the least. He is nineteen years old but, with youthful arrogance, he was expecting to be nominated. So, too, was his mother, Berrach – I mean that she was expecting her son to be nominated and, so it is said, she has made her displeasure known to her husband.'

'It is not unusual for a mother to have ambition for her child.'

'Berrach is more than tenacious for her son's future. She dotes on him and panders to his every wish. Now he has outgrown her and nothing will ever bring him to discipline.'

Fidelma smiled softly.

'Remember what Aristotle wrote? That the reason why mothers are more devoted to their children and have more ambition for them than their fathers is that they have suffered more in giving them birth and are more certain that they are their own.'

Declan pulled a face.

'It is true that Augaire is more akin to Berrach than Cúan and therein is the reason why Cúan has nominated Talamnach instead. Augaire lacks modesty, he is quick to anger and slow to forgive. A hint of any insult will have him reaching for his dagger. He is an immature youth, vain, pretentious and unable to withstand any hint of criticism. That is why he is unfit to be the heir apparent to the chieftain of the Uí Liatháin. I can say that with authority as his cousin.'

Fidelma stared at Declan's animated features for a moment as he finished his vehement declaration.

'So you also have a vote in the *derbhfine*?'

He shrugged and suddenly smiled.

'I beg your pardon, Fidelma. In expressing my prejudice I overstep the bounds of my calling which is to be at my chief's side and see that the proper forms are observed for the meeting of the *derbfine* of the chief, the electoral college to proclaim who is next heir apparent. I am technically of the *derbhfine* but, as Brehon, I shall abstain in the vote.'

'Well, we cannot help being human, Declan. We cannot pretend that we do not have feelings. What is important is that we, as members of the legal profession, must subordinate our feelings so that the law is followed and the views of the *derbhfine* are made plain and carried through.'

Declan inclined his head.

'Have no fear on that score. But I am sure that Augaire and his mother are up to something. And then there is Selbach.'

Fidelma paused for a moment or two and then prompted: 'Who is Selbach?'

'My uncle. He is Cúan's own younger brother but has disapproved of his brother for many years. He so disapproved of some of Cúan's methods that he took ship ten years ago and went to rule the Uí Liatháin community that lives across the seas in the kingdom of Kernow. Now he has returned with the expectation that his supporters will name him as heir apparent. He has made a fortune abroad and now struts about like a turkey-cock, all dressed up in those clothes rich and fashionable Britons wear with their new-fangled Roman style pockets.'

Fidelma's eyes widened slightly at his ardour.

'You say that he has expectations that his supporters will name him heir apparent. How valid are such expectations?'

'There are some cousins who would support him. Probably only a small group. But the majority are for Talamnach. But the trouble that will arise at the meeting, and the trouble that I fear, is the plotting and planning.'

'You would say that Talamnach is a good choice as heir apparent?'

'Undoubtedly. He has all the qualities. He has even studied law . . .'

'If that is a recommendation,' smiled Fidelma mischievously.

Declan was serious. 'He is temperate in all things. A good judge. A good negotiator and, above all, he keeps the interest of all the people in mind, not just certain influential sections of the people.'

'He sounds a paragon,' observed Fidelma drily.

They had reached the great hall of Cúan and people, recognising Declan in the glow from the torches that lit the entrance, began to greet him and Fidelma. They were all relatives of Cúan the chief and formed the *derbhfine* who were to elect from their number the heir apparent to the chieftainship who would take over when Cúan resigned or died in office. Chiefs, provincial kings and even the High King might die after a lifetime in office. Many times, however, they simply retired. Sometimes, when they had not promoted the commonwealth of their people, the same *derbhfine* who elected them to office would meet and strip them of their rank and confirm the heir apparent as new chief, king or High King.

Declan had guided her to a seat among the rows of witnesses. These were the religious, lawyers and historians who were not part of the *derhbfine* but who were the observers of the event and bore witness to the legality of its proceedings. Declan left her, as he had to see about the preparations, exiting the hall through a side door.

The great hall, lit by flickering torches and lamps, smoky and hot, seemed packed. There were at least three generations of Cúan's family there, predominantly the male members. There were several women there, it was true, and prominent among them, seated to one side, was a tall, austere woman, with a sharp face and dark eyes. Fidelma had already met Berrach, who had come from the neighbouring clan of the Déices. She was attending out of courtesy, not because she had any public voice in the election of an heir to her husband, for a woman belonged to the *derbhfine* of her father and not of her husband.

It was rare that a woman was elected to chieftainship or kingship. This was not because women were excluded from office, because the law gave equal status to women. In fact, only one woman had ever become High King of the five kingdoms of Éireann. Fidelma learned this from the ancient king lists. But there were several tribes who elected women not only as chieftains but as military leaders. The female heir apparent, the *banchomarba*, appeared usually when there was no acceptable male heir. Because the social system was based on the clan, female succession might lead to the alienation of the title and lands of the clan by marriage with people from another clan.

Fidelma knew that the Cáin Lánamna law text stipulated that the inheritance of a title or office, and especially inheritance of land, could only be used for the life of the female and then it had to revert to her father's family. Any movable property could go to her husband and children even if outside the clan but land had to remain within the clan. This was so that the clan could protect its chieftainship and its territory. A female chief or king could not, therefore, nominate one of her own children as heir apparent to her title as it had to remain with her father's *derbhfine*. It was not so long ago, Fidelma recalled, that the Brehon Sencha Mac Ailella had given a wrongful judgement on female rights regarding this very matter and a female Brehon, Brígh Briugaid, had, on appeal, corrected it.

Fidelma suddenly awoke from her reverie to find that Declan had entered the hall and was making his way across to where a group of the more elderly of the *derbhfine* was seated. He looked serious and paused before one man, who stood up to speak to him face to face. Even at the angle from which she was observing, Fidelma could see that he was remarkably like Cúan, except that he was younger and bore deep lines on his face and had a weather-beaten look. The exchange, which Fidelma could not hear, appeared to be curt and hardly one of friendship. Declan then turned, and seemed to trip and stumble, colliding with the man. He caught himself and obviously apologised without enthusiasm before leaving the hall again.

A moment later Declan reappeared leading into the hall Cúan, the chief of the Uí Liatháin. The stocky, red-bearded chieftain took his seat. At his right hand side sat the handsome young man she knew to be Talamnach, smiling and looking confident. An attendant, following them, brought in two mugs of mead and placed them on a table standing between the chief and his nominee. Fidelma glanced to where Berrach was sitting. The woman was scowling but staring straight ahead. Nearby she noticed Berrach's son Augaire was sprawled in his seat. He was about nineteen and Fidelma could see how Declan's description of him as a weak, indolent youth seemed apt. He seemed totally uninterested in the proceedings.

Declan, as Cúan's Brehon and adviser, had taken his place standing at the chief's side and began to call for order.

'The matter that brings us here today is a simple one. It is to elect the heir apparent to Cúan, chief of the Uí Liatháin.' He turned to Cúan. 'Is there a nominee?'

The chief rose from his seat.

'I nominate, as my successor, Talamnach,' he announced and reseated himself.

'Does Talamnach accept this nomination?'

The young man rose and smiled.

'I do.'

'Is there any here that will speak out against Talamnach?' intoned Declan in formal manner, still following the ancient ritual.

'There is!'

All eyes turned to the elderly man who had risen in the hall. Fidelma realised it was the man seated next to the one whom Declan had spoken to earlier. Fidelma suppressed a smile. Declan had obviously been making sure that there were no surprises by ensuring that he had foreknowledge of them. He had always been like that even at the college run by the Brehon Morann where they had both studied for eight years. Indeed, some fellow students had whispered that Declan was too fond of making sure he knew the answers before the questions were asked. She shook her head and turned to listen to the man who had risen.

'I am Illan of Cluain Mult, cousin to Cúan and to his brother Bressal, father of Talamnach, and to their brother Selbach. I claim, as member of the first generation of this *derbhfine*, the right of challenge.'

There was no surprise expressed by either Cúan or Talamnach, who continued smiling though somewhat fixed in expression. Nor was there any consternation among those gathered. It was clear that this was the 'trouble' that Brehon Declan had prophesied and which everyone was expecting.

'State your challenge, Illan of Cluain Mult,' intoned Declan in almost a monotone.

'My challenge is that there is one among us who is more fitted to be the heir apparent, one who is filled with wisdom, who has travelled beyond our borders and seen the ways of other peoples. He has returned from his self-imposed exile among those of our people who migrated in recent centuries to the land called Kernow, settling there as our cousins, the Déices, did when they sailed to the kingdom of Dyfed. He brings temperance, knowledge and wisdom.'

'And his name?'

'His name is well known among us for it is my cousin, brother to Cúan – the man I nominate is Selbach. He sits at my side.'

'Stand, Selbach, and say if you accept the nomination.'

The elderly man to whom Declan had earlier spoken now stood.

'I do.'

Brehon Declan stood for a moment looking at the silent audience in the hall.

'Is there any other challenge or nomination?'

Fidelma saw that he was glancing towards the group surrounding

142

Augaire. They were young men, arrogant, whose glances showed that they were taking their cue from Augaire. Fidelma saw Augaire frown at his companions and shake his head quickly.

'If none,' went on Declan, 'then we must proceed with the debate on the rival nominees.'

There was a silence.

'It behoves each nominee to make statements on their merits and attitudes for being considered,' Declan announced. 'We must start with the first nominee, Talamnach, for he has been chosen by Cúan, our chief.'

Talamnach rose slowly. He still wore his smile of confidence.

'You all know me and must judge of yourselves what my merits are. You know that they satisfy our great chief, Cúan. The test of a great leader, as Cúan undoubtedly is, is that he leaves behind him an heir who has the determination and ability to continue his achievements. I believe that I am such an heir. Cúan commanded wisely and was, therefore, obeyed cheerfully. He had no need to lead but was content to point the way – and in that fact lay the greatness of his leadership. But he always accepted the responsibility in all things – he would say "I am in error"; he would never say "my followers were in error" – that, again, is the mark of great leadership . . .'

Fidelma listened to the young man with a certain degree of admiration for his oratory for not once had he, so far, sung his own praises as to his ability. Yet in praising the ability of the man who had nominated him, Talamnach was winning the hearts and minds of the *derbhfine*.

'I have watched Cúan deal with many difficult problems. That is the responsibility of being a chief for only difficult problems are laid before the chief. If problems were easy to resolve then someone else would have already resolved them.'

Talamnach paused to cough, as it was clear his throat had become dry from the acrid atmosphere put out by the burning brand torches that lit the great hall.

He turned to pick up one of the small mugs of mead and sipped it before turning back to the *derbhfine*.

'I say this, that I would . . . I would . . .' He paused and coughed again. His smile became a frown and then an expression of agony. He took a sudden step forward, hand outstretched, and then, with a croaking sound in his throat, he pitched headlong on to the floor.

Consternation arose suddenly among the people. Most were on their feet, shouting and moving about in agitation.

Fidelma rose, too, hearing Declan calling for an apothecary. She began to push her way through the crowd, finally emerging to see Declan and another man bending over Talamnach. The second man was shaking his head. Declan glanced up and saw Fidelma and gave an angry grimace.

'He is dead,' he said angrily. 'Did I not warn that there would be trouble?'

Fidelma pushed her way to the pottery mug which Talamnach had just drunk from, and placed a fingertip in it. Holding it to her nose, she sniffed. Then she repeated this action with the mug nearer to Cúan.

She turned swiftly back to Declan.

'No one must drink from these mugs. It is *tre luib eccineol*,' she said sharply. 'I recognise its odour. He has been poisoned.'

Declan was looking shocked.

'Are you sure?' he demanded. *Tre luib eccineol* was a deadly herb. It was said that the herb's being introduced in his food had murdered the satirist Cridenbél. The look that she gave him was enough for him not to question her further.

'Everyone, everyone return to your seats. No one is to leave the hall,' Declan was shouting. Warriors were called from outside the hall to stand guard at the doors and while people were still milling around looking bewildered, Declan had ordered the attendant who had brought in the mead to be seized and escorted back to the hall.

Cúan was seated in his chair, looking stunned. Fidelma glanced quickly round. The crowd around Selbach was huddled together and talking animatedly among themselves. Augaire was sprawled in his seat now wearing a supercilious smile as if something amusing had happened although his companions looked shocked and nervous. Only Berrach, the wife of Cúan, had not changed her expression, which was one of total detachment and disinterest.

Declan stepped forward, hand raised to still the muttering of the *derbhfine*.

The body of Talamnach lay sprawled before him.

'Talamnach has been poisoned, murdered before our eyes,' he announced. 'If we need look for a motive, we should remind ourselves as to why we are gathered here.'

Several people now turned their suspicious gaze towards Selbach. The man rose from his seat.

'I object!'

'To what do you object, Selbach?' inquired Declan blandly.

'Why . . . why, to your implication!' spluttered the man indignantly.

'I have implied nothing. I have indicated a motive, that is all. I have sent for the attendant who brought in the poisoned mead. It is fortunate that we have among us Sister Fidelma, Fidelma of Cashel, whom most of you know by reputation as a *dálaigh*, an advocate of the courts. That she is sister to our king, Colgú, makes her well placed to sit in judgement on the Uí Liatháin. I will ask her to assist me in resolving this crime.'

He glanced towards Fidelma as if seeking her permission and she hesitated only for a moment before acknowledging her acceptance.

'Is the attendant who brought in this poison apprehended?' demanded Declan of one of the warriors.

'He is,' the man said.

'Bring him forth.'

The attendant was an elderly man, white-haired, and as he was pushed, none too gently, before the assembly, he looked understandably bewildered and frightened. He seemed to be shivering in fear.

'Well, Muirecán, things look bad for you,' Declan declared, his tone threatening.

Fidelma frowned in disapproval. It was not the way she would examine a suspect. She moved forward and touched Declan's arm gently.

'As you have invited me to assist you, perhaps I might question this man?'

Declan glanced at her in surprise and then shrugged.

'By all means.'

Fidelma turned on the ageing servant and smiled reassuringly.

'Your name is Muirecán, I believe?'

'It is.'

'How long have you been in service to the chief?'

'Ten years to Cúan, lady, and twenty-three years to his father, Cú Chongelt, who was chief before him.' The man was holding his shaking hands clasped tightly before him. He was glancing from side to side, like some animal seeking a means of escape.

145

'There is no need to worry, Muirecán, provided you tell us the truth,' Fidelma said gently.

The man nodded quickly.

'I swear it on the Holy Cross, lady. I will tell the truth.'

'You brought in the mead to this hall. We all saw you do that.'

'I did. I don't deny that. But I did not know it was poisoned.'

'So tell us how you came to bring in the mead. Did you draw the mead yourself?'

'I did. From the large barrel in the kitchen.'

'A new barrel?'

He shook his head.

'It is half full and many a drink has been served from it.'

'Who instructed you to draw the mead and bring it into the hall?'

The man looked blank and shook his head.

'No one, lady. It is the custom of Cúan and his *tánaiste* to have a drink placed at their side during any official meeting in the great hall.'

Fidelma glanced to the still shocked and numbed-looking chieftain and had to prompt him for confirmation. He eventually nodded in agreement.

'It was the custom,' he echoed hollowly.

'And everyone knew of this custom?' she asked, turning back to the attendant.

'Everyone,' affirmed Muirecán.

Fidelma was silent for a moment and then smiled encouragingly.

'So let us continue. You drew the two mugs of mead and placed them on the tray. Did you come straight into the hall?'

Muirecán shook his head.

'I did not. I came straight from the kitchen to the antechamber outside and there I found that Cúan had not arrived yet. So I put down the mead on a table that is there . . .'

'Was anyone in the antechamber?'

'The Brehon,' he nodded to Declan, 'my lady Berrach, the wife of Cúan, the chief's son Augaire, and the chief's brother, Selbach . . . oh, and Talamnach entered shortly afterwards.'

'And so you stood by the tray awaiting the arrival of the chief?'

Muirecán shook his head.

'Talamnach asked me to go to Cúan's quarters and warn him that everyone was waiting. The Brehon was with Talamnach at the time and had been speaking with him when Talamnach gave me the order.'

Fidelma glanced at Declan who nodded.

'It is true. I went to the antechamber and found it as this man has described. I spoke to Talamnach and mentioned that everyone was ready and suggested that the servant be sent in search of Cúan.'

The chief of the Uí Liatháin suddenly leaned forward and spoke, recovering something of his equilibrium.

'I can confirm that Muirecán came to my chamber and warned me that everything was prepared and awaiting my presence. He accompanied me back to the antechamber where Declan and Talamnach were awaiting me.'

Fidelma raised her head sharply.

'Only Declan and Talamnach were in the room? In what order did the others leave?'

From the hall the elderly man, Selbach, stood up.

'I left first, lady. I had hoped to have a word with my brother before he came to preside here and forewarn him about my protest. But with Talamnach there and my brother's wife and son, it seemed a pointless exercise to seek privacy with my brother. So I left and came into the hall.'

There was a soft bark of laughter. It came from Augaire.

Fidelma swung round and examined the young man.

Augaire was still sprawling in his seat, his expression seeming to indicate that he was bored with the proceedings. His face was still masked in a supercilious smile.

'And when did you leave the anteroom?' Fidelma asked in a deceptively pleasant tone.

Augaire did not alter his position.

'After him,' he drawled, nodding his head to Selbach.

There was a sharp cough.

'If I may be allowed a voice . . . ?'

Fidelma turned to the haughty-looking Berrach.

'No woman outside the *derbhfine* can speak, Mother,' interrupted Augaire in a sneering tone.

Fidelma smiled quickly.

'But this is no longer a *derbhfine* meeting but a legal investigation. Berrach, you have the right to speak.'

147

Berrach inclined her head towards Fidelma for a moment.

'My son and I left the antechamber a moment or so after Selbach. I had noticed that Selbach was having a word with Talamnach and I am unsure what passed between them. But I know that Talamnach left the room but not to come into the hall. After which, Selbach waited a while and then left. Then Augaire and I left to enter this hall. That is all I have to say.'

'And all this while the mugs of mead remained on the table in the antechamber?'

Augaire chuckled softly.

'That is obvious, even for a *dálaigh* to deduce.'

Fidelma's features did not alter as she turned to face him.

'In all matters of observation, young man,' she added emphasis on the 'young' which made the youth flush for he obviously prided himself on his manhood, 'in all matters of observation, people often see only what they are prepared to see, so nothing should be deemed obvious without confirmation.'

She suddenly turned back to Declan.

'You have just been placed alone in the antechamber with the mead.'

Brehon Declan stared at her a moment and then smiled broadly.

'Not exactly. Talamnach had returned by the time Augaire and his mother were leaving.'

'So you were not alone there.'

'In fact,' Declan said thoughtfully, 'Talamnach himself was alone because shortly after he re-entered, I went out to see if I could see if Cúan was approaching.'

'And do you suggest that Talamnach took the opportunity to poison his own mead?' Fidelma smiled thinly.

'Maybe the mead was meant for my father.' Augaire's sneering tone came again. 'My guess is the poor fool mixed up the mugs and drank from the one which he meant my father to drink out of.'

Fidelma looked at him in exasperation.

'We have spoken of observation. I would suggest that you spend time in developing the art, Augaire. Had you been observant, you would have noticed that I tested both mugs. Both were laced with poison. I suspect the person who did this was not particular as to whether Cúan or Talamnach died. Perhaps they hoped they both would.'

There was a sudden hush in the great hall.

Fidelma looked towards Selbach.

'You were talking to Talamnach and then he left the room. Is that a correct observation?'

Selbach thought for a moment.

'It is correct.'

'What did you speak to Talamnach about?'

Selbach grinned wryly.

'There was one matter preoccupying us. That is the reason why we gathered here tonight. I told Talamnach that Illan would challenge him and nominate me. I wondered if we might reach a compromise in order to keep our family together. He laughed at the idea. He was confident of overwhelming support.'

'How confident were you, Selbach?' intervened Declan, speaking after some time of silence.

'I would not have allowed myself to be named as a nominee if I was not assured of support.'

'And now it seems that you are the only surviving candidate,' sneered Declan.

Selbach flushed.

'Again you seem to imply something, cousin Brehon. Do you have the courage to be honest in your accusation?'

Declan took a step forward.

'You have come back from exile – albeit a self-imposed one, because you did not agree with the way your brother Cúan ruled. You abrogated your responsibility in this clan and now, seeing a chance for power, you return. You seek office. The question is just how ambitious are you for that office and what are you prepared to do in order to obtain it?'

Selbach was red with anger now and only Illan, at his side, restrained him from coming forward.

'Declan!' Fidelma was quietly outraged by her former colleague's behaviour. 'This is not the way for a Brehon to conduct himself.'

Declan stood still for some moments, his mouth thin in a tight expression. Then he relaxed.

'I apologise, Fidelma.' He turned and smiled, although it was a smile without any warmth. 'I suppose that I am not a very good Brehon. But this is also a family matter and my cousin, Talamnach, lies dead on the ground.'

Fidelma nodded.

'This is why I must conduct the rest of this inquiry. You are too close to it and not detached in your judgement.'

Declan compressed his lips for a second and then shrugged.

'Carry on.' The Brehon walked to the vacant seat left by Talamnach and sat down in an attitude of expectancy.

Fidelma turned to the chief. 'I think, at this stage, and with your permission, Cúan, your warriors might remove the body of Talamnach.'

The chief turned to one of the warriors and indicated this should be so.

The people in the hall were getting restless.

'Selbach, a few more questions, if I may,' she began again. 'I am intrigued. There is only one office open for this *derbhfine* to vote on. What compromise did you seek with Talamnach?'

'I suggested to him that if he stand down in favour of my nomination, when I am chief he would be my chosen heir apparent.'

There was an audible gasp from some sections of the hall.

Cúan's face was creased in anger.

'Do you expect my departure so soon, brother?' he said menacingly. 'You are younger than I am by merely one year. When did you expect to become chief if you had been elected my heir?'

Selbach was not abashed.

'I have not heard that age debarred a person from office, brother,' he retorted.

Declan's voice was accusing but he remained seated.

'It is true, Selbach. But I think many here will draw conclusions.'

Fidelma wheeled round in annoyance.

'The only conclusion to be drawn here will be when we have the facts and can conclude the truth. At the moment, Selbach has been open in his opinions when it might best have served his purpose had he not been so. What made Talamnach leave the chamber?' she suddenly asked, turning back to Selbach.

The chief's brother shrugged.

'No great mystery, I am afraid. Nothing more sinister than the call of nature. However, it was clear that he would not entertain my compromise and so I left. As I said, at the time Augaire and his mother and our cousin the Brehon were left in the room.'

'Had you noticed the mead?'

'Oh yes. When the servant, Muirecán, put it on the table, young Augaire went to grab one of the mugs.'

Fidelma's eyebrows lifted slightly.

'Did he drink?'

'Thanks be to God, I did not!' roared Augaire, his laughter echoed by his friends. 'I think even your observation will show that I still live, *dálaigh*.'

'It is a moot point whether your existence has life in it, young man,' snapped Fidelma. 'It strikes me that it has more of dissoluteness than real life. However, you seem certain that the mead was already poisoned when it was placed on the table in the antechamber. Can you share your knowledge with us? How did you know it was poisoned?'

Augaire flushed angrily.

'I did not know. I . . . I assumed.'

Fidelma smiled cynically.

'Ah, assumption? Only a short time ago, we had your attempts at conjecture, did we not?' Then sharply: 'Why did you not drink the mead if you took up the mug?'

'I stopped him,' came Berrach's firm tone.

Fidelma swung round on her.

'For what reason?'

The woman still bore her expressionless face. She did not even bother to look at Fidelma.

'The reason is simple enough. The mead was there as was normal practice to be carried in for the use of my husband and his *tánaiste*. Also . . .'

'Also?' prompted Fidelma when she paused.

'Also, my son had, in my opinion, drunk too much already before coming to this *derbhfine*.'

Augaire gave an angry hiss, which Fidelma ignored.

'Thank you for your honesty, Berrach,' she said softly. 'It is hard to acknowledge the faults of one's offspring.'

Augaire had stood up with two or three of his young friends and they were moving towards the door.

'Stop!' cried Fidelma. 'You have no permission to leave.'

Augaire glanced back mockingly.

'You have no authority in this place, woman of Cashel,' he sneered. 'You can resume your cackling to others but I am a chief's son and will do what I like. No woman who hides behind religious robes will tell me what to do.'

He turned and urged his companions to leave with him.

'Warriors! Stop them!'

It was Cúan's sharp voice that echoed through the hall. Two of his warriors came forward and barred the young men's path. The chief was shaking with rage.

'That my own son shames me thus!' he growled. 'You and your sycophants will return to your seats and will not leave until you have permission. Had you concentrated on your education you would know that the powers of a *dálaigh*, and the powers of the sister of our king, Colgú of Cashel, are not to be challenged lightly. Your ignorance puts shame not only on me as chief, but on our family, on our clan. That display of ignorance is demonstration of why you will never be elected as chief nor will you ever be able to aspire to any office. You are worthless!'

The silence in the hall was deathly. Augaire and his youthful companions returned to sit in white-faced silence as Cúan rebuked them.

'Fidelma of Cashel, accept my apologies. I know that apologies are not enough for this insult to your office. We stand ready to pay the fine.'

Fidelma nodded gravely.

'Let Augaire rise from his seat and face me.'

The young man hesitated, bringing forth the sharp cry 'Augaire!' from his father. Augaire rose to his feet, sullen and defiant.

'Know this, young man, and spread light in the darkness of your ignorance. Insult is regarded with the utmost seriousness in our law. I am now talking about insult to office, for I am a *dálaigh*, conducting a murder inquiry. In that respect, even a king has to accept that I take precedence in the procedure. The law text called the Bretha Nemed Déidenach is quite clear on the ways of insulting people and the penalties that are incurred. Any offence relating to insult requires the payment of the honour price of the person insulted.'

'Lady,' the cry was wrung from Berrach, 'the boy does not have such a sum. You are sister to the king and also a *dálaigh* of renown. That means your honour price is at least seven *cumals*, the value of twenty-one milch cows. I know that the law then says if he does not or cannot pay he must lose all rights and freedoms until he works to gain sufficient in order to pay the honour price. He will become a servant without honour or land. Is there no other way? No other way?'

Augaire had gone pale as he listened to his mother's plea, perhaps realising for the first time the magnitude of his offence.

Fidelma stood thoughtful for a moment.

'The offence cannot be ignored, for it is written in the law that the king or chieftain who tolerates insult must themselves lose their honour price,' she said. 'The boy may be immature and stupid but he is two years older than the "age of choice" and should know right from wrong. However, there is a way in which the boy himself may reduce the penalty. Sincere apology made in the presence of those who were also present when the insult was made may reduce the proscribed fine.'

'He will apologise, lady,' Berrach said, moving anxiously forward, but Fidelma held up her hand.

'An apology made while the blood is still tempered and there still exists anger is not valid. Augaire has been forced to return, to stand, and there he is, brooding and sullen. But knowing the penalty, he will say words without meaning. Let him sit down and wait for this hearing to end. Let him think of his responsibility, for the three young men whom he led from this place did not know what they were doing but followed him out of misguided loyalty. Therefore, the penalty is his, not theirs. Let others advise him of the law and the fines and why our law denounces insults so strongly. Then let us all return at noon tomorrow and hear whether he truly understands and truly repents.'

Cúan nodded quickly.

'It shall be as you say, Fidelma, and we thank you for your justice and your wisdom. Sit down, Augaire, and do not let me hear from you again unless you are asked a specific question by the *dálaigh*. Then you may answer with respect.'

Fidelma turned back to those gathered in the hall.

'I do not think we need to detain you much longer. The facts of this murder are becoming clearer.'

That caught their attention.

Brehon Declan was nodding.

'We are agreed on that, Fidelma,' he said. 'One person benefits from this and one person had the opportunity.'

Fidelma glanced at him. 'Broadly speaking, there is no disagreement in that. But can that person be identified?'

'Well, I think it is easy,' replied Declan confidently.

Fidelma looked towards Muirecán the attendant.

'Surely Muirecán had the opportunity to poison the mead?'

The elderly servant groaned and swayed.

'I did not, I did not,' he almost whimpered.

'Of course he did not,' affirmed Declan. 'The poor man's only involvement was to draw the mead from the barrel and bring it to the antechamber where his guilt lay in leaving it unattended for the murderer to slip in the contents of the phial of poison.'

'Very well, Declan. Let us examine first the motive. Remember what our old mentor, Brehon Morann, used to say? That in such cases, if one found motive, then the culprit was never far away. Deeds are either stimulated by hope or driven by fear. If the motive here was not one of fear then it must be one of hope. Hope for gain? What gain?'

Declan grinned.

'Now you are talking as of old, Fidelma. Indeed, this deed was done for gain. To be rid of Talamnach and thus secure the office of *tánaiste*. That was the object and that was the gain. And, of course, there was one person here that stood to gain once Talamnach was out of the way. That person was not Augaire for we have already seen demonstrated that he would not have any more votes in this *derbhfine* than those of his three friends and cousins.'

'True enough,' agreed Fidelma. 'Continue on along your path of logic.'

Selbach had arisen again.

'He does not need to.'

There was gasp among the people.

Fidelma frowned.

'Why not?' she demanded.

'Because the goal of his logic is obvious. He points the finger, as he has done throughout these entire proceedings, at me.'

'And do you admit to this deed?'

'I am innocent before God!' snapped Selbach.

'But you admit that you had the motive and the opportunity?' Declan said triumphantly.

'Motive yes, but opportunity . . . ?'

Fidelma's words were hardly more than a sigh but they caused all eyes to be turned towards her.

154

'Reflect on this,' she went on, when she had their attention. 'Muirecán comes into the antechamber with the mead and sets down the tray. Who is there?' When no one answered her, she continued. 'Brehon Declan was there. Talmanach was there. Selbach was there. Berrach was there. Augaire was there.'

She counted off the names on the fingers of her left hand.

'At this stage we have accepted the assurance of Muirecán that no poison had entered the mead. Now, Declan and Talamnach are speaking together. They realise it is late and Cúan has not arrived. So Muirecán is despatched to the chief's chamber to tell him that the meeting is ready. The mead is left on the table. Augaire makes to drink the mead and is prevented from doing so by his mother. Wouldn't that be an ideal opportunity for Augaire to introduce the poison? Wait!' She held up her hand to still a protest from Berrach. 'I did not say that he did. But let us consider. He, too, has the motive. For in spite of what Declan says, I think this young man is arrogant enough not to realise that he stands little chance of being supported by this *derbhfine*. He might be arrogant enough to think that once rid of Talamnach, he would stand a chance and find favour in his father's eyes. However, he picks up one mug and makes to drink it and is prevented and drawn away. True he could have introduced the poison into that mug but not into both mugs.'

There was a quiet murmuring as her logic was followed.

'Meanwhile, Talamnach leaves Declan and goes to speak to Selbach. Selbach puts his proposition. Stand down this time and I'll make you my *tánaiste* when I am chief. Not a particularly subtle proposal. I am sure that Selbach offered something more.'

She turned to gaze at the chief's brother.

'I have some small wealth in the land of Kernow. That was offered,' he admitted.

'Very well. And Talamnach treated your offer with contempt. He then leaves the antechamber and goes to answer, as Selbach tells us, a call of nature. Is that correct?'

Selbach nodded.

'And you say that as soon as Talamnach left, you came in here?'

'I did.'

'Berrach confirms this. After Selbach left she and her son came into the hall as well.'

155

'That is true,' said Berrach. 'A moment or so after Selbach went into the hall, we followed.'

Fidelma nodded, smiling softly.

'Now, we were all witness to the entrance of Selbach, Berrach and Augaire. Can anyone give a good estimate between their entrance and when Cúan, Talamnach and the attendant with the drinks entered this hall?'

It was Illan of Cluain Mult who answered.

'It was no more than ten minutes.'

'So, Cúan and the attendant, Muirecán, inform us that when they reached the antechamber, Talamnach was there, having returned from his call of nature. He was there with Declan. Is this right?'

Cúan agreed.

'One person was alone in the antechamber for a while,' Fidelma said softly.

Declan rose.

'If you are accusing me, Fidelma,' he said angrily, 'you have forgotten one thing. I followed Berrach and Augaire out here to speak to Selbach and if Selbach does not acknowledge that then Illan is my witness.'

Illan of Cluain Mult looked unhappy.

'That is true,' he agreed. 'You did speak to Selbach.'

'Don't worry, Declan,' Fidelma went on. 'I observed you come and speak to Selbach.'

Declan relaxed and smiled.

'Then I suggest we end this game. There is only one person who gains and I now order Selbach to submit to a search. I am sure we will find the phial that contained the poison on him.'

'This is a lie!' protested Selbach.

Fidelma raised her hands for order as the hall went into an uproar.

'There is no need to search. The phial of poison, emptied of its contents, will be found in the pocket of Selbach's leather jerkin.'

Immediately, Selbach thrust his hand into the pocket and his face went white.

'Is it not so, Selbach?' called Fidelma.

The man could not speak but he was holding a small phial in his hand.

'Warriors, arrest Selbach,' called Declan with triumph in his voice.

156

'Do not!' cried Fidelma, staying them in mid-stride. 'Arrest the Brehon Declan, for his is the hand that placed that phial in Selbach's pocket.'

There came a stunned silence.

Declan stared at her in amazement.

'What are you saying, Fidelma?' He tried to sound angry but his tone was somehow deflated.

'It does not take long to introduce poison into two drinking mugs. I am not sure whether your planning was precise or opportunist. You suggested that Talamnach despatch the attendant to fetch Cúan, leaving the drinks unguarded. As soon as Berrach and her son left, it took a moment to empty the phial and follow them out into this hall. I suspect had the antechamber not emptied you would have found some other ruse to poison the drinks. Then you came out and pretended that you wanted to speak to Selbach.'

'I wanted to ask him if he meant to go on with his challenge. He will tell you that.'

'Why could you not ask in the antechamber? Why come into the hall to challenge him in front of people? You turned, stumbled and by sleight of hand placed the phial in his pocket. Even before this meeting you had told me, disparagingly, of Selbach's tendency to wear the new fashions that have been introduced among the Britons, of Roman pockets in robes.'

'But what motive have I? I am a Brehon,' protested Declan.

'Is a Brehon precluded from chiefship?' returned Fidelma. 'You are of this *derbhfine* and can be accepted in office. Indeed, you are first cousin to Talamnach and Augaire. Your ultimate hope, I think, was both Cúan and Talamnach would be poisoned. You did your best to point the finger at Selbach. With him under suspicion you knew no one would support Augaire and that would leave you open to declare yourself *rechtaire*, steward of this clan, until you could dispose of your rivals and get yourself installed properly as chief. As it was, with Talamnach dead, you were prepared to go through your plan and eliminate Selbach and then persuade Cúan to nominate you his heir apparent anyway.'

Fidelma shook her head slowly.

'You almost had me fooled, Declan.'

Cúan had stood and motioned to his warriors to secure the pale-faced Brehon.

157

'What stopped you being fooled, Fidelma?' he asked softly.

'I was suspicious at how aggressive Declan was in laying the blame at Selbach's door. No Brehon worth his salt would be so forgetful of his office, and the need for impartiality, as to act as he did. However, what really alerted me and make me realise what had happened was the fact that Declan had mentioned a phial of poison. How did he know that the poison had been introduced into the mugs by means of a phial and not by some other method? There are many other ways of introducing poison other than a phial. Only the murderer would know this and then the meaning of the pantomime of his stumbling against Selbach became clear to me.'

Fidelma watched with sad eyes as the warriors escorted Declan from the hall.

'Nobody has a more sacred obligation to obey the law than those who take on the robes of Brehons to judge others by the law.'

Who Stole the Fish?

Sister Fidelma glanced up in mild surprise as the red-faced religieux came bursting through the doors into the refectory where she and her fellow religieuses were about to sit down at the long wooden tables for the evening meal. In fact, Abbot Laisran had already called for silence so that he could intone the *gratias*.

The man halted in confusion as he realised that his abrupt entrance had caused several eyes to turn questioningly upon him. His red cheeks, if anything, deepened their colour and he appeared to wring his hands together for a moment in indecision. He knew well that this was no ordinary evening meal but a feast given in welcome to the Venerable Salvian, an emissary from Rome who was visiting the Abbey of Durrow. The patrician Roman was even now sitting by the side of the abbot, watching the new arrival with some astonishment.

The red-faced monk apparently summoned courage and hurried to the main table where Abbot Laisran stood with an expression of irritation on his rotund features. He bent forward. A few words were whispered. Something was wrong. Fidelma could tell that by the startled look which formed momentarily on the abbot's face. He leaned across to his steward, who was seated at his left side, and muttered something. It was the steward's turn to look surprised. Then the abbot turned to his guest, the Venerable Salvian, and seemed to force a smile before speaking, waving his hand as if in emphasis. The old patrician's expression was polite yet puzzled.

The abbot then rose and came hurrying down the refectory in the wake of the religieux who had delayed the meal. To her surprise, Fidelma realised the abbot was making directly towards her.

Abbot Laisran was looking very unhappy as he bent down with

lowered voice. 'I have need of your services, Fidelma,' he said tersely. 'Would you follow me to the kitchens?'

Fidelma realised that Laisran was not prone to dramatic gestures. Without wasting time with questions, she rose and followed the unhappy man. Before them hurried the red-faced brother.

Beyond the doors, just inside the kitchen, Abbot Laisran halted and looked around. There were several religieux in the long chamber where all the meals of the abbey were prepared. Curiously, Fidelma noted, there was no activity in the kitchen. The group of religieux, marked as kitchen workers by the aprons they wore and rolled-up sleeves, stood about in silent awkwardness.

Laisran turned to the red-faced man who had conducted them hither. 'Now, Brother Dian, tell Sister Fidelma what you have just told me. Brother Dian is our second cook,' he added quickly for Fidelma's benefit.

Brother Dian, looking very frightened, bobbed his head several times. He spoke in rapid bursts and was clearly distressed.

'This afternoon, our cook, Brother Roilt, knowing that the Venerable Salvian was to be the guest of the abbey at this feast, went down to the river with his fishing rod and line, intent on hooking a salmon to prepare as a special dish.'

Laisran, fretting a little at this preamble, cut in: 'Brother Roilt caught a great salmon. He showed it to me. It was just right for the dish to present to Salvian. It would show him how well we live in this part of the world . . .'

Brother Dian, nodding eagerly, intervened in turn. 'The fish was prepared and Brother Roilt had started to cook it a short while ago for we knew that the *gratias* was about to be said. I was in charge of preparing the vegetables, so I was working at the far end of the kitchen. Brother Roilt was cooking the fish over there . . .' He indicated the respective positions with a wave of his hand. 'A short while ago, the chief server entered and told me that everyone was ready at the tables. I looked up to see whether Brother Roilt was ready also so that the servers could take in the fish. I could not see Brother Roilt. I came down to where he had been cooking the fish and . . . and the fish was gone.'

Abbot Laisran gave a groan. 'The fish has been stolen! The delicacy that we were to present to the Venerable Salvian! What shall I do?'

Fidelma had not said a word since she had been summoned from the

160

refectory. Now she spoke. 'The fish is missing. How do you deduce it was stolen?'

It was Brother Dian who answered. 'I made a thorough search of the kitchens and questioned the kitchen staff.' He gestured to the half-dozen or so brothers who stood gathered in their silent group. 'Everyone denies knowledge of the missing fish. It has simply vanished.'

'But what of the cook, Brother Roilt?' Fidelma demanded, irritated by the lack of explanation of the obvious. 'What does he say about this matter?'

There was a pause.

'Alas,' moaned Brother Dian. 'He, too, has disappeared.'

Fidelma arched an eyebrow. 'Are you saying that one moment he was cooking the salmon over a fire in this kitchen, with half a dozen others around him, and the next moment he had vanished?'

'Yes, Sister,' the man wailed. 'Maybe it's sorcery. *Deus avertat!*'

Fidelma sniffed disparagingly. 'Nonsense! There are a hundred reasons why the cook might have disappeared with his fish.'

Brother Dian was not convinced. 'He took such care with it because he knew it was going to be placed before the emissary from Rome. He caught the fish in the River Feoir itself, a great, wise salmon.'

'Show me exactly where he was last seen with this fish,' Fidelma instructed.

Brother Dian took her to a spot at the far end of the kitchen beside an open door leading into the abbey gardens. There was a table below an open window to one side and next to this was a hearth over which hung both a *bir*, or cooking spit, and an *indeoin*, or gridiron.

'It was at this gridiron that Brother Roilt was cooking the fish,' the red-faced brother informed her. 'He was basting it with honey and salt. See there.' He pointed to a large wooden platter on the table before the open window. 'There is the platter he intended to put it on.'

Fidelma bent forward with a frown. Then she put a finger to the platter where she had seen grease stains and raised it to her lips.

'Which he did put it on,' she corrected gently.

Then her eyes fell to the floor. There were several spots on the oak boards. She crouched down and looked at them for a few seconds before reaching forward, touching one with her forefinger and bringing it up to eye level.

161

'Has anyone been slaughtering meat in this part of the kitchen?' she asked.

Brother Dian shook his head indignantly. 'This area of the kitchen is reserved for cooking fish only. We cook our meat over there, on the far side of the kitchen, so that the two tastes do not combine and ruin the palate.'

Fidelma held her red-tinged fingertip towards Abbot Laisran.

'Then if that is not animal blood, I presume our cook has cut himself, which might account for his absence,' she observed drily.

Abbot Laisran frowned. 'I see. He might have cut himself and dropped blood over the fish and, seeing that it was thus tainted, might have been forced to discard it?'

Sister Fidelma smiled at the chubby-faced abbot.

'A good deduction, Laisran. We might make you a *dálaigh* yet.'

'Then you think that this is the answer?'

'I do not.' She shook her head. 'Brother Roilt would not simply have vanished without telling his staff to prepare some substitute dish. Nor would he have deserted his kitchen for such a long period. There are more blood spots on the floor.'

Keeping her eyes on the trail of blood, Fidelma followed it to a small door on the other side of the open door to the garden.

'Where does that lead?'

'A storeroom for flour, barley and other grains. I've looked inside. He is not hiding there, Sister,' Brother Dian said.

'Yet the spots of blood lead in there.'

'I did not see them before you pointed them out,' confessed the second cook.

Fidelma opened the door and peered inside. There were several large cupboards at the far end, beyond the stacked sacks of grains. She walked swiftly towards them, having observed where the blood spots led, and opened the door of the central one.

The body of an elderly monk fell out on to the floor to gasps of horror from those about her. A large butcher's knife protruded from under the corpse's ribcage.

'This, I presume, is Brother Roilt?' she inquired coldly.

'*Quod avertat Deus!*' breathed the abbot. 'What animals are we that someone kills the cook to steal a fish?'

One of the younger brothers began to sob uncontrollably. The abbot glanced across in distraction. 'Take Brother Enda and give him a glass of water,' he instructed another youth who was trying to comfort his companion. He turned back to Fidelma apologetically. 'The sight of violent death is often upsetting to the young.'

'I know who must have done this evil deed,' interposed one of the young men, who was wearing a clean white baker's apron over his habit. 'It must be one of those wandering beggars that were camping by the river this morning.'

The term he actually used was *daer-fuidhir*, a class of people who were more or less reduced to penury and whose labour was as close to slavery as anything. These were criminals or prisoners taken in warfare who could not redeem themselves and had lost all civil rights in society. They often wandered as itinerant labourers hiring themselves out to whoever would offer them food and lodging.

Abbot Laisran's face was grave. 'We will take our revenge on this band of miscreants if—'

'There is no need for that,' interrupted Fidelma quietly. 'I have a feeling that you will not find your fish thief among them.'

They all turned towards her expectantly.

'Abbot Laisran, you must return to your distinguished guest. Is there some other dish which can replace the fish that you were to serve him?'

The abbot glanced at Brother Dian.

'We can serve the venison, Father Abbot,' the second cook volunteered.

'Good,' Fidelma answered for Laisran. 'Then get on with the meal and while you are doing that I shall make some inquiries here and find out how Brother Roilt came by his death and who stole the fish.'

The abbot hesitated but Fidelma's expression was determined and confident. He nodded briefly to her and, as an afterthought, directed Brother Dian to obey all her instructions.

Fidelma turned to the table under the window and stared down at the empty wooden platter with the now drying grease marks on it. After a moment or two, she raised her eyes to gaze into the tiny plot beyond. It was a small, enclosed herb garden.

It was clear, from the blood spots, that Brother Roilt had been standing here when he was stabbed. He could not have walked to the store cupboard on his own. The killer would have had to drag him there, probably on his back, pulling him by his two arms. Had he been dragged on his stomach then the blood trail would have been more noticeable. The physical removal of the body would not have been difficult for Brother Roilt was elderly, small and frail in appearance. Indeed, he did not look remotely like the typical cook. But why had no one else in the kitchen seen anything?

She swung round.

The kitchen staff were busy handing platters to the servers who were waiting to take them to the tables in the refectory beyond.

There were six workers in the kitchen. It was a long, large chamber but, she realised, it actually was L-shaped. Part of it was hidden from the other part. Brother Roilt would not have been seen by anyone beyond the angle. Furthermore, the centre of the room, along its entire length, contained preparation tables and a central oven. The kitchen was fairly wide but, with a series of wooden supports running along its centre, it was obvious that certain lines of sight would be met with visual obstruction. Yet while these might obscure vision from various points, it was surely impossible that no one had been in a position to see the killer stab the cook and then drag him to the storeroom, even if the murder had been executed almost soundlessly.

That a murder could have been done in full view and no one had noticed it was also impossible.

She glanced back down to the platter. Who stole the fish? Why kill someone to steal a salmon? It was not logical. Not even an itinerant worker would come forward and attempt such a thing in these circumstances.

She went to the open door and stood looking out into the herb garden. It was no more than ten metres square, surrounded by a high wall and with a wooden gate at the far end. She walked down the paved pathway towards it and saw that it carried a bolt. The bolt was firmly in place and this would have prevented any access into the garden from the outside. Furthermore, anyone leaving by this means could not have secured the bolt behind them.

She turned and walked back to the kitchen door. There was nothing unusual; nothing out of place. By the door stood a spade and some other gardening tools. Next to them, on the ground, was an empty tin dish. Presumably, the tools were used for tending the garden. Fidelma realised that there was only one conclusion.

Brother Roilt must have been killed by someone who had been in the kitchen.

She was so engrossed in contemplating this fact as she re-entered the kitchen and took her stand by the empty fish platter that she did not see Brother Dian return to her side until he cleared his throat in order to regain her attention.

'The dishes have been taken into the refectory, Sister. What do you wish us to do now?'

Fidelma made a quick decision. 'I want everyone who was working in the kitchen to come forward,' she instructed.

Brother Dian waved the men forward. 'I was here: then there was Brother Gebhus, Brother Manchán, Brother Torolb, Brother Enda and Brother Cett.'

He indicated them each in turn. They stood before her looking awkward, like small boys caught in some naughty escapade and brought before their senior. It had been the youthful Brother Enda who had given way to his emotions at the sight of the dead body. Now he seemed more in control, although his eyes were red and his facial muscles pinched in maintaining his calm.

'I want each one of you to go to the position where you were working at the time when it was noticed that Brother Roilt was missing.'

Brother Dian frowned. 'To be truthful, Sister, it was the fish which I noticed was missing first. I was, as I said, at the far end of the kitchen preparing the vegetables. Brother Gebhus was my assistant, working at my side.'

'Go there, then,' Fidelma instructed.

Brother Dian walked to the far end of the room with Brother Gebhus trotting after him. They were obscured from sight by the central obstructions but did not go into the area which was hidden by the angle of the L. She stood at the spot where the murdered man must have worked. She could not see the second cook or his assistant from that point.

'Now repeat your actions when you came to check on the readiness of the fish,' she called.

Brother Dian appeared around an obstruction at the top of the kitchen, hesitated, and then came towards her.

'What made you take the trouble to do this?' she inquired.

'The server who was to take the fish to the table had entered from the refectory. The door as you know is at the top end of the chamber near where I was working. He told me that the *gratias* was about to be said. That was why I turned and saw Brother Roilt was not at his position and when I came along I saw that the fish was missing.'

'How many entrances are there to the kitchen?'

'Three.'

'And these are . . . ?'

'The garden entrance, the door from the refectory and the one which leads into a small anteroom in which the servers prepare their trays and plates to go into the refectory.'

'So if anyone left the kitchen they would have to go directly into the refectory or into the servers' room?'

'In which case,' Brother Dian pointed out, 'they would have been observed. The only way in and out without going through one of those rooms is through the kitchen garden. That is why I agree it was the itinerants who slunk in—'

Fidelma held up a hand. 'The garden is surrounded by a high wall. There is a wooden door which gives the only exit or entrance. That door is bolted from the inside.'

Brother Dian pursed his lips. 'The reason it is locked, Sister, is because I locked it. When I noticed the fish had gone, I went out to see if the culprit was still in the garden.'

Fidelma gestured in exasperation. 'And was the door shut or open at that time?' she demanded.

'It was open. That was very unusual. Indeed, I clearly remember that when we arrived to start the meal this evening the gate was shut and locked. That's why I threw the bolt on it, to make sure no one else came through that way.'

'I am glad that you have told me.' She was reflective. 'It could have led to a wrong conclusion.' She did not explain further but turned to the others.

'Will everyone now go to the positions that they occupied?'

She saw that Brother Enda and Brother Cett immediately went into the area beyond the angle of the L at the far end of the kitchen. It was obvious that they could not see round the corner.

She called them out into her line of vision again. 'How long were you in that area, Brothers?'

The two young religieux exchanged glances. Brother Cett spoke for them both for the red-eyed Brother Enda was clearly still upset.

'This is where we prepare the fruit. We were washing and cutting pieces for the dessert course. That is our only task and so we were here most of the time. There was no reason for us to be anywhere else.'

'When did you last see Brother Roilt?'

'When we arrived in the kitchen to start to prepare our dishes. As head cook we had to report to him.'

'Stay there then.' She walked back to her original position. 'Now the rest of you . . .'

Brother Gebhus still remained out of sight at Brother Dian's original position. Brother Torolb stood on the far side of the kitchen in front of another big range supporting meat spits, while Brother Manchán took a position at the centre table next to some clay ovens where he had obviously been preparing bread.

Fidelma regarded their positions carefully. If Torolb and Manchán had been glancing in Roilt's direction, then they would have seen him, although with various obstructions depending on what they were doing. For example, if Brother Torolb had been bending to his cooking range he would have been facing the opposite wall, and even when he turned there would have been a central table with a low central beam from which a number of metal pots and pans hung which would have obstructed his view. He could only have seen the midsection of Brother Roilt.

She checked each of their views carefully before sighing in exasperation.

If everyone had been totally engrossed with their work, it might just have been possible for someone to enter from the herb garden, stab Roilt, drag his frail body to the storeroom and then steal the fish. Yet she was sure that the murderer had not come in from the garden. It made no sense. Why kill Roilt for a fish? The plate was by the window. If they were so desperate, they could have waited until Roilt's attention was distracted, leaned forward across the window sill and grabbed the fish. Why take such an extraordinary risk of discovery and resort to murder? And there was the matter of the gate.

Perhaps she was looking at this from the wrong viewpoint?

'I shall speak to each of you individually, starting with Brother Dian,' she announced. 'The rest of you will continue about your duties until you are called.'

With the exception of Brother Dian, the others, reluctantly it seemed, resumed their tasks in other parts of the kitchen.

'How long have you been second cook here?' Fidelma began.

Brother Dian reflected. 'Five years.'

'How long had Roilt been cook here?'

'Is this relevant? We should be searching for the itinerants,' he began, and then caught the glint in her eye. 'Roilt had been here for a year longer than I. That was why he was head cook.'

'Did you and the others get on with him?'

'Roilt? No one liked him. He was a weasel of a man.' He stopped, flushed and genuflected. '*De mortuis nil nisi bonum*,' he muttered. Of the dead say nothing but good.

'*Vincit omnia veritas*,' replied Fidelma sharply. Truth conquers all things. 'I prefer to hear the truth than false praise.'

Brother Dian glanced around. 'Very well. It is known than Roilt liked the company of the young novitiates, if you know what I mean. Male novitiates,' he added with emphasis.

'There was hatred towards him because of this?'

Dian nodded. 'Many brothers disliked his abuse of the young.'

'Abuse? Do you mean that he forced his attentions on them against their will?'

Dian gave an expressive shrug by way of reply.

'Did Roilt have affairs with any of the kitchen staff?' she demanded.

Dian blinked at the directness of the question. 'I must protest, Sister . . . you are here to find out who stole the fish . . .'

'I am here to find out who murdered Brother Roilt,' snapped Fidelma, causing Brother Dian to start.

'It is clear that he was killed for the fish,' Dian said doggedly after a moment to recover.

'Is it?' Fidelma glanced to the far end of the kitchen. 'Ask Brother Enda to come to me.'

Brother Dian looked surprised at being summarily dismissed. A moment later the youthful, red-eyed Brother Enda arrived at her side.

'Are you feeling better now?' Fidelma asked him.

The young man nodded slowly. 'It was a shock, you see . . .' he began hesitantly.

'Of course. You were close to Brother Roilt, weren't you?'

Brother Enda flushed and pressed his lips firmly together, saying nothing.

'Were you currently in a relationship with him?' demanded Fidelma.

'I was not.'

'He preferred someone younger?'

'He was the only person who was kind to me in this abbey. I shall not speak ill of him.'

'I do not ask you to say anything that is not the truth and will not help us find out who killed him.'

The young man seemed bewildered for a moment. 'I thought he was killed for . . .'

'For the fish?' Fidelma's expression did not change. 'Did he have a current lover?'

'I think there was a young novitiate that he had just taken a liking to.'

'When did he end his relationship with you?'

'Six months ago.'

'Were you angry about that?'

'Sad. I was not—' The young man's eyes abruptly widened. 'You think that I . . . that I killed him?' His voice rose on a high note causing some of the other kitchen workers to turn in their direction.

'Did you?' Fidelma was unperturbed.

'I did not!'

'How about Brother Cett? He is your age. Did he have a relationship with Roilt or with yourself?'

Enda laughed harshly. 'Brother Cett is not like that. He loves women too much.'

'There is no feeling, beyond fraternity, between you and Cett?'

'We are friends, that is all.'

'I am told that Roilt was disliked. Perhaps he was disliked for his sexuality? Often people kill out of fear of things they cannot comprehend.'

'I can only tell you what I know,' insisted the young man stubbornly.

'That is all that is asked of the innocent.' Fidelma smiled thinly. 'Send Brother Torolb to me.'

Torolb was a man about twenty years of age. He was handsome and still in the vigour of youth, though not so young as Enda or Cett. He was dark-eyed and had determined features, an expression as though he would not suffer fools gladly. He wore a short leather apron around his habit.

'Your task is to cook the meat dishes?' she asked. Torolb nodded warily.

'How long have you worked in the kitchens here?'

'Since I came to the abbey at the "age of choice".'

'Three or four years ago?'

'Four years ago.'

'So you learned your art in this kitchen?'

Torolb smiled thinly. 'Part of it. I was raised on a farm and taught to butcher and cook meat when I was young. That was why I specially asked to work in the kitchens.'

Fidelma glanced down at his clothing. 'You have blood on your apron,' she observed.

Torolb uttered a short laugh. 'You cannot butcher and cut meat without blood.'

'Naturally,' sighed Fidelma. 'How well did you know Brother Roilt?'

An expression of displeasure crossed Torolb's features. 'I knew Roilt,' he replied shortly.

'You did not like him?'

'Why should I?'

'He was head cook and you were under his direction. People have feelings about those they work with and an elderly man usually influences the young.'

'Roilt could only influence gullible youths like Enda. Others despised him.'

'Others, like yourself?'

'I do not deny it. I obey the law.'

'The law?' Fidelma frowned.

'The law of God, the Father of Christ Jesus,' replied the young man fiercely. 'You will find the law in Leviticus where it says, "If a man has intercourse with a man as with a woman, they both commit an abomination. They shall be put to death; their blood shall be on their own heads." That is what is written.'

Fidelma examined the saturnine young man thoughtfully. 'Is that what you believe?'

170

'That is what is written.'

'But do you believe it?'

'Surely we must believe the word of the Holy Scripture?'

'And would you go so far as to carry out the word of that Scripture?'

The young man glanced at her, his eyes narrowing suspiciously for a moment. 'We are forbidden to take the law into our own hands and to kill. So if you are trying to accuse me of killing Brother Roilt, you are wrong. Yet if those who are given authority under the law had said he should be executed, then I would not have lifted a hand to prevent it.'

Fidelma paused for a moment and then asked: 'When you came here as a young novice, did Roilt make any advances towards you?'

Brother Torolb was angry. 'How dare you imply—'

'You forget yourself, Brother Torolb!' snapped Fidelma 'You are talking to a *dálaigh*, an advocate of the Laws of the Féncchus. I ask questions to discover the truth. Your duty is to answer.'

'I tell you again, I obey the laws of the Faith as given in Scripture. Anyway, you forget one thing in desperately seeking to find the guilty.'

'What is that?'

'The missing fish. If I were called to be God's instrument to punish Roilt, what reason would I have to steal a fish that I did not want? Or would you like to come and search my cupboards for it?'

Fidelma gazed coldly at him. 'That will not be necessary. Tell Brother Manchán to come to me.'

Torolb turned away, his attitude one of barely controlled anger

Brother Manchán came forward smiling. He was a fleshy bright-faced young man, scarcely older than Torolb. He gave the impression that he had just stepped from a bath and was freshly scrubbed. His smile seemed a permanent part of his features.

'And you, Brother, I observe, are the baker of this abbey?' Fidelma said in greeting.

Manchán wore a pristine white apron over his habit, yet this had not prevented the fine dust of flour settling over his clothing like powder.

'I have been baker here for two years and was three years assistant baker until the death of poor Brother Tomaltach.'

'So you came here as a young novitiate five years ago?'

171

Manchán bobbed his head and his smile seemed to broaden. 'Even so, Sister.'

'How well did you know Roilt?'

'I knew him well enough, for he was head cook here. Poor Brother Roilt.'

'Why do you say "poor"?'

'The manner of his death, what else? Death comes to us all but it should not visit us in such a terrible fashion.' The young baker shuddered and genuflected.

'Any untimely death is terrible,' Fidelma agreed. 'Yet I believe that many in this kitchen do not feel grief at this man's passing.'

Manchán glanced quickly in the direction of Brother Dian, still at the far end of the kitchen.

'I can imagine that some would even feel pleased at it,' he said quickly.

'Pleased?'

'A matter of ambition, Sister,' the young man replied.

'Do you imply that Brother Dian was ambitious to be head cook here?'

'Isn't that natural? If one is second then it behoves him to strive to be first.'

'I was not particularly thinking about ambition.'

Brother Manchán regarded her for a moment or two and then grimaced. 'I suppose you refer to Roilt's sexual inclinations?'

'What were your views?'

'Each to his own, I say. *Quod cibus est aliis est venenum.*' What is food to some is poison to others.

'That is laudable, but not a view shared by some of your colleagues.'

'You mean Torolb? Well, pay no attention to his fundamentalism. It is so much baying at the moon. Who knows? It may even be an attempt to hide his own inclinations, even from himself?'

'Yet a man who can wield a knife and slaughter an animal might have no compunction in slaughtering a human being.'

Brother Manchán reflected for a moment.

'Are you really sure that Roilt was killed by one of us? That he was not killed by itinerants determined to feed well on the salmon that disappeared? After all, wasn't the garden gate open and unbolted? One of the itinerants must have come in.'

172

'And you can think of no other explanation?' countered Fidelma.

The young man raised a hand to rub his chin thoughtfully.

'Anything is possible. I agree some did not like Roilt. But I think you are wrong about Torolb. Brother Dian coveted Roilt's position as head cook and disliked him because he thought himself a better cook.'

Fidelma smiled. 'But Brother Dian was at the far end of the kitchen. He would have had to leave his position and walk down the length of the kitchen to where Roilt was cooking his fish. He would have been seen by either yourself or Torolb or, indeed, by Brother Gebhus who was working beside him and would have noticed him leave.'

'But he did come by me. He did leave his position,' pointed out Brother Manchán.

'That was when he went to check whether the fish was ready; when he noticed that the fish and Roilt were missing.' Fidelma frowned as an idea occurred to her. 'Did you see Dian pass by?'

Brother Manchán nodded. 'I had my head down rolling dough but I was aware that he passed my table.'

'How long was it before he announced that Roilt was missing?'

Brother Manchán thought for a moment.

'I think that some time passed between my being aware of him passing my table and the moment I thought I heard a door hang. That made me look up and go to the corner where I could see without obstruction. I saw Brother Dian standing by the kitchen door. He was looking rather flushed, as from exertion. I asked him what was wrong and that was when he said that the fish was missing and that he could not find Brother Roilt.'

Fidelma was thoughtful. 'Thank you, Brother Manchán.'

She went forward to where Brother Gebhus was standing nervously awaiting her.

'Now, Brother Gebhus.' She drew him to one side of the kitchen, away from where Brother Dian was now intent on ensuring the fruit dishes were being handed to the servers.

'I don't know anything, Sister,' the young man began nervously.

Fidelma suppressed an impatient sigh. She pointed to a hearth where a fire crackled under a hanging cauldron.

'Would you like to put your hand in that fire. Brother Gebhus?' she asked.

Brother Gebhus looked startled. 'Not I!'

'Why?'

'I don't want my hand burnt.'

'Then you do know something, Gebhus, don't you?' she replied acidly. 'You know that the fire will burn your hand.'

Brother Gebhus stared blankly at her.

'Think about the meaning of what you are saying before you answer my questions,' explained Fidelma. 'I need them to be answered with accuracy. How long have you worked here?'

'Two years in this kitchen.'

'You assist Brother Dian?'

He nodded briefly, eyes warily on her.

'How well did you know Brother Roilt?'

'Not well. I . . . I tried to avoid him. I did not like him because . . .' He hesitated.

'He made advances to you?'

The young man sighed deeply. 'When I first came to the abbey. I told him that I was not like that.'

'You were standing here when Dian went to look for Roilt?'

'He went to look for the fish,' corrected Gebhus. 'The chief server had come in and said that the *gratias* was about to be said and Brother Dian turned and looked down the aisle there to where Brother Roilt was cooking the fish for the guest of honour. He could not see him and so he went to find him.'

'And you remained here?'

'I was here from the moment I came into the kitchen this evening.'

'Was Brother Dian with you the whole time?'

'Not the whole time. He had to discuss the meal with Brother Roilt before we began and once or twice he went to consult with him and the other cooks.'

The refectory door opened at that point and Abbot Laisran came in, looking worried. He approached Fidelma.

'I just had to come to see if you had any news. Have you decided who stole the fish?'

Fidelma smiled her curious urchin-like grin.

'I knew who stole the fish some time ago. But you are just in time, Father Abbot.'

She turned and called for everyone to gather round her. They did so, expectantly, almost fearfully.

'Do you know who murdered Brother Roilt?' demanded Brother Dian, asking the question that was in everyone's minds.

Fidelma glanced swiftly at them, observing their growing anticipation.

'Brother Manchán, would you mind removing your apron?' she asked.

The young brother suddenly turned white and began to back away.

Brother Torolb grabbed him and tore the apron off. Beneath the pristine white apron, Brother Manchán's habit was splattered with bloodstains.

Abbot Laisran was bewildered. 'Why would Brother Manchán kill Roilt?'

'Reasons as old as the human condition: jealousy, love turned to hatred; an immature and uncontrollable rage at being rejected by a lover. Manchán had been Roilt's lover until Roilt turned his attentions to a new young novitiate. Roilt rejected Manchán for a younger man. Presumably Roilt was neither sensitive nor tactful in bringing an end to his relationship and so Manchán killed him.'

The young man did not deny her accusation.

'How did you know?' asked the Abbot.

'Brother Manchán was very eager to point an accusing finger at others in the kitchen and out of it, especially at Brother Dian. I realised that he was just too eager.'

'But you must have had something else to go by?' Brother Dian asked. 'Something made you suspect him.'

'Brother Manchán was, of course, best placed to kill Roilt. When everyone had their attentions fixed on their tasks he seized the opportunity. He went forward, struck so quickly that Roilt did not have time to cry out, and then he dragged Roilt to the storeroom. He even went into the garden and opened the wooden gate, which was usually kept shut and bolted, in an attempt to lay a false trail. He pointed out to me that the gate had been open. Yet Dian, finding it so, had shut it and bolted it again almost immediately. How had he known that it had been open?'

'And he also took the fish to lay a false trail?' suggested Brother Dian.

Fidelma shook her head with a smile. 'He did not have time to do that. No; the fish was actually stolen by someone else. The

175

opportunity to take the fish was seized when Roilt was no longer there to prevent it.'

'Just a minute,' interrupted Abbot Laisran. 'I still do not understand how you initially came to suspect Manchán. Suspicion because he tried to lay the blame on others is not sufficient, surely?'

'You are right, as always, Father Abbot,' conceded Fidelma. 'What alerted me was the problem of his apron.'

'His apron?' frowned the abbot.

'Manchán would have us believe that he was working away making bread. Indeed, there was a fine dust of flour over his clothing with the exception of his apron which was clean; pristine white. It was clearly not the apron that he had been wearing while he was working. Why had he changed it? When Roilt was killed blood had splattered on the floor. It would have splashed on his clothes, especially on a white apron. He changed the apron in the storeroom. covering the bloodstains that had seeped through on to his habit. Seeing that clean white apron made me suspicious and his eagerness to point the finger at others simply strengthened my instinct. The reference to the gate merely confirmed matters. Now you have the proof,' she added with a gesture at Manchán's bloodstained robes.

Abbot Laisran stood nodding his head thoughtfully as he considered the matter. Then he suddenly looked at her in bewilderment. 'But the fish? Who stole the fish?'

Sister Fidelma moved across to the kitchen door and pointed down to the empty tin dish by the door.

'I noticed this earlier. It looks as though it is used to contain milk. Therefore, would I be correct in presuming that there is a cat who frequents the kitchen area?'

Brother Dian gave a gasp which was enough acknowledgement of this surmise.

Fidelma grinned. 'I suggest that a search of the garden will probably disclose the remains of the fish and your cat curled up nearby having had one of the best meals of its life. It was the cat who stole the fish.'

Cry 'Wolf!'

∾

'Is that all the petitions and statements?' asked Sister Fidelma with a sigh of relief.

It had been a long morning and Sister Fidelma had been fulfilling the job that she liked least as a *dálaigh* or an advocate of the courts of the five kingdoms of Éireann. Having qualified to the level of *anruth*, only one level below the highest degree accorded by the ecclesiastical and secular colleges of Ireland, she would often be asked by the Chief Brehon, the senior judge, of the kingdom of Muman, which her brother Colgú ruled from Cashel, to hear minor cases. This usually meant visiting outlying corners of the kingdom where there was no permanent Brehon. She would judge such cases, or study submissions from plaintiffs to see whether there was some case of civil or criminal law that should be heard by a more senior Brehon.

She had spent the night in her least favourite part of her brother's kingdom. It was a disputed territory claimed by the princes of the Uí Fidgente and those of the Eóghanacht Áine. The Eóghanacht Áine were related to her own family and there had been many conflicts between them and the Uí Fidgente. Yet, these conflicts apart, she admitted that the area was a beautiful country. It was a large, fertile valley land; a lush green plain which was sheltered by surrounding hills and stretched north to a great sea inlet.

The main township was set at a river bend where the river of the plain, the Maigue, and the little crooked river Camoge intersected at a spot called Cromadh, or the crooked ford. At this juncture stood the Wood of Eóghan, rising on a hill surmounted by the ancient fortress of the chief, Díomsach the Proud. Fidelma had discovered that the man's name had not been given lightly for he was, indeed, a proud man and conscious of his lineage from the ruling family of the kingdom, albeit a branch that had long separated from the Eóghanacht of Cashel. The Eóghanacht Áine were one of the seven main branches of the family establishing their rule over Muman. The Áine claimed precedence as second to the senior branch at Cashel. They were proud and arrogant.

But the area in which Díomsach claimed his power spread into this fertile valley which the Uí Fidgente also claimed as their territory. The Uí Fidgente were just as stubborn and proud. Many times had they risen up in rebellion against Cashel itself, even asserting a claim to the kingship. The continuing dispute as to who should rule in Cromadh made the presence of any *dálaigh*, let alone the sister of the King of Cashel, a subject of great tension. At all such courts held at Cromadh, the local chief of the Uí Fidgente claimed it was his right to attend and sit with the chief of the Tuatha Cromadh. It was a demand that was reluctantly agreed upon.

Fidelma now glanced at the haughty face of Díomsach as he sat on her right hand side in his great hall. She had heard a number of complaints that morning, none of them major. Then she turned to the equally stony face of Conrí, local chieftain of the Uí Fidgente. Both kept silent.

'Is that all the submissions and statements?' she asked again, more sharply.

'I see no more supplicants,' replied Conrí of the Uí Fidgente in a bored voice.

Brother Colla, the *scriptor* who was taking a record of the proceedings, coughed nervously, looking towards Fidelma.

'You have something to say, Brother Colla?' she inquired.

'There is one other person who demands a hearing,' he said quietly. Then he hesitated.

Sister Fidelma looked at him with curiosity.

'Then why isn't this person brought before me?'

The *scriptor* shuffled his feet awkwardly.

'He has been detained outside by Fallach, the . . .'

Díomsach's brows came together sharply.

'Fallach will doubtless have a good reason,' he snapped, adding quickly to Fidelma, 'He is my chief of warriors. Who is this man apprehended by Fallach?'

'Lord, it is the farmer Febrat.'

To Sister Fidelma's surprise, Díomsach burst out chuckling.

'Febrat? That half-wit? Then there is no more to be said. Our hearing is ended and we may retire for the feasting and entertainment.'

He made to rise but Sister Fidelma said quietly, 'I am afraid that it is I who must say when my court may disperse, Díomsach. I would know more about this man Febrat and why you would exclude him from the right of petition to the courts of this land.'

Díomsach reseated himself and looked momentarily uncomfortable.

'The man is mad, Fidelma of Cashel.'

Sister Fidelma smiled cynically. 'Are you saying that he is adjudged insane and without responsibility in law?'

The chief shook his head but was silent.

'I am still, then, awaiting an answer.'

'I am also intrigued,' Conrí of the Uí Fidgente added, not disguising his delight at Díomsach's discomfort.

Díomsach sighed softly.

'Febrat may not be legally insane but I think we are approaching a point where he must be adjudged as such. Febrat is a farmer. His farmstead is across the river, in the valley. It is the farthest farmstead in my territory bordering on the lands of my good friend, Conrí.' Díomsach inclined the upper half of his body towards the Uí Fidgente chief. It was an ironic gesture of deference, which was returned in kind by Conrí.

'I know the area,' Conrí confirmed with a polite smile.

'Then know this,' went on Díomsach. 'Twice in the last two weeks he has come to my fortress claiming that the Uí Fidgente were raiding his farmstead.'

The smile vanished from Conrí's lips.

'That is a lie!' he snapped. 'There have been no such raids.'

'Nevertheless, we were not initially surprised when Febrat came here with his story,' Díomsach went on grimly. 'It cannot be said that the Uí Fidgente are the most trustworthy neighbours . . .'

Fidelma raised a hand as Conrí clapped a hand to his empty sword sheath, half rising from his seat. It was a firm rule that no weapons could be carried into a feasting hall or into a Brehon's court.

'Sit down, Conrí, and calm yourself,' she admonished sharply. 'Let us hear out this story. Did you investigate Febrat's complaint?' she turned back to ask of Díomsach.

The chief nodded swiftly.

'Of course. Fallach and some of our warriors rode out and found nothing. Not broken blades of grass, a missing sheep nor dog in frenzied mood. There was no sign of any movement of horses being ridden around the farmstead. Fallach questioned one or two people, including Febrat's own wife, Cara, and she dismissed the idea as a figment of his imagination. Not being able to discover anything, Fallach returned.'

'Then there had been no raid?' asked Fidelma.

'Of course there had not,' snapped Conrí. 'My men would not raid a farmstead without my knowing of it, and they would know their punishment would be that much more harsh should I have discovered it. This man Febrat was indulging in liquor or was a liar.'

Díomsach nodded slowly.

'In this we find agreement, my friend. But then, two days afterwards, Febrat came to me with the same tale. He had the same sincerity and anguish as he had the first time he reported such an event. He named his neighbour, claiming this farmer was the man leading the raid. We had to take him seriously and so I accompanied Fallach and some warriors to investigate again, only to find that once more there was nothing to justify his complaint.'

Sister Fidelma sat with raised eyebrows.

'He came twice to you claiming that his farmstead was being raided and each time you found nothing? Did you question his wife and did you also question the man against whom he laid the charge of leading the raid?'

Díomsach nodded quickly.

'We did. The man that he claimed led the raid was a farmer named Faramund. He was aghast at the accusation and as we found nothing, nothing further was done.'

'And what did Febrat's wife say? What did you say her name was? Cara?'

'Cara said that she thought her husband was imagining such things for she knew nothing.'

'What did Febrat say to this?'

'He was trying to persuade his wife that it had happened.'

'But if she was there and if it happened she would know,' Fidelma pointed out. 'How could he persuade her otherwise?'

180

'That's just it. On both occasions Febrat's wife was away that night. I think she was staying with her mother.'

'On both occasions?' pressed Fidelma.

Díomsach nodded. 'That is the sum total of it, Fidelma of Cashel.'

'Has the man a history of instability?'

'I do not know,' Díomsach replied.

'And what does his wife say about this imagining?'

The chief shrugged. 'Only that perhaps her husband was working too hard or drinking too much.'

Conrí nodded in grim satisfaction.

'So long as the good name of the Uí Fidgente has been cleared on this matter, I care not about the man.'

'But he is here and wishes to make another supplication,' Fidelma pointed out. 'Why?'

There was a silence.

'Maybe he wishes to test our wits again,' Díomsach replied at last. 'Or he is truly mad and we must bring in a physician to judge him.'

'Brother Colla,' Sister Fidelma instructed the *scriptor* quietly, 'ask Fallach the warrior to come before us . . . but without his prisoner.'

Fallach was a lean, but muscular, dark-haired man. He came to stand before them with an expression of detached disdain.

'Fallach, I understand that a farmer called Febrat came to make supplication before this court,' Fidelma said. 'You hold him prisoner. Tell me why and what you know of this man.'

Fallach frowned for a moment, glancing swiftly towards his chief, Díomsach.

'Lady,' he began, addressing her as such for her knew her to be sister to the King of Muman and not merely a religieuse or simple *dálaigh*. 'I did not want you to be bothered by the fantasies of this man Febrat. That is why I detained him before he could enter the court.'

'What do you know of these fantasies?'

Fallach shifted his weight for a moment.

'Lady, twice he has come to my chief, Díomsach, claiming that the Uí Fidgente were raiding his land and harming his livestock. Twice have these claims proved to be untrue. On both occasions we have gone to his farm and found it to be in perfect peace. No harm has come to his farm or to his livestock. His wife, Cara, cannot explain

181

her husband's attitude. She has told us that nothing has ever happened to make her husband behave in this manner.'

Sister Fidelma nodded thoughtfully.

'Yet I am told that Febrat has been specific in his charge?'

Fallach frowned. 'Specific? Ah, you mean on the second occasion when he laid a claim against Faramund, a neighbouring farmer? We went to see him . . .'

Conrí's eyes narrowed.

'I have just realised that to speak to Faramund, you went into Uí Fidgente territory. That is an act of aggression. Compensation must be . . .'

Sister Fidelma cut in sharply.

'The territory is part of the kingdom of Muman and I am sitting in judgement on a matter pertaining to the kingdom. We will hear no more about disputed boundaries. Díomsach and Fallach were quite right to pursue an investigation relating to a potential criminal raid against a peaceful farmstead. That is the law.' She turned to the warrior. 'And what did Faramund say?'

'He assured us that he was nowhere near the farmstead of Febrat and with the testimony of Cara and the lack of evidence of a raid, there was only one conclusion. To be honest, Faramund, while an Uí Fidgente, is trustworthy. He even studied law at one time.'

'Then is your opinion that the man, Febrat, is lying for some reason or that he has become deranged?'

Fallach shrugged expressively.

'I would say that the man is deranged. He has dwelt within this community for as long as I can recall, though I scarcely know him well. He was merely a *daer-fuidhir*, one of the itinerant labouring classes. Then he was able to buy a little unfertile land and afterwards . . .'

Díomsach interrupted with a smile.

'Well, I think that decides the matter. Despatch him back to his farm. There is little we can do until his wife, who is his next of kin, declares him incapable and has him examined by the physicians. Then it will be a decision for the law as to whether he should be declared a *dásachtach*.'

Fallach made to turn but Sister Fidelma stayed him.

'Since the man is here, we might as well examine him. You, Díomsach, have reminded me of the law Do Brethaib Gaire that is concerned to protect society from the insane. If the man is truly displaying manic symptoms then we should not let him wander back to his farmstead. He is married and therefore his wife may have to become the *conn*, the guardian, who will be responsible for his behaviour.'

Conrí shrugged with studied disinterest while Díomsach frowned with displeasure. He was looking forward to the feasting and did not want to delay any longer. He had ordered a boar to be roasted and had bought red Gaulish wine from a merchant. Nevertheless, the court could only be brought to a close by the presiding lawyer and he had to defer to Fidelma.

'Bring Febrat before us,' instructed Fidelma and Fallach inclined his head in acknowledgement and left them.

When Febrat stood before Sister Fidelma she almost smiled. He reminded her of a pine marten, the sloping forehead, pointed features, dark restless eyes seemingly without pupils, and greying hair. He stood stock-still, erect, hands in front of his stomach, twisting together. The only movement was his head, looking from side to side as if seeking for an enemy, while it seemed his neck and body stayed motionless.

'Well, Febrat,' Sister Fidelma began, speaking softly to put the man at his ease. 'I understand that you have come to make a supplication to this court. Is this correct?'

'Indeed, indeed, indeed.' The rapidity of the repeated word made her blink.

'What is the plea?'

'My wife, my wife, Cara, Cara. She has disappeared, disappeared. Carried off in an Uí Fidgente raid, a raid.'

Sister Fidelma felt Conrí stir and glanced quickly at him to still any outburst.

'And when was this raid?'

'Last night, maybe this morning. Yes, this morning.'

'I see. And they carried off your wife?'

'They did, they did.'

'Tell us about it, in your own words.'

Febrat glanced to his left and then his right in quick nervous motions and then his dark eyes focused on Fidelma. He spoke rapidly and with many repetitions.

He and his wife, Cara, had gone to bed at the usual hour. Around dawn they had been awoken by the noise of horses and men riding about the farmstead. He had taken his billhook, his only weapon, and gone out to see what was happening. In the yard, he recognised men of the Uí Fidgente apparently trying to steal his livestock. He was aware that his wife was behind him for he heard her cry out. That was the last thing that he had heard for something must have hit him. He awoke on the floor beside his bed and all was quiet. His wife had disappeared.

He ended his swift recital and stood looking at Sister Fidelma waiting for her reaction.

Díomsach stifled a yawn at her side.

'Febrat, this is the third time you have come before me with tales of raids by the Uí Fidgente . . .'

'False tales,' interrupted Conrí in annoyance.

'In the other two instances,' went on the chief of the Tuatha Cromadh, 'we have investigated and found your stories to be untrue. Do you expect us to believe you now?'

Febrat glanced quickly at him and then back to Fidelma.

'All true, all true,' he replied. 'I never told a lie, a lie. Not before and not now. My wife has been taken by the raiders, by the raiders. True, I swear it.'

'As you have sworn before and been found to be a liar!' snapped Díomsach.

'Come here, Febrat,' Sister Fidelma instructed quietly.

The man hesitated.

'Come and stand before me here!' she repeated more sharply.

He did so.

'Now kneel down.'

Her eyes glinted as he hesitated for a fraction and then he dropped to one knee.

'Bow your head.'

He did so. She peered into the grey tousled mess of hair, much to the surprise of Díomsach and Conrí.

'Stand back,' she instructed after a moment or two, and when he had resumed his place, Fidelma pursed her lips. 'This blow that knocked you unconscious, it was on the head?'

'It was, it was.'

'There is an abrasion on the side of your head,' she confirmed.

'The story is false, Fidelma,' Díomsach said. 'Let him return to his farmstead and we will discuss what is to be done later.'

Fidelma compressed her lips for a moment and then said to the warrior Fallach: 'Take Febrat outside for a moment.'

When they had gone, Fidelma turned to her companions.

'This case intrigues me.'

The chief of the Tuatha Cromadh made a sound like a cynical chuckle.

'You surely don't believe the man, do you? Because he has an abrasion on the side of his head does not prove his ridiculous story!'

'Did I say that it did prove his story? What I believe is not relevant to the case. I know that this matter cannot be left as it is. Either there is something substantial that motivates this man to come to you with his stories, or it is something that is due to a dementia. Either way, one should investigate so that the good of the people may be safeguarded. I would like you, Díomsach, to keep Febrat in your custody while I will ride out to Febrat's farmstead and speak to his wife, Cara. And I shall take your chief warrior, Fallach, as escort in case of trouble.'

'I can tell you this, Fidelma of Cashel, there has been no Uí Fidgente raid,' Conrí announced belligerently.

Fidelma returned his sour look with a bright smile.

'I am sure that had such a raid taken place you, as an Uí Fidgente chieftain, would have the honesty to admit it,' she said softly.

Conrí's jaws snapped shut for a moment.

'I can give you this assurance, lady, that if there had been a raid, word of it would have come to my ear,' he said stiffly.

'Excellent.' Fidelma rose and looked across to where Brother Colla, the *scriptor*, was still working away. 'You may say that this court has ceased its hearing *sine die* while I investigate the matter of Febrat.'

'You are not going before the feasting?' demanded Díomsach in dismay.

'I think this matter demands my immediate attention. But I shall return, I hope, before evening to enjoy your feasting.'

Díomsach's face fell for he had been expecting to start the entertainment within that very hour and now the laws of hospitality would prevent his starting before his chief guest, the sister of the king, was ready to join him.

*   *   *

Febrat's farmstead stood in lush fields by the river of the plain, the Maigue, about an hour's ride from Díomsach's fortress. The nearest hills were a mile or two to the south and east.

Fallach, riding at Fidelma's side, stretched out a hand to indicate the group of buildings sheltering behind a small copse of oaks and yew.

'There is Febrat's farm, lady.'

Fidelma's eyes narrowed as they rode nearer. There came to her ears the sound of some cows in distress, a bellowing which she was able to interpret immediately.

'It sounds as though the cows have not been milked,' Fallach announced, interpreting the sound as she had but before she could articulate it.

They rode into the yard and looked round. Sure enough, two cows were bellowing in plaintive tones in a nearby paddock. Chickens ignored them and continued pecking their haphazard way around the yard. Other animals meandered here and there, a few sheep, several goats. Apart from that the place seemed deserted.

Fidelma dismounted and stood looking around.

Fallach had also slid from his horse and tied their mounts to the rail before striding forward to the house, shouting loudly for the wife of Febrat. There was no response.

'Shall we search inside, lady?' he asked.

Fidelma sighed deeply.

'Our first duty is to put those animals out of their misery,' she said, indicating the two cows. 'Find buckets. You take one and I will take the other.'

Fallach looked shocked.

'But lady, I am a warrior . . .'

'I am sure the poor beasts will overlook that fact as they will overlook the fact that I am a *dálaigh* and sister to the king,' she replied with a smile of sarcasm.

He flushed and turned to search for buckets.

A while later when the lowing of the cows had ceased and the buckets were almost full, Fidelma and Fallach stood up and moved the milk into the shade of the farmhouse.

'Well, it is clear that no one is here,' Fallach announced, peering around.

'We will search. You try the outbuildings and also watch out for any sign that a raid might have taken place. I will look inside.'

Fallach frowned. 'You do not think that this time Febrat is right . . . ?'

'The time to think about conclusions is after we have found some facts,' she replied, and went inside.

Febrat and Cara certainly kept a tidy house. Not just tidy but Fidelma found that, surprisingly for a farmer, there were several rich artefacts adorning the place and tapestries of good quality hanging from some of the walls and on the bed. She examined them with interest.

She frowned suddenly. The tapestry on the bed covered it neatly. She swung round. Certainly everything in the farmhouse was neat and placed in order. Her eyes dropped to a rug by the bedside. Again she was slightly surprised for this was a sign of wealth and quality of living. Most farm folk did not concern themselves with floor coverings; even those with higher standards would simply have bare boards on the floor while the great majority made do with earthen floors, trodden hard into an almost marble-like surface by the stamp of generations of feet upon it. But Febrat and Cara obviously liked to live well or were used to living well. This thought caused something to stir in her mind, something that was not quite right. It was the fact that Febrat had been described as an itinerant labourer. The thoughts went through her mind quickly as she glanced at the bedside rug, a sheepskin.

Then her eyes narrowed. There appeared to be a discoloured patch on the rug.

She stooped down and placed her hand on it. It was damp. She sniffed at her fingertips but there was no odour. It seemed that only water had been spilt on it. But water would have dried long before Febrat had completed his journey to her court that morning.

She picked up the rug and moved to the door. As she did so the sunlight shot through the clouds. It caught on the sheepskin that she was holding; on the creamy white of the wool. Something caught her eye among the patch of white woollen tufts. It was a few dark spots, which had been missed by the water.

She licked her fingertip and rubbed. A tinge of red remained on her finger. The spots had been dried blood.

She stared at her finger for a time before returning the sheepskin and turning to the cupboards and examining the contents. She noticed that Cara had a large wardrobe compared with the average farmer's wife and she found a box of personal items of jewellery. Cara was obviously someone who believed in personal adornment. And the jewels were valuable.

She went outside to join Fallach.

'Did you find anything?' she asked as he came out of a barn door.

He shook his head. 'Nothing. There are no signs of violence or destruction. I am afraid that Febrat has let his imagination run wild again.'

'But what of the missing wife, Cara?' Fidelma pointed out.

Fallach shrugged. 'Maybe she has gone to visit friends or relatives.'

'Again?'

Fallach looked puzzled at her inflection.

Fidelma did not answer his questioning glance but began to walk across the farmyard to the barn. Suddenly she bent down and picked up a branch.

'What tree would you say that came from?'

Fallach barely glanced at it.

'It's an alder, of course.'

Fidelma gazed round at the trees surrounding them. Oaks and yew but there was no sign of an alder. She dropped the branch and continued to the barn. Inside was a cart, the usual type of cart found on a farm, which could be pulled by a single ass. Its large wheels were still damp with drying mud. On the cart was a large metal-bladed spade, a *ráma* for digging earth. The blade had similar wet mud on it.

She glanced round the interior of the barn. There seemed nothing out of place. Certainly no sign of anything that could be interpreted as an indication of an attack or violence. Her eye caught sight of a wooden chest in a corner. Part of its exterior had drying mud clinging to it and the muddy imprint of a hand. The chest was fastened with an iron lock and there was no sight of a key. She turned to Fallach.

'Find a hammer and open that,' she instructed.

Fallach whistled in surprise.

'But, lady . . .'

'I take responsibility.'

He paused only a moment more and then did as he was told.

Inside the chest was a small hand pick and wrapped in sacking a large number of what seemed to be lumps of metal. Fallach looked puzzled and reached in to pick one up.

'Silver!' he whispered. 'Great nuggets of silver.'

'And excavated recently,' agreed Fidelma, bending down and pointing to the bright marks on the nuggets and the marks on the hand pick.

'I know there are places to the north-east of here, mountains where those who mine lead and other metals say that veins of silver are to be seen. But these are nuggets. Rich ones.'

Fidelma rose to her feet.

'Replace them and let us continue with our task. If, as you say, Febrat's wife was staying with friends or relatives, exactly who would she have gone to visit?'

Fallach grimaced as he replaced the lid of the box.

'You mean near here?'

'Near here will do to start with,' affirmed Fidelma patiently.

'Well, Cara's mother, the lady Donn Dige, lives half an hour's ride in that direction.' He pointed to the south.

Fidelma's eyes widened a fraction at the name.

'Donn Dige? Isn't she . . . ?'

'She was sister to a prince of the Eóghanacht Áine,' Fallach confirmed. 'Her brother was killed at the battle of Cnoc Áine just two years ago.'

Fidelma sighed. So that explained the comparative wealth displayed in the farmhouse. Cara was not the average farmer's wife but the daughter of a princely ruling house.

'Someone should have explained that to me,' she muttered almost petulantly.

'Does it matter?' inquired Fallach innocently. 'It does not bear on the fact that Febrat is mad.'

'Perhaps, perhaps not,' agreed Fidelma. She glanced at the cart again. 'Those wheels have been through a lot of mud. Let's see if we can pick up the trail of its last journey.'

Fallach looked at her curiously.

'Why would you want to do that? The cart is just a normal farm cart. I have often seen Febrat driving it. It has nothing to do with any imagined Uí Fidgente raid.'

'Indulge me, Fallach,' said Fidelma, mounting her horse.

They rode out of the farmyard, eyes on the ground seeking the tracks of the cart. To Fidelma's surprise they found no tracks at all. Some

189

instinct told her to circle to the north, following a stony track. They had to go some distance from the farm buildings before they found traces of the almost obscured tracks they wanted. They moved down a narrow path through fields of cereal crops and then cut across a ploughed field and then over coarse uncultivated land. It began to be very stony. She suddenly paused when she saw several newly cut branches of alder lying discarded on the rocky soil. She slid from her horse and examined them. Sections about ten or fifteen feet in length had been cut, spreading out their twigs and leaves like a broom. She peered around and to Fallach's surprise spent some time peering at the stony ground.

'We seem to be some way from an alder wood,' she observed. 'And these branches appear to have been dragged here.'

Fallach did not reply, as he had no idea what to answer.

'If I am not mistaken, that is Uí Fidgente territory,' Fidelma said, pointing to the north as she remounted her horse. 'I presume that Faramund's farmstead lies in that direction?'

'It does. He is a good man, even though he is one of the Uí Fidgente. Even Febrat's wife Cara told us that he was a good neighbour. Febrat confirmed that before he became sure that Faramund was leading these imaginary raids, he and his wife often invited him over to feast with them.'

Fidelma nodded.

'You found him reasonable enough when you questioned him with Díomsach? You felt no threat from him?'

'None.'

Fidelma halted and looked back towards the southern hills.

'I have changed my mind,' she said. 'Let us go and see if Cara is at the home of her mother.'

'The homestead of the lady Donn Dige?' Fallach was surprised but he shrugged and turned his horse in that direction.

The house of Donn Dige was a small fortified building, which spoke of the wealth that the sister of a petty king would have. There were a few men working in neighbouring fields. It was a far richer farmstead than the house of Febrat and his wife.

A short, almost muscular woman awaited them at the entrance. She had greying hair and coarse features and watched them suspiciously.

'Good day, Doireann,' called Fallach as they approached. 'Is the lady Donn Dige at home?'

The woman's narrowed eyes continued to rest on Sister Fidelma.

'Who wants to know?' she said ungraciously.

Fallach glanced in embarrassment at his companion and was about to open his mouth when Fidelma intervened.

'Tell her that it is Fidelma of Cashel who wants to know,' she snapped. 'And if she hesitates to welcome the sister of the King of Muman, tell her it is a *dálaigh* of the courts that seeks her out. And be quick, woman.'

The woman called Doireann blinked for a moment and then, with deliberate slowness, she turned and made her way into the house while Fallach and Fidelma dismounted in the courtyard and hitched their horses to a rail erected for that purpose. By the time they had done so, the woman had reappeared and waved them forward into the building.

Donn Dige received them. She was a dignified and elderly woman, whose rank showed in her stature and clothing. Had she stood, she would have been tall. Fidelma noticed the crutch at her side. The woman saw the glance and smiled ruefully.

'A riding accident, so you will forgive my inability to rise to greet you. Alas, it also confines me to the house.'

The greetings were pleasant and in contrast with the curtness of her servant, Doireann. Refreshments were offered and accepted.

'What can I do for you, Fidelma of Cashel?' inquired Donn Dige after the rituals had been observed.

'Let me begin by asking whether your daughter, Cara, is staying with you?'

The elderly woman's eyes narrowed suspiciously.

'I have not seen my daughter this last month. Why do you ask?'

Fidelma hid her surprise. 'Not for a month?'

'Why do you ask?'

'Her husband has reported her missing and claims his farm was raided by the Uí Fidgente.'

Donn Dige compressed her mouth for a moment.

'Again? Is this the same claim that he made last week?'

'It is a claim he made this morning,' intervened Fallach.

'If you have not seen your daughter for a month how do you know about the previous claims?' pressed Fidelma.

'Simple enough. Doireann is my messenger and news-bringer.'

'Though it is surely a short ride from Febrat's farmstead to here,' Fidelma reflected, 'which makes me wonder why your daughter has not visited you this last month.'

Donne Dige smiled, perhaps a little sadly.

'My daughter has her own worries and she will come in her own good time. Doireann tells me that she has been greatly worried about Febrat.'

'In what way?' demanded Fidelma.

'What way would anyone be worried when one's husband starts to claim that events are happening when one knows that they are not?'

'Your daughter believes that her husband is losing his reason?'

'Of course. What else can it be?'

'Doireann has reported to you that Cara is absolutely sure that there is no reason for Febrat to make these claims?'

'None. Have you been to the farm yet? What does Cara say about this latest claim?'

'Your daughter is not at the farm.'

Donn Dige's eyes widened slightly.

'Is there any sign of a raid?' she asked anxiously.

'None at all,' Fallach said quickly. 'The animals are there, the house is untouched by any sign of an attack . . .'

'Then she has gone visiting.' The elderly woman smiled in relief. 'I shall send for Doireann to . . .'

She was about to reach for a bell on a side table when Fidelma stayed her.

'Let us sort out a few things first,' she insisted gently. 'Are there any problems between your daughter and her husband?'

'Problems?'

'Marital problems.'

'As far as I am aware, there were none before Febrat started these hallucinations. However, if you must know, I disapproved of my daughter's choice of husband.'

'Why?'

'He was of inferior rank. My brother was prince of a territory whose honour price was seven *cumals*. My daughter, by rank and learning, had an honour price of a full *cumal* while Febrat had the value of a *colpach*, no more.'

A *colpach* was the value of a two-year-old heifer compared to a *cumal* equivalent to the value of three milch cows.

Fidelma frowned.

'Do you mean that he did not own the farmstead?'

Donn Dige sniffed in disgust.

'Of course not. Apart from some gifts from my family to Cara, they have no substance to call their own. Since my brother's death in battle, our branch of the family has been in reduced circumstances.'

'Then the rich tapestries and objects in the farmhouse . . . ?'

'A few gifts and loans by my family so that Cara would have some semblance of the rank to which she had been accustomed.'

'Who owns the farm?'

'My cousin, the lord of Orbraige. Febrat is simply his tenant at will.'

'Was the fact that Febrat was of inferior rank to your daughter, and thereby without wealth, your only objection to their marriage?'

'It was a major factor,' confirmed the elderly woman. 'But, in truth, and I admit that I am prejudiced, I simply did not like him. He had the look of a hungry wolf, the bright intensity of his eyes, longing and underfed.'

'So all the wealth in the house belongs to your daughter?'

'He had nothing at all apart . . .'

'Apart from what?' prompted Fidelma.

'He had a little patch of land on a hill beside the river of the plain. A piece of worthless stone that used to mark the boundary of the Uí Fidgente land. It was all he could buy with money he had saved as an itinerant labourer. A stupid waste, for it is useless for grazing and useless for planting. A stony, infertile tract of land called Cnoc Cerb.'

Beside her, Fallach let out a sharp breath.

'Isn't *cerb* the ancient word for . . . ?'

'It's an old name, Hill of Silver,' replied Fidelma, swiftly moving on. 'But apart from your reservations, Donn Dige, I presume that there were no other objections to this marriage? Your daughter was in love with him?'

'Love!' sniffed Donn Dige as if such a thing were not even worth discussing.

'When was the marriage?'

193

'Six months ago.'

'And the marriage has proved a happy one?'

'As I said, the only thing that worried my daughter, according to Doireann, was this recent business of imagining the Uí Fidgente were raiding the farmstead. I understand that it happened twice and both times it was shown to be in his imagination.'

'And at the time these raids were supposed to take place, your daughter was not at the farmstead. Was she staying with you?'

'I am not my daughter's keeper. I have no idea where she was.'

'Tell me something about Febrat's background.'

'There is nothing to tell. I believe that his parents died when he was a child. The mother died in childbirth and the father later on. The father was a *sen-cleithe*, a herdsman, and that was the occupation Febrat followed until he met my daughter . . . But where is my daughter?' Donn Dige suddenly demanded.

'I intend to find out,' Fidelma said softly as she stood up.

Donn Dige suddenly looked pale. For all her hauteur, and desire to keep her emotions to herself, the hurt that her daughter had not visited her shone in her eyes.

'Has Febrat killed her and pretended that the Uí Fidgente have carried her off?'

'What makes you ask that?'

'It stands to reason. The man has become mad . . . or cunning. He went to Díomsach the chief with outlandish tales of raids twice. Twice the claims were investigated. According to you he went a third time today and it is likely that he thought that Díomsach would not even bother to investigate and simply throw him out of his fortress.'

Fallach nodded slowly.

'That is certainly what Díomsach intended to do.' He turned eagerly to Fidelma. 'Had it not been for your presence, Febrat would have been sent to his farm and it would not have been discovered that Cara was missing for several days. Then Febrat would have simply said that he had told us so and we would have felt guilty for not looking for her. We would not have suspected him.'

Fidelma silenced him with an upraised hand.

'That is leaping to the conclusion that Febrat possesses enough cunning to plan such a complicated method of murder,' she observed.

'What other explanation is there?' demanded Donn Dige wearily.

194

'I shall endeavour to discover what has happened to your daughter, Donn Dige. I hope to have an answer to your question before nightfall.'

As they rode back in the direction of the farmstead of Febrat and Cara, Fallach was still shaking his head in bewilderment.

'I don't understand, lady. You seem to know something that I don't.'

Fidelma smiled briefly.

'Let us say that I now have a presentiment.'

'I still do not understand. Where are we making for, lady?'

'The farmstead of Faramund.'

He stared at her for a moment.

'You surely don't believe that Faramund and the Uí Fidgente did raid Febrat's farmstead?'

'I will tell you what I believe when we reach Faramund's farmstead.'

The farmstead lay at the foot of a hill. As they were crossing its gentle sloping shoulder, Fallach pointed to another jagged, stony hillock about a half-mile distant.

'That is Cnoc Cerb, the Hill of Silver, lady,' he said. 'That's where Febrat must be digging out those silver nuggets.'

Dogs were barking a warning below them as they rode down the track that led to the farm buildings.

A young man, tanned, with dark hair and handsome features, had come out of the building and now stood leaning on a gate watching their approach. His pleasant face wore a smile of welcome as he waited for them to ride up.

'This is Faramund,' muttered Fallach in explanation at her side.

'Good day, Fallach. Good day, Sister,' the young man sang out. 'What can I do for you this fine afternoon?'

Fidelma halted her horse and dismounted. Fallach followed her example.

'You can tell Cara to come out from where she is hiding,' Fidelma smiled back.

Faramund's expression changed to one of momentary shock before he controlled himself. Fallach's jaw had also dropped slightly at her opening words.

'Cara?' Faramund's voice was puzzled. 'Do you . . . you mean Febrat's wife? I don't know where . . .'

The corners of Fidelma's mouth turned down in disapproval.

'It will save us a lot of time if you are honest, Faramund. You have placed your chieftain, Conrí, in an embarrassing position, organising mock raids on Febrat's farmstead and conspiring with his wife to have him declared insane.'

'Conspiring . . . ?' The good humour in the young man seemed to evaporate into visible anger 'Who are you to come here and make these accusations?'

'Fallach, explain to Faramund who I am.'

The warrior did so.

'So, Faramund, you have a choice,' went on Fidelma calmly. 'You will co-operate with me now, or you will do so later under duress before your chieftain. If you choose the latter, your punishment when you are judged will be that much more severe.'

Faramund stared malevolently at her. He was not intimidated.

'You threaten to carry me off to be judged? You are either very brave or very stupid, *dálaigh*. There are only two of you, one warrior and one woman. Within my call there are half a dozen of my men. I have but to summon them . . .'

'And then what? Díomsach and your own chieftain Conrí await our return. Do you think that you can threaten harm to a *dálaigh* and the sister of the King of Muman with impunity?'

Faramund was still truculent and threatening.

'The King of Muman is not here and I . . .'

A female voice interrupted.

'Enough, Faramund! You cannot defy her by physical threats. She is too powerful.'

A young woman emerged from the door. She had dark hair and was good-looking in a voluptuous way. She knew that she was attractive and her whole body moved in a manner that seemed to exploit the animal-like quality. Fidelma noticed that she was holding a wooden mallet in her hand as if as a defensive weapon.

Faramund turned as if to protest.

'Cara! So you are here?' Fallach greeted her in astonishment.

The young woman laughed. There was bitterness in her tone. 'That is obvious.' She turned to stare at Fidelma. 'But I don't know how you knew.'

Fidelma sighed softly.

196

'When did you think of this crazy scheme, Cara? Was it before or after you married Febrat?'

The young woman looked defiant.

'I have nothing to say. You can prove nothing. Is it a crime to have a lover? My husband could not fulfil all my wants.'

Faramund nodded eagerly at her words.

'Cara's right. We are simply lovers. What else are you accusing us of?'

Fidelma regarded them patiently.

'I was not aware that I had accused you of anything. But, since you have raised the matter, it's quite simple. You want Febrat out of the way so that you can take over the silver mine at Cnoc Cerb.'

Faramund gave an angry hiss as he exhaled sharply but Cara's shoulders suddenly drooped in resignation.

'You will have to prove it,' she said quietly but submissively.

'If Febrat could be pronounced without legal responsibility, as a *mer*, one who is confused or deranged, then you would be in control of his land at Cnoc Cerb.'

'I don't understand what you are talking about,' Cara said suddenly. 'I know nothing of law.'

'But you do, don't you, Faramund? What level of law did you achieve in your studies?'

Faramund flushed.

'Who says that I . . . ?'

'Do not waste my time!' she snapped.

'There has been no secret that you once studied law before you became a farmer,' Fallach pointed out. 'I know it and so does Díomsach.'

The young man hesitated and then shrugged.

'I studied to the level of *freisneidhed*.'

'So you reached your third year of study?' mused Fidelma. 'And thus you have read the text Do Drúithaib agus Meraib agus Dásachtaib which deals with the use of land belonging to an insane person.' It was a statement not a question. 'So it was you who suggested a way by which Cara might take over her husband's land at Cnoc Cerb without killing poor Febrat? Have him declared a *mer* and, being guardian, she would gain control of the riches that he had discovered there.'

Cara was defiant.

'So what? No harm would have come to Febrat. The law says that I would have to look after Febrat for so long as he lives and if I did not I would have to pay five *séds* and suffer forfeiture of the land. He would not have suffered . . .'

Faramund frowned at her.

'You are talking too much, Cara,' he warned sharply. 'She cannot prove . . .'

'I expect,' Fidelma wheeled round on him, 'that was not your plan, was it? An accident, perhaps, some months in the future? Or perhaps something more subtle? An insane person attacking his wife? The insane person can be killed in self-defence or by someone else acting to defend the person being attacked.' She turned back to Cara, who was sobbing quietly. 'What I would like to know is when did this plan first materialise in your mind – before or after you married Febrat?'

'Faramund and I were lovers before Febrat started paying me court. My mother was a princess of Áine and so was I but we had no wealth, no backing. You don't know what that means. It was then we found out that there was silver in the hill which Febrat owned. It was Faramund who suggested the idea of obtaining ownership without even hurting Febrat by having him declared insane. I married him and waited for a while before we put the plan into operation.'

'And you really think that Faramund would remain your secret lover while Febrat lived? Once you had your hands on the silver mine, Faramund would have wanted to own it by seeking marriage with you and becoming your heir. How long before not only Febrat perished but you as well?'

Faramund's eyes narrowed. His look was murderous.

'You don't think that you will be able to get back to Díomsach and tell him this, do you?' he asked quietly.

Fidelma smiled softly.

'Are you proposing to start your killing spree already? First Fallach and myself and then . . . who? Cara next, I suppose.'

Faramund drew out a vicious-looking long-bladed knife but before anyone could move he suddenly gave a grunt and went down senseless to the ground.

Cara was standing behind him looking at the wooden mallet in her hand.

'I presume that you used the same method to knock out your

husband? Faramund and his farmhands came last night and rode around the farmstead hooting and yelling to convince your husband the farm was under attack. They trailed alder branches behind them to disguise the passage of their horses.'

Cara gestured helplessly.

'I could not stand to kill anyone. I told Faramund that. He made his plan seem so plausible. No one would get hurt. Febrat would be taken care of and we would have the silver. But I could not bear to kill anyone.'

Fallach, who had been bending by the slumped form of Faramund, glanced up and grimaced.

'I am afraid that you will have to come to terms with that, Cara. You have hit him too hard.'

Scattered Thorns

⁊

'The boy is innocent.'

The chief magistrate of Droim Sorn, Brehon Tuama, seemed adamant.

Sister Fidelma sat back in her chair and gazed thoughtfully at the tall man who was seated on the other side of the hearth. She had received an urgent request from Brehon Tuama to come to the small township of Droim Sorn in her capacity as *dálaigh*, advocate of the law courts. A sixteen-year-old lad named Braon had been accused of murder and theft. Brehon Tuama had suggested that Fidelma should undertake the boy's defence

In accordance with protocol, Fidelma had first made her presence in the township known to the chieftain, Odar, in whose house the boy was being held. Odar seemed to display a mixed reaction to her arrival but had offered her a few formal words of welcome before suggesting that she seek out Brehon Tuama to discuss the details of the case. She had decided, on this brief acquaintance, that Odar was not a man particularly concerned with details. She had noticed that the chieftain had an impressive array of hunting weapons on his walls and two sleek wolfhounds basking in front of his hearth. She deduced that Odar's concerns were more of the hunt than the pursuit of justice.

Brehon Tuama had invited her inside his house and offered her refreshment before making his opening remark about the accused's guilt.

'Are you saying that the boy is not to be tried?' asked Fidelma. 'If you have already dismissed the case against him, why was I summoned . . . ?'

Brehon Tuama quickly shook his head.

'I cannot dismiss the matter yet. Odar is adamant that the boy has to go through due process. In fact . . .' The Brehon hesitated. 'The victim's husband is his cousin.'

Fidelma sighed softly. She disliked nepotism.

'Perhaps you should explain to me the basic facts as you know them.'

Brehon Tuama stretched uneasily in his chair.

'Findach the smith is reputed to be one of the most able craftsmen in this township. His work is apparently widely admired and has graced abbeys, chieftains' raths, and kings' fortresses. He has been able to refuse such mundane tasks as shoeing horses, or making harnesses, ploughs, and weapons, to pursue more artistic work.'

'It sounds as though you do not share others' appreciation of his work?' interposed Fidelma, catching the inflection in his tone.

'I don't,' agreed the Brehon. 'But that is by the way. Findach was commissioned to make a silver cross for the high altar of the Abbey of Cluain. He had completed the commission only a few days ago.

'The cross was extremely valuable. Findach had polished it and taken it to his house ready for collection by one of the religious from the abbey. Yesterday morning, Findach had gone to his workshop, which is a hundred yards beyond his house, to commence work. The silver cross was left in his house. His wife, Muirenn, was there.

'It was that morning that Brother Caisín had been sent by the Abbot of Cluain to collect the cross. I have questioned Brother Caisín who says that he arrived at Findach's house early in the morning. He noticed that the door was open and he went in. Muirenn lay on the floor with blood on her head. He tried to render assistance but found that she was dead, apparently killed by a sharp blow to the head.

'Brother Caisín then said that he heard a noise from a side room and found the boy, Braon, hiding there. There was blood on his clothes.

'It was then that Findach arrived back at his house and found Brother Caisín and Braon standing by the body of his wife. His cry of anguish was heard by a passer-by who, ascertaining the situation, came in search of me as Brehon of Droim Sorn.'

Fidelma was thoughtful.

'At what point was it discovered the silver cross was missing?' she asked.

Brehon Tuama looked surprised.

'How did you know that it was the silver cross that had been stolen? The object of the theft was not specified when I sent for you.'

Fidelma made an impatient gesture with her hand.

'I did not think that you would spend so much time and detail telling me about Findach's commission from Cluain if it had no relevance to this matter.'

Brehon Tuama looked crestfallen.

'What did the boy have to say?' Fidelma continued. 'I presume the boy's father was sent for before you questioned him?'

Brehon Tuama looked pained.

'Of course. I know the law. As he is under the "age of choice", his father is deemed responsible for him in law.'

'So the father was summoned and the boy was questioned?' pressed Fidelma impatiently.

'The boy said that he had been asked to go to Findach's house by Muirenn, who often used to employ him to look after a small herd of cattle they kept in the upper pastures behind the house. Braon said he found the door open. He saw the body and went inside in order to help, but Muirenn was already dead.'

'And bending by the body accounted for blood on his clothes?'

'Precisely. He said that he was about to go for help when he heard someone approaching. Fearing the return of the killer, he hid in the room where Brother Caisín discovered him.'

'And those are all the facts, so far as you know them?'

'Exactly. It is all circumstantial evidence. I would be inclined to dismiss the charge for lack of evidence. However, Odar insists that the boy should be prosecuted. A chieftain's orders are sometimes difficult to disregard,' he added apologetically.

'What about the cross?'

Brehon Tuama was baffled for a moment.

'I mean,' went on Fidelma, 'where was it found? You have not mentioned that fact.'

The Brehon shifted his weight.

'It has not been found,' he confessed.

Fidelma made her surprise apparent.

'We made a thorough search for the cross and found no sign of it,' confirmed Brehon Tuama.

'Surely, that further weakens the case against the boy? When could he have had the time to hide the cross before being discovered by Brother Caisín?'

'Odar argues that he must have had an accomplice. He favours the boy's father. He suggests the boy passed the cross to his accomplice just as Brother Caisín arrived.'

'A rather weak argument.' Fidelma was dismissive. 'What I find more interesting is the motivation for your chieftain's apparent determination to pursue the boy and his father. You tell me that it is because the dead woman's husband is his cousin? That does not seem sufficient justification. I would agree with your first conclusion, Tuama. The whole affair is based on circumstantial evidence. By the way, how big was this silver cross?'

'I do not know. We would have to ask Findach. Findach said it was valuable enough. The silver alone being worth . . .'

'I am more interested in its size, not value. Presumably, a high altar cross would be of large size and therefore of great weight?'

'Presumably,' agreed the Brehon.

'Also too heavy, surely, for the boy, Braon, to have hidden it by himself?'

Brehon Tuama did not reply.

'You say that Findach's forge was a hundred yards from his house. Isn't it unusual for a smith to have a workshop at such a distance from his house?'

Brehon Tuama shook his head.

'Not in this case. Findach was a careful man. Do you know how often smiths' forges burn down because a spark from the furnace ignites them?'

'I have known of some cases,' admitted Fidelma. 'So Findach and his wife Muirenn lived in the house. Did they have children?'

'No. There were just the two of them . . .'

There was a sudden noise outside and the door burst open.

A wild-looking, broad-shouldered man stood on the threshold. He was dressed in the manner of a man who worked long hours in the fields. His eyes were stormy.

Brehon Tuama sprang up from his seat in annoyance.

'What is the meaning of this, Brocc?' he demanded.

The man stood breathing heavily a moment.

'You know well enough, Brehon. I heard that the *dálaigh* had arrived.

She's been to see Odar and now you. Yet you told me that she was coming to defend my boy. Defend? How can she defend him when she consorts only with his persecutors?'

Fidelma examined the man coolly.

'Come forward! So you are the father of Braon?'

The burly man took a hesitant step towards her.

'My son is innocent! You must clear his name. They are trying to lay the blame on my son and on me because they hate us.'

'I am here to listen to the evidence and form my opinion. Why would people hate you and your son?'

'Because I am a *bothach*!'

In the social system of the five kingdoms of Éireann, the *bothach* was one of the lowest classes in society, being a crofter or cowherd. *Bothachs* had no political or clan rights, but they were capable of acquiring their own plots of land by contract. While there were no restrictions placed on whom they could work for, they were not allowed to leave the clan territory except by special permission. If they worked well, they could eventually expect to acquire full citizen's rights.

'Aye.' Brocc was bitter. 'It is always the lower orders who are blamed when a crime is committed. Always the bottom end of the social scale who get the blame. That is why Odar is trying to make out that my boy and I were in league to rob Findach.'

Fidelma was beginning to understand what Brehon Tuama had been trying to tell her about Odar's insistence that Braon stand trial.

'You and your son have nothing to fear so long as you tell the truth,' she said, trying not to let it sound like a platitude. 'If I believe your son is innocent then I will defend him.' Fidelma paused for a moment. 'You realise that under the law it will be your responsibility to pay the compensation and fines if your son is found guilty? Are you more concerned about that or whether your son is innocent?'

Brocc scowled, his features reddening.

'That is unjust. I will pay you seven *séds* if you simply defend him. That is a token of my faith in my son.'

The sum was the value of seven milch cows.

Fidelma's face showed that she was not impressed.

'Brehon Tuama should have informed you that my fees, which are payable directly to my community and not to me, do not vary but stand at two *séds* and only change when they are remitted because of exceptional circumstances such as the poverty of those who seek my assistance.'

Brocc stood uncertainly with lips compressed. Fidelma went on: 'Since you are here, Brocc, you may tell me a little about your son, Braon. Did he frequently work for Findach?'

'Not for Findach, that mean . . . !' Brocc caught himself. 'No, my boy worked for his wife Muirenn. Muirenn was a kindly soul, a good soul. My boy would never have harmed her.'

'How often did he work for Muirenn and in what capacity?'

'My boy and I are cowherds. We hire our labour to those who need an expert hand.'

'So you knew Braon was going to work for Muirenn that morning?'

'I did. She had asked him to tend her cows in the pasture above the house.'

'And that was a usual task for him?'

'Usual? It was.'

'Did anyone else know he was going to Muirenn's house that morning?'

'The boy's mother knew and doubtless Muirenn told that mean husband of hers.'

Fidelma was interested.

'Why do you call Findach mean?'

'The man was tight-fisted. It was well known. He behaved as if he was as poor as a church mouse.'

Fidelma glanced to Brehon Tuama for confirmation. The tall magistrate shrugged.

'It is true that Findach was not renowned for his generosity, Sister. He always claimed he had little money. The truth was he spent a lot on gambling. In fact, only the other day Odar told me that Findach owed him a large sum. Ten *séds*, as I recall. Yet Findach would not even employ an assistant or an apprentice at his forge.'

'Yet he did pay for help with his cattle.'

Brocc laughed harshly.

'The herd was his wife's property and she paid my son.'

A wife, under law, remained the owner of all the property and wealth that she brought into a marriage. Fidelma appreciated the point.

'So, as far as you knew, your son went off to work as usual. You noticed nothing unusual at all?'

'I did not.'

'And during that day, you never went near Findach's house nor his forge?'

'Nowhere near.'

'You can prove it?'

Brocc glowered for a moment.

'I can prove it. I was in Lonán's pastures helping him thresh hay. I was there until someone came with the news of Braon's arrest.'

'Very well.' Fidelma rose abruptly. 'I think I would like to see Findach's house and speak with this renowned smith.'

The house of Findach the smith stood on the edge of the township. It was isolated among a small copse of hazel and oak.

Findach was a stocky, muscular man of indiscernible age. He had a short neck and a build that one associated with a smith. He gazed distastefully at Fidelma.

'If you seek to defend my wife's killer, *dálaigh*, you are not welcome in this house.' His voice was a low growl of anger.

Fidelma was not perturbed.

'Inform Findach of the law and my rights as a *dálaigh*, Tuama,' she instructed, her eyes not leaving those of the smith.

'You are obliged by law to answer all the *dálaigh's* questions and allow free access to all . . .'

Findach cut the Brehon short with a scowl and turned abruptly inside the house, leaving them to follow.

Fidelma addressed herself to Brehon Tuama.

'Show me where the body was lying.'

Tuama pointed to the floor inside the first room, which was the kitchen.

'And where was the boy found?'

Findach answered this time, turning and pushing open a door sharply.

'The killer was hiding in here,' he grunted.

'I understand that you knew that Brother Caisín would be arriving to collect the silver cross you had made for his abbey?'

Findach glanced at Brehon Tuama who stood stony-faced. Then he shrugged. His voice was ungracious.

206

'I expected someone from the abbey to come to collect the piece. It was the agreed day.'

'You brought the cross from your forge to the house. Wasn't that unusual?'

'I brought it here for safekeeping. There is no one at my forge at night and so I do not leave valuable items there.'

'How valuable was this cross?'

'My commission price was twenty-one *séds*.'

'Describe the cross, its weight and size.'

'It was of silver mined at Magh Méine. Just over three feet in height and half of that across the arms. It was heavy. The only way I could carry it was by means of a rope slung across my back.'

'Brother Caisín was to carry it in the same fashion?'

'I believe he arrived on an ass, realising the weight to be transported.'

'And where did you leave the cross?'

'It was standing in that corner of the room.'

Fidelma went and looked at the corner that he indicated.

'You believe that the boy, Braon, came into your house, saw this cross, killed your wife, and took it, heavy as it was, and then – presumably having hidden it – returned to this house? Having done that, hearing the arrival of Brother Caisín, he then hid himself in that room, where he was discovered.'

Findach scowled at her smile of scepticism.

'How else do you explain it?'

'I don't have to, as yet. What time did you leave that morning to go to your forge?'

Findach shrugged.

'Just after dawn.'

'Did you know the boy was coming to help with your wife's herd?'

'I knew. I never trusted him. His father was a *bothach*, always cadging money from the better off.'

'I understand that you were not one of them.' Fidelma's riposte caused Findach's face to go red.

'I don't know what you mean,' he said defensively.

'I heard that you were regarded as poor.'

'Silver and gold costs money. When I get a commission, I have

207

to find the metals and don't get paid until the commission is complete.'

'Braon had worked for your wife often before, hadn't he?' Fidelma changed the subject.

'He had.'

'And you had no cause to complain about him before? Surely you have left valuable items in your house on other occasions?'

'My wife is murdered. The silver cross is gone. The boy was a *bothach*.'

'So you imply that you were always suspicious of him? As you say, he was a *bothach*. Yet you left the silver cross in your house and went to the forge. Isn't that strange?'

Findach flushed in annoyance.

'I did not suspect that he would be tempted . . .'

'Quite so,' snapped Fidelma. She turned to Brehon Tuama. 'I suppose that you have asked Brother Caisín to remain in Droim Sorn until the case is concluded?'

'Indeed I have. Much to his annoyance. But I have sent a message to his abbot to explain the circumstances.'

'Excellent.' Fidelma swung round to Findach. 'Now, I would like to see your forge.'

Findach was astonished.

'I do not understand what relevance . . . ?'

Fidelma smiled mischievously.

'You do not have to understand, only to respond to my questions. I understand the forge is a hundred yards from here?'

Findach bit his lip and turned silently to lead the way.

The forge lay one hundred yards through the trees in a small clearing.

'The furnace is out,' observed Fidelma as they entered.

'Of course. I have not worked here since yesterday morning.'

'Obviously,' Fidelma agreed easily. Then, surprising both Findach and Brehon Tuama, she thrust her right hand into the grey charcoal of the brazier. After a moment, she withdrew her hand and without any comment went to the *umar* or water trough to wash the dirt off. As she did so, she surveyed the *cartha*, the term used for a forge. It was unusual for a forge to be so isolated from the rest of the township. Smiths and their forges were usually one of the important centres of a district, often well frequented. Findach seemed to read her mind.

'I am a craftsman only in silver and gold these days. I do not make harnesses, shoe horses, or fix farm implements. I make works of art.'

His voice possessed arrogance, a boastfulness.

She did not answer.

The great anvil stood in the centre of the forge, near the blackened wood-charcoal-filled brazier and next to the water trough. A box containing the supply of wood charcoal stood nearby ready for fuelling the fire. There was a bellows next to the brazier.

'Do you have examples of your work here?' she asked, peering round.

Findach shook his head.

'I have closed down my forge out of respect to my wife. Once this matter is cleared up . . .'

'But you must have moulds, casts . . . pieces you have made?'

Findach shook his head.

'I was just curious to see the work of a smith who is so renowned for his fine work. However, to the task at hand. I think, Brehon Tuama, I shall see the boy now.'

They retraced their steps to Odar's house. The chieftain was out hunting, but his *tánaiste*, his heir apparent, led them to the room where the accused boy was held.

Braon was tall for his sixteen years. A thin, pale boy, fair of skin and freckled. There was no sign that he had yet begun to shave. He stood up nervously before Fidelma.

Fidelma entered the room while Brehon Tuama, by agreement, stayed outside as, under law, if she were to defend the boy, it was her privilege to see him alone. She waved him to be seated again on the small wooden bed while she herself sat on a stool before him.

'You know who I am?' she asked.

The boy nodded.

'I want you to tell me your story in your own words.'

'I have already told the Brehon.'

'The Brehon is to sit in judgement on you. I am a *dálaigh* who will defend you. So tell me.'

The young boy seemed nervous.

'What will happen to me?'

'That depends if you are guilty or innocent.'

'No one cares if a *bothach* is innocent when there is a crime to be answered for.'

'That is not what the law says, Braon. The law is there to protect the innocent whoever they are and to punish the guilty whoever they may be. Do you understand?'

'That is not how Odar sees it,' replied the boy.

'Tell me the events of that morning when you went to work for Muirenn,' Fidelma said, thinking it best not to pursue the matter of Odar's prejudice.

'I did not kill her. She was always kind to me. She was not like her husband, Findach. He was mean, and I heard her reprimanding him often about that. He claimed that he did not have money but everyone knows that smiths have money.'

'Tell me what happened that morning.'

'I arrived at the house and went inside . . .'

'One moment. Was there anything out of the usual? Was there anyone about, so far as you saw?'

The boy shook his head thoughtfully.

'Nothing out of the usual. I saw no one, except for Odar's hunting dogs . . . he has two big wolfhounds. I saw them bounding into the woods by Findach's forge. But there was no one about. So I went to the house and found the door ajar. I called out and, receiving no answer, I pushed it open.'

'What did you see?'

'From the open door I could see a body on the floor of the kitchen beyond. It was Muirenn. I thought she had fallen, perhaps struck her head. I bent down and felt her pulse, but the moment my hand touched her flesh I could feel a chill on it. I knew that she was dead.'

'The flesh felt chilled?'

'It did.'

'What then?' she prompted.

'I stood up and . . .'

'A moment. Did you see any sign of the silver cross in the room?'

'It was not there. Something as unusual as that I would have noticed even in such circumstances. In fact, I was looking round when I heard a noise. Someone was approaching. I panicked and hid myself in an adjoining room.' He hesitated. 'The rest you must know. Brother Caisín came in and discovered me. There was blood on my clothes where I had touched Muirenn. No one listened, and hence I am accused of theft and murder. Sister, I swear to you that I never saw such a cross nor would I have killed Muirenn. She was one of the few people here who did not treat me as if I were beneath contempt!'

Fidelma found it difficult to question the sincerity in the boy's voice. She joined Brehon Tuama outside.

'Well?' asked the Brehon morosely. 'Do you see the difficulty of this case?'

'I have seen the difficulty ever since you explained it to me,' she replied shortly. 'However, let us now find this Brother Caisín and see what he has to say.'

'He has accommodation in the hostel.'

They went to the town's *bruighean*, which was situated in the centre of Droim Som and provided accommodation and hospitality to whoever sought it there.

Brother Caisín was well built and, in spite of his robes, Fidelma noticed that he was muscular and more of a build associated with a warrior than that of a religieux. It was when she examined his features that she found herself distrusting the man. His eyes were close set in the narrow face, shifty and not focusing on his questioner. The lips were too thin, the nose narrow and hooked. He spoke with a soft, lisping voice that seemed at odds with his build. The line from Juvenal came to her mind: *fronti nulla fides* – no reliance can be placed on appearance.

'Brother Caisín?'

Caisín glanced quickly at her and then at Brehon Tuama before dropping his gaze to focus on a point midway between them.

'I suppose you are the *dálaigh* from Cashel?'

'You suppose correctly. I am Fidelma of Cashel.'

The man seemed to sigh and shiver slightly.

'I have heard of your reputation, Sister. You have a way of ferreting out information.'

Fidelma smiled broadly.

'I am not sure whether you mean that as a compliment, Brother. I will accept it as such.'

'I must tell you something before you discover it for yourself and place a wrong interpretation on it.' The monk seemed anxious. 'Have you heard of Caisín of Inis Geimhleach?'

211

Fidelma frowned and shook her head.

'I know Inis Geimhleach, the imprisoned island, a small settlement in Loch Allua, a wild and beautiful spot.'

At her side, Brehon Tuama suddenly snapped his fingers with a triumphant exclamation.

'Caisín . . . I have heard the story. Caisín was a warrior turned thief! It was ten years ago that he was found guilty of stealing from the church there. He claimed that he had repented and went into the service of the church and disappeared . . .'

Brehon Tuama's voice trailed off. His eyes narrowed on the religieux before him.

'Caisín of Inis Geimhleach? Are you saying that you are that man?' Fidelma articulated the conclusion of his thoughts.

The monk bowed his head and nodded.

Brehon Tuama turned to Fidelma with a glance of satisfaction. 'Then, Sister, we . . .'

Fidelma stilled him with a warning glance.

'So, Caisín, why do you confess this now?'

'I have paid penance for my crime and have continued to serve in the Abbey of Cluain. You might discover this and leap to the wrong conclusion.'

'So why did you not reveal this before when the Brehon questioned you?' she demanded.

Caisín flushed.

'One does not always do the correct thing at the correct time. This last day, I have had a chance to think more carefully. I realised it was foolish not to be completely honest even though it has nothing to do with the current matter.'

Fidelma sighed.

'Well, your honesty does you credit in the circumstances. Tell me, in your own words, what happened when you discovered the body of Muirenn, the wife of the smith.'

Caisín spread his arms in a sort of helpless gesture.

'There is nothing complicated about it. My abbot told me that some time ago he had commissioned a new silver cross for our high altar from Findach the smith. I was instructed to come to Droim Sorn to collect it.'

'How was payment to be made to Findach?' asked Fidelma.

Caisín looked bewildered.

'The abbot made no reference to payment. He simply asked me to come and collect the cross. As it was for the high altar, I understood it to be heavy, and so I asked permission to take one of the mules from the abbey. I had been to Droim Sorn before and so I knew where to find Findach's forge.'

Fidelma glanced quickly at him.

'You went to the forge directly?'

'Oh yes. Where else would I go to collect the cross?'

'Where, indeed? What then?'

'Findach was at the forge, and when I arrived he told me that the cross was at his house and I should precede him there. He would join me once he had doused his furnace.'

'Was anyone else at the forge when you arrived?'

'No . . . well, I did see a man riding away.'

'I don't suppose you knew who it was?'

Brother Caisín surprised her by an affirmative nod.

'I recognised him later as Odar, the chieftain. He had his hunting dogs with him. I left Findach and went to the house. I arrived at the door. It was slightly ajar. I caught sight of clothing on the floor. I pushed the door open and then I realised the clothing was a body. It was a woman. I was standing there when I heard a noise beyond an interior door. I opened it and found the youth, Braon, hiding there. He had blood on his clothes and instinct made me grasp hold of him. A moment later, Findach, who followed me from the forge, entered and cried out when he recognised the body of his wife. His cry brought someone else who ran to fetch Brehon Tuama. That is all I know.'

Outside Brehon Tuama looked worried.

'Do you think he is being honest? Once a thief . . . ? Isn't it said that opportunity makes the thief, and this man had opportunity.'

'Publilius Syrus once wrote that the stolen ox sometimes puts his head out of the stall,' smiled Fidelma, mysteriously.

Brehon Tuama looked bewildered. Fidelma went on without enlightening him: 'I am going to ride to Cluain to see the abbot. When I return I hope to have resolved this mystery.'

Brehon Tuama's eyes lightened.

'Then you think that Caisín is responsible?'

'I did not say that.'

Cluain, the meadow, was the site of an abbey and community founded by Colmán Mac Léníne some sixty years before. It was evening when she reached the abbey and demanded to be announced to the abbot immediately. The abbot received her without demur for he knew that Fidelma was also the sister of the young King of Cashel.

'You have come from Droim Sorn, lady?' asked the elderly abbot when they were seated. 'I suppose that you wish to speak to me of Brother Caisín?'

'Why do you suppose that?'

'His background and the circumstances make him suspect in the murder and theft there. I have had word of the event from Brehon Tuama. Caisín is a good man in spite of his history. He came to this abbey ten years ago as a penitent thief. Like the penitent thief of the Bible, he was received with rejoicing and forgiveness and never once has he given us cause to question his redemption.'

'You trusted him to go to Droim Sorn to bring back a valuable cross of silver.'

'It was the new cross for our high altar.'

'But you did not trust him with the money to pay for it, I understand.'

The old man blinked rapidly.

'There was no payment to be made.'

'You mean that Findach undertook to make this cross out of charity for the abbey?' Fidelma was puzzled.

The old abbot laughed, a slightly high-pitched laugh.

'Findach never gave anything out of charity. I should know for I was uncle to his wife Muirenn. He is an impecunious man. He made the cross for us in repayment for his indebtedness to the abbey.'

Fidelma raised an eyebrow in query.

'Findach spent money like water. His wife owned the house in which he dwells and kept her own money as the law allows. In fact, all Findach owns is his forge and tools.'

Fidelma leaned forward quickly.

'You mean that Findach will benefit from his wife's wealth now that she is dead?'

The abbot smiled sadly and shook his head.

'He does not benefit at all. Half of her money is returned to her own family in accordance with the law. She was an *aire-echta* in her own right.'

Fidelma was surprised, for it was not often that a smith's wife held an equal honour price to that of her husband.

The abbot continued: 'She has bequeathed the residue of her property to this abbey in my name, for she knew how I had helped her husband over the years.'

Fidelma hid her disappointment at being first presented with and then deprived of another motive for the murder of Muirenn.

'Findach had been asked to make some artefact for Imleach; and rather than admit to the Abbot of Imleach that he had no money to purchase the silver needed to make it, he asked me for a loan. When he later confessed he could not repay it, I offered to provide him with enough silver to construct a cross for our high altar. His craftsmanship was to be the repayment.'

'I am beginning to understand. I am told that Caisín had been to Droim Sorn before?'

'I sent him myself,' agreed the abbot. 'Last month I sent him to see Findach to remind him that the time to deliver the cross was approaching. He returned and told me that Findach had assured him that the cross would be ready at the appropriate time.'

Fidelma, fretting at the delay, had to spend the night at Cluain, and rode back to Droim Sorn the following morning.

She was met by Brehon Tuama whose face mirrored some degree of excitement.

'It seems that we were both wrong, Sister. The boy, Braon, announced his guilt by attempting to escape.'

Fidelma exhaled sharply in her annoyance.

'The stupid boy! What happened?'

'He climbed out of a window and fled into the forest. He was recaptured early this morning. Odar let loose his hunting dogs after him and it was a wonder that the boy was not ripped apart. We caught him just in time. Odar has now demanded the imprisonment of his father as an accomplice.'

Fidelma stared at the Brehon.

'And you have agreed to this?'

Brehon Tuama spread his hands in resignation.

'What is there to be done? Whatever doubts I had before are now

215

dispelled by the boy's own admission of guilt . . . his attempt to escape.'

'Does it not occur to you that the boy attempted to escape out of fear rather than out of guilt?'

'Fear? What had he to fear if he was innocent?'

'He and his father seemed to fear that, as they are of the class of *bothach*, looked down on and despised by many of the free clansmen of this place, they would not be treated fairly,' she snapped. 'The law is there so that no one should fear any unjust action. I regret that Odar does not appreciate that fact.'

Brehon Tuama sighed.

'Sadly, the law is merely that which is written on paper. It is human beings who interpret and govern the law, and often human beings are frail creatures full of the seven deadly sins that govern their little lives.'

'Are you telling me the boy is again imprisoned at Odar's rath and is unhurt?'

'Bruised a little, but unhurt.'

'*Deo gratias*! And the father?'

'He has been imprisoned in the barn behind the chief's house.'

'Then let us go to the chief's house and have all those involved in this matter summoned. If, after hearing what I have to say, you feel that there is a necessity for a formal trial, so be it. But the boy is not guilty.'

Half an hour later they were gathered in Odar's hall. Along with Odar and his *tánaiste* were Brehon Tuama, the boy Braon and his father Brocc, with Findach and Brother Caisín.

Fidelma turned to Brocc first. Her voice was brusque.

'Although you are a *bothach*, you have worked hard and gathered enough valuables to soon be able to purchase your place as a full and free clansman here. Is that correct?'

Brocc was bewildered by her question, but gave an affirmative jerk of his head.

'You would be able to pay the honour price for the death of Muirenn, the compensation due for her unlawful killing?'

'If my son were judged guilty, yes.'

'Indeed. For everyone knows that your son is under age. The payment of compensation and fines incurred by his action, if found guilty, falls to you.'

'I understand that.'

'Indeed you do. The law is well known.' Fidelma turned to Findach. 'Am I right in believing that your wife Muirenn was of the social rank of *aire-echta*, and her honour price was ten *séds* – that is the worth of ten milch cows?'

'That is no secret,' snapped Findach belligerently.

Fidelma swung round to Odar.

'And isn't that the very sum of money that Findach owed you?'

Odar coloured a little.

'What of it? I can lend money to my own kinsman if I wish to.'

'You know that Findach is penniless. If Braon was found guilty, Findach would receive the very sum of money in compensation that he owed to you, perhaps more if the claim of theft to the value of twenty-one *séds* is proved as well. Would that have any influence on your insisting on the boy's prosecution?'

Odar rose to his feet, opening his mouth to protest, but Fidelma silenced him before he could speak.

'Sit down!' Fidelma's voice was sharp. 'I speak here as *dálaigh* and will not be interrupted.'

There was a tense silence before she continued.

'This is a sad case. There never was a cross of silver that was stolen, was there, Findach?'

The smith turned abruptly white.

'You are known to be a gambler, often in debt to people such as Odar . . . and to your wife's uncle, the Abbot of Cluain. You are also lazy. Instead of pursuing the work that you have a talent for, you prefer to borrow or steal so that you may gamble. You were in debt to your wife's uncle, and when he gave you silver to fashion a cross as a means of repaying him you doubtless sold that silver.

'Having sold the silver, you had no cross to give to the Abbey of Cluain. You have not used your forge in days, perhaps weeks. Your furnace was as cold as the grave. And speaking of coldness . . . when Braon touched the body of Muirenn to see if he could help, he remarked the body was cold. Muirenn could not have been killed that morning after you left. She had been dead many hours.'

Findach collapsed suddenly on his chair. He slumped forward, head held in his hands.

'Muirenn . . .' The word was a piteous groan.

'Why did you kill Muirenn?' pressed Fidelma. 'Did she try to stop you from faking the theft of the cross?'

Findach raised his eyes. His expression was pathetic.

'I did not mean to kill her, just silence her nagging. Faking the theft was the only way I could avoid the debts . . . I hit her. I sat in the kitchen all night by her body wondering what I should do.'

'And the idea came that you could claim that the silver cross, which you had never made, was stolen by the same person who murdered your wife? You knew that Braon was coming that morning and he was a suitable scapegoat.' She turned to Brehon Tuama. '*Res ipsa loquitur*,' she muttered, using the Latin to indicate that the facts spoke for themselves.

When Findach had been taken away and Braon and his father released, Brehon Tuama accompanied Fidelma as she led her horse to the start of the Cashel road.

'A bad business,' muttered the Brehon. 'We are all at fault here.'

'I think that Odar's chiefship is worthy of challenge,' agreed Fidelma. 'He is not fit to hold that office.'

'Was it luck that made you suspicious of Findach?' queried Tuama, nodding absently.

Sister Fidelma swung up into the saddle of her horse and glanced down at the Brehon with a smile.

'A good judge must never rely on luck in deduction. Findach tried to scatter thorns across the path of our investigation, hoping that the boy or Caisín would pierce their feet on them and be adjudged guilty. He should have remembered the old proverb: he that scatters thorns must not go barefooted.'

Gold At Night

⁓

'**B**y this time tomorrow, thanks be to God, it will be all over for another three years. I have to admit that I am quite exhausted.'

Sister Fidelma smiled at her companion as they walked along the banks of the broad river of Bearbha. Abbot Laisran of Durrow was a portly man, short of stature, with silver hair and a permanent air of jollity about him. He had been born with a rare gift of humour and a sense that the world was there to provide enjoyment to those who inhabited it. In this he was in contrast with many of his calling. In spite of his statement, he looked far from fatigued.

Fidelma and Laisran paused a while to watch some boys fishing in the river, the abbot watching their casts with a critical eye.

'Was it worth your coming?' he suddenly asked.

Fidelma considered the question before answering. She did not like to give glib answers for the sake of politeness.

'The great Fair of Carman is an experience not to be missed,' she replied with studied reflection.

The Aenach or Fair of Carman was held once every three years over the days of the Feast of Lugnasadh, the first days of what the Romans called the month of Augustus, and it was one of the two major fairs held within the kingdom of Laighin. It was attended in person by Fáelán of the Uí Dúnláinge, King of Laighin, and no less than forty-seven of his leading nobles. During the period of the fair, there were games, contests in sports and the arts. Poets would declaim their verses and strong men would contest with one another in all manner of feats of skill as well as strength. So would women because there were special times set aside for contests between women. In addition to the entertainment, there were markets for all manner of livestock, produce and goods.

219

In fact, Laisran had been telling Fidelma how he had to chase a stallkeeper from the fairground because the man had been selling potions for destroying pests such as foxes and wolves. But the very noxious brews that would kill a fox or a wolf could kill other animals and, as such, were prohibited from sale at the fair. Yet it was true that many wonderful and curious things were to be found on sale in the stalls of the Aenach Carman.

But there was also a serious side to the Aenach Carman, unlike the Aenach Lifé, which was Laighin's other great fair and devoted to great horse racing.

During the days of the Aenach Carman, the assembly of the kingdom met. All the nobles, the chiefs of clans, the Brehons and lawyers, the professional men and women gathered to discuss the laws. On the first day, the men and women of the kingdom held separate councils at which the other sex was not allowed. The women's council admitted no man and the men's council admitted no women. Each council met and decided matters pertaining to their sex and elected representatives to go forward to attend the formal meetings of the Great Assembly of Laighin. Both sexes attended this and matters pertaining to all the people were discussed and decided upon. The king, his Brehons, or judges, and representatives of all the people would discuss any necessary amendment to the laws and agree the fiscal policies of the kingdom for the next three years.

While Fidelma was from the neighbouring kingdom of Muman, and therefore not qualified to voice any opinion in the councils or assembly, she had been invited by the women's council to attend and speak to them as their guest. She was asked to advise them on certain laws in her own kingdom and how they might be applicable to Laighin. For while the great law system applied equally in all five kingdoms, there was a section of laws called the Urrdas Law which were the minor variations that applied from kingdom to kingdom. But now such serious matters were over and one more day of festivity would end the fair.

Fidelma had been delighted, although not surprised, to find her distant cousin and friend, Laisran, Abbot of Durrow, the great teaching college, attending the fair. Not only attending it, but being present as adviser to the Great Assembly. It had been Laisran who had persuaded her to join the nearby abbey of Brigid at the Church of the Oaks, not far from the plain by the river Bearbha on which the Aenach Carman was held. But Fidelma had long since left the abbey of Brigid to return to her own land.

'What did you think of the competence of our law-makers?' Laisran was asking. 'Do we pass good laws and have good government?'

Fidelma chuckled.

'Did not Aristotle say that good laws, if they are not obeyed, do not constitute good government?'

Laisran answered his young cousin's infectious humour.

'I might have expected that from a lawyer,' he said. 'Seriously, have you enjoyed the Aenach Carman?'

Fidelma assured him she had, but added: 'Although I have often wondered why it is so called. Wasn't Carman a malevolent female figure who had three sons and didn't they blight all the crops in Éireann until the children of Danu defeated them and drove them into exile? How, then, does it come about that the people of Laighin do honour to her by naming their principal festival after her?'

Laisran's eyes had a twinkle.

'Well, if I were to tell you . . .'

'My lord!'

A man who came running towards them cut the abbot's words short. The newcomer was well dressed and wore a chain of office.

'Lígach, chieftain of the Laisig,' whispered Laisran in quick explanation. 'The Laisig are the hereditary organisers and stewards of the fair.'

The man halted somewhat breathlessly before the abbot. He was clearly disturbed about something.

'My lord abbot . . .' He had to pause to gulp some air.

'Calm yourself, Lígach. Catch your breath and then state calmly the matter that is troubling you.'

The chieftain took several breaths.

'We need your services. Ruisín is dead. I have sent for an apothecary but we cannot find one on the field. I know you are not without some medical skills, lord abbot.'

'Ruisín dead? How did he die?'

'Ruisín?' intervened Fidelma, interested by Laisran's concern. 'Who is he?'

Laisran replied immediately.

'He is . . . he was,' he corrected, 'a champion of the Osraige.' He turned back to Lígach. 'What has happened? An accident?'

221

Lígach shook his head.

'We think a surfeit of alcohol has killed him.'

Fidelma raised an eyebrow in query. Lígach saw the look.

'He was taking part in a challenge. Crónán, the champion of the Fidh Gabhla, had challenged him as to how much ale each of them could consume. Suddenly, with no more than the first jug taken, Ruisín collapsed. He was carried to his tent but when we laid him down we found his pulse no longer beat.'

'A drinking contest?' Fidelma's features twisted into a grimace of disapproval. Drink in moderation, wine with a meal, there was nothing better. But to drink to destroy the senses was pathetic, something she could never understand.

Lígach was defensive.

'There are often such contests between the champions of the clans. A clan can lose all honour if their champion fails.'

She sniffed in distaste.

'Far be it for me to condemn anyone when a man lies dead, but my mentor, the Brehon Morann, always said that alcohol is lead in the morning, silver at noon and gold at night and lead always follows the period of gold. So excessive drinking is merely a pursuit of fool's gold.'

'Please, my lord,' urged Ligach, ignoring her, 'come, confirm his death and perform the last rite of the Faith. Ruisín's wife Muirgel is with the body and is in distress.'

'Lead me to his tent, then,' Laisran said, and then glanced at his cousin. 'Perhaps you would like to accompany me, Fidelma? You might be able to formulate some words to the widow, for I feel myself inadequate to utter comfort in such circumstances.'

Reluctantly, Fidelma fell in step with the abbot. She, too, could not think what might be said to comfort the widowed spouse of someone who drank him or herself into an early grave for the sake of a wager. They followed the nervous chieftain to the area of the field where the tents of those participating in the fair were raised. A small group stood outside one tent, which marked it off as the one in which Ruisín's body had been laid. The group of men and women parted before them.

Lígach went in first.

Inside a woman was kneeling beside the body of a man. She was young and fairly attractive. She glanced up as they entered. Fidelma noticed that her face wore an almost bland expression. The eyes were large and round and dry. There was no discernible grief in the face, no tearful lines of one struck by sudden sorrow.

'This is Muirgel,' Lígach said quickly.

The young woman regarded them curiously. She seemed almost a somnambulant. It was as if she was not quite cognisant of her surroundings.

'Muirgel, this is Abbot Laisran and Sister . . . Sister . . . ?'

'Fidelma,' supplied Laisran, bending down to the body.

Fidelma glanced down. Ruisín had been a big, broad-shouldered man with a shock of red curling hair and a beard that covered most of his barrel chest. He had obviously been a strong man.

A thought struck Fidelma.

'What work did Ruisín do?' she asked Lígach quietly.

'He was a blacksmith, Sister,' replied the chieftain.

'Didn't you say that he collapsed after the first jug of ale had been consumed?'

'I did so.'

Laisran, kneeling beside the body, suddenly expelled the air from his lungs with a hiss.

'The man is, indeed, dead. I am sorry for the anguish that has been visited upon you, Muirgel. Lígach, would you take Muirgel outside for a moment?'

Fidelma frowned at the studied seriousness of Laisran's voice.

Lígach hesitated and then reached forward to help Muirgel to her feet. She did not actually respond willingly but she offered no resistance. It was as if she had no will of her own. She allowed Lígach to lead her out of the tent without a word.

'Shock, perhaps,' Fidelma commented. 'I have seen death take people so.'

Laisran did not seem to hear her.

'Take a look at the mouth, Fidelma,' he said quietly. 'The lips, I mean.'

Puzzled a little, Fidelma bent down. She found that the man's beard was so full and wiry that she had to pull it back a little to view his mouth and lips. Her brows came together. The lips were a bright purple colour. Her eye travelled to the skin. She had not noticed it before. It was mottled as if someone had painted a patterning on it.

223

She looked up.

'This man has not died from an excess of alcohol,' Laisran said, anticipating her conclusion.

'Poison?'

'Some virulent form,' agreed Laisran. 'I have not practised the apothecary's art for some time, so I would not be able to identify it. Death was not from excessive alcohol, that is obvious. He was young, strong and fit, anyway. And if it was poison that caused his death, then . . .'

'Then it was either an accident or murder,' concluded Fidelma.

'And no poison would enter a jug in a drinking contest by mere accident.'

'Murder?' Fidelma paused and nodded slowly. 'The local Brehon must be summoned.'

There was a movement behind them. Lígach had re-entered the tent unnoticed by them. He had heard their conclusion.

'Are you sure that Ruisín has been murdered?' he demanded, aghast.

Laisran confirmed it with a quick nod of his head.

'And are you Fidelma of Cashel?' Lígach added, turning to Fidelma. 'I heard that you were attending the fair. If so, please undertake the task of inquiring how Ruisín came by his death, for I have heard great things of you. As organiser of the fair, this is my jurisdiction and I willingly grant you the right to pursue these inquiries. If we do not clear this matter up then the reputation of the Aenach Carman will be blighted, for it will be said murder can be done within the king's shadow and the culprit can escape unknown and unpunished.'

Before Fidelma could protest, Laisran had agreed.

'There is none better than Fidelma of Cashel to dissect any web of intrigue that is woven around a murder.'

Fidelma sighed in resignation. It seemed that she had no choice. It was time to be practical.

'I would like another tent where I may sit and examine the witnesses to this matter.'

Lígach was smiling in his relief.

'The tent next to this one is at your disposal. It is my own.'

'Then I shall want all involved to be gathered outside, including the widow, Muirgel. I will tarry a moment longer here.'

Lígach hastened off while Laisran stood awkwardly as Fidelma bent down again.

'What should I do?' he asked.

Fidelma smiled briefly up at him.

'You will witness my inquiry,' she replied, 'for I would not like to be accused of interference by the Chief Brehon of Laighin.'

'I will guarantee that,' confirmed Laisran.

Fidelma was carefully examining the body of the dead man.

'What are you looking for?' the abbot asked after a while.

'I do not know. Something. Something out of the ordinary.'

'The extraordinary thing is the fact that the man was poisoned, surely?'

'Yet we have to be sure that we do not miss anything.' She rose to her feet. 'Now, let us question the witnesses.'

Fidelma and Laisran seated themselves on camp stools within Lígach's tent. There was a table and a scribe had been sent for to record the details. He was a young, nervous man, who sat huddled over his inks and leaves of imported papyrus.

'Who shall I bring in first, Sister?' asked Lígach.

'Who organised this drinking contest?'

'Rumann, who was Ruisín's friend, and Cobha, who supplied the ale.'

'Bring in Rumann first.'

First through the tent door came a young, eager terrier, its ears forward, its jaws slightly opened, and its neck straining against a rope. The dog hauled into the tent a burly man who was clutching the leash. It leapt towards Fidelma in its excitement, but in a friendly fashion, with short barks and a furiously wagging tail.

The man on the end of the leash snapped at it and tugged the animal to obedience at his heel. Then he gestured apologetically.

Rumann was almost the twin image of Ruisín, but with brown tousled hair. He was another burly man who had the look of a smith about him. Indeed, such was the craft he pursued.

'Sorry, Sister, but Cubheg here is young and excitable. He won't harm you.'

He turned to a tent post and tied the rope around it. The dog continued to tug and pull forward. Rumann glanced round.

'With your permission, Sister?' He indicated a bowl on the table. There was a jug of ale nearby. He poured some ale in the bowl and set it down before the animal which began to lap noisily at it with great relish. 'Cubheg likes a drink of ale. I can't deny him. Now, how can I help you?'

'This contest: whose idea was it?' demanded Fidelma without preamble.

'Crónán of the Fidh Gabhla issued the challenge.'

'For what purpose?'

Rumann shrugged.

'The rivalry between the Fidh Gabhla and the Osraige is generations old.'

'This is so,' whispered Abbot Laisran at her side.

'During the games these last few days, there have been several contests and the Osraige have held their own with the Fidh Gabhla,' went on Rumann. 'Crónán then challenged my friend Ruisín to a contest which would finally decide who were the greater at this fair, Osraige or the Fidh Gabhla.'

Fidelma's mouth turned down in disapproval.

'A clan made great simply by whoever could drink the most?'

'Sister, you must know that it is an old contest known in many lands? Whoever can drink most and still remain on their feet is the champion. This was to be the last great contest between us at the Aenach Carman.'

'Why was Ruisín chosen to take part?'

'He was our champion. And he was a great drinker,' Rumann said boastfully. 'He would drink a barrel of ale and still lift the empty barrel above his head at the end of it.'

Fidelma hid her cynicism.

'So the challenge was to him or to the Osraige?'

'Ruisín was champion of Osraige. It was the same thing.'

'So explain what happened at this contest.'

'Ruisín and Crónán met at the tent of Cobha the ale-maker. He supplied the ale. And . . .'

'And which side was Cobha on?' queried Fidelma sharply.

'He was from the Fidh Gabhla. But the supplier of the ale in these contests is supposed to maintain neutrality.'

'Was there an impartial referee?'

'We were all referees. The men of Osraige and the men of Fidh Gabhla were there to see fair play.'

'No women?'

Rumann looked pained.

'It was not a contest that appealed to women,' he said.

'Quite so,' replied Fidelma grimly. 'So a crowd was gathered round?'

'Cobha poured two jugs of ale . . .'

'From the same barrel?'

Rumann frowned and thought.

'I think so. One jug apiece. Each man took up his position at either end of a wooden table on which the jugs were set. At a word from Cobha, they began to drink. Each man drained the first jug without a problem. Cobha brought the second jug . . . my friend Ruisín had just picked up the second jug when he staggered. He dropped the jug and suddenly fell back. How the men of the Fidh Gabhla jeered, but I saw him writhing on the ground. I knew he was ill. Within a moment he was dead. That is all I know.'

Fidelma was quiet for a moment.

'You say that Ruisín was your friend?'

'He was.'

'He was a smith?'

'Like myself. We often worked together when our chieftain needed two pairs of bellows instead of one.'

'Would you say that Ruisín was a strong man, a healthy man?'

'I have known him since he was a boy. There was never a stronger man. I refuse to believe that a surfeit of alcohol would kill him. Why, just one jug of ale and he went down like a cow at the slaughter.'

Fidelma sat back and gazed at the man with interest.

'Did your friend have enemies?'

'Enemies? Why, was he not our champion and being challenged by the Fidh Gabhla? The Fidh Gabhla had motive enough to ensure that their man should win.'

'But in these circumstances, there would be no victory.'

Rumann pursed his lips as though he had not thought of that.

'Did he have any other enemies?'

Rumann shook his head.

'He was regarded as a first-class craftsman, had plenty of work. He was happily married to Muirgel and had no other cares in the world except how to enjoy his life more fully. No one would wish him harm . . .'

'Except?' prompted Fidelma as his voice trailed away and the cast of thought came into his eyes.

'Only the men of the Fidh Gabhla,' he replied shortly. Fidelma knew that he had thought of something and was hiding it.

Crónán, the drinking champion of the Fidh Gabhla, was shown in next; a surly man with a mass of dark hair and bright blue eyes which flickered nervously as if seeking out potential danger.

'We have had many a drinking contest in the past, Ruisín and I. We were rivals. Our clans were rivals. But we were friends.'

'That's not what Rumann seems to imply,' Fidelma pointed out.

'Rumann has his own way of looking at things. Sometimes it is not reality.'

'Why would anyone put poison into Ruisín's drink during this contest?'

Crónán raised his chin defiantly.

'I did not, that you may take as the truth. I swear that by the Holy Cross.'

'I would need more than an oath if I were to attempt to use it as evidence in court. You were both given separate jugs. I am told that the ale was poured from the same barrel.'

'It was. There were many witnesses to that. Cobha opened a new barrel so that the measure could be strictly witnessed.'

'What were the jugs?'

'The usual pottery jugs, which contain two *meisrin* each. We watched Cobha fill them and we all watched carefully so that the measure was equal. We had to double check because of Rumann's damned dog.'

'His dog?' Fidelma frowned.

'That young terrier. He broke loose from Rumann just when Cobha was pouring my first jug. He had set Ruisín's on the table while he poured mine. Then the dog went between his legs and nearly had him over. Rumann was apologetic and tied the dog up for the rest of the contest. I and Lennán, who was my witness, had to double check to make sure that Cobha had poured an equal measure for me.'

'And when you had ensured that he had . . . ?'

'He brought it to the table and placed the jugs before us. The signal was given. We took them and downed the contents, each being equal in time to the other.'

'Cobha then filled a second pair of jugs?'

The man shook his head.

'No, he retrieved the empty jugs from us and refilled them with the same measure, no more than two *meisrin* each. He put the jugs on the table in front of us as before. The signal was given and I began to drink mine. It was then that I noticed that while Ruisín had picked up his jug, he held it loosely. Then he staggered and fell back, dropping it.'

'Did it break?'

'What?'

'The jug, I mean. Did it break?'

'I think so. Yes, it cracked on the side of the table. I remember now, the damned dog ran forward to try to lap at the contents and Rumann had to haul him away with a good smack on the nose.'

Fidelma turned to Lígach.

'Can the broken pieces of the jug be found?'

The man went off about the task.

'Tell me, on this second time of filling, Crónán, I presume the same jugs were returned to you both? The jug that you first drank from was returned to you and the jug Ruisín drank out of was returned to him? Can you be sure?'

'Easy enough to tell. The jugs had different coloured bands around them, the colours of the Fidh Gabhla and Osraige.'

'What craft do you follow, Crónán?' asked Fidelma suddenly.

'Me? Why, I am a hooper.'

'You make barrels?'

'I do indeed.'

Lígach returned. The broken jug could not be found. A more than diligent assistant to Cobha the ale keeper had apparently cleaned the area and taken the pieces to a rubbish dump where the results of several days of broken jugs and clay goblets were discarded in such manner that it was impossible to sort them out at all.

'I thought it best to take the broken jug to the rubbish dump immediately,' the assistant said defensively when summoned. 'It was dangerous. Broken pieces and jagged. Rumann had difficulty dragging his dog away from it. He was very perturbed that the animal would injure itself. There were sharp edges.'

When Cobha entered to give his account, Fidelma had to disguise her instant dislike of the man. He was tall, and so exceedingly thin that he gave the appearance of someone on the verge of starvation.

His looks were sallow and the sunken eyes filled with suspicion. The only touch of colour was the thin redness of his lips. He came before Fidelma with his head hanging like someone caught in a shameful act. His speech was oily and apologetic.

His account basically confirmed what had been said before.

'Did you examine the jugs before you poured the measure?' asked Fidelma.

Cobha looked puzzled.

'Were they clean?' Fidelma was more specific.

'Clean? I would always provide clean drinking vessels to my customers,' Cobha said, with an ingratiating air. 'I have been coming to the Fair of Carman for two decades and no one has ever criticised my ale . . . or died of it.'

'Until today,' Abbot Laisran could not help but add, showing he, too, disapproved of the aleman's character.

'My ale was not to blame.'

'Do you have any idea what or who might be to blame?'

Cobha shook his head. 'Ruisín was not liked by everyone.'

Fidelma leaned forward quickly.

'Is that so? Who did not like him?'

'Lennán, for example. He hated Ruisín.'

'Why?'

'Because of his sister.'

'Explain.'

'He once told me that his sister was having an affair with Ruisín. He disliked that.'

'Who is his sister and who is Lennán?' asked Fidelma. 'He has been mentioned before as being Crónán's witness.'

'Lennán is a farmer. His farm straddles the borders of Osraige and the lands of the Fidh Gabhla. His sister is Uainiunn. Lennán hated Ruisín but, to be honest, I think Lennán was trying to find an excuse for his hate. I have seen Uainiunn and Muirgel together and they were close friends.'

Fidelma sat back thoughtfully.

'And Lennán was Crónán's witness today?'

Cobha nodded.

'Let us go back to the jugs. How did you decide which jug to give to whom?'

'Easy enough. One jug had a yellow band on it, the colour for Osraige. The other jug had a red band for the Fidh Gabhla.'

'Who put the colour bands on them?'

'I did.'

'Before the contest?'

'About half an hour before.'

'And where did the jugs stand while the contestants readied themselves before you finally took them up to fill?'

'On the table by the cask.'

'I want you to think clearly. Did you examine the jugs before you began to fill them?'

This time Cobha thought more carefully.

'I looked into them to make sure that they were still clean and no creature had crept into either, a fly or some such creature.'

'And they were clean?'

Cobha nodded emphatically.

'I would not serve ale, even in such circumstances as this contest, in dirty vessels. I have my licence to consider. My alehouse has always been *dligtech* for it has passed the three tests according to law.'

Fidelma was looking puzzled.

'The contestants were standing with the table between them. Is that so?'

'It is.'

'How near were the onlookers?'

Cobha rubbed his jaw thoughtfully.

'Gathered around,' he said with a shrug.

'Such as? Who was, say, near Crónán? I presume this witness, Lennán?'

'Lennán was next to him,' Cobha agreed and added, 'Lennán would not miss an opportunity to see Ruisín worsted.'

'That he certainly saw,' commented Fidelma drily.

Cobha suddenly looked nervous.

'I did not mean to imply that . . . I only meant to say . . . You asked me where Lennán was.'

'And you told me,' agreed Fidelma. 'Who else was there?'

Cobha compressed his lips for a moment, then shrugged.

'Uainiunn was with her brother.'

'I thought Rumann said that there were no women present?' Fidelma frowned.

Cobha shrugged indifferently. 'She was the only woman present apart from Muirgel. Perhaps that is what Rumann meant?'

Fidelma's eyebrows shot up.

'Muirgel as well? Where was she standing? You say that Uainiunn stood by her brother, Lennán? So they were close to Crónán?'

'That is so. Rumann and Muirgel were standing at the opposite end of the table on either side of Ruisín.'

'And you were the only person to pour the ale and place the jugs on the table?'

'True enough.'

She gestured for him to withdraw and turned with a fretful expression to Abbot Laisran.

'So far as I can see, there are only two possibilities. One possibility is that the poison was introduced into the jug destined for Ruisín between the time of its being poured and the time of his drinking it.'

'That surely means that Cobha is chief suspect for if anyone else had introduced the poison then they would surely be seen?' replied Laisran. 'But I fail to see the second possibility?'

'That would involve introducing the poison to Ruisín before the contest so that it would affect him later?'

Laisran immediately shook his head.

'I know of no poison that could have such a long-term effect as has been described. By all accounts Ruisín was well until the second jug was placed before him.'

'Importantly, we are told that he did not drink from it. So the poison must have been in the first jug.'

There was a moment of silence between them.

'It seems an impossible crime for it was carried out in front of so many witnesses.' Laisran sighed. 'We don't even know how the crime was committed, let alone who committed it. Although a young *dálaigh* I knew would say, solve the one and find the other.'

Fidelma shook her head with a wry smile.

'That young *dálaigh* was being a little glib,' she confessed.

'You were correct then. The principle also applies now.'

'Let us see what Lennán has to say,' she said. 'At least he is the only person who seems to have had some dislike for Ruisín.'

She called to Lígach to bring in the man.

Lennán was another of those people that she felt should be distrusted on sight. Shifty weak eyes, light and flickering here and there but never focusing on the person he was addressing. He was not thin but wiry; the mouth seemed malleable and he had a weak jaw. Nothing seemed firm about him. A vivid white line curved across his forehead, the scar of some terrible wound. The aura he gave out was intangible; that was the word Fidelma came up with. There seemed nothing substantial about the man that would even give a reason for her feeling of distrust.

'Well, Lennán,' she began sharply. 'We understand that you did not like Ruisín.'

The man actually cringed before her. It was not a pleasant sight.

'With good reason, Sister. With good reason,' he whined.

'And what good reason?'

'He was having an affair with my sister and he being married to Muirgel. It is a matter of her honour.'

'How did you know Ruisín was having an affair with your sister?'

'How do I know the midday sun is bright?' retorted the man.

'Sometimes the midday sun is obscured by grey cloud,' Fidelma pointed out drily. 'I ask again, how did you know this?'

'She was always going to Ruisín's house.'

'But isn't that naturally explained? Ruisín's wife was her friend.'

Lennán sniffed in annoyance, the closest he came to defiance of her.

'Ruisín's wife was an excuse. It was not Muirgel that she was going to see.'

'I still cannot see how you can be so sure. I presume you asked her?'

'She denied it.'

'Did you ask Ruisín?'

'He also denied it.'

'So did you kill Ruisín?'

The question was put in the same tone and without pause so that Lennán was about to answer before he realised what he was being asked. He frowned in annoyance.

'I would have done so if I had had the chance,' he replied in a surly tone.

'That seems honest enough,' admitted Fidelma. 'You take your sister's honour seriously. I think you take it more seriously than she does. I wonder why?'

The man said nothing.

'You can offer no facts about this affair between your sister and Ruisín?'

'I don't need facts. I base my knowledge on logic.'

'Ah, logic. My mentor, Brehon Morann, once said that anything could be demonstrated by logic. By logic we can prove whatever we wish to. Very well. During this contest, I am told you were standing at the table next to Crónán?'

'I was. My sister was beside me, mooning across the table at that oaf Ruisín.'

'And you saw no one interfere with the drinking vessels?'

'I would not stoop to poison, Sister. If I had reached the point where I wished to kill Ruisín, my weapon would have been a sword or an axe.'

Abbot Laisran was smiling in satisfaction when Lennán left the tent.

'That is our man, Fidelma. A whole *screpall* on it. That's worth a good barrel of Gaulish wine.'

'I think you are a little free with your money, Laisran.' She smiled. 'Before taking the wager, let us have a word with his sister, Uainiunn.'

Uainiunn looked nothing like her brother. She was fleshy; almost voluptuous, with an animal magnetism and a provocative way of looking at one from under half-closed eyelids. She was dark of hair and eyes and had full red lips.

'I understand that you attended this drinking contest.'

'With my brother. He insisted.'

'He insisted?'

'He wanted to see Ruisín beaten by Crónán.'

'And you?'

The girl shrugged. 'It was a matter of indifference to me.'

Fidelma examined her closely.

'Why would that be so?' she asked.

Uainiunn sniffed. 'What entertainment is there in watching men drink themselves senseless?'

'True enough, but didn't you want to see Ruisín win the contest?'

'Not particularly. I am sad for Muirgel, though. The loss of Ruisín is going to be a heavy blow for her. However, I do not doubt that she will find another man to take care of her. Rumann for example. It might stop Rumann chasing me. He does not interest me.'

'Ruisín's death does not affect you in any way?' demanded Abbot Laisran, slightly outraged at the seeming callousness of the girl.

Uainiunn frowned.

'Only inasmuch as it affects my friend Muirgel.'

'It sounds as though you did not care much for Ruisín,' Fidelma reflected.

'He was my friend's husband, that is all.'

'I understand that is not what your brother thought.'

The girl's eyes blazed for a moment. It was like a door opening suddenly and for a moment Fidelma glimpsed something equivalent to the hot fires of Hell beyond. Then they snapped shut.

'I am not responsible for what Lennán thinks,' she snapped.

'So you would deny his claim that you were having an affair with Ruisín?'

The girl threw back her head and laughed. Yet it was not a pleasant sound. There was no need to press her further on her opinion.

'Very well,' Fidelma said quietly. 'You may leave us.'

Abbot Laisran turned eagerly after she left.

'You think that she did it? She is callous enough.'

Fidelma raised an eyebrow.

'Are you about to place another wager, another *screpall*, on it?' she asked.

Laisran flushed. 'Perhaps either one of them did it,' he countered.

Fidelma did not reply directly. She turned to Lígach.

'Let Muirgel come in.'

Laisran looked slightly crushed and sat back. He whispered stubbornly, 'No, she didn't do it. A *screpall* on Lennán. He's your man, I am now certain. After all, he confessed that he wanted to murder Ruisín.'

'But says that he did not. If he were guilty of the fact, he would surely have attempted to hide his intention?' replied Fidelma.

'A subtle way of deflecting you from the truth. He has motive and . . .'

'And opportunity? How so? He was with Crónán on the far side of the table.'

Laisran shook his head. 'This is worse than the mystery you had to solve in my abbey, when Wulfstan was found stabbed to death in his cell which had been locked from the inside. Do you remember?'

'I remember it well.'

'No one could have entered or left – so who had killed Wulfstan? Here we have a similar problem.'

'Similar?'

'There is Ruisín. He is in full view of a large number of people and he is poisoned. No one can have administered the poison without being seen.'

Fidelma smiled softly. 'Yet someone did.'

Muirgel came in; her face was still mask-like, displaying no emotion. Fidelma pointed to a chair and invited her to sit down.

'We will not keep you long.'

The woman raised a bland face to them as she sat.

'The gossip is that my husband did not die from excess of drink but was poisoned.'

'It is a conclusion that we have reached.'

'But why? There was no reason to kill him.'

'There obviously was and we require your help in discovering that reason. What enemies did he have?'

'None except . . .' She suddenly looked nervous and paused.

'Lennán?'

'You know about him?'

'I know only that he hated your husband.'

Muirgel sat silently.

'Was your husband having an affair with Uainiunn?' demanded Fidelma brutally.

At once Muirgel shook her head vehemently.

'What makes you so positive?' pressed Fidelma.

'Uainiunn is my friend. I have known her longer than Ruisín. But I also know Ruisín. You cannot live in close proximity with a man day in and day out without knowing whether he is seeing another woman, especially if the woman is your best friend.'

Fidelma grimaced. She had known women who had been fooled, as well as men come to that. But she did not comment further. Then another thought occurred to her.

'Rumann was your husband's friend?'

'He was.'

'And your friend also?'

The woman frowned. 'Of course.'

'Rumann is not married?'

'He is not.'

Fidelma was watching the woman's expression intently when she posed the questions with their subtle implication. But there was no guile there. Nothing was hidden.

'I suppose that you and Ruisín, Rumann and Uainiunn were often together?'

Again, Muirgel looked puzzled.

'Uainiunn was my friend. Rumann was Ruisín's friend. It was inevitable that we would be together from time to time.'

'What of Uainiunn's brother – Lennán? Was he in your company?'

Muirgel looked annoyed.

'I thought we had cleared up that matter. He was never in our company.'

Fidelma nodded with a sigh.

'You see, I would like to understand why Lennán has developed this idea about his sister and your husband?'

'If you can peer through a person's skull, through into the secrets of their mind, then you will find the answer. All I know is that Lennán was not so extreme until after he returned from the cattle raid against the Uí Néill.'

'You will have to explain that.'

'Over a year ago Lennán decided to join a raiding party to retrieve some cattle stolen by the one of Uí Néill clans. When he came back he was a changed man. You saw the scar across his forehead?'

'He was wounded?'

'The rest of the raiding party did not return,' went on Muirgel. 'Only he returned out of the score of men who went off.'

'Did he explain what had happened to them?'

'An ambush. A fight. He was, indeed, wounded, and left for dead. A hill shepherd cared for him until he was well enough and then he returned. That was when he became suspicious of everyone and when he began to make those silly accusations against Ruisín.'

Fidelma leaned forward a little with interest.

237

'So this started only after his return. And you say there was no reason that you knew of?'

'Perhaps he had become deranged.'

'Did you speak about this to Uainiunn?'

Muirgel grimaced. 'Of course. Lennán was her brother.'

'And what comment did she make?'

'That we should ignore him. She said that most people knew he had become a changed man since his return from the cattle raid. No one would take him seriously.' Muirgel suddenly paused and her eyes widened as she gazed at Fidelma. 'Lennán? Do you suspect Lennán of killing Ruisín? How? He was standing on the far side of the table when the contest started. How could he have killed my husband?'

'You've no idea who killed your husband?' Fidelma asked, ignoring her question.

'None.'

'That is all then.'

Muirgel rose and went to the flap of the tent.

'Oh, just one question more,' called Fidelma softly.

The woman turned expectantly.

'You were not having an affair with Rumann, were you?'

Muirgel's eyes widened for a moment in shock and then a cynical smile slowly crossed her face. She made a sound, a sort of suppressed chuckle, and shook her head.

'I am not. And Rumann is too interested in Uainiunn to bother with me and I would have discouraged him. I loved Ruisín.'

Fidelma nodded and gestured her to leave.

Abbot Laisran was staring at Fidelma in surprise.

'That was surely an insensitive question to ask of a newly widowed woman?' He spoke in a tone of stern rebuke.

'Sometimes, Laisran, in order to get to firm ground one has to tread through bogland, through mire,' she replied.

'Do you really suspect that Muirgel poisoned her husband because she was having an affair with his friend, Rumann?'

'Every question I ask is for a purpose. You should know my methods by now, Laisran.'

'I am still at a loss. I thought it was clear that Lennán must be the culprit. But your question to Muirgel . . . ?'

Fidelma had turned to Lígach who had entered the tent again.

The chieftain bent down and whispered in her ear. She nodded firmly.

'Bring Rumann back,' she ordered.

Rumann came in with his dog again but this time immediately tied it to the tent post so that it would not leap up.

'Well, Sister? Have you found out who killed my friend?'

Fidelma regarded him with grave chill eyes.

'I think I have a good idea, Rumann. You did.'

The man froze. He tried to form a sentence but the words would not come out. He managed a nervous laugh.

'You are joking, of course?'

'I never joke about these matters, Rumann.'

'How could I have done such a thing?'

'Is that a practical question or a philosophical one?'

Rumann stood defiantly before her, having regained his composure. He folded his arms across his chest.

'You must be mad.'

'I think you will find that you have been the victim of madness, but it does not emanate from me. How did you do it? The drinking contest had been arranged. Early in the fair you saw the stall which sold poisons. Abbot Laisran had told me how he had to chase the stallholder away because the noxious brews that he was selling to control pests could also be used to kill other animals. They would also kill human beings. You acquired some of that brew before Abbot Laisran forced the stall to close.'

For the first time Rumann looked nervous.

'You are guessing,' he said uncertainly. 'And am I supposed to have slipped this poison into his drink in full view of everyone gathered to watch the contest?'

'Supposed to and did so,' agreed Fidelma. 'It was very simple. You were standing by his side. Your terrier is always with you. It seems to like ale. You let slip the leash of your dog just after Cobha set down Ruisín's jug and while he was filling the one for Crónán. The immediate concern was to save Crónán's jug. No one noticed you slipping the phial of poison into Ruisín's jug while they were fussing over the proper measurement in Crónán's.'

Rumann was silent.

'You retrieved your dog and tied it to a post. When Ruisín fell dead and his jug shattered to pieces, your dog sprang forward to lap the ale in the broken pieces. You don't mind your dog lapping at ale. I asked myself why you were so concerned to drag him away from the ale in those broken pieces. A fear that he might injure himself on the broken pieces? Dogs have more sense. You thought some residue of the poison might be left, didn't you? You didn't want your dog to be poisoned.'

Rumann was still silent. Fidelma glanced towards the open tent flap.

'I could bring forth the stallholder who sold you the poison but I am sure you won't want to give us that trouble,' mused Fidelma softly.

Laisrean went to say something and then put a hand in front of his features and coughed noisily. Rumann did not seem to notice him and his jaw came up defiantly.

'Even if I admitted that I purchased poison from that stall, you have yet to argue a good cause why I would want to kill my friend Ruisín.'

Fidelma shook her head.

'Sadly, that is not difficult. It is a cause, if you would call it so, that is as old as time itself. Jealousy.'

'I? Jealous of Ruisín's wife? Ridiculous!'

'I did not say who you were jealous of. It was not Ruisín's wife. You are desperately in love with Uainiunn although she does not appear to care for you. In your justification for this, you came to believe the stories that Lennán was putting about – that his sister was having an affair with Ruisín. She was not. But you chose to believe Lennán because you could not accept that Uainiunn was simply not interested in you. Your jealousy knew no bounds. Pitifully, you believed that if you killed Ruisín, then Uainiunn would turn to you. It is not love that is blind, Rumann, but jealousy.'

'I loved Uainiunn. Ruisín stood in my way,' replied the smith firmly.

'He did not. That was no more than a deranged mind's fantasy which a frustrated and suspicious ear picked up and was then nurtured among the gall of rejection. The bitter fruits of this harvest have destroyed minds as well as lives. Love that is fed only on jealousy dies hard. So it will die in you, Rumann.'

She gestured to Lígach to remove the man from the tent.

Abbot Laisran was wiping the sweat from his brow.

'I swear that you had me worried there, Fidelma. A *dálaigh* is not supposed to tell an untruth to force a confession. What if Rumann had called your bluff and demanded that you bring in that stallholder that I chased from here?'

Fidelma smiled wanly.

'Then I would have asked him to come in. As soon as I saw that poison was involved, I remembered what you said and asked Lígach to find the man. You did not think that an entrepreneur would meekly depart from such a good source of revenue as this fairground just because you chased him away from his stall? He had not gone very far at all.'

'I think I shall need a drink after this – but an amphora of good Gaulish wine.' Laisran shuddered. 'Certainly not ale!'

Fidelma looked cynical.

'What was it that you were going to wager with me – a *screpall*? A barrel of Gaulish wine? Lucky for you I did not accept it. You'll find wine is sweet but sour its payment.'

'I'm willing to fulfil my obligation,' the abbot said defensively.

Fidelma shook her head.

'A share of the amphora will do. You are not searching for the gold at night, surely? Tomorrow will only bring lead.'

Abbot Laisran grimaced wryly.

'Poor Ruisín found lead earlier than most. Moderation, Fidelma. I agree. I invite you to the hospitality of the abbey.'

'And is it not an old saying that it is not an invitation to hospitality without a drink?' smiled Fidelma.

Death of an Icon

'I cannot understand why the abbot feels that he has to interfere in this matter,' Father Maílín said defensively. 'I have conducted a thorough investigation of the circumstances. The matter is, sadly, a simple one.'

Sister Fidelma regarded the Father Superior of the small community of St Martin of Dubh Ross with a mild expression of reproach.

'When such a respected man as the Venerable Gelasius has met with an unnatural death, then it is surely not an interference for the religious superior of this territory to inquire into it?' she rebuked gently. 'Portraits of the Venerable Gelasius hang in many of our great ecclesiastical centres. He has become an icon to the faithful.'

Father Maílín coloured a little and shifted his weight in his chair.

'I did not mean to imply a censure of the abbot or his authority,' he replied quickly. 'It is just that I have carried out a very thorough investigation of the circumstances and have forwarded all the relevant details to the abbot. There is nothing more to be said unless we can track down the culprits and that, as I pointed out, will be impossible unless, in some fit of repentance, they confess. But they have long departed from this territory, they and their ill-gotten spoils.'

Fidelma gazed thoughtfully at the Father Superior for a moment or two.

'I have your report here,' her hand lightly touched the *marsupium* at her waist, 'and I must confess to there being some matters which puzzle me, as, I hasten to say, they have also puzzled the abbot. That is why he has authorised me, as a *dálaigh*, an advocate of the courts, to visit your small community to see whether or not the questions might be clarified.'

Father Maílín raised his jaw, slightly aggressively.

'I see nothing at all that is confusing or which requires any further explanation,' he replied stubbornly. Then, meeting her icy blue eyes, he added brusquely, 'However, you may ask me your questions and then depart.'

Fidelma's mouth twitched a fraction in irritation and she shook her head briefly.

'Perhaps it is because you are not a trained advocate of the law and thus do not know what is required that you take this attitude. I, however, will conduct my inquiries in the way prescribed by the law. When I have finished my investigation, then I shall depart.' She paused to allow her words to penetrate and then said, in a brighter tone: 'First, let us begin with you recounting the general details of the Venerable Gelasius's death.'

Father Maílín's lips compressed into a thin, bloodless line in order to disguise his anger. His eyes had a fixed look. It seemed, for a moment or two, that he would challenge her. Then he appeared to realise the futility of such an action and relaxed. He knew that he had to accept her authority however reluctantly. He pushed himself back in his chair, sitting stiffly. His voice was an emotionless monotone.

'It was on the morning of the sabbath. Brother Gormgilla went to rouse the Venerable Gelasius. As he grew elderly, Gelasius required some assistance in the morning and Brother Gormgilla would help him rise and dress and then escort him to the chapel for morning prayer.'

'I have heard that Brother Gelasius was of a great age,' intervened Fidelma. Everyone knew he was of considerable age but Fidelma's intervention was more to break Father Maílín's monotonous recital so that she would be able to extract the information she wanted.

'Indeed, but Gelasius was also frail. It was his frailty that made him needful of the helping hand of Brother Gormgilla.'

'So, this Brother Gormgilla went to the chamber of the Venerable Gelasius on the morning of the sabbath? What then?' encouraged Fidelma.

'The facts are straightforward enough. Gormgilla entered and found the Venerable Gelasius hanging from a beam just above his bed. There was a sign that a valuable personal item had been taken, that is a rosary. Some valuable objects were also missing from the chapel which adjoins the chamber of the Venerable Gelasius.'

'These discoveries were made after Brother Gormgilla had roused the community having found the body of the Venerable Gelasius?'

'They were.'

'And your deduction was . . . ?'

'Theft and murder. I put it in my report to the abbot.'

'And to whom do you ascribe this theft and murder?'

'It is also in my report to the abbot.'

'Remind me,' Fidelma insisted sharply.

'For the two days previous to the death of the Venerable Gelasius, some itinerants were observed to be camping in nearby woods. They were mercenaries, warriors who hired themselves out to anyone who would pay them. They had their womenfolk and children with them. Our community, as you know, has no walls around it. We are an open settlement for we have always argued that there is no need at all to protect ourselves from any aggressor, for who, we thought, would ever wish harm to our little community?'

Fidelma treated his question as rhetorical and did not reply.

'You have suggested that these itinerant mercenaries entered the community at night to rob your chapel.' Her tone was considered. 'You have argued that the Venerable Gelasius must have been disturbed by them; that he went to investigate and that they turned on the old man and hanged him from his own roof beam and even robbed him.'

'That is so. It is not so much an argument as a logical deduction from the facts,' the Father Superior added stiffly.

'Truly so?' Fidelma gave him a quick scrutiny and Father Maílín read a quiet sarcasm there.

The Father Superior stared back defiantly but said nothing.

'Tell me,' continued Fidelma. 'Does it not strike you as strange that an elderly man, who needed help to rise in the morning as well as to be escorted to the chapel, would rise in the night on hearing intruders and go alone into the chapel to investigate?'

Father Maílín shrugged.

'People, *in extremis*, have been known to do many extraordinary things: things that are either out of character or beyond their capabilities.'

'If I have the right information, the Venerable Gelasius was nearly ninety. In that case . . . ?' Fidelma eloquently spread her hands.

'In his case, it does not surprise me,' affirmed Father Maílín. 'He was frail but he was a man of a very determined nature. Why, twenty and five years ago, when he was entering the latter years, Gelasius insisted on bearing the cross of Clonmacnoise in the battle of Ballyconnell when Diarmuid Mac Aodh was granted a victory over the Uí Fidgente. Gelasius was in the thick of the battle and armed with nothing but Christ's Cross for self-protection.'

Fidelma suppressed a sigh for all Ireland knew of the story of the Venerable Gelasius which was why the old monk's name was a byword for moral and physical courage throughout the five kingdoms of Éireann.

'Yet five and twenty years ago is still a quarter of a century before this time and we are talking of an old man who needed help to rise and go to chapel as a regular course.'

'As I have said, he was a determined man.'

'Therefore, if I understand your report correctly, you believe that the Venerable Gelasius, hearing some robbers moving in the chapel, left his bed and went to confront them without rousing anyone else. That these robbers then overpowered him and hanged him in his own bedchamber?'

'I have said as much.'

'Yet doesn't it also strike you as strange that these thieves and robbers, thus disturbed, took the old man back to his chamber and hanged him there? Surely a thief, so disturbed, might strike out in fear and seek to escape. Was Gelasius a tall man who, in spite of his frailty, might have appeared a threat?'

Father Maílín shook his head.

'Age had bent him.'

'Then the Venerable Gelasius could not have prevented the escape of the thieves nor even pursued them. Why would they bother to take him and, presumably, get him to show them the way back to his chamber to kill him?'

'Who knows the minds of thieves and murderers?' snorted Father Maílín. 'I deal with the facts. I don't attempt to understand their minds.'

'Nevertheless, that is the business in which I am engaged because in considering the "why" and "wherefore", often one can solve the "how" and "who".' She paused for a moment and when he did not respond, she added: 'After this barbaric act of sacrilege, you reported

245

that they then removed some valuable items and went calmly off into the night?'

'The itinerants were certainly gone by the next morning when one of the outraged brethren went to their camp. The emotional attitude of the itinerants, as to whether they were calm or otherwise, is not for me to comment on. I will leave that to you to judge.'

'Very well. You say that Brother Gormgilla was the first to discover the body of the Venerable Gelasius?'

'Brother Gormgilla always roused the Venerable Gelasius first.'

'Ah, just so. I shall want to see this Brother Gormgilla.'

'But I have told you all . . .'

Fidelma raised an eyebrow, staring at him with cold, blue eyes.

Father Maílín hesitated and shrugged. He reached for a hand bell and jangled it. A member of the community entered but when the Father Superior asked that Brother Gormgilla be summoned, Fidelma intervened. She did not want Father Maílín interfering in her questioning.

'I will go to the brother myself. I have trespassed on your valuable time long enough, Father Maílín.'

The Father Superior rose unhappily as Sister Fidelma turned and accompanied the religieuse from the room.

Brother Gormgilla was a stocky, round-faced man, with a permanent expression of woe sitting on his fleshy features. She introduced herself briefly to him.

'Had you known the Venerable Gelasius for a long time, Brother?' she asked.

'For fifteen years. I have been his helper all that time. He would soon be in his ninety-first year had he been spared.'

'So you knew him very well?'

'I did so. He was a man of infinite wisdom and knowledge.'

Fidelma smiled briefly.

'I know of his reputation. He was spoken of as one of our greatest philosophers not merely in this kingdom but among all five kingdoms of Éireann. He adopted the Latin name of Gelasius; why was that?'

Brother Gormgilla shrugged as if it was a matter of little importance.

'It was a Latinisation of the name he was given when he was received into the Church – Gilla Isu, the servant of Jesus.'

'So he was a convert to the Faith?'

246

'As were many in our poor benighted country when he was a young man. At that time, most of us cleaved to the old gods and goddesses of our fathers. The Faith was not so widespread through our kingdoms. Gelasius's own father was a Druid and a seer. When he was young, Gelasius told me, he was going to follow the arts of his father's religion. But he was converted and took his new name.'

'And became a respected philosopher of the Faith,' added Fidelma. 'Well, tell me . . . in fact, show me, how and where you discovered his body?'

Brother Gormgilla led the way towards the main chapel around which the various circular buildings of the community were situated. Next to the chapel was one small circular building outside the door of which the monk paused.

'Each morning, just before the Angelus, I came here to rouse and dress the Venerable Gelasius,' he explained.

'And on that morning . . . ? Take me through what happened when you found Gelasius was dead.'

'I came to the door. It was shut and locked. That was highly unusual. I knocked upon it and not being able to get an answer I went to a side window.'

'One moment. Are you telling me that you did not possess a key to Gelasius's chamber?'

'No. There was only one key which the Venerable Gelasius kept himself.'

'Was it usual for Gelasius to lock his door?'

'Unusual in the extreme. He always left it open.'

'So the door was locked! You say that you went to the window? Was it open?'

'No. It was closed.'

'And secured?'

'Well, I had to smash the glass to open it and squeeze through.'

'Go on. What did you find inside?'

'I had seen through the window that which caused me to see the smashing of the window as my only course. I saw the body of the Venerable Gelasius hanging from a beam.'

'Show me.'

Brother Gormgilla opened the door and conducted her into a spacious round chamber which had been the Venerable Gelasius's living quarters and study. He pointed up to the roof rafters. Great beams of wood at the height of eight feet from the ground crossed the room.

'See that one, just near the bed? Old Gelasius was hanging from it. A rope was twisted round it and one end was tied in a noose around his neck. I think that he had been dead for some hours. I knew at once that I could do nothing for him and so I went to rouse Father Maílín.'

Fidelma rubbed her jaw thoughtfully.

'Did you stop to search the room?'

'My only thought was to tell the Father Superior the catastrophic news.'

'You have told me that the door was locked. Was the key on the inside?'

'There was no sign of the key. That was why I had to squeeze back out of the window. Our smith then came and picked the lock when Father Maílín arrived. It was the missing key that confirmed Father Maílín in his theory that thieves had done the deed, locking Gelasius in his own chamber after they had hanged him.'

Fidelma examined the lock and saw the scratch marks where it had been picked. There was little else to decipher from it, except that the lock had apparently not been forced at any other stage. Fidelma moved to the window, where she saw the clear signs of broken glass and some scratching on the frame which might have been made by a body pushing through the aperture. It was certainly consistent with Brother Gormgilla's story.

She went to the bed and gazed up. There was some scoring on the beam.

'Is the bed in the same position?'

'It is.'

Fidelma made some mental measurements and then nodded.

'Let me get this perfectly clear, Brother Gormgilla. You say that the door was locked and there was no key in the lock on either side of the door? You also say that the window was secured and to gain access you had to break in from the outside?'

'That is so.'

'Let me put this question to you, as I have also put it to your Father Superior: his theory is that the Venerable Gelasius was disturbed by marauders in the night. He went into the chapel to investigate. They overpowered him and brought him back here, hanged him and then robbed him. Does it occur to you that something is wrong with this explanation?'

Brother Gormgilla looked uncomfortable.

'I do not understand.'

Fidelma tapped her foot in annoyance.

'Come now, Brother. For fifteen years you have been his helper; you helped him rise in the morning and had to accompany him to the chapel. Would such a frail old man suddenly start from his bed in the middle of the night and set off to face intruders? And why would these intruders bring him back here to hang him? Surely one sharp blow on the head would have been enough to render Gelasius dead or beyond hindrance to them?'

'It is not for me to say, Sister. Father Maílín says . . .'

'I know what Father Maílín says. What do you say?'

'It is not for me to question Father Maílín. He came to his conclusion after making strenuous inquiries.'

'Of whom, other than yourself, could he make such inquiries?'

'It was Brother Firgil who told the Father Superior about the itinerants.'

'Then bring Brother Firgil to me.'

Brother Gormgilla scurried off.

Sister Fidelma wandered around the chamber and examined the manuscripts and books that lined the walls. Gelasius had, as hearsay had it, been an extraordinary scholar. There were books on philosophy in Hebrew, Latin, Greek and even works in the old tongue of the Irish, written on wooden wands in Ogham, the earliest Irish alphabet.

Everything was neatly placed along the shelves.

Gelasius had clearly been a methodical and tidy man. She glanced at some of the works. They intrigued her for they concerned the ancient stories of her people: stories of the pagan gods, the children of the Mother Goddess Danu whose 'divine waters' fertilised the earth at the beginning of time itself. It was a strange library for a great philosopher and teacher of the Faith to have.

At a little desk were vellum and quills where the Venerable Gelasius obviously sat composing his own works which were widely distributed among the teaching abbeys of Ireland. Now his voice would be heard no more. His death at the hands of mere thieves had robbed the Faith of one of its greatest protagonists. No wonder the abbot had not been satisfied with Father Maílín's simple report and had asked Fidelma, as a trained *dálaigh* of the courts, to make an inquiry which could be presented to the king himself.

Fidelma glanced down at the vellum. It was pristine. Whatever Gelasius had been working on, he must have finished before his death, for his writing materials were clean and set out neatly; everything placed carefully, ready and waiting . . .

She frowned suddenly. Her wandering eye had caught something tucked inside a small calf-bound book on a nearby shelf. Why should she be attracted by a slip of parchment sticking out of a book? She was not sure until she realised everything else was so neat and tidy that the very fact that the paper was left so untidily was the reason which drew her attention to it.

She reached forward and drew it out. The slip of parchment fluttered awkwardly in her hands and made a slow glide to the floor. She bent down to pick it up. As she did so she noticed something protruding behind one of the stout legs of Gelasius's desk. Retrieving the parchment she reached forward and eased out the object from its hiding place.

It was an iron key, cold and greasy to the touch. For a moment, she stood gazing at it. Then she went to the door and inserted it. The key fitted into the lock and she turned it slowly. Then she turned it back and took it out, slipping it into her *marsupium*.

Finally, she reverted her attention to the piece of parchment. It was a note in Ogham. A line, a half constructed sentence, no more. It read: 'By despising, denigrating and destroying all that has preceded us, we will simply teach this and future generations to despise our beliefs. *Veritas vos liberabit!'*

'Sister?'

Fidelma glanced round. At the door stood a thin, pale-faced religieux with a hook nose and thin lips.

'I am Brother Firgil. You were asking for me?'

Fidelma placed the piece of parchment in her *marsupium* along with the key and turned to him.

'Brother Fergal?' she asked, using the Irish name.

The man shook his head.

'Firgil,' he corrected. 'My father named me from the Latin Vergilius.'

'I understand. I am told that you informed Father Maílín about the itinerants who were camping in the woods on the night of the Venerable Gelasius's death?'

'I did so,' Brother Firgil agreed readily. 'I noticed them on the day before that tragic event. I took them to be a band of mercenaries, about a score in number with womenfolk and children. They were camped out in the woods about half a mile from here.'

'What made you think that they were responsible for the theft and killing of the Venerable Gelasius?'

Brother Firgil shrugged.

'Who else would dare such sacrilege than godless mercenaries?'

'Are you sure that they were godless?' Fidelma asked waspishly.

The man looked bewildered for a moment and then shrugged.

'No one who is at one with God would dare rob His house or harm His servants, particularly one who was as elderly as the Venerable Gelasius. It is well known that most of those mercenaries are not converted to the Faith.'

'Is there proof that they robbed the chapel?'

'The proof is that a crucifix from the chapel and two gold chalices from the altar are gone. The proof is that the Venerable Gelasius had a rosary made of marble beads from a green stone from the lands of Conamara, which was said to have been blessed by the saintly Ailbe himself. That, too, is gone. Finally, the Venerable Gelasius was found dead. Hanged.'

'But nothing you have said is proof that these itinerants were the culprits,' Fidelma pointed out. 'Is there any proof absolute?'

'The itinerants were camping in the wood on the day before the Venerable Gelasius's death. On the morning that Gelasius was discovered and the items were found missing, I told Father Maílín of my suspicions and was sent to observe the itinerants so that we could appeal to the local chieftain for warriors to take them. But they were gone. That is proof that guilt bade them hurry away from the scene of their crime.'

'It is circumstantial proof only and that is not absolutely proof in law. Was the local chieftain informed?'

'He sent warriors immediately to follow them but their tracks vanished in some rocky passes through the hills and could not be picked up again.'

'Did anyone observe anything strange during the night when these events happened?'

Brother Firgil shook his head.

'The only person who must have been roused by the thieves was poor Gelasius.'

'How many brethren live in this community?'

'Twenty-one.'

'It seems strange that an elderly man would be the only one disturbed during the night.'

'You see that this chamber lies next to the chapel. Gelasius often kept late hours while working on his texts. I see no strangeness in this.'

'In relationship to the chapel, where are the quarters of the other brethren?'

'The Father Superior has the chamber next to this one. I, as steward of the community, have the next chamber. The rest of the brethren share the *dormitorium*.'

'Is the Father Superior a sound sleeper?'

Brother Firgil frowned.

'I do not understand.'

'No matter. When was it discovered that the artefacts had been stolen?'

'Brother Gormgilla discovered the body of Gelasius and raised the alarm. A search was made and the crucifix, cups and rosary were found missing.'

'And no physical damage was done in the chapel or to this room before Brother Gormgilla had to break in?'

'None, so far as I am aware. Had there been, it might have aroused the community and we might have saved Gelasius.'

'Was Gelasius an exceptionally tidy person?'

Brother Firgil blinked at the abrupt change of question.

'He was not especially so.'

Fidelma gestured to the chamber.

'Was this how the room was when he was found?'

'I think it has been tidied up after his body was removed. I think that his papers were tidied and his clothes put away until it was decided what should be done with them.'

'Who did the tidying?'

'Father Maílín himself.'

Fidelma sighed softly.

'That is all, Brother Firgil.'

She hesitated a moment, after he had left, and looked at the area where Gelasius would have been working, examining the books and papers carefully.

She left Gelasius's chamber and went into the chapel. It was small and with few icons. Two candles burnt on the altar. A rough-hewn, wooden crucifix had been positioned in obvious replacement of the stolen one. She examined the interior of the chapel for a few minutes before deciding that it would tell her nothing more.

She left the chapel and paused for a moment in the central courtyard looking at the buildings and judging their relation to the chapel. Again, it merely confirmed what Brother Firgil had said. Gelasius's chamber was the closest.

She felt frustrated. There was something that was not right at all.

Members of the brethren of the community went about their daily tasks, either avoiding her eyes or nodding a greeting to her, each according to their characters. There was no wall around the community and, in that, there was nothing to contradict the idea that a band of thieves could easily have infiltrated the community and entered the chapel.

Half a mile away, crossing a small hill, was a wood and it was this wood where Brother Firgil had indicated that the itinerants had encamped.

Fidelma began to walk in that direction. Her movement towards the woods was purely automatic. She felt the compulsion to walk and think matters over and the wood was as good a direction as any in which to do so. It was not as though she expected to find any evidence among the remains of the itinerant camp.

She had barely gone a few hundred yards when she noticed the figure a short distance behind her. It was moving surreptitiously: one of the brothers following her from the buildings of the community.

She imperceptibly increased her pace up the rising path towards the woods and entered it quickly. The path immediately led into a clearing where it was obvious that there had been an encampment not so long ago. There were signs of a fire, the grey ashes spread in a circle. Some of the ground had been turned by the hooves of horses and a wagon.

'You won't find anything here, Sister.'

Fidelma turned and regarded the figure of the brother who had now entered the clearing behind her.

'Good day, Brother,' she replied solemnly. He was a young man, with bright ginger red hair and dark blue eyes. He was young, no more than twenty, but wore the tonsure of St John. 'Brother . . . ?' She paused, inviting him to supply his name.

'My name is Brother Ledbán.'

'You have followed me, Brother Ledbán. Do you wish to talk with me?'

'I want you to know that the Venerable Gelasius was a brilliant man.'

'I think most of Christendom knows that,' she replied solemnly.

'Most of Christendom does not know that the Venerable Gelasius hungered for truth no matter if the truth was unpalatable to them.'

'*Veritas vos liberabit*. The truth shall make you free,' Fidelma quoted from the vellum in her *marsupium*.

'That was his very motto,' Brother Ledbán agreed. 'He should have remembered the corollary to that – *veritas odium parit*.'

Fidelma's eyes narrowed slightly.

'I have heard that said. Truth breeds hatred. Was Gelasius getting near a truth that caused hatred?'

'I think so.'

'Among the brethren?'

'Among certain of our community at St Martin's,' agreed Brother Ledbán.

'Perhaps you should tell me what you know.'

'I know little but what little I know, I shall impart to you.'

Fidelma sat down on a fallen tree trunk and motioned Brother Ledbán to sit next to her.

'I understand that the Venerable Gelasius must have been working on a new text of philosophy?'

'He was. Why I know it is because I am a scribe and the *delbatóir* of the community. I would often sharpen Gelasius's quills for him or seek out new ones. I would mix his inks. As *delbatóir* it was my task to make the metal covers that would enshrine and protect the books.'

Fidelma nodded. Many books considered worthy of note were either enshrined in metal boxes or had finely covered plates of gold or silver, some encrusted with jewels, sewn on to their leather covers. This was a special art, the casting of such plates called a *cumtach*, and the task fell to the one appointed a *delbatóir* which meant a framer or fashioner.

254

'We sometimes worked closely and Gelasius would often say to me that truth was the philosopher's food but was often bitter to the taste. Most people preferred the savoury lie.'

'Who was he annoying by his truth?'

'To be frank, Sister, he was annoying himself. I went into his chamber once, where he had been poring over some texts in the old writing . . .'

'In Ogham?'

'In Ogham. Alas, I have not the knowledge of it to be able to decipher the ancient alphabet. But he suddenly threw the text from him and exclaimed: "Alas! The value of the well is not known until it has dried up!" Then he saw me and smiled and apologised for his temper. But temper was not really part of that wise old man, Sister. It was more a sadness than a temper.'

'A sadness at what he was reading?'

'A sadness at what he was realising through his great knowledge.'

'I take it that you do not believe in Father Maílín's story of the itinerant thieves?' she suddenly asked.

He glanced swiftly at her.

'I am not one to point a finger of accusation at any one individual. The bird has little affection that deserts its own brood.'

'There is also an old saying, that one bird flies away from every brood. However, I am not asking you to desert your own brood but I am asking you to help in tracking down the person responsible for the Venerable Gelasius's death.'

'I cannot betray that person.'

'Then you do know who it was?'

'I suspect but suspecting would cast doubt on the good name of Gelasius.'

Fidelma frowned slightly.

'I fail to understand that.'

'The explanation of every riddle is contained in itself,' Brother Ledbán replied, rising. 'Gelasius was fond of reading *Naturalis Historia* . . .'

'Pliny?' queried Fidelma.

'Indeed – Gaius Plinius Secundus. Gelasius once remarked to me that he echoed Pliny in acknowledging God's best gift to mankind.'

He had gone even before Fidelma felt that she should have pointed out that he could be ordered to explain by law under pain of fine. Yet, somehow, she did not think it was appropriate or that she would be able to discover his suspicions in that way.

She sat for some time on the log, turning matters over in her own mind. Then she pulled out the piece of parchment and read it again, considering it carefully. She replaced it in her *marsupium* and stood up abruptly, her mouth set in a grim line.

She retraced her steps back down the hill to the community and went straight to the Father Superior's chamber.

Father Maílín was still seated at his desk and looked up in annoyance as she entered.

'Have you finished your investigation, Sister?'

'Not as yet,' Fidelma replied and, without waiting to be asked, sat down. A frown crossed Father Maílín's brow but before he could admonish Fidelma, she cut in with a bored voice, 'I would remind you that not only am I sister to the King of Cashel but, in holding the degree of *anruth* as an advocate of the court, I have the privilege of even sitting in the presence of the High King. Do not, therefore, lecture me on protocol.'

Father Maílín swallowed at the harshness of her tone.

He had, indeed, been about to point out that a member of the brethren was not allowed to sit in the presence of a Father Superior without being invited.

'You are a clever man, Father Maílín,' Fidelma suddenly said, although the Father Superior missed the patronising tone in her voice.

He stared at her, not knowing how to interpret her words.

'I need your advice.'

Father Maílín shifted his weight slightly in his chair. He was bewildered by her abrupt changes of attitude.

'I am at your service, Sister Fidelma.'

'It is just that you have been able to reason out an explanation for a matter which is beyond my understanding and I would like you to explain it to me.'

'I will do my best.'

'Excellent. Tell me how these thieves were able to overpower and hang an old man in his chamber and leave the room, having secured the window on the inside and locking the door behind them, leaving the key in the room?'

256

Father Maílín stared at her for some moments, his eyes fixed on her in puzzlement. Then he began to chuckle.

'You are misinformed. The key was never found. The thieves took it with them.'

'I am told that there was only one key to that room which the Venerable Gelasius kept in his possession. Is that true?'

Father Maílín nodded slowly.

'There was no other key. Our smith had to pick the lock for us to gain entrance to the room.'

Fidelma reached into her *marsupium* and laid the key before him.

'Don't worry, I tried it in Gelasius's lock. It works. I found the key on the floor behind his desk.'

'I don't . . . I can't . . .'

His voice stumbled over the words.

Fidelma smiled sharply.

'Somehow I didn't think you would be able to offer an explanation.'

Father Maílín ran a hand, distractedly, through his hair. He said nothing.

'Where are the writings that the Venerable Gelasius was working on?' went on Fidelma.

'Destroyed,' Father Maílín replied limply.

'Was it you who destroyed them?'

'I take that responsibility.'

'*Veritas odium parit*,' repeated Fidelma softly.

'You know your Terence, eh? But I did not hate old Gelasius. He was just misguided. The more misguided he became, the more stubborn he became. Ask anyone. Even Brother Ledbán, who worked closely with him, refused to cast a mould for a bookplate which carried some Ogham script because he thought Gelasius had misinterpreted it.'

'You felt that Gelasius was so misguided that you had to destroy his work?'

'You do not understand, Sister.'

'I think I do.'

'I doubt it. You could not. Gelasius was like a father to me. I was protecting him. Protecting his reputation.'

Fidelma raised an eyebrow in disbelief.

'It is the truth that I tell you,' insisted the Father Superior. 'Those papers on which he was working, I had hoped that he would never release to the world. He was the great philosopher of the Faith and yet he grew senile and began to doubt his faith.'

'In what way did he grow senile?'

'What other condition could account for his doubt? When I reproved him for it he told me that one must question even the existence of God for if God did exist then He would approve of the homage of reason rather than fear born out of ignorance.'

Fidelma inclined her head.

'He was, indeed, a wise man,' she sighed. 'But for those doubts . . . you killed him!'

Father Maílín sprang to his feet, his face white.

'What? Do you accuse me of his murder? It was the itinerants, I tell you.'

'I do not believe your itinerant theory, Father Maílín,' she said firmly. 'No one who considers the facts could believe it.'

The Father Superior slumped back in his seat with hunched shoulders. There was guilt written on his features. He groaned softly.

'I only sought to protect Gelasius's reputation. I did not kill him,' he protested.

'You, yourself, have given yourself a suitable motive for his murder.'

'I didn't! I did not . . .'

'I will leave you for a moment to consider your story. When I return, I shall want the truth.'

She turned out of his chamber and made her way slowly to the chapel. She was about to pass the Venerable Gelasius's door when some instinct drew her inside again. She did not know what made her enter until she saw the shelf of books.

She made her way across the room and began to peer along the line of books.

'Gaius Plinius Secundus,' she muttered to herself, as her eyes rested on the book which she was unconsciously looking for – *Naturalis Historia*.

She began to flip through the pages seeking the half-forgotten reference.

Finally, she found the passage and read it through. The passage contained what she expected it would.

She glanced quickly round the room and then went to the bed. She climbed on it and stood at the edge, reaching her hands up towards the beam above. It was, for her, within easy arm's length. She stepped down again to the floor. Then she made her way to the chapel and stood inside the door as she had done a short time before.

Her gaze swept around the chapel and then, making up her mind on some intuition, she walked to the altar and went down on her hands and knees but it was not to pray. She bent forward and lifted an edge of the drape across the altar.

Beneath the altar stood a silver crucifix and two golden chalices. In one of them was a rosary of green stone beads. Fidelma reached forward and took them out. She regarded them for a moment or two and then heaved a deep sigh.

Gathering them in her arms she retraced her steps to Father Maílín's chamber. He was still seated at his desk. He began to rise when she entered, and then his eyes fell to the trophies she carried. He turned pale and slumped back in his seat.

'Where did you . . .' he began, trying to summon up some residue of sharpness by which he hoped to control the situation.

'Listen to me,' she interrupted harshly. 'I have told you that it is impossible to accept your story that thieves broke in, killed Gelasius and left him in a room secured from the inside. I then find that you disapproved of the work which Gelasius was doing and after his death destroyed it. Tell me how these matters add up to a reasonable explanation?'

Father Maílín was shaking his head.

'It was wrong to blame the itinerants. I realise that. It seemed that it was the only excuse I could make. As soon as I realised the situation, I distracted the brethren and quickly went into the chapel and removed the first things that came to hand. The crucifix and the cups. These I placed under the altar where you doubtless discovered them. I returned to Gelasius's room and seized the opportunity to take his rosary from the drawer. Then it was easy. I could now claim that we had been robbed.'

'And you destroyed Gelasius's work?'

'I only collected the text that Gelasius had been working on at the time and destroyed it lest it corrupt the minds of the faithful. Surely it was better to remember Gelasius in the vigour of his youth when he took up the banner of the Faith against all comers and destroyed the idols of the past? Why remember him as he was in his dotage, in his senility – an old embittered man filled with self-doubts?'

'Is that how you saw him?'

'That is how he became, and this I say even though he had been a father to me. He taught us to overthrow the idols of the pagans, to recant the sins of our fathers who lived in heathendom . . .'

'By despising, denigrating and destroying all that has preceded us, we will simply teach this and future generations to despise our beliefs. *Veritas vos liberabit!*'

Father Maílín stared at her quizzically.

'How do you know that?'

'You did not destroy all Gelasius's notes. Gelasius, towards the end of his life, suddenly began to realise the cultural wealth he had been instrumental in destroying. It began to prey on his mind that instead of bringing civilisation and knowledge to this land, he was destroying thousands of years of learning. Benignus writes that the Blessed Patrick himself, in his missionary zeal, burnt a hundred and eighty books of the Druids. Imagine the loss to learning!'

'It was right that such books of pagan impropriety be destroyed,' protested the Father Superior.

'To a true scholar it was a sacrilege that should never have happened.'

'He was wrong.'

'The burning of books, the destruction of knowledge, is a great crime against humanity. No matter in whose name it is done,' replied Fidelma. 'Gelasius saw that. He knew he was partially responsible for a crime which he had committed against his own culture as well as the learning of the world.'

Father Maílín was silent for a moment and then he said: 'I did not kill him. He took his own life. That was why I tried to blame the itinerants.'

'Gelasius was murdered,' Fidelma said. 'But not by the itinerants. He was murdered by a member of this community.'

Father Maílín was pale and shocked.

'You cannot believe that I . . . I only meant to cover up his own suicide and hide the nature of his work. I did not kill him!'

'I realise that . . . now. The thing that had misled me was the fact that you and the real killer both shared a fear of the nature of Gelasius's work. But you both took different ways of dealing with it. When the killer struck, he wanted to make it appear that Gelasius committed suicide and so discredit him. However, you, believing that Gelasius's suicide was genuine, and would bring discredit on the Faith, then tried to disguise what you thought was a suicide and blame itinerants for murder.'

'Who killed the Venerable Gelasius, then?' demanded Father Maílín. 'And how? There was only one key and you say that you found it in the room.'

'Let me first explain why I did not think Gelasius took his own life. The obvious point was that it was physically impossible for him to do so. He was old and frail. I stood on the bed and reached to the roof beam. I am tall and therefore could reach it. But for an elderly and frail man, and one of short stature, it was impossible for him to stand on the bed, tie the rope and hang himself.

'Yet one of your brethren went to considerable lengths to draw attention to the nature of the work that Gelasius was doing, pretending to express approval for it but, at the same time, hinting that Gelasius was so overawed by his revelations that he could not face the fact of his complicity in the destruction of our ancient beliefs and rituals. He even said that Gelasius had approved of a quotation by Pliny which, cunningly, he left for me to find, having whetted my curiosity. It was the passage where Pliny wrote that "amid the suffering of life, suicide is the gods' best gift to men". The murderer was Brother Ledbán.'

'Ledbán?' Father Maílín looked at her in amazement. 'The *delbatóir*? But he worked closely with the Venerable Gelasius . . .'

'And so knew all about his work. And one of the mistakes Ledbán made was in pretending he had no knowledge of Ogham when, as you yourself testify, he knew enough to accuse Gelasius of wrong interpretation.'

'But there is one thing you cannot explain,' Father Maílín pointed out, 'and in this your whole argument falls apart. There was only one key and that you confess you found inside Gelasius's room.'

Fidelma smiled knowingly.

'I think you will find a second key. What is the task of Brother Ledbán?'

'He's the *delbatóir* . . . why?'

261

'He makes the metal book plates and book shrines, casting them from moulds in gold or silver. It is not beyond his capability to cast a second key, having made a mould from the first. You simply take the key and press it into wax to form the mould from which you will make your cast. You will note, as I did, the key I found – Gelasius's own key – was covered in grease. A search of Ledbán's chamber or his forge should bring the second key to light if he does not confess when faced with the rest of the evidence.'

'I see.'

'However, it was wrong of you, Father Maílín, to try to disguise the manner of Gelasius's death.'

'You must understand my position. I did believe Gelasius had committed suicide. If so, the nature of his work would be revealed. Would you rather Christendom knew that one of its great theologians committed suicide in protest at being responsible for the destruction of a few pagan books?'

'I would rather Christendom might learn from such an act. However, it was a greater guilt to fabricate the false evidence.'

'My desire was to save Gelasius from condemnation,' protested Father Maílín.

'Had Gelasius resorted to suicide, then he would have been condemned for his action,' Fidelma said. 'What was it that Martial wrote?

When all the flattery of life is gone
The fearful steal away to death, the brave live on.

'But, as you frequently remarked, the Venerable Gelasius was a brave man and would have lived to argue his case had he not been murdered. I will leave it to you to arrest Brother Ledbán and await instructions from the abbot.'

She smiled sadly and turned towards the door.

'Must everything come out?' called Father Maílín. 'Must all be revealed?'

'That is up to the abbot,' replied Fidelma, glancing back. 'Thankfully, in this case, it is not in my purview to make such moral judgements on what took place here. I only have to report the facts to the abbot.'

The Fosterer

'Fidelma! I am glad that you have come.'

Brehon Spélan was looking somewhat harassed as Fidelma entered the old judge's chamber. She had known Spélan for many years and had ridden to the fortress of Críonchoill, the place of the withered wood, in answer to his summons. He had sent her a message that he required some urgent assistance. Now his face was wreathed in a tired smile of relief as he came forward to welcome her.

'What ails you, Spélan?' Fidelma examined him with concern. He did not seem physically ill and a moment later he confirmed that fact to her.

'I did not mean to alarm you, Fidelma.' He was apologetic. 'I was due to hear a case this morning; a case of death by neglect and now I have been called to hear a case of kin-slaying in the neighbouring territory. The kin-slaying concerns a cleric of noble rank and, as you will know, takes precedence. I am afraid that I must leave at once and yet all the witnesses of the death by neglect case have already been summoned here. It is too late to cancel the hearing. I asked you here to beg a favour of you.'

Fidelma smiled wryly.

'You want me to hear this case of death by neglect?'

'You are qualified to do so,' pointed out the elderly Brehon, as if it might be a matter for dispute.

She nodded in agreement. Being qualified to the level of *anruth*, only one degree below the highest the law courts could bestow, she could sit in judgement on certain cases but her main task as a *dálaigh* was to prosecute or defend and, more often than not, simply to gather information for presentation to the higher courts.

263

'Of course I will do so. A case of death by neglect? Do you have details?'

'A father whose son has died while in fosterage brings the charge. That is all I know, except that such a case should be fairly simple. I have a copy of the Cáin Íarraith, the law on fosterage, should you need it.'

Fidelma inclined her head slightly.

'I would be grateful, Spélan. While I know generalities of the law pertaining to fosterage, I may need to refresh myself on the specifics.'

The old judge moved to his table, picked up a well-thumbed manuscript book and handed it to her. He seemed in a hurry to depart for he glanced at her in embarrassment.

'Thank you for standing in for me, Fidelma. I must be on my way now. My clerk is Brother Corbb. I am leaving him behind. He will guide and advise you.'

He raised his hand in a sort of salutation, picked up the leather satchel, which he had just finished packing as she entered, and left the room.

Fidelma stood for a moment regarding the closed door with a faint smile of amusement. Brehon Spélan had not really given her time to think and she hoped that she had not been pushed into a wrong choice. She dropped her eyes to the law text that the old judge had thrust into her hand and sighed deeply. What did she really know of fosterage? She seated herself at the desk vacated by Brehon Spélan and placed the book before her.

Altram – fosterage – was the keystone of society and practised in the five kingdoms of Éireann since remote times and by all social ranks. Children were sent away to be reared and educated and those who undertook the task became foster parents of the child. Usually children were sent to fosterage at the age of seven years. They remained in fosterage until the age of fourteen for girls and seventeen for boys when they were deemed to have reached the 'age of choice'.

There were two types of fosterage: fosterage for affection and fosterage for payment. Kings sent their sons to other kings to be fostered. Had not Lugaid, son of the High King Conn Cétchathach of the Uí Néill, been sent to the Eóghanacht King of Muman, Ailill Olum, to be raised and educated? From fosterage grew close ties between families. The relationship was regarded as something sacred and often the foster children became more attached to their foster parents than to members of their own family. Cases had occurred where a warrior had voluntarily laid down his own life to save that of his foster father or foster brother.

Fidelma had been told that in the year of her birth, at the great battle of Magh Roth, the High King, Domhnall mac Aedo, had been concerned for the personal safety of his rebellious foster son, Congal Cáel, King of Ulaidh, against whom he was fighting. In spite of Congal's attempt to oust his foster father from the kingship both foster father and foster son regarded one another with affection and when Congal was slain, Domhnall lamented as if he had lost the battle.

The law on fosterage was written down in minute detail.

For a while Fidelma thumbed through the text and then she suddenly realised the passage of time. She reached forward and picked up the small silver hand bell and shook it. The door opened immediately to its summons and a thin-faced religieux with rounded shoulders scurried into the room to stand before her.

Brother Corbb had been Brehon Spélan's clerk for many years. He did not look prepossessing but Fidelma knew that he understood his job thoroughly and was as well versed in law as many who had qualified.

'Has Brehon Spélan told you that he has asked me to hear this case of death by neglect in his absence?' she began.

The thin-faced man inclined his head. It was a swift almost sparrow-like movement.

'He has, lady.' Brother Corbb preferred to ignore her religious office and address her as the sister to Colgú, King of Muman.

'I am told it concerns a death in fosterage. Who is the plaintiff?'

'Fécho is the father of the dead child. He is a smith.'

'And the defendant?'

'Colla, a wainwright, lady, a maker of wagons.'

'Are they both in attendance in the Hall of Hearings? And all who are witness to this matter also present?'

'They are. Shall I give you the details about them?'

Fidelma shook her head.

'I do not want to prejudge anything, Brother Corbb. I will hear from the witnesses themselves and make my own interpretations and judgements as we proceed.'

'Be it as you wish, lady.'

She rose from the desk and Brother Corbb moved to the door to hold it open for her to pass through. Then with nimble movements he contrived to close the door behind her and move back into a position to lead her into the Hall of Hearings.

There were many people there, drawn from the two extended families involved – the families of both the plaintiff and the defendant. Young as well as old were included. As Brother Corbb led Fidelma into the hall and up to the raised platform on which she would sit as judge, a murmuring broke out which was quickly hushed by a movement from Brother Corbb, who banged a wooden staff on the floor to indicate that the court was in session. Fidelma had put down the manuscript book and taken her seat. She examined the expectant upturned faces slowly before speaking.

'I am Fidelma of Cashel,' she announced. 'In the absence of Brehon Spélan it is I who will hear this case. Does anyone present object?'

There was a silence and she smiled drily.

'*Qui tacet consentit*,' she intoned. Silence implies consent. 'Let the plaintiff or the *dálaigh* for the plaintiff stand forward and state their case.'

A man with dark hair, short of stature but well muscled, with clothes that betrayed his calling, a leather jerkin and trousers, stood up hesitantly and coughed as if to clear his throat.

'We are poor folk in Críonchoill,' he began. 'We can't afford the ten *séds* that a lawyer would charge to represent us. I will speak for my family.'

Fidelma frowned.

'I presume that you are Fécho the smith?' On receiving a gesture of confirmation, she continued: 'Before you commence, I would offer a word of advice. If you do not have funds to pay for legal representation, have you considered the possible outcome of legal action? If you cannot present a good case and I find it so then you have to pay the court fees, that is the *aile déc*, which is called the judge's fee. And if your testimony is found false against him that you accuse, you may find yourself having to pay fines and compensation also.'

Fécho compressed his lips and shuffled his feet as he stood before her.

'I have discussed the matter.' He waved his hand to encompass his entire family. 'They have agreed that they will support me in this matter.'

'So long as you are aware of this fact,' Fidelma said. 'I, myself, have to lodge five ounces of silver with this court to ensure that I carry out my duties as judge in an appropriate manner. If I do not, that is my loss. And if, on appeal, my decision is overturned because it is found in error, then I am fined one *cumal* – the value of three milch cows.'

She did not have to explain this but she saw the trusting and unlettered people anxiously regarding her and felt that she had to make an effort to reassure them.

'Where is the defendant?'

The man who stood up was almost a replica of Fécho the smith, except his hair was a dirty, corn yellow, but he too was tanned and muscular.

'I am Colla the wainwright,' he announced nervously.

'Understand, Colla, that what I have told Fécho also applies to you. If you are found guilty, you will have to pay the fines and the court costs. Do you understand?'

'I am not guilty, and Fécho . . .'

'You will have an opportunity to speak later,' she interrupted him sharply. 'I am telling you the course of the law. I presume that you have no legal representation?'

'I do not.'

'Then having warned you of the consequence I presume your *fine*, your kindred, are prepared to pay if the case goes against you?'

'But it will not . . .' he began to protest.

A plump woman at his side tugged at his sleeve, and said loudly: 'The kindred are prepared to pay and will appeal if the judgement goes against us.'

'So long as you both understand. Colla the wainwright is classed, I see, as a chief expert wright, and his honour price is adjudged in law as even greater than the highest grade of judge. Some twenty *séds* is the sum. Likewise, Fécho, the smith, is similarly classed as having an honour price of twenty *séds*.'

'We know this,' interrupted Colla brusquely. 'The equality of our honour prices is why we exchanged the contract for this fosterage.'

Fidelma sighed softly and indicated that the wainwright should be reseated. It was little use explaining to him the etiquette of court procedure.

'Let us hear your case, Fécho. Keep only to the facts as you know them and do not indulge in any story that you have heard or cannot prove.'

The blacksmith ran a hand nervously through his hair.

'My son was called Enda and he was seven years old. I claim he was murdered.'

'Murdered?' Fidelma was startled. 'I thought that this was a case of death by neglect?'

'So I thought at first until Tassach . . .'

Fidelma raised a hand to still him.

'Let us begin at the beginning. You may start by telling me how Enda came to be in fosterage with Colla?'

'As a wainwright Colla was well known to me for he often brought work to my forge. His workshop is on the other side of the hill. It occurred to me that Colla, who has several children and two apprentices whom he instructs in his art of wagon-making, would be the ideal person to foster my son. One month ago we agreed on this course of action.'

'And was this fosterage done for affection or for fee?'

Fécho shrugged.

'As we have explained, we are poor here, and so we agreed that I would supply my services without cost, if Colla fostered the child and taught him his arts.'

Fidelma nodded thoughtfully.

'And this, you say, was agreed just a month ago?'

'It was.'

'Proceed.'

'A week ago, Colla came to me in his wagon. He told me that there had been an accident. That Enda, my son, had fallen into a pool near the house and drowned. That poor little Enda . . .'

There was a sudden catch in the man's throat.

'Take your time,' Fidelma advised him gently. 'Tell me what created

268

the suspicion in your mind that this was not an accident as Colla maintained?'

'Things were blurred for a while. I was shocked, and so was my wife, who even now remains at home prostrate with grief, for little Enda was our only child. I recall that Colla had brought the body in his wagon and I lifted it down and carried it into my *bothán*. We sat a long time before the body. Colla had left. Then it was that my cousin Tassach arrived and he said . . .'

'Just a moment. Who is Tassach, apart from being your cousin, and is he in this court?'

A stocky young man stood up.

'I am Tassach, learned Brehon. I am a physician as well as cousin to Fécho.'

'I see. In that case, we will interrupt Fécho's testimony to hear what you said at this time.'

The young man gestured with his hand towards Fécho.

'I came to visit my cousin and found him and his wife kneeling before the body of little Enda, their only son. His little body was laid out on the table. They were upset; Fécho and his wife, that is. Fécho told me that the child had drowned while in the care of Colla. I was puzzled at this.'

'Puzzled? Why?'

'Because Enda swam like a fish. He was a strong little swimmer. I have seen him fight the torrents of the Siúr like a salmon racing upriver.'

'Even the strongest swimmers can sometimes have accidents and drown,' observed Fidelma.

'That is certainly true,' replied Tassach. 'However, to drown in the pool by Colla's house would take an accident of exceptional character.'

'You speak as if you know that pool?'

'This is a small community, learned Brehon. We all know one another and know the territory of our clan as we know the interior of our own *bothán*.'

'So you were suspicious and told Fécho so?'

'Not at once. I examined the body of Enda.'

Fidelma had been forming a theory that the claim was being brought by parents motivated by grief and hurt and not able to accept the loss

269

of their only child. But with a physician involved, the evidence was changing. Fidelma turned her undivided attention on Tassach.

'And, as a physician, what do you say was the result of your examination?'

'The child had the appearance of having been immersed in water but on the back of his skull was an abrasion, a deep cut as though he had been hit from behind with something heavy. Perhaps a rock. I believe the child was dead before he was immersed.'

Brother Corbb had to bang his staff several times to still the hubbub that had broken out from Colla and his family.

Fidelma gazed thoughtfully at the physician.

'What you are saying is that the boy was murdered.'

Tassach compressed his lips for a moment.

'That is a matter that only you can decide, learned Brehon. I can only report what I found. What is clear is that the boy did not fall into the pool and drown.'

'And did your findings persuade Fécho to bring this action?'

'I would not say that it was my findings alone.'

'Really? What, then?'

'Obviously, as one of the *fine*, the kindred of Fécho, even though I am a physician and have taken the oath of Diancecht to uphold the honour of my profession, my word would not carry as much weight as someone who was unconnected with our two families.'

Fidelma stared at the physician in surprise. The man obviously knew the law of evidence.

'And did someone unconnected with the families of Fécho and Colla make an examination of the body of Enda?'

Tassach turned slightly to where an elderly man with long white hair rose to his feet.

'If it please you, learned Brehon, I am the physician Niall. I can confirm the findings of my young colleague Tassach, in so far as the boy had received a sharp blow on the back of the head.'

Fidelma pursed her lips.

'It seems, in this case, it is a curious coincidence that two learned physicians were on hand at the same time as Colla brought the body of Enda to his parents' home.'

Niall snorted indignantly.

'I was not at hand, learned Brehon, but had to be sent for. Tassach wisely, because of his relationship with Fécho and the dead boy, and because of his concerns as to the nature of the injuries, summoned me to attend at Fécho's forge. I arrived there about an hour later. I am well known in Críonchoill and anyone will tell you that I have no connection with either family in this case.'

Fidelma stirred a little in discomfort, rebuking herself for thinking aloud so publicly.

'In your opinion, then, Niall, the injury on the boy's head was one that was inconsistent with a drowning accident?'

To her surprise, he shook his head.

'I thought that you agreed with Tassach?' she demanded sharply.

Niall smiled gently.

'We can each only give testimony as to what we know. I confirmed Tassach's medical opinion that the body was more likely than not dead when it became immersed in the water. That the death was due to the blow the child received, which not only cut him deeply but splintered pieces of his skull. But whether this was an *accident* or not, I cannot express an opinion. I do not know the pool in which the child is said to have met his death. Were any rocks there? Was the child thrown against a rock by a surge of water? These are things that others must consider.'

Fidelma sat back, unconsciously drumming her fingers on the arm of her chair.

'Very well. Let me return to Fécho.'

The smith rose again.

'You have heard the evidence of Tassach and Niall?'

'I have.'

'It was on this basis that you charged Colla with death by neglect? Death by neglect and not unlawful killing.'

Fécho spread his hands.

'Lady, I am no lawyer. I do not know what happened except that Colla brought my son home and he was dead. Colla said he had drowned. The physicians said he had not. They say some rock struck him on the head. I can only raise the questions and only Colla can provide the answers.'

There was a murmur of agreement in the court.

'Then we shall ask Colla what he has to say about this matter.'

The burly wainwright stood slowly up.

'Fécho has told you the truth in that we agreed that I would take his son Enda into fosterage and instruct him in the art of building wagons. In return for this, Fécho promised that he would do all the work I needed in terms of his smith's art.'

'Then proceed to how Enda came by his death. You do not deny it occurred while in your care?'

'He was in my care as fosterer when the death occurred,' agreed Colla. 'I deny that his death occurred through any neglect or any action of mine.'

He paused for a moment, as if summoning his thoughts.

'It was in the morning. My wife was washing clothes while I went to my carpenter's shop with my two apprentices. We were turning spokes for wheels for a cart. The young children, my daughters Una and Faife and my son Maine, with young Enda, had been allowed an hour of play. My wife, having finished the washing, was going to teach them their letters.' Colla glanced at Fécho. 'This was in accordance with our agreement, that Enda would be taught to read and write alongside my own children.'

Fidelma nodded. 'As is customary in such fostering agreements. Continue.'

Colla made a gesture with his shoulder that was not quite a shrug.

'I suppose it was less than an hour later when I heard a shout. My son, Maine, who is nine years of age, came running to me and said there had been an accident in the pool. That Enda had fallen in and drowned.'

'Fallen in?' queried Fidelma sharply. 'So the child was not swimming?'

Colla shook his head.

'None of them were.'

'Just describe this pool.'

'It is about one hundred yards from the house. It is hidden by trees but it is a small pool and not at all deep. It is fed by a small spring and it is where my cattle are watered.'

'Can you hazard its dimensions?'

'A circular pool about twelve feet in diameter. I can wade across it without the water's coming to my chest.'

'What happened next?'

'I went running to the pool, my apprentices with me, and I saw the child floating face down in the middle of the pond. I waded in and brought him to the bank but he was already dead.'

'Did Maine explain what happened?'

Colla grimaced.

'My son said that he was wandering by the pool when he saw Enda floating there and came to fetch me.'

'Were the other children, your daughters, there?'

He shook his head.

'So Enda was alone when he fell in the water?'

'I asked my children what they knew. They had gone to the woods just beyond the pool. They were going to play *folacháin* – hide and seek. It seems, according to Faife, that after a while Enda tired of the game and went off on his own. Later Maine also tired and was returning to the house when he saw Enda. That is all they knew.'

'And then?'

'Then I could do no more than take the body of the young boy in my wagon to his father. What more could I do? I am not responsible for his death. I did not neglect him. It was an accident.'

Fidelma sighed softly.

'Tell me one more thing, Colla. Are there sharp rocks around this pool?'

The wainwright immediately shook his head.

'I told you, my cattle water there. The banks are muddy and slope gently into the pool.'

'And you found Enda in the pool, fully clothed?'

'I did.'

'How do you imagine he came there?'

'How . . . ? I suppose . . .' Colla paused and frowned.

'Did you not consider how he could have fallen into the pool?' pressed Fidelma. 'For I see that you are now thinking that it is curious that a child could fall into a pool when it is surrounded by gentle sloping banks on which cattle might safely drink.'

'Maybe he waded in to fetch something, slipped, and fell . . .'

'Causing the wound on the back of his head?' sneered Tassach from across the courtroom.

'Of course the boy fell. He was always getting into mischief. The boy was a thief and a liar!'

273

The woman who had been silent at Colla's side suddenly rose to her feet as she delivered her outburst.

Fidelma met her eye with a stern expression and waited until Brother Corbb had restored some order among the outraged members of Fécho's family.

'And you are?' she asked coldly.

'I am Dublemna, wife to Colla.'

'What have you to tell us of Enda that is pertinent to this case?'

'Of the death, I know nothing. But let it not be thought that this Enda was a blameless sweet child.'

Fidelma raised an eyebrow in surprise at her anger.

'You have to explain yourself.'

'We agreed to the fosterage but we found that the child was wayward and undisciplined. My daughter Faife revealed to me that the boy was stealing eggs from my own kitchen. Later I discovered that he had been stealing honey from our neighbour's hives. I told my husband and said that the boy should be returned to Fécho or disciplined severely.'

Fécho was on his feet.

'My boy was not a thief. This is a lie.'

'It was no lie!' returned Dublemna with equal vehemence. 'The reason why I tell it is to show that if ever there was neglect of the child, it was not our neglect. We should have been warned of the child's behaviour by its parents.'

The hubbub of anger and insults now rose between the two families and Brother Corbb had his work cut out to bring them to order again.

'Any further outbursts such as that will require everyone to pay fines to this court,' Fidelma said quietly before turning to Fécho.

'Had the boy ever been in trouble before he went into fosterage? On your word, now. Lies have a habit of catching up with you.'

Fécho shook his head.

'No one will tell you otherwise, Brehon,' he asserted with passion. 'He was a good child. Ask anyone in Críonchoill except that woman.' He jerked his head to Colla's wife.

Fidelma turned to Dublemna.

'Your daughter Faife told you that Enda had been stealing eggs? When was this?'

'The day before the boy fell into the pool,' she asserted.

'Were the eggs found?'

'Faife had them. I found her with them. I asked what she was doing with them and she told me that it was Enda who had stolen them and she had taken them from him. We were going to discipline the boy. A good thrashing would have worked wonders.'

'I am bound to point out,' Fidelma spoke sharply, 'that the law of fosterage allows no corporal punishment. Fosterage should be without blemish, so the law says. And as for evidence, all I have heard is accusations and little proof.'

Dublemna's face was red with anger.

'No proof? Then what of this for proof . . . ? Later that very same day our neighbour called by to say that during the last few weeks – from the time that Enda came to us as foster child – he had been missing honeycombs from his beehives. He made no accusations but wondered if we had been missing anything. After the boy died, when we were clearing out his things, we found a remnant of a honeycomb in the little box where he kept his personal possessions. Is that proof enough for you?'

Brother Corbb commented drily: 'Crimes committed by the foster child are the responsibility of the foster father. Technically, if the boy was guilty of these thefts then Colla was facing a fine for the crime . . .'

Before Fidelma could rebuke Brother Corbb for ignoring court etiquette, Tassach, the physician, was on his feet, his face showing his excitement.

'I have it! The poor boy was drowned so that Colla would not be held responsible for the theft of the honey from the neighbour's hives! It was an attempt to hide his responsibility.'

Fidelma raised a hand to stifle the angry murmuring that arose again. Brother Corbb had to thump the floor with his staff.

'This second warning will be my last to you. The next time everyone here will pay a *screpall* apiece as a fine for contempt of this court. Let me remind you all of something,' Fidelma said grimly. 'This *is* a court. At the moment, I am giving you maximum latitude in the presentation of evidence. I shall even give latitude when people speak out of turn.' Her steely eyes glanced at Brother Corbb, who had the grace to blush. It was unseemly for a steward to comment on law in the presence of a Brehon sitting in judgement. 'However, what is law outside this room is also law inside this room. Claims such as the one you have just made, Tassach, cannot be tolerated unless you are prepared to offer proof. You are not allowed to make accusations without proof.'

The physician was silent but his expression was one of anger.

At her side, Brother Corbb coughed discreetly and leaned forward to whisper in her ear.

'Pardon, lady. I am uncertain how you intend to proceed, but so far I have heard no proof that the boy met his end by either neglect or foul play. Should not this matter be addressed?'

Fidelma shot him an irritated glance.

'I know my duty, Brother Corbb. We have not heard all the witnesses yet,' she snapped, causing the steward to blink and step back.

She turned back to the court, which had grown expectantly quiet.

'In the circumstances, the court wishes to examine the three last people to see Enda alive . . . are the children Faife, Una and Maine in the court room?'

There was a murmur of surprise. Fidelma felt Brother Corbb take a step forward and raised her hand to still his protest, but he would not be silenced.

'A child under fourteen years of age has neither legal responsibility nor any right to independent legal action. That means that the children cannot be sworn in as witnesses or their statements be given the same weight of authority as an adult's. A *fiadu*, a witness, can only give evidence about what they have seen or heard. What does not take place before a witness's eyes is invalid. We have heard some supposition in this case about what may or may not have happened. I have to tell you that this is not evidence in the strict sense. However, the law acknowledges that one can accept into judgement indications of guilt other than the direct evidence of an eyewitness, such as incriminating behaviour in the one suspected of the offence.'

Fidelma restrained her anger at his presumption.

'I am well aware of the law in this matter,' she said tightly. 'Had you also been qualified to bring a judgement . . .' she paused to let her sharp words sink in, 'then you might have known that there is a precedent which gives me the authority to question the three children I have named.'

Brother Corbb flushed and took an involuntary step backwards.

'I was . . .'

'I do not know what leeway the Brehon Spélan gives you as his clerk. In my court there is only one judge. Remember that, Brother Corbb.' She then turned to the court. 'There is a precedent where a young child's testimony can be made without oath and can be accepted for consideration. The example given is the case of a stolen animal believed to have been eaten on the previous night. The child was asked, "What did you have to eat last night?" and his reply was taken into consideration in proving the case against the suspect. I will give the reference to Brother Corbb here to enter when he makes a record of this procedure. Are the children here?'

'They are,' admitted Colla the wainwright, after some moments of delay.

'Then bring Maine to sit beside me and let me speak to him.'

A young boy, dragging reluctant feet, moved to the platform and Brother Corbb produced a chair.

Fidelma smiled at the child encouragingly.

'Now, Maine, I understand that you had a shock when you found the body of poor Enda.'

The boy nodded slowly.

'Did you like him?'

Maine looked surprised at the question and then gave it some consideration before responding.

'He was all right,' he said dismissively. 'He was my *comaltae*, my foster brother.'

'Did you like having a foster brother?'

'I had two sisters. It was good to have a *comaltae*.'

'That's natural,' agreed Fidelma. 'Was Enda liked by everyone in your family . . . your sisters, for example?'

'My sisters don't like boys anyway. That's why I liked having a *comaltae*. My father's apprentices were too old to have time for me. All they cared about was their work and soppy girls in the village when they went to dances . . . *dances!*' The boy shuddered as he gave expression to the word.

'So only you were friends with Enda.'

'I suppose so. He was two years younger than me.'

'But you liked him?'

'I suppose so.'

'How did your parents treat him? No, don't look at them, Maine. Look at me,' she added quickly when Colla and his wife started to rise from their seats. She glanced quickly at them and said: 'You will both be silent while I am examining a witnesses.' She turned back and repeated: 'How did your parents treat him?'

Maine shrugged.

'My father didn't have much to do with us, except when he was teaching us about carpentry and the like. Mother was always moaning about something. I don't think Enda liked her but that's just her way.'

'She finds fault with all of you?'

Maine shrugged. 'More with Enda than me or my sisters.'

'Now, when you found the body. I understand that you were all playing together that morning?'

The boy kicked at the floor.

'Because Faife said we should. She's my eldest sister and . . . well, you know what elder sisters are like.'

Fidelma smiled softly. 'Tell me.'

'Bossy. You know.'

'So you all went off to play because Faife told you to? What did you play?'

'Hide and seek. In the woods. It was boring, 'cos the girls are so easy to find. Enda finally got fed up and said he was going back to the house.'

'But you stayed on?'

'For a while. It was Faife's turn to hide and it took a long time to find her. This time she hid herself well. Had it not been for the business of Enda, I think our mother would have been very angry with her.'

'Angry? Why?'

'I found her hiding under some bushes where it was wet and muddy. Her dress was in a terrible mess. Mother would have given her a good hiding had it not been . . . well, you know.'

'So what did you do then?'

'Faife wanted another game but I was bored, like Enda. I decided to go to look for him.'

'And that is when you found him in the pond?'

The boy nodded quickly.

'When I saw him in the middle of the pond, I ran off to find my father.'

'Two more questions. How far was the pond from where you were playing your game?'

The boy frowned. 'Not very far.'

'Did you know about the theft of the eggs?'

Maine nodded quickly.

'What did Enda say when he was accused of taking the eggs?'

'He said he had not taken them. That it was a story that had been made up by the girls 'cos they didn't like him. Mother wanted Father to wallop him good but Father said he couldn't but would speak to Enda's father when he could.'

Fidelma dismissed him and called for Una to come forward.

She was eight years old and nervous.

'Did you like Enda?' Fidelma asked.

'Not much. Boys are rough creatures. I don't see why we had to have him living with us and he was . . .'

Fidelma looked at her sharply. 'He was – what?'

'A thief. Mummy said so. Thieves are punished. That's probably why he drowned in the pool. God probably drowned him. Mummy said so.'

'But Enda denied he was the thief.'

'He would, wouldn't he? He's a liar because Mummy said so.'

'And you always believe your mother?'

'She's my mother,' the girl replied with simplicity. Fidelma let her return to her seat.

Faife was eleven years old, solemn and trying to behave as a grown-up. When Fidelma posed her initial question the girl frowned in thought.

'I did not dislike him.'

'Not even when you discovered that he was a thief?'

The girl sniffed. 'I knew he had done wrong. I told my mother that he had stolen the eggs.'

'Did he admit that he had stolen the eggs?'

'I found him with the eggs. He could not deny it.'

'Why would he steal eggs from the kitchen?'

Faife frowned. 'I don't understand.'

'He was living with your family and being fed by your family. What need had he of eggs?'

She shrugged as if either it was not important or she did not care.

'I can't answer for him.'

'What makes you so sure that he did steal the eggs?'

'I said so, didn't I?' A note of belligerence crept into her voice.

'But how do you know?' pressed Fidelma, not put out by the girl's tone.

'Because I found him with the eggs.'

'What happened?'

The girl hesitated and then nodded quickly.

'Enda shared a room with my brother and my dad's two apprentices. I went there.'

'Why?' Fidelma's voice interrupted sharply.

There was no hesitation.

'I went looking for Enda to come for the daily lesson my mother gave us in how to tell our letters.'

'And?'

'He was on his bed with the eggs. It is my job to go to the hen house and collect the eggs each morning. I had done so that morning and put them in the kitchen. He had stolen them from there.'

'Did you ask him where the eggs came from?'

The little girl chuckled.

'He told me that he found them under his bed. Of course, no one believed him. Anyway, I said that I would take charge of them and return them.'

'Did you do so?'

'I was taking them back to the kitchen when my mother came. Enda had already scuttled off. My mother asked me what I was doing with the eggs and I had to tell the truth, 'cos that's important, isn't it?'

Fidelma looked at the earnest expression on Faife's face and sighed.

'What did your mother say?'

'Mummy said that Enda would be in for a good beating when Daddy returned.'

'And was he?'

Faife pouted, almost in disapproval.

'Daddy said he was not allowed to touch Enda. We get hit when we do something wrong, why was it wrong to hit Enda?'

'In what way do you get hit?'

'Mummy usually hits us with a switch across the back of the legs.'

'Go back to your place, Faife,' Fidelma said quietly. She paused for a moment. The law, according to her reading of it, was quite clear and did not only apply to foster children. Corporal punishment of a child was prohibited except for a single smack in anger with the palm of the hand. She wondered if she should make a point of this. She decided to leave it to judgement.

'Is the neighbour whose honey was stolen here?' she demanded, when Faife returned to her seat.

'It was my honey that was stolen.' A man with thin, sallow looks rose from his seat. His dress was leather-patched woollen trousers and a short-sleeved jacket and boots. 'My name is Mel, lady. I am a neighbour of Colla and Dublemna.'

'And you keep bees?'

'Don't worry,' grinned the man. 'I know all about the Bechbretha, the law of bees, and I can assure you that I have given the necessary pledges to my four neighbours allowing them to keep swarms from my hives to guarantee me immunity from any claim of trespass. However, as Colla had no wish to keep bees, I guaranteed him combs of honey from my hives in fair exchange. So I am aware of the law and I keep the law.'

Fidelma regarded the farmer with a solemn look.

'That is good. We have heard it suggested that you found that honeycombs were being removed from your hives?'

'I can confirm it. I noticed the missing combs a few weeks ago and I went round my neighbours to warn them that there might be a thief about. However, only one comb went missing at a time, and that on very few days. It seemed so petty. It was only a few days ago, after the boy – this boy Enda – drowned in the pool, that Dublemna told me that they had found part of a honeycomb in his belongings. Of course, I would not prosecute my neighbours for what the boy had done, even though Colla had taken on this role as *aite* – foster father.'

Fidelma heaved a long inward sigh as she dismissed the beekeeper. She sat in thought for a while.

'I am going to adjourn this case for an hour or so,' she suddenly announced. 'I want to see where this death occurred so that I might fully understand the situation.'

It took them just under an hour to reach Colla's homestead. Fécho, Tassach and Niall, and Colla and Dublemna and their children as well as Mel the neighbour accompanied Sister Fidelma and Brother Corbb.

The party, at Fidelma's request, made straight for the pond where Enda had been found. A copse of alder trees obscured it from the homestead. They all halted at a respectful distance while Fidelma went forward to make her examination. It was as Colla had described it. Indeed, it did not take long to realise that with such gently sloping banks, it was beyond question that the boy could have fallen in by accident. She walked round the pond several times, scrutinising the area in search of rocks, stones or anything else that could have made the wound described by Tassach and Niall.

She turned and waved Maine forward.

'I want you to show me where you were playing that morning,' she told him.

The boy pointed to a section of woodland.

'Exactly where?' she pressed.

The boy led her across to the woodland. The trees pressed close and within a dozen feet one could be hidden along its paths. Fidelma noticed the ground was fairly hard and stony. There was an outcrop of boulders in one clearing. It was useless looking for the precise stone that came into contact with Enda's head. Fidelma turned to the boy.

'Just tell me again, Maine, because I would like to be absolutely sure of this . . . when you were playing here and Enda became bored with the game. He left.'

The boy nodded.

'And you all continued to play until you became bored and went off after him?'

'We did so.'

'Any idea of how long this was?' She did not ask with any hope, knowing that children really did not have the same sense of time as adults.

'I think it was a long time. Long enough for Faife to insist we play another game of hide and seek. And I know that she was a long time being found. That's when I got fed up. Una thought that Faife had gone home, for I was the seeker and I easily found Una. Then we both looked for Faife.'

'But you found her eventually, under a bush?'

'We did.'

'Near here?'

'She was under that big bush there.' He pointed.

Fidelma moved forward and glanced quickly at it.

Maine led the way back to where the others were still waiting by the pool. There was little else to be seen that would help her. Fidelma examined their expectant faces.

'I will reserve my judgement in this matter. You will have my judgement on the seventh day from now.'

She hurried away so as not to see the crestfallen, puzzled expressions.

Three days later she was sitting in front of a fire in Brehon Spélan's chambers. The old judge was seated on the opposite side of the fire, sipping mulled wine. Fidelma had just finished recounting the details of the case to him.

'I see your difficulty, Fidelma.' The old judge sighed. 'It is not often that it seems obvious what happened but there is insufficient evidence to pronounce the guilt of the person involved.'

'This is, indeed, a sad case,' she agreed. 'Poor little Enda was placed in an environment that was hostile to him and that very hostility led to his murder. Indeed, not death by neglect but murder. Colla tolerated him simply as a business transaction so that he would get all his smithy work done by Fécho. Colla's wife Dublemna hated the boy. I think she is a bad woman who is not averse to physically punishing her children . . .'

'Even though corporal punishment is against the law?' interposed Spélan.

'Even so,' agreed Fidelma. 'That much Faife made clear. And Colla only seems to have protected Enda because he had obviously been told the law of fosterage when he made the contract.'

'So, from what you say, only little Maine welcomed Enda, and only in him did the child find any sense of companionship?' queried Spélan.

'That is so. But Dublemna was a vindictive and cruel foster mother as well as mother.'

'So you think it was she who actually killed Enda in some rage against the boy?' The old judge was frowning.

Fidelma shook her head.

'Enda left his game of hide and seek that morning and walked back to the homestead. At the pond he was hit over the head by someone wielding a stone and then pushed into the pond. Maine found him and then ran to fetch help.'

'But who did it?'

'Dublemna's influence was strongest on her daughters. Both of them took their cue of hatred for Enda from her. I suspect they were both hated by their mother and sought to please her. One of them, in fact, went out of her way to please the mother. That was Faife.'

'But why?' Spélan was astonished. 'Why would this child resort to murder?'

'The logic of a child is not the same as that of an adult. I think that Faife, overhearing her mother's anger at her husband for having brought the child into fosterage with them, her dislike of the child, thought it would please her mother if Enda was punished – especially when her father refused to do so.'

'It is strange thinking, but I have heard similar tales of children trying to appease parents by doing things they think will please them.'

'In fact, I believe that Faife even decided to provide some ammunition for her mother to justify her dislike. She was the one taking the honey. She stole the eggs and planted them under the bed and then came to accuse Enda.'

'But what happened at the pond?'

'I believe that when they were playing hide and seek, Faife decided – having overheard the conversation between her mother and father – to physically hurt Enda as her mother wanted. Enda had left the game. The next game began – we heard from Maine that it took a long time to find Faife. In the time she was supposed to be hiding and Maine and Una were trying to find her, she went after Enda, found a stone, and hit him on the back of the head. We may never know if her intention was to kill him. When she discovered he was dead she pushed his body in the pond. That's how she muddied and soaked her dress. She tried to disguise it by pretending she was hiding under a bush. But the bush grew in stony, dry ground. It would not have been soaked or muddied, merely dirtied.'

Brehon Spélan whistled softly.

'But we cannot prove that Faife killed the boy. You are Brehon enough to know that your reconstruction would not stand up as proof in court.'

Fidelma sighed deeply.

'I know. That is the sad thing. There is no redress in law for Fécho unless he is persuaded to change his claim back to death by neglect.

They have a good chance of being compensated by Colla's paying half the *dire* or honour price. Enda was over the age of seven, and after that age the child's honour price becomes half that of his father. Under law we can do no more. I can also fine Dublemna for hitting her own children as an infraction of the law but I don't think I will make her see that her hatred of Enda, indeed her dislike even of her own children, led to this tragedy. Colla and Dublemna will stop up their ears. The next recommendation is that due to the fines they be refused any position as fosterers in the future.'

Brehon Spélan shook his head sadly.

'This is one of those times when justice and law are not the same thing, Fidelma. I am sure that we will be able to get Fécho to accept that he press for the lesser charge. I agree about Colla and Dublemna. But what about Faife? What is to stop her the next time she feels like using violence as a solution? I know that you are fond of quoting Publilius Syrus, Fidelma. Didn't he say that the judge is condemned when the guilty one goes free?'

'He did. But then we are here to interpret and maintain the law, for when the rule of law ends rule by tyranny begins. At least we have our great *féis* every three years at which we can argue, with others, and attempt to change the laws that are wrong and expand those that need such amendment. But here and now it is not the law which is wrong but lack of evidence.'

'Perhaps sometimes circumstantial evidence should be taken into judgement when it is very strong . . . such as when you find an overturned and empty pail of milk and a cat sleeping beside it. It is clearly the cat that is guilty.'

Fidelma smiled mischievously.

'Yet a good lawyer might argue that perhaps a dog happened by, overturned the pail, emptying the milk, which evaporated, and afterwards a cat came along and merely went to sleep beside it. Who can with certainty say that the cat was the guilty party?'

The Lost Eagle

$\mathcal{C}\mathcal{D}$

'This is Deacon Platonius Lepidus, Sister Fidelma. He is a visitor from Rome and he wishes a word with you.'

Fidelma looked up in surprise as the stranger was shown into the *scriptorum* of the abbey. She was a stranger in the abbey of Augustine herself. Augustine was the former prior of St Andrews in Rome who had died here scarcely sixty years ago, having been sent as missionary to the king of the Cantware. It was now the focal point of the Jutish Christian community in the centre of the *burg* of Cantware. Fidelma was waiting for Brother Eadulf to finish some business with the Archbishop Theodore. The religieux who had announced the deacon's presence had withdrawn from the library, shutting the door behind him. As Fidelma rose uncertainly the deacon came forward to the table where she had been seated.

Platonius Lepidus looked every inch of what she knew to be a Roman aristocrat; there was arrogance about him in spite of his religious robes. She had been on a pilgrimage to Rome and knew that his aristocratic rank would immediately be recognisable there. He was tall, with dark hair, and swarthy of complexion. His greeting and smile were pleasant enough.

'The Venerable Gelasius told me that you had rendered him a signal service when you were in Rome, Sister. When I heard that you were here in Cantwareburg, I felt compelled to make your acquaintance.'

'How is the Venerable Gelasius?' she rejoined at once, for she had warm memories of the harassed official in the Lateran Palace where the Bishop of Rome resided.

'He is well, and would have sent his personal felicitations had he known that I would be meeting you. The *scriptor* has informed me that you are on a visit with Brother Eadulf, whom the Venerable Gelasius also remembers fondly. I was also informed that you are both soon to leave for a place called Seaxmund's Ham.'

'You are correctly informed, Deacon Lepidus,' Fidelma replied with gravity.

'Let us sit awhile and talk, Sister Fidelma,' the deacon said, applying action to the word and inviting her to do the same with a gesture of his hand. 'I am afraid that I also have a selfish interest in making your acquaintance. I need your help.'

Fidelma seated herself with an expression of curiosity.

'I will help if it is a matter that is within my power, Deacon Lepidus.'

'Do you know much about the history of this land?'

'Of the kingdom of these Jutes? Only a little. I know that the Jutes drove out the original inhabitants of Kent scarcely two centuries ago.'

The deacon shook his head swiftly.

'I meant knowledge of this land before the Jutes came here. Before they drove the Britons out. The time when it was called Britannia and a province of Rome. You know that in the days of the great Roman Empire our legions occupied and governed this land for several centuries?'

Fidelma bowed her head in amused affirmation at the slight tone of pride in his voice.

'I do know something of that history,' she replied softly.

'One of the legions that made up the garrison here was called the Ninth Hispana. It was an élite legion. You might have heard of it?'

'If my memory serves me right, this élite legion was reduced by a queen of the Britons called Boudicca.' Fidelma smiled ironically. 'Something like six thousand foot soldiers and almost an equal number of auxiliaries were killed when she ambushed them. I have read your historian, Tacitus, who wrote about the battle.'

'The Britons were lucky,' snapped Deacon Lepidus in sudden irritation. Clearly his pride was patriotic even though the incident was an ancient one. It had happened a full six centuries before.

'Or Queen Boudicca was the better general,' Fidelma murmured quietly. 'As I recall, the legion was cut to pieces and its commander, Petilius Cerialis, barely escaped to the shelter of his fortress with some of his cavalry. I think that there were only five hundred survivors out of the thousands of troops.'

For a moment Lepidus looked annoyed and then he shrugged.

'It is clear that you have read Tacitus, Sister. The Venerable Gelasius was fulsome in his praise of your knowledge. The Legion, however, saved its eagle and was later brought back to fighting strength. Cerialis, in fact, went on to become governor of the province in recognition of his ability. You know what the eagle symbolises for a Roman legion?'

'The eagle is the standard of each Roman legion, thought to be divinely blessed by being bestowed personally by the hand of the emperor, who was then thought to be divine. If the eagle fell into enemy hands, then the disgrace was such that the entire legion had to be disbanded,' replied Fidelma.

'Exactly so,' agreed the deacon with satisfaction. 'The Ninth Legion survived and served the emperors well. It pacified the northern part of this island, which was peopled by a fierce tribal confederation called the Brigantes . . .'

The man's voice was enthused and Fidelma, who disliked militarism, found herself frowning.

'All this is ancient history, Deacon Lepidus,' she interrupted pointedly. 'I am not sure why you are recalling it nor what advice you seek from me.'

Deacon Lepidus made a quick gesture of apology.

'I shall come to that immediately. Did you know that the Ninth Legion disappeared while on active service among the Britons?'

'I did not know. I have read only Tacitus and some of Suetonius, neither of whom mention that.'

'They would not have been alive to record the event for it happened some sixty or seventy years later. My ancestor, the Legate Platonius Lepidus, was the officer in command of the Ninth Legion at that time. He was commanding it when it vanished.'

Fidelma began to realise why the deacon was interested in ancient history but not why he was raising the subject.

'So, your ancestor disappeared with six thousand men or more?'

'He did. He and the eagle of the Ninth Hispana vanished as well as the men. There were rumours that the Legion had disgraced itself and was disbanded. Other stories say that it was sent to fight against the Parthans and eliminated. Yet other stories say that it had lost its eagle and all record of it was then stricken from the books. A few claimed that the legion was marched north across the great wall built by the Emperor Hadrian to protect the northern border of this province from the unconquered country of the Caledonii. You see, all the record books are now destroyed and so we have no knowledge of what happened . . .'

'It happened a long time ago,' observed Fidelma patiently. 'What is it that you want of me?'

'It happened well over five hundred years ago,' Deacon Lepidus agreed. He was silent for a moment or so as if preoccupied with some thoughts. Then he stirred, as if making up his mind. 'The fate of my ancestor, the eagle and the legion has become a matter of contention within our family. Pride bids us attempt to resolve the mystery.'

'After so long?' Fidelma could not help but sound sceptical.

The deacon smiled disarmingly.

'The truth is that I am writing a history of the Ninth Legion and want to insert into that history the facts of what their fate was and also exonerate the name of my ancestor. He has been blamed for the loss and even now the aristocracy of Rome does not readily forget this besmirching of our family's good name.'

'Ah.' That Fidelma could understand. 'But I cannot see how I might help you? I am not of this country and the area in which this legion disappeared, the land of the Brigantes, has been occupied for over one hundred years by the Angles, so any local traditions will have vanished when their culture and traditions replaced those of the Britons.'

'But you are an adept at solving mysteries,' pressed Deacon Lepidus. 'The Venerable Gelasius has told me of how you investigated the murders at the Lateran Palace.'

'What do you expect from me?'

The deacon gave an almost conspiratorial glance around him and leaned forward.

'The name Lepidus is well known in Rome. We are a princely family. We descend from Marcus Aemilius Lepidus who was a member of the great Julius Caesar's council and formed the triumvirate to govern Rome with Mark Antony and Octavian Caesar.' He halted, perhaps realising that the history of his family in ancient Rome was of little interest to her. He went on: 'Some months ago a merchant arrived seeking our family villa. He had been trading between here and Frankia.'

289

'Trading between here and Frankia? How then did this merchant get to Rome?'

Deacon Lepidus absently placed a hand inside his robe.

'The merchant brought with him a piece of ancient vellum that he had acquired. He thought it valuable enough to come to Rome and seek out our family. He sold it to my father because it bore a name on it.'

'The name of Lepidus, undoubtedly.' Fidelma smiled, trying not to sound sarcastic.

'The name of the Legate Platonius Lepidus,' affirmed the other significantly. 'The name of my ancestor who commanded the Ninth Hispana Legion at the time of its disappearance.' He paused dramatically. 'The merchant bargained for a good price for that vellum.'

'He obviously expected it, having travelled all the way from these shores to Rome to sell it,' murmured Fidelma.

'The vellum was worth much to me and my family,' agreed Deacon Lepidus.

'And will you now produce this vellum?' asked Fidelma. When a suspicious frown crossed Lepidus's face, she added: 'I presume, because you placed your hand inside your robe when you spoke of it, the vellum reposes there?'

Deacon Lepidus drew forth the piece of fine burnished calfskin.

'The original is now in my family archive in Rome but I have made a precise copy of what was written on that ancient vellum.'

Fidelma reached out a hand.

'I observe that you have also used vellum on which to make your copy.'

'I made the copy as close as I could to the original. The text is as it was written nearly five hundred years ago.'

Fidelma spread the copy on the table and looked at it for a moment before asking: 'You have copied the exact wording? You have not altered anything at all?'

'I can assure you that the wording is exactly as it was. Shall I translate it for you?' the deacon asked eagerly.

'My knowledge of Latin is adequate, I believe. Although five centuries have intervened, the grammar and vocabulary seem clear enough to me.'

She began to read.

'. . . his wounds and weakness having prevented the legate from falling upon his sword in his despair, I bound his hands to prevent such a disaster's occurring in future should consciousness return after he had fainted. Thereupon, we lay hidden in a culvert until darkness descended while our enemies revelled and caroused around us. They had much to celebrate. They had annihilated the greatest legion that had marched from Hispania under the burnished eagles of the empire.

'All that remained of the famous band of six thousand fighting men was the wounded legate and their eagle. History must record how Lepidus, the last survivor of those fighting men, grasped the eagle in that final overwhelming attack and stood, surrounded by the dead and dying, his *gladius* in one hand and the eagle in the other until he, too, was struck down. Thus it was that I found him. I, a mere *mathematicus* whose job was only to keep the legion's account books. His grasp on the eagle was so tight, even in unconsciousness, that I could not sever his grip and thus I dragged him and the eagle to the culvert which ran not far away from that bloody field. Mars looked down on us for we were not observed by our enemies.

'How we survived was truly the decision of the gods. The legate had become feverish from his wounds and I dragged and hauled him along the culvert further away from that grim field of slaughter until we reached the safety of a copse. There we lay a further day but, alas, the legate's condition deteriorated. By morning, a calm had seized him. He knew he was dying. He gripped my hand and recognised me.

'He spoke slowly: "Cingetorix," he addressed me by name, "how came you here?"'

'I replied that I had been with the baggage train when the Caledonii attacked it and fled, I knew not whither. Only after being led blindly by fate did I come upon the remarkable scene of the commander and a few men about the eagle, making their last stand. When they were overcome I saw the Caledonii had neglected to gather up the eagle, and knowing of its value I had made my way to the now deserted bodies in an endeavour to save it. That was when I saw the legate was still alive, albeit barely.

'The Legate Lepidus was still gripping my arm. "Cingetorix, you know what the eagle means. I am done for. So I charge you, take the eagle and place it in the hands of the emperor of Rome whence it came that he might raise it once again and declare that the Ninth Hispana is not yet dead even though the men have fallen. Proclaim that Lepidus shed his life's blood in its defence and died with the eagle and his honour intact."'

Fidelma paused and looked up from the vellum.

'This text is surely the authority you need to write your history?' she asked. 'What now brings you to this country?'

'Read on,' the deacon urged.

'The legate tarried not a moment more in this life. Therefore I removed the eagle from the shattered remains of its wooden pole and wrapped it in cloth to make it easier to carry. I then waited until night fell again and slowly began to make what distance I could from the still celebrating Caledonii. However, they were blocking the roads to the south and so I resolved to move westward into the country of the horse people – the Epidii.

'My story is long and complicated and I will transcribe it as and when I can. However, I must insert at this point that I could not fulfil my promise to the Legate Lepidus, may the gods honour him. It took me years to return to my own town of Darovernum and the gods smiled on me for I brought the eagle with me. But there is much disorder here at this time and age has spread a shadow over me. I cannot take the eagle to Rome and I fear to give it to the Governor Verus lest he take the credit himself. He is a man not to be trusted in such matters. I have therefore determined to hide it with some account in the tiny house I have which lies close to Tower Eight towards the north-east corner of a building some Christians have erected to honour one of their leaders named Martin of Gaul. I have hidden the honour of the Ninth Hispana in the hypocaust. There it will remain until my son has grown and can, under my instruction, resume the journey to Rome and can fulfil my . . .'

The vellum ended and Fidelma stopped reading. She looked up at Deacon Lepidus with eyes narrowed slightly.

'Now that I have read this document, what is it you want of me?'

Deacon Lepidus gave a winning smile.

'I had thought that there were clues in the document which might tell you where this man came from and where the eagle might be hidden. If I could take the eagle and more details back to Rome, if I could have a trustworthy witness to its rediscovery, then I could write my history with confidence. My family, the family of Lepidus, would be able to raise their heads in Rome and aspire to all the great offices without a cloud hanging over the past. Why, I might aspire to bishop or cardinal . . . there is no limit to the temporal and spiritual ambitions that . . .'

He paused and smiled quickly as if in embarrassment.

'My concern, however, as an historian, is simply to discover the truth. Perhaps this man, Cingetorix, was writing lies. Perhaps . . . but if we could discover where he lived and where he hid the eagle, if it was his to hide, then what a great historical mystery would be solved.'

Fidelma sat back and examined the man carefully.

'There are many Britons who are more qualified than I am to examine this document and point to the clues.'

Lepidus shrugged.

'The Britons? They never venture now beyond the new borders of the kingdoms into which the Saxons have confined them. They certainly would not venture into the country of the Saxons. And have they not consistently fought against us Romans? Not simply in the days when our legions ruled their lands but even in recent times when they refused to obey the rule of the Mother Church in Rome. Their kings refused to bend their necks before Augustine, who was the Bishop of Rome's personal envoy and missionary here. They preferred to stick to their idolatry, to the heretic Pelagius and their own leaders.'

Fidelma raised an amused eyebrow.

'Surely we of Éireann are also condemned by Rome? For our churches, too, believe in the theology of Pelagius rather than the attitudes adopted by Augustine of Hippo.'

Lepidus smiled disarmingly.

'But we can always argue with you folk of Éireann, whereas the Britons are proud people, inclined to test their belief at sword point.'

Fidelma was about to say 'just like the Romans' but thought better of it.

'I know a little of the history and language of the Britons, but I am not an expert.' She glanced at the vellum again and smiled thinly. 'Certainly there are many clues in this account.'

Deacon Lepidus leaned forward eagerly.

'Enough to track down where this man Cingetorix came from?'

Fidelma tapped the manuscript with her forefinger.

'That is simple. See, the man has written the exact location.'

The deacon frowned.

'Certainly he has. He has written Darovernum. But where is that place? I have asked several people and none seem to know.'

Fidelma chuckled.

'It is a name recorded by the geographer Ptolemy about the time when the deeds mentioned in this story are said to have taken place.'

'What does it mean?'

'In the tongue of the Britons, *duro* means a fort and *verno is* an alder swamp. Therefore it is the fort by the alder swamp.'

Lepidus looked dismayed.

'That is a fine example of linguistics, Sister Fidelma, but where can we find the location of this place?'

Fidelma regarded him steadily.

'The Romans called the place Darovernum Cantiacorum – the Cantiaci fort by the alder swamp.'

'I am at a loss still,' Deacon Lepidus confessed.

'You are in the very town. The Cantiaci fort by the alder swamp is what the Jutes now call the *burg* of the Cantware.'

Deacon Lepidus's features dissolved into an expression of amazement.

'Do you mean that the eagle might be hidden here? Here, in this very town?'

'All I mean, so far, is that the place mentioned in this document is this very town,' replied Fidelma solemnly.

'But this is incredible. Are you saying that this man, Cingetorix, the man who took the eagle from my ancestor, brought the eagle to this town? Is there anything else you can tell me?' Deacon Lepidus was clearly excited.

Fidelma pursed her lips thoughtfully.

'Since you have mentioned it, the name Cingetorix is a name that is also associated with the Cantiaci. Any student of Julius Caesar's account of his landing here would recognise it. But it is a strange name for a lowly *mathematicus* in the employ of a legion to have – it means "king of heroes". It was one of the names of the four kings of the Cantiaci who attacked Caesar's coastal camp during his landings.'

Deacon Lepidus sat back with a sigh. After his moment of excitement, he suddenly appeared depressed. He thought for a while and then raised his arms in a hopeless gesture before letting them fall again.

'Then all we have to do is find the location of the house of this man, Cingetorix. After five hundred years, that is impossible.'

Fidelma shook her head with a sudden smile.

'The vellum gives us a little clue, doesn't it?'

The deacon stared at her.

'A clue? What clue could it give to be able to trace his house? The Romans have gone, departing with the Britons, and the Jutes have come and settled. The town or *burg* of the Cantware has changed immeasurably. Most of the original buildings are old and decaying. When the Jutes broke out of the island of Tanatos and rose up against the Britons it took a generation to drive them out and for Aesc to make himself king of Jutish Kent. In that time much of this city was destroyed.'

'You appear to have learned much history in the short time you have been here, Deacon Lepidus,' Fidelma murmured. She rose, a whimsical expression crossing her features, and turned to a shelf behind her. 'It is by good fortune that the librarian here has some old charts of the town. I was examining them only this morning.'

'But they do not date from the time of my ancestor. Of what use are they to us?'

Fidelma was spreading one before her on the table.

'The writing mentions that his house stands near a tower; Tower Eight. Also that the house is situated at the north-east corner of a building which some Christians had erected in honour of one of their leaders, Martin of Gaul.'

Deacon Lepidus was perplexed.

'Does that help us? It is so many years ago.'

'The ten towers built by the Romans along the ancient walls of the town can still be recognised, although they are crumbling away. The Jutes do not like occupying the old buildings of the Britons or the Romans and prefer to build their own. However, there is still the chapel dedicated to Martin of Gaul, who is more popularly known as Martin of Tours. The chapel is still standing. People still go there to worship.'

A warm smile spread across the deacon's face.

'By all that is a miracle! What the Venerable Gelasius said about you was an underestimate, Sister Fidelma. You have, in a few moments, cleared away the misty paths and pointed to . . .'

Fidelma held up a hand to silence him.

'Are you truly convinced that if we can locate the precise spot you will find this eagle?'

'You have demonstrated that the writer of the vellum has provided clues enough to lead us not only to the town but to the location where his house might have stood.'

The corners of Fidelma's mouth turned down momentarily. Then she exhaled slowly.

'Let us observe, then, where else the writer of the vellum will lead us.'

Deacon Lepidus rose to his feet with a smile that was almost a grin of triumph and clapped his hands together.

'Just so! Just so! Where shall we go?'

Fidelma tapped the map with a slim forefinger.

'First, let us see what these charts of the town tell us. To the east of the township we have the River Stur. Since you are interested in these old names, Deacon Lepidus, you might like to know that it is a name given by the Britons, which means a strong or powerful river. Now these buildings here are the main part of the old town. As you observe, they stand beyond the west bank of the river and beyond the alder swamp. The walls were built by the Romans and then later fortified by the Britons, after the Roman withdrawal, to keep out the Angles, Saxons and Jutish raiders.'

Deacon Lepidus peered down and his excitement returned.

'I see. Around the walls are ten towers. Each tower is numbered on the chart.'

It was true that each tower had a Roman numeral, and among them was VIII on which Fidelma tapped lightly with her forefinger.

'And to the west, we have the church of Martin and buildings around it. What buildings would be at the north-west corner?'

'North-east,' corrected the deacon hurriedly.

'Exactly so,' agreed Fidelma, unperturbed. 'That's what I meant.'

'Why,' cried the deacon, jabbing at the chart, 'this building here is on the north-east corner of the church. It is marked as some sort of villa.'

'So it is. But is it still standing after all these centuries?'

'Perhaps some building is standing there,' Deacon Lepidus replied enthusiastically. 'Maybe the original foundations are still intact.'

296

'And would that help us?' queried Fidelma. Her voice was gently probing, like a teacher trying to help a pupil with a lesson.

'Surely,' the deacon said confidently. 'Cingetorix wrote that he would hide the eagle in the hypocaust. If so, if the building was destroyed, whatever was hidden in the foundations, where the hypocaust is, might have survived. You see, a hypocaust is . . .'

'It is a system for heating rooms with warm air,' intervened Fidelma. 'I am afraid that you Romans did not exactly invent the idea, although you claim as much. However, I have seen other ancient examples of the basic system. The floors are raised on pillars and the air underneath is heated by a furnace and piped through the flues.'

Deacon Lepidus's face was a struggle to control a patriotic irritation at Fidelma's words. He finally produced a strained smile.

'I will not argue with you on who or what invented the *hypocaustrum*, which is a Latin word.'

'*Hypokauston* is a Greek word,' pointed out Fidelma calmly. 'Clearly, we all borrow from one another, and perhaps that is as it should be. Let us return to the problem in hand. We will have to walk to this spot and see what remains of any building. Only once we have surveyed this area will we see what our next step might be.'

Fidelma had only been in the town a week but it was so small that she had already explored the location around the abbey. It was sad that during the two centuries since the Britons had been driven out by Hengist and his son Aesc, the Jutes and their Angle and Saxon comrades had let much of it fall into disuse and disrepair, preferring to build their own crude constructions of timber outside the old city walls. A few buildings had been erected in spaces where the older buildings had decayed. Only recently, since the coming of Augustine from Rome and his successors, had a new dynamism seized the city and buildings started to be renovated and repaired. Even so, it was a haphazard process.

Fidelma led the way with confidence to the crumbling towers that had once guarded the city walls.

'That is Tower Eight,' she said, pointing to what had once been a square tower now standing no more than a single storey high.

'How do you know? Just from the map?' demanded the deacon.

She shook her head irritably.

'It bears the number on the lintel above the door.'

She pointed to where 'VIII' could clearly be seen before turning to survey the piles of stone and brickwork that lay about. Her eyes widened suddenly.

'That wooden granary and its outbuilding appear to stand in the position that is indicted. See, there is the church dedicated to the Blessed Martin of Tours. Curious. They are the only buildings near here, as well.'

Deacon Lepidus followed her gaze and nodded.

'God is smiling on us.'

Fidelma was already making her way towards the buildings.

'There are two possibilities,' she mused. 'The granary has been built over the villa so that the hypocaust is under there. Or, that smaller stone building next to the granary may have been part of the original villa and we will find the hypocaust there.' She hesitated a moment. 'Let us try the stone building first. It is clearly older than the granary.'

While they were standing there, a thick-set man, dressed in Saxon workman's clothing, stepped out of the shadow of the granary.

'Good day, reverend sir. Good day, lady. What do you seek here?'

He smiled too easily for Fidelma's taste, giving her the impression of a fox assessing his prey. His Jutish accent was hard to understand, although he was speaking in a low Latin. It was the deacon who explained their purpose, playing down the value of the eagle but offering a silver coin if the man could help them locate what they were looking for.

'This is my granary. I built it,' the man replied. 'My name is Wulfred.'

'If you built it, did you observe whether it had holes in the ground or tunnels underneath it?' Fidelma inquired.

The man rubbed his jaw thoughtfully.

'There were places we had to fill in with rubble to give us a foundation.'

Deacon Lepidus's face fell.

'The hypocaust was filled in?'

Wulfred shrugged. 'I can show you the type of holes we filled in, if you are interested. The little stone building has such holes under the floor. Come, I have a lantern. I'll show you.'

They were following the man through the doorway when Fidelma suddenly caught sight of something scratched on one of the side pillars supporting the frame of the door. She called Deacon Lepidus's attention to it, simply pointing. It was a scratch mark. It looked like 'IX'. There was something before it, which neither of them could make out.

'Nine?' whispered Lepidus, with sudden excitement. 'The Ninth Legion?'

Fidelma made no reply.

It was cold and dirty inside. Dirt covered the floor. Wulfred held his polished horn lantern high. It revealed a room of about twelve feet square. It was totally empty. In one corner was a hole in the floor.

'Down there is where you can see the tunnels under the floor,' volunteered Wulfred.

Fidelma went across and knelt down. The smell of decay was quite prevalent. She asked for the lantern and peered down. A space of about three inches lay underneath the floor. Little brick piers supported the timbers at intervals of three feet from one another, forming little squares.

'A hypocaust,' she said, raising herself and handing the lantern back. 'But now what?'

Deacon Lepidus made no reply.

'Perhaps some sign was left . . . ?' he ventured.

Fidelma glanced on the floor. What she saw made her frown and began to scrape at the floor with the point of her shoe. The earth came away to reveal a tiny patch of mosaic. This was the type of floor she had seen in Rome. She asked Wulfred if he had a broom of twigs. It took half an hour to clear a sizeable section. The mosaic revealed a Roman figure clad in a senatorial toga, one hand held up with a finger extended. Fidelma frowned. Something made her follow the pointing figure. She suddenly noticed a scratch mark on the wall. There was no doubt about it this time. The figure IX had been scratched into the stonework and a tiny arrow pointed downwards beneath it.

'We'll break into the hypocaust here,' she announced. 'With the permission of Wulfred, of course,' she added.

The Jute readily agreed when Deacon Lepidus held out another coin.

Lepidus himself took charge of making the hole. It was the work of another half an hour to create a space through which a small person could pass into the hypocaust below. Fidelma volunteered. Her face was screwed into an expression of distaste as she squeezed into the confined darkness, having to lie full length on her stomach. It was not merely damp but the walls below were bathed in water. It was musty and reminded Fidelma of a cemetery vault. She ran her hand in darkness over the wet brickwork.

'Pass me down the lantern,' she called up.

It was Lepidus who leaned down and handed her the polished horn lantern, giving its opaque glow in the darkness.

Fidelma breathed out softly.

By its light she could see the brickwork and almost immediately she saw scratch marks on the brickwork. 'IX Hispana'. She put the lantern down and began to tug at the first brick. It was loose and gave way with surprising ease, swinging a little so that she could remove it. The other long, thin bricks were removed with the same ease. A large aperture was soon opened. She peered into the darkness. Something flickered back in the lantern light. She reached forth a hand. It was metal, cold and wet.

She knew what it was before her exploring hand encompassed the lines of the object. She knew it was a bronze eagle.

'What is it?' called Deacon Lepidus above her, sensing her discovery.

'Wait,' she instructed sharply.

Her exploring hand felt around the interior of the alcove. Water was seeping in, damp and dark. Obviously the alcove was not waterproof.

Then her exploring hand felt a piece of material. It too was wet from the seepage. She drew it forth. It was a piece of vellum. She could not make out the writing by the limited light of the lantern. Then, turning, she handed the eagle upwards. It was only a few feet in length for it was lacking its wooden haft. Ignoring the gasps from Deacon Lepidus, she passed up the vellum and the lantern to Wulfred, twisted on her back, and scrambled back into the room above.

A moment or so later she was able to see the fruits of her sojourn in the dank darkness below. Wulfred was holding the lantern high while Deacon Lepidus was almost dancing as he clutched his prize.

'The eagle! The eagle!' he cried delightedly.

It was a dark bronze eagle surrounded by laurel wreaths, its claws apparently clutching a branch, and below it a scroll on which the letters 'SPQR' were engraved. *Senatus Populusque Romanus*. Lepidus tapped

300

the letters with his forefinger. 'The ultimate authority for any Roman legion. The Senate and People of Rome.'

'Let us not forget these finds have been made on Wulfred's property,' she pointed out, as Lepidus seemed to forget the presence of the Jutish granary owner.

'I will come to an accommodation with Wulfred. A third silver coin should suffice, for he has no use for these relics. Is that not so?'

Wulfred bowed his head.

'I am sure that the reverend sir is generous in rewarding me for my services,' he replied.

'My ancestor's eagle has induced such generosity.' Lepidus smiled.

'What of the vellum that was with it?' Fidelma asked.

Wulfred handed it to her.

She took it, carefully unrolling it. She examined the handwriting closely, and then the text.

'At least it is short,' Deacon Lepidus observed.

'Indeed,' she agreed. 'It simply says – "I, Cingetorix of the Cantiaci and *mathematicus* of Darovernum, place the eagle of the Ninth Hispana Legion, for safe keeping, in this place. My son is dead without issue. So should a younger hand find it, I entreat whoever you are, take the eagle to Rome and hand it to the emperor and tell him that the Legate Platonius Lepidus gave his life in its defence having exhorted me to make the journey to Rome so that the legion might be raised again under this divine standard. I failed but I hope the words I have written will be testament to the honour and glory of the Ninth and of its commander, Platonius Lepidus, may the gods give him eternal rest."'

Fidelma sighed deeply.

'Then there is no more to be said. You have what you wanted, Deacon. Let us return to the abbey.'

Deacon Lepidus smiled appreciatively.

'I have what I want thanks to you, Sister Fidelma. You are witness to these events, which will ensure no one questions them. I shall go to the Archbishop Theodore and tell him what has transpired, and that you will confirm my testimony.'

Fidelma grimaced.

'Immediately, I need to bathe after crawling around in that hypocaust. I will join you and the archbishop later.'

*   *   *

Archbishop Theodore sat in his chair of office and was smiling.

'Well, Fidelma of Cashel, the Deacon Lepidus has much to say in praise of you.'

Fidelma had entered the archbishop's chamber with Eadulf at her side. Deacon Lepidus was standing to one side nodding happily.

'It seems that you have done a signal service by solving an ancient riddle for him and his family.'

'Not so, my lord,' replied Fidelma quietly.

'Come, Sister Fidelma, no undue modesty,' intervened Deacon Lepidus. 'You have discovered the truth of what happened to my ancestor and to the fate of six thousand soldiers of Rome, the fate of the Ninth Hispana.'

'The truth?' Fidelma glanced towards him, suddenly scornful. Her voice was sharp. 'The truth is that Deacon Lepidus wished to perpetuate a hoax, a fraud, an untruth, in order to give himself and his family prestige. He sought to write a fabricated history, which would elevate him in society in Rome where his ambitions know no bounds.'

'I don't understand,' frowned Archbishop Theodore.

'Simple to understand once told,' replied Fidelma. 'Deacon Lepidus faked an eagle which he claimed was the five-hundred-year-old regimental emblem of the Ninth Hispana Legion which disappeared in Britain at a time when his ancestor was supposed to be its legate or commanding officer. He wrote two accounts on vellum which explained what supposedly happened to the legion and how the eagle could be found.'

'This is nonsense!' snapped Lepidus. 'I will not stay here to be insulted.'

'Wait!' Archbishop Theodore said quietly as Lepidus turned to go. 'You will stay until I give you leave to go.'

'And you will stay to hear the truth,' added Fidelma. 'Do you think I am a simpleton that you could fool me? Your complicated plot merely needed me, my reputation, to confirm the veracity of your claim. You came with a vellum, pretending that you needed my help to solve the clues given in it. There were enough clues for an idiot to follow. It was to lead me to a house in this town and to the old hypocaust where I would find another vellum and the bronze eagle.'

'This is an insult to me, an insult to Rome,' spluttered the deacon.

Archbishop Theodore raised a hand.

'I will judge what insults Rome, Deacon Lepidus. Sister Fidelma, have you some evidence behind this accusation?'

Fidelma nodded.

'Firstly, I demand Lepidus produce the two pieces of vellum. The first is a text said to be written five hundred years ago . . .'

'I never said that!' snapped Lepidus triumphantly. 'I said it was my copy from the original which resides in my family library in Rome.'

'So you did. And I asked you very clearly whether you had altered the text in any way or whether it was an exact copy of the original. True or false?'

He nodded reluctantly.

'What you neglected to take into account is that languages change over the centuries. In my own land we have our modern speech but we also have the language that has been used in the inscriptions which we put up in the alphabet we called Ogham, named after Ogma, the old god of literacy. That language is called the Bérla Féine which many of our professional scribes cannot even understand today. I have seen Latin texts of ancient times, having read Tacitus and Caesar and others. This text of five hundred years ago is the Latin that is used today, called vulgar or popular Latin.

'Next, I found it strange that Cingetorix, who is supposed to have written this, is a *mathematicus*, an accountant employed by the legion, yet bearing a kingly name which Romans would have found extraordinary in one so lowly in their eyes. Cingetorix is a name well known to those who read Caesar. Lepidus's Cingetorix is a Cantii but he calls himself a Cantiaci, which is the Roman form, just as he describes his native town as Darovernum in the form recorded by Ptolemy, as I recall. Had he been a native he would have recorded it as Duroverno. Both these things were strange to me but not conclusive of fraud, as Cingetorix is writing in Latin.'

'That is exactly what I was about to point out,' intervened Deacon Lepidus. 'All this is just foolish speculation to show how clever the woman is.'

'I was interested when I said that the abbey library had some old charts of the town and turned to get them,' went on Fidelma calmly. 'You immediately said that the charts did not date to the time of your ancestor. How would you know unless you had first checked out everything? You seemed to know so much of the history of the town as well. When I was speculating on the destruction of buildings in the town since the coming of the Jutes, you were quick to point out that while buildings might be destroyed the foundations could remain. You emphasised that the text claimed the eagle was hidden in the hypocaust and thus in the foundations. So it proved . . . as if you knew it already. The house had long since vanished and a new granary stood on the site. But a small part of the villa, one room, stood and under it was the hypocaust. Amazing.'

'It is still speculation,' observed the archbishop.

'Indeed. I have had some dealings with the people of this country. The owner of the granary did not seem perturbed at our demands to search under his property. Nor surprised by what we found there. Whereas some might have demanded either the property or some high reward, the man Wulfred was quite happy for Lepidus to take eagle and vellum away on payment of a few coins. Not typical merchant's behaviour.'

'Not typical but not proof of any wrong-doing,' Archbishop Theodore pointed out.

'I concede that. When we found the alcove in which the eagle and the second vellum lay, I was surprised that the interior was really damp. Not just damp but almost running with water. My hand was covered in water as if I had immersed it.'

'What does that prove?'

'While a bronze object might have survived in those conditions, it would undoubtedly have deteriorated significantly. The other item – the vellum with writing on it – would hardly have lasted months, let alone centuries.' Fidelma turned to the deacon. 'You were not that clever, Deacon Lepidus.'

The deacon was finally looking less than confident.

Brother Eadulf was smiling broadly.

'My lord archbishop, if we could persuade Deacon Lepidus to allow us to have his precious eagle for an hour, there are smiths of quality in this town who would, I am sure, be able to estimate whether the bronze was cast over five centuries ago, or recently?'

'That is a good idea,' agreed Archbishop Theodore.

Fidelma intervened with a quiet smile.

'I am sure that Deacon Lepidus would not wish to trouble us to do so. It is too time-consuming and wearisome. I am sure that on reflection he would prefer to admit the truth. The truth of what he was attempting was plain from the very moment he presented me with the first vellum in the abbey library. The fact that it was a fake leapt from the text immediately I saw it.'

Brother Eadulf was smiling brightly. Archbishop Theodore's eyes had widened.

'Do you mean that when you saw that the Latin was so modern, you realised that it could not have been written five centuries ago?'

Fidelma shook her head.

'When I read how Cingetorix described the position of his house, the forgery stood out like a sore thumb.'

Archbishop Theodore was shaking his head.

'But you found the hypocaust of an ancient Roman building exactly where he said it was. And there was the ruined defensive tower on the old city wall, which is marked with the number eight. Each tower bears a Roman numeral.'

'Surely, and his house was by the north-east corner of a church being raised by Christians to Martin of Gaul, whom we call the Blessed Martin of Tours,' agreed Fidelma.

'So? What is significant about that? There were Christians and Christian communities in Britain for about a hundred years before the time when the Ninth Legion was said to have disappeared here.'

'Indeed. But Martin of Tours, who had such a profound effect on the Christian communities not only in Britain but in my own land of the five kingdoms of Éireann, was not born until a century and a half after the events supposedly recounted by Cingetorix. Deacon Lepidus had done some research, but not well enough. I went along with him to see where he was leading me. In my own language, Archbishop, there is a saying *is fearrde a dhearcas bréug fiadhnuise* – a lie looks the better for having a witness. He wanted me to be witness to his lie, to his fraud. But even a clever man cannot be wise all the time.'

305

Acknowledgements

The stories contained in this volume first appeared as follows:

'Whispers of the Dead' – originally published in *Murder Most Catholic*, ed. Ralph McInery, Cumberland House, Nashville, Tennessee, July 2002.

'Corpse on a Holy Day' – originally published in *And the Dying is Easy*, ed. Joseph Pittman and Annette Riffle, Signet Books, New York, May 2001.

'The Astrologer Who Predicted His Own Murder' – originally published in *Death By Horoscope*, ed. Anne Perry, Carroll & Graf, New York, July 2001.

'The Blemish' – originally published in *The Brehon*, Vol. I, No. 3, September 2002.

'Dark Moon Rising' – originally published in *The Brehon*, Vol. II, No. 3, September 2003.

'Like a Dog Returning . . .' – originally published in *Murder Most Medieval*, ed. Martin H. Greenberg & John Helfers, Cumberland House, Nashville, Tennessee, June 2000.

'The Banshee' – originally published in *Ellery Queen Mystery Magazine*, February 2004.

'Who Stole the Fish?' – originally published in *Murder Through the Ages*, ed. Maxim Jakubowski, Headline, London, November 2000.

'Scattered Thorns' – originally published in *Murder Most Celtic*, ed. Martin H. Greenberg, Cumberland House, Nashville, Tennessee, May 2001.

'Gold At Night' – originally published in *Great Irish Drinking Stories*, ed. Peter Haining, Souvenir Press, London, November 2002.

'Death of an Icon' – originally published in *The Mammoth Book of Historical Whodunnits II*, ed. Mike Ashley, Robinson, London, August 2001.

'The Lost Eagle' – originally published in *The Mammoth Book of Ancient Roman Whodunnits*, ed. Mike Ashley, Robinson, London, August 2003.

'Cry "Wolf!"', 'The Fosterer' and 'The Heir Apparent' have all been written as original contributions to this volume.